At nineteen, I was already married with a child on the way, Becky thought. And yet there was Michelle, twenty-two years old and apparently showing not the slightest interest in lads. Maybe all those loud men who claimed that women shouldn't be well educated because it would destroy their femininity were not just spouting a load of hot air after all. No, that's a stupid way to think! Becky told herself angrily. But even so, she wished Michelle would be a little more . . . well . . . normal.

When Billy had finished his breakfast and gone off to work, Becky walked over to the mantelpiece and, almost reverently, picked up her husband's photograph. She remembered when it had been taken, in the early summer, three years earlier. It was just before Michael had been due to sail. They had walked hand in hand through a field of foxgloves. They had seen a yellow wagtail sitting on a tree stump – fresh from Africa to which Michael was soon to return – and at dusk they had spotted a couple of fox cubs, gambolling near their earth.

The next morning, Becky had travelled with Michael to Liverpool. She had stood on the dock, waving, as his ship sailed slowly out of sight. It was the last time that she would ever see him alive.

Sally Spencer was born and brought up in Marston, Cheshire, but now lives in Spain.

By the same author

Salt of the Earth
Up Our Street
Old Father Thames
A Picnic in Eden
South of the River

Those Golden Days

SALLY SPENCER

An Orion paperback
First published in Great Britain by Orion in 1996
This paperback edition published in 1997 by Orion Books Ltd,
Orion House, 5 Upper St Martin's Lane, London WC2H 9EA

A CIP catalogue record for this book
is available from the British Library.

ISBN: 0 75280 911 3

Printed and bound in Great Britain by
Clays Ltd, St Ives plc

This book is dedicated to the local historians throughout Britain, but especially to: John Simcock, who, though he would deny it, has an encyclopaedic knowledge of the village in which I grew up; Colin Lynch, whose painstakingly acquired collection of photographs have been of immense help to me in writing about Marston, the setting for three of my books; Bev Blain, whose excellent drawings and paintings have done so much to retain an image of a vanishing world; and Keith Fahrenholz, whose pub, the Salt Barge, would be well worth visiting even without the outstanding work he has done to capture the history of the village within its walls.

Author's Note

Marston is a real village in Cheshire, and the house in which Becky Worrell – and I – were brought up is still standing, as are other buildings described in this book. Many of the events described are also rooted in historical reality, though, as in *Salt of the Earth*, I have taken some liberties with the time-scale. The characters, however, are based on no one either living or dead, and are purely the products of my imagination.

Sally Spencer

THOSE GOLDEN DAYS

PROLOGUE

Spring 1913

Michelle Worrell sat on her metal trunk, waiting for the taxi which would take her to the station – and wished she were dead. Was it only two and a half years earlier that she had first come to Oxford? she asked herself. Two and a half years since she'd reached the end of the rainbow and fulfilled her wildest dream?

She laughed – inwardly and bitterly. Oxford had been no dream. It had been a nightmare. And though she had fought back, even after her father's . . . after her father's . . .

She took a deep breath. There was no point in blaming anyone else, she thought. Nor could she put the blame on Fate, which had visited her family with tragedy. The failure was hers and hers alone.

'I should have been stronger,' she said.

She spoke only in a whisper, but her words seemed to echo round the archway. 'Should have been stronger . . . stronger . . .'

She glanced around her. Happy, confident students were everywhere – books under their arms and smiles on their faces. None of them looked at her. She was an embarrassment who, once removed, would soon be forgotten.

She did not want to stay in Oxford, but she did not want to go home, either. Back home, in Marston, were the people she had grown up amongst – people who remembered her as she'd once been. What would they think of her now, seeing her come home defeated, her tail between her legs?

Yet what choice did she have *but* to go home? Even if people did despise her? Or worse – pitied her?

Two porters appeared, one on either side of her. 'Taxi's just coming, Miss,' said the senior of the pair.

Michelle looked up and saw the black cab. So this was it – the end.

The senior porter coughed, as if to hide an awkwardness. 'So if you'll just get up, Miss, we'll load your trunk into it.'

'Of course.'

They couldn't wait to get rid of her, she thought as she rose to her feet. It wasn't that they hated her. She just didn't fit in. Why, oh why, had it taken her two and a half soul-destroying years to realise that?

The taxi drew up, the porters hefted the trunk into it. Michelle gazed, for the last time, on the City of Sleepy Spires. Then, with legs that felt as heavy as lead, she walked to the taxi.

'Good luck, Miss,' the senior porter called after her.

'Thank you,' Michelle replied.

The two men watched the cab drive away. The senior porter sighed. 'Poor little bugger,' he said. 'I wonder if she'll ever get over it.'

PART ONE

Distant Thunder
Summer 1914

Chapter One

Marston had only three streets. The longest, Ollershaw Lane, pointed towards Warrington in one direction, Northwich in the other, and ran through the centre of the village. The other two streets, Cross Street and The Avenue, dissected the lane just beyond the mineral railway line.

The terraced red-brick houses groaned under the weight of heavy blue slate roofs. Each house had a front garden the size of a bed sheet, and a larger back yard where the wash-house and outside lavatory could be found.

All the dwellings had four rooms – two up and two down. The back room downstairs was the kitchen, where a fire burned all year round to heat the oven which stood next to it. The downstairs front room was used as a bedroom for growing families, but once the girls had gone into service and the boys had set up homes of their own, it quickly reverted to its rightful function – a parlour only used for weddings, funerals and Christmas.

No one pretended that Marston was a pretty village – it had been thrown up hurriedly to accommodate the workers in the saltmines and the brine works – but the villagers thought it suited them well enough, and most of them would never have considered living anywhere else.

Spudder Johnson stepped out of what had once been a front parlour – but was now his fish and chip shop – and looked up Ollershaw Lane to the hump-backed bridge over the canal. On his right was Worrell's saltworks, with its two chimneys belching out thick black smoke and the steam from its brine evaporation pans floating almost lazily into the sky. On his left was the salt store, a huge, domed wooden building, which some people said resembled a beached whale. But Spudder had never seen a whale, let alone a beached one – whatever *that* was – so he had no way of knowing whether they were right or wrong.

He turned the other way. Apart from a few little kids playing hopscotch, the lane was as quiet as it ever got.

'It won't stay quiet for long,' Spudder said to no one in particular. In a few minutes the hooters would sound at Worrell's, and at the Adelaide mine on the other side of the bridge. Then the chip shop would start filling with hungry saltworkers who had put in a twelve-hour shift and wanted their pieces of haddock pretty damn quick.

How long had he been living in the village? Spudder wondered. He had first come to Marston in the summer of 1893, and now it was 1914, so that made it . . . He shook his head defeatedly. He'd never been very good at doing figures.

He saw Michelle Worrell come out of the alley which ran along the side of her house. He'd known her since she was a little girl, and she always called him Uncle Spudder, though he wasn't her uncle really. He'd missed her, those three years she'd been away down south. He'd been surprised, too, when she returned home at the end of her studies, because he was almost sure that her mam – Mrs Becky – had told him that she was going to stay on and become a doctor of something or other. Still, he often got things wrong, so maybe Mrs Becky hadn't said that at all.

One thing he was sure of was that Michelle wasn't the same girl who'd gone away. She been so chirpy and confident before she'd left the village. Now she almost seemed afraid of her own shadow.

'Time to start fryin', Spudder!' called Aggie Spratt, the huge woman who helped him to run both his chip shop and the boarding house.

'Be with you in a minute,' Spudder replied, watching Michelle make her way down the lane, and wondering again what had happened to the girl he'd once known.

As Michelle hurried down the lane, she cursed herself for her own forgetfulness. She had known she would need Lightfoot's account books in the afternoon, so what had ever possessed her to leave them in her bedroom when she set out that morning? Now she'd wasted an hour – an hour she could never replace – and she'd have to spend the rest of the week trying to catch up on herself.

She heard the sound of horses' hooves coming towards her, but she didn't look up to see who it was, because she knew that only one man rode a horse through Marston. Gerald Worrell – her cousin Gerald! The son of the man who had seduced her mother, then tried to ruin her father – his own brother. The two branches of the family hadn't spoken to each other since before she and Gerald were born.

The hoofbeats grew nearer, and Michelle kept her eyes fixed on the ground, as if she were afraid of tripping. 'Think of something else!' she ordered herself.

Though she couldn't see her cousin, she could picture him in her mind's eye – his shining black hair, his strong nose, his wide mouth with lips that . . . Her heart was beating at a gallop and she suddenly felt hot. She gripped the account books more tightly in her hands, as if that would help to control her trembling.

Rider and horse were past her. Now she lifted her head and looked over her shoulder. It was only a second's glance, but it was enough to take in the proud carriage, broad back and powerful thighs. Michelle shifted the account books to a more comfortable position and tried to plan her afternoon's work.

Becky Worrell gazed down at the black marble gravestone and read the words she knew off by heart, the words she had composed herself:

'Michael Worrell 1865–1911
He left the world a better place than he found it.'

She sighed.

'How long has he been gone now?' asked her older brother Jack, sympathetically.

Becky sighed again. 'Three years, two months and six days.'

'An' you still miss 'im a lot, don't you?' Jack said, then, looking as if he could have bitten out his own tongue, he added, 'Now that was a bloody stupid thing for me to say, wasn't it? Of course you still miss him.'

Becky didn't reply. Instead she looked across the road at the school, erected thanks to voluntary subscription some fifty years before. It was a large building, with three slate-covered gables which seemed to frown down disapprovingly at the children in the playground. The playground itself had once been as level as anyone could wish, but the land under Marston was honeycombed with saltmine workings, and that had caused subsidence. Now, it was possible to place a glass marble on the ground at the top end of the playground, and chase it as it rolled, faster and faster, towards the bottom.

Becky watched the children running around, letting out all their pent-up energy in furious games and loud shrieking.

How quickly time passes, she thought. It seemed like only five minutes since she'd been in that playground herself. Yet she hadn't been what they called a scholar for over thirty years. Almost without realising it, she had grown up, got married, given birth to one child, adopted another, opened her bakery – and lost her beloved husband to a tropical disease the doctors didn't even have a name for.

'I always knew that Michael would die young,' she said to her brother. 'The risks he took, it was bound to happen. But that was my husband for you. He thought he could put all of the wrongs of the world right by himself, and once he'd got an idea in his head, there was no holding him.'

And she wouldn't have had it any other way, she thought. It was that fire – that drive – in her Michael which had made her fall in love with him in the first place. And which kept her loving him even now he was gone.

Jack coughed uncomfortably, and Becky turned to look at the man who, even in his early fifties, had still not lost the appearance of a wild-eyed gypsy boy. 'You've got somethin' on your mind, haven't you?' she asked.

Jack grinned ruefully. 'You allus could read me like a book, our Becky.'

Becky put her hands on her hips, a sign of exasperation she had unconsciously copied from her late mother. 'Well, out with it, then,' she said.

Jack shrugged his shoulders. 'I was just wonderin' if you'd looked in the mirror lately,' he muttered.

'Well, of course I have. I look in it every day, first thing in the morning when I brush me hair.'

'I mean *really* looked,' Jack persisted.

Becky shook her head. 'You're a right funny 'ap'orth, an' no mistake, our Jack,' she told her brother. 'I've known you all me life, an' yet there's times when I still don't understand what the heck you're talkin' about.'

Jack stepped back so he could get a better view of her. His sister was no longer a young girl, as the faint lines around her eyes showed. But the eyes themselves were as deep a blue as they'd ever been, and her long hair – tucked in now, under her demure, broad-brimmed hat – was as golden as the day she'd married Michael Worrell. Add to that her long, straight nose with only the slightest suggestion of a tilt at its end, her wide, generous mouth, and a chin which was firm without being aggressive, and Becky still presented a very striking picture. In some ways, Jack realised, age had actually improved his sister. There was a grace about Becky which only comes with time. Yes, she might be what some folk would call past the first flush of girlhood, but there was no doubt that she could still turn any number of heads on the street.

'Is your inspection over yet, our Jack?' Becky asked, though not unkindly.

Jack jumped slightly, startled out of his musings. On the oil rivers of West Africa, where there was little to do for most of the time but think, he had thought a great deal about Becky. However much she had loved Michael, widowhood was not a natural state for his sister, he had decided, and during this brief visit to Britain, he had planned to steer Becky away from it as skilfully as he steered his steamer between the sand bars and up the narrow creeks.

That *had* been the plan. But somehow when he was actually with Becky, all his plans came to pieces, and now he blurted out, 'Have you ever thought of getting married again?'

'Now where did that idea come from?'

It was ridiculous to feel so embarrassed, but nevertheless Jack did. Still, he had started, so he might as well go on. 'You're a beautiful woman, still in your prime,' he said. 'I know you loved Michael, but you can't go on mournin' him for ever.'

Becky smiled sadly. 'I don't mourn him. When I think of him, it's more like I'm celebratin' the time we had together.' She blushed. 'Now that's just the kind of fanciful thing Michael would have said if I'd been the one who'd gone first.'

'You're right there,' Jack agreed.

'But just because it's fanciful doesn't make it any less true,' Becky said fiercely.

'No, it doesn't,' Jack replied awkwardly, 'but you can't afford to spend all your time lookin' back. You have to consider the future. Now I know a couple of fellers in Liverpool – decent, honest chaps with their own business – who'd consider it a real privilege to take you out once in a while. It doesn't have to lead to anythin' if you don't want it to, but . . .' He trailed off.

Becky was no longer listening to him, but had turned her head and was looking at the school yard again. 'Where *does* the time go?' she asked herself for a second time.

Half a lifetime, over in a click of the fingers. Maybe Jack was right and she should try to grab a little happiness while she still had the chance. Michael wouldn't mind, she thought. If there really was a heaven, he would be up there now, urging her on. But how could she ever settle for anything less than what she'd had? And how could she ever hope to find a man who could replace Michael?

One of the monitors appeared in the playground, staggering under the weight of the great brass handbell which for generations had been used to summon the children back into their classrooms.

With an effort, the boy swung the bell, and the sound of its harsh tone drifted across to the quiet graveyard. The kids, as terrified of their teachers as Becky had been of hers, stopped their skipping and jumping and began to make their way reluctantly to their separate entrances – one for boys, one for girls.

The sound of Jack's voice drifted into her consciousness. 'Just think about what I been sayin',' he implored her.

Becky surreptitiously wiped a tear from her eye. 'You're a good big brother, our Jack,' she said. 'You always were. But you're wastin' your time with this one. I'll never marry again.'

'Won't you at least give it a try?' Jack suggested. 'Meetin' other men, I mean.'

Becky shook her head. 'It's time I got back to the bakery,' she said. 'They'll be needin' me.'

The sun was low in the sky, and in a few minutes it would begin to sink into the horizon, drenching the grounds of Peak House – only a couple of miles from Marston, but a world apart from it – in glowing red light.

From his study window, Richard Worrell watched his son, Gerald, putting his new horse, a chestnut mare, through its paces in the grounds outside.

'The boy's a natural horseman,' he told himself proudly for probably the thousandth time. Although perhaps it was wrong to think of Gerald as a boy at all. He had already celebrated his twenty-second birthday, was six foot two inches tall, and as strong and handsome a young man as you could hope to find in the county.

'He takes after his father,' Richard murmured with considerable satisfaction. It was no idle boast. Years of hard drinking might have taken their toll on Richard Worrell, but he still cut a fine figure.

There were other ways in which Gerald took after him, too – his love of horses, for example. And his love of – or perhaps his lust for – women. Gerald had been just sixteen when Richard took him to his first brothel, and the lad had settled into it as quickly as he'd taken to the other kind of riding. All part of the plan, Richard thought.

Richard had always been a planner, and patience was his greatest – if not his only – virtue. The way he'd dealt with Becky Taylor had been a good example. He could have had her that night at the fairground, when she was only thirteen, but he had waited – savouring the thought of what was to come – until she was nineteen. Only then, when she had ripened into full womanhood, had he seduced her.

'You could still have been mine, Becky,' he growled to the empty room. She *should* have been his. Marrying her had been out of the question – a saltminer's daughter was no proper match for the saltworks owner – but he had offered to set her up as his mistress, and that should have been enough for her.

Yet she had had the nerve to turn him down. Then, as if to add insult to injury, she had married his brother Michael.

There were other scores, besides that, which he had to settle with Becky. Like the part she had played in getting his wife, Hortense, released from the lunatic asylum he had confined her to after she had given birth to her second child – *her* second, not his. What a deal of trouble Hortense's release had caused him! What legal battles he'd been forced to fight for custody of Gerald.

'Let your wife have the boy,' Richard's lawyer, Horace Crimp, had advised him.

'Never!'

'With respect, I really don't think you've thought this through carefully enough, Mr Worrell. If the case goes to court, then it is bound to come out that . . .'

'That what?'

'Well, that your wife has . . .'

'Cuckolded me with one of my own servants?'

'Something like that.'

'I don't care.'

'You'll be a laughing stock.'

'I told you, I don't care. As long as I can keep my son, I'm willing to tolerate anything.'

It *had* come out in court and, as Crimp had predicted, there had been much sniggering behind Richard's back. He had been willing to pay the price for Gerald's sake, but he had never forgotten that without Becky's interference there would have been no price at all.

But perhaps the worst of all the wrongs Becky had done him had been to insist – while Hortense was still in the asylum – on adopting the child of his wife's shame. So that now, every time Richard drove up Ollershaw Lane to the saltworks, he ran the risk of catching sight of Billy Worrell – and of being reminded of his own humiliation.

Oh yes, Becky had a great deal to account for, but soon – very soon – he would have his revenge for all she had done to him.

The door to the study swung open, and Gerald walked in.

How handsome he was, with his broad shoulders, jet-black hair, dark eyes and a mouth which could seem cruel, but had an appeal few women could resist.

'Are we planning to go out "visiting" tonight, Father?' the young man asked.

Richard took a reflective sip of his malt whisky. 'Why not?' he said. 'I'm told there's a new house opened in Liverpool which is supposed to have some very interesting young girls on offer. Would you like to go there?'

Gerald smiled. 'Do you know, I think that I would like that very much indeed.'

Darkness settled over Rudheath, but though the bakers and deliverymen had long since gone home, a light still burned in the converted barn which was now the shiny-clean home of Worrell's Famous Cakes and Bread.

At the big table, which was situated near the main door, Michelle Worrell was poring over the columns of figures in a huge, leather-bound ledger. This had once been her mam's job, but ever since she'd left Oxford, Michelle had taken over the task herself.

She didn't work exclusively for her mother. A number of other businesses in Northwich had soon come to appreciate the advantages of employing a quick-minded young woman like Michelle, and though she'd only been back home for a little more than a year, she already had more work than she could really handle.

'I'll turn down the next person who asks me if I've got any free time,' she promised herself. But she knew she wouldn't, because it was good to keep busy.

She had never imagined she'd end up a kind of glorified book-keeper, she thought as she scanned another column. When she'd set off for university she'd had other plans. She was going to get her degree as a first step, and then, if she was good enough, a university teaching post. Even before she left Marston, she could already see herself lecturing to enthralled young students, filling them with the same enthusiasm she felt, inspiring them to go on and make great discoveries.

Dreams! Dreams which had crumbled around her. Yet it wasn't her studies which had defeated her. It had been Oxford – or rather, the people she had met in Oxford.

She remembered the first social event she had attended – a gathering in the Junior Common Room, where all the new 'young ladies' were expected to get to know one another. The problem was, from Michelle's point of view, that many of the young ladies seemed to know each other already. She had stood alone in the centre of the room, watching groups of old friends catch up on the gossip, and never felt lonelier. Finally, she had plucked up the courage to approach a slightly haughty girl who was standing by herself, impatiently consulting her watch every few seconds.

'Hello, I'm Michelle Worrell,' she said hesitantly.

The haughty girl looked her up and down, the expression clearly saying that she did not really consider Michelle passed muster. 'One of the Hampshire Worrells?' she asked.

Michelle laughed awkwardly. 'No. One of the Marston Worrells, actually.'

The haughty girl raised an eyebrow. 'And where on earth is that, may I ask?'

'Near Northwich.'

'I'm none the wiser.'

'Have you heard of Warrington?'

'Vaguely. I think.'

'Well, it's near there an' all.'

The girl had grimaced at 'an' all', and Michelle, who was always considered to talk posh by most people in the village, realised that her accent must sound very common to this well-bred young lady.

'Isn't all that area very . . . well . . . industrial?' the haughty girl asked, as if she was giving Michelle an opportunity to correct her misapprehensions.

'There's a lot of saltmines an' brine works around there,' Michelle admitted.

The haughty girl had put her hands up to her face in mock horror. 'Oh, my dear, how awful for you! I imagine it was a great relief for you to go away to school.'

'I didn't go away to school.'

The haughty girl looked like she could hardly believe her ears. 'Then where did you receive your education?'

'At Marston School until I was fourteen, an' then at the technical college in Northwich. You see, me mam – my mother – didn't want me goin' away from home.'

The haughty girl sighed as if she had finally given up. 'Well, I'm sure you'll have a wonderful time here after the technical college in . . . Northwich, was it?' A new group of chattering young women entered the room, and the relief was evident on her face. 'And now if you'll excuse me,' she said to Michelle, 'there are some people I simply have to talk to.'

Michelle soon learned that the other students fitted neatly into two categories: there were the country set, who regarded Oxford as little more than a finishing school, and there were the professional types, the daughters of big city solicitors and doctors, who were more serious, but no less at ease in their new surroundings.

Michelle, a baker's daughter – a *tradesman's* daughter – fitted in with neither group. Conversations, when she had them, were awkward, and she was always conscious of the girls looking out of the corners of their eyes, as if what they wanted most in the world was to get away from her. And so, since they didn't seem to want to talk to her, she stopped trying to talk to them.

She fell into a routine, once her lectures were over, of cycling straight back to her lodgings in Brewers Street, a pile of books in her bicycle basket to keep her occupied during the long night.

A couple of weeks into the term, she started to hear whispered references to someone called 'the mouse', references which were usually followed by giggles, and it did not take her long to work out the mouse in question was her.

She threw herself even deeper into her studies. While the other girls went to dances, drove out to the country in young men's cars, or had riverside picnics, Michelle pored over books on the binomial theory.

It was like being trapped in an unreal world, where time passed, but she was not allowed to grow. She had her nineteenth birthday, and then her twentieth – both spent alone in her room – and she felt no more like an adult than she had at eighteen. If anything, she felt even *less* like one, because she was losing the knack of talking about anything but her work.

She lasted for two and a half years before she finally cracked. The college doctor said it was a mild nervous breakdown brought about by worry over her studies, and the death of her father. But it wasn't. The work had been going well, and though Michael's death had shocked her, she could have survived that. No, it wasn't either of those things. It was the loneliness and isolation which she could no longer take.

'You'll wear your eyes out with all that studyin',' said a voice from the doorway of the bakery.

Michelle looked up into the grinning face of her brother Billy, who was the head baker. 'What are you doing here?' she asked. 'You should have gone home hours ago.'

'I did,' Billy admitted, 'but then Mam told me that you'd be workin' late tonight, so I thought I'd drop in an' make sure that you were all right.'

Michelle smiled fondly at her brother. He was nearly two years younger than she was, but they had always been close, and as he had grown older, Billy had become more and more protective of her.

Michelle remembered when Mam had rescued him from the dirty old coal barge which had been his foster home. He'd been such a pathetic little thing with barely more meat on him than a half-starved rabbit. He hadn't been able to speak a word and had crawled round the house like a crab. That was what Richard Worrell had done to him, she thought, and though she knew the man was really *Uncle* Richard, she just couldn't bear to use the term.

'Are you?' Billy asked.

'Am I what?'

'Are you all right?'

'And just how do you think I'd manage to be *all wrong* in a quiet place like Rudheath?'

Billy shrugged. 'Well, you know . . .'

'No, I don't know. Now stop pestering me, our Billy, and get yourself off home,' Michelle said.

'If you're sure you'll . . .'

'I'll be fine.'

Billy shifted his weight awkwardly from one foot to the other. 'I'll be off, then,' he said.

Michelle smiled weakly. 'Good idea. You've got an early start in the morning.'

Billy left, and Michelle returned to her ledger, but her mind refused to settle back on work. Thoughts of Richard Worrell had naturally led her to thoughts of Gerald Worrell. How handsome he always looked riding through the village – how dashing.

What did *he* see when he looked at *her*? She took a pocket mirror out of her bag, removed her spectacles, and gazed down at her silvered image. She had the same hair-colouring as Mam, she thought, but whereas Mam usually let her hair flow free, she had hers tied up tightly in a bun.

Her eyes were blue, again like Becky's, but weren't they a little further apart? A little *too* far apart? Then there was her nose. That was like her mother's, too, but whereas the slight tilt always looked so attractive on Becky, it only seemed awkward on her.

Her mouth was all right, she supposed, the teeth were regular and white, although maybe the lips were a little thin.

Not a bad face, all in all, but certainly not the kind of face which could ever be expected to captivate a man like Gerald Worrell.

'So there's not much point in even thinking about it, Mouse,' she said, glancing around the bakery and then turning back to the leather-bound ledger.

Gerald would never look at her. When he fell in love, it would be with one of the brown-limbed country girls who had wanted nothing to do with her at Oxford.

Chapter Two

Aggie Spratt was a large woman who made even plumping up a feather bed seem a noisy process, and as she unloaded the breakfast crockery from the Welsh dresser, the boarding-house dining-room reverberated to crashing and clattering.

'Lodgers! Who needs 'em?' Aggie asked, as she slammed the plates down on the table. But though she would not admit it, even to herself, she loved her job and would have been lost without it.

'Boardin' houses!' she said to the knives and forks. 'A boardin' house is nothin' but slavery.'

The boarding house was, in fact, two houses. Three of the lodgers slept in number 49, where they also ate, and the fourth had a room over the chip shop in number 47. Spudder Johnson, who was probably the most unlikely landlord in the world, slept in the back room of 47, but ate all his meals with his lodgers because he liked their company.

The back door opened, and Spudder walked in. As usual, his skin glistened as if he'd just been given a thorough scrubbing in a very hot tub, and his blue eyes had that slightly vacant look which immediately told people that he was not quite all there.

'Lovely day again,' he said, as Aggie banged the frying pan down on the hob over the fire.

'Best early summer that I can ever remember,' Aggie agreed. 'Do you want me to get the lodgers up?'

A look of alarm came to Spudder's face. 'Give 'em a couple more minutes,' he said hastily, because he knew from experience that Aggie's way of getting anybody up was to shake them unceremoniously out of their beds.

There was the sound of footsteps on the stairs, and the first of the paying guests appeared in the doorway, a dapper man in his fifties, with short grey-black hair which formed a widow's peak.

'Mornin', Mr Marvello,' Spudder said cheerfully.

'Good morning to you, my young friend. And how is my favourite local entrepreneur feeling today?'

'Very well,' Spudder replied, assuming that Marvello was talking about him, but really having no idea what an entre . . . entre . . . the thing he'd been called . . . had meant.

Mr Marvello, or the Great Marvello, as he much preferred to be known, had moved into the boarding house when Mary Taylor – Becky Worrell's mam – was still running it. He was a magician who travelled the music halls of the North of England and had once, as he never tired to telling anyone who would listen, 'performed before royalty'.

What he didn't usually mention, perhaps wisely, was that the 'performance' had consisted of a few card tricks on a tree stump on a private estate near Lymm. And what he *never* mentioned was that though his audience had been the late king, then the Prince of Wales, he hadn't realised it until he'd seen the prince's picture in the paper later that day.

A second boarder entered the room. He said a curt good morning, and took his customary seat at the table. He was a tall man, of around forty-five, with sharp, intelligent eyes and a short, tightly clipped moustache.

'You goin' to be stoppin' with us long this time, Mr Bingham?' Spudder asked.

'A few days. Perhaps a week. I'm not entirely sure.'

Which is about as much as he ever says, Spudder thought. Mr Bingham really was a bit of a mystery. He had arrived at the boarding house shortly after Ned Spratt had left to marry Aggie. That had been years ago, yet nobody knew any more about him now than they did then.

Though he paid for his lodgings all the year round, Mr Bingham wasn't really a full-time lodger at all. He disappeared for months on end, and even when he was in Marston, he seemed to do nothing but go for long strolls. And it was a little strange that such a gentleman as he obviously was should choose to live in a humble establishment like Spudder's.

The last two men to take their seats at the table were both watermen – or flatmen as they were sometimes called – who worked on the steam barges which carried Northwich salt up the River Weaver to the bustling port of Liverpool.

The elder of the two, Captain Fred Davenport, was a grizzled old seaman with a balding head and a white beard. He had sailed the tall ships as far as China in his day, but said that now he was getting old, a gentle trip up the River Weaver was more than enough excitement for him.

The other flatman, Jim Vernon, was much younger. He could not have been called handsome – his face was perhaps a little too rounded, his cheeks a little too like crab apples – but he had kind brown eyes and a generous mouth. He had just finished his apprenticeship, and was now the mate on Captain Davenport's barge.

Spudder liked both the watermen immensely, but then he found it very difficult to *dislike* anybody at all, even when he knew that he should.

Aggie brought the food to the table, and the lodgers attacked it with pleasure because, for all her noise, she was one of the finest cooks in mid-Cheshire.

'Will you be goin' to Liverpool today?' Spudder asked the two flatmen as he speared a piece of sausage.

'Aye, we are that,' Captain Davenport replied. 'They finished loadin' th'old tub last night, so it'll be waitin' for us when we get there this mornin'.'

'I, myself, shall be leaving straight after breakfast,' the Great Marvello announced. 'I have secured an engagement in one of the finer palaces of entertainment in Bolton, where I will, no doubt, mesmerise the local inhabitants with my feats of prestidigitation.'

'You mean, you've got yourself another job?' Spudder asked.

The Great Marvello sighed. After all these years, he should have learned that while such fancy words routinely dazzled his audiences, they had no effect on his host. 'Yes, Spudder, I have got myself another job,' he said.

'What about you, Mr Bingham?' Spudder asked. 'What will you be doin' today?'

The tall man looked up from his bacon and eggs. 'Oh, I

expect that I will find something to amuse myself with,' he said, and then resumed eating.

In an identical terraced house just a few doors down from the boarding house, Becky Worrell dropped a dollop of lard into the frying pan and swung the hob over the open fire. As if it had been waiting for the signal, the door by the stairs swung open and her son Billy entered the room.

'Mornin', Mam,' he said chirpily. 'What are you cookin' up for me today?'

'Sausages an' eggs suit you?'

'Just the job.' Billy sat down at the table and opened the *Northwich Guardian* at the classified advertisements section. 'Have you given any thought to what I said about us movin' house?' he asked.

Instead of answering, Becky pulled the hob clear of the fire and dropped two sausages into the frying pan.

'Well, have you?' Billy repeated.

Becky shrugged her shoulders irritably. 'You always ask me that kind of question when I'm busy.'

'Come on, Mam!' Billy replied.

Though she had her back to him, Becky knew her son well enough to know that he was grinning. 'What do you mean, "Come on"?' she asked.

'I've seen you prepare a meal for twenty people, and still find time to natter while you were doin' it.'

He was right, Becky thought. It wasn't that she *couldn't* discuss it while she was cooking, it was just that she didn't *want* to.

'We've got money,' Billy said, as Becky placed a piece of bread into the frying pan. 'We can easily afford somethin' better. So why should we stay in a saltminer's cottage with only one tap, an' that in the wash-house? It's very inconvenient.'

Becky turned the sausages. 'I've got used to it,' she said. 'I don't really find it very inconvenient at all.'

'An' I suppose you don't find it inconvenient goin' to the outside lavvy in the middle of winter, either, do you?'

Becky laughed again. 'I've done that nearly all me life.'

She had. True, for a while she and Michael had lived in a

grand house in Northwich, but she'd never really been comfortable there, and moving into the cottage had been more about feeling at home again than it was about freeing money to invest in the business.

'Just because you've always done it isn't any reason to *keep on* doin' it,' Billy said.

No it wasn't, but for all its drawbacks, Becky loved her little house. It was there that she'd brought up her two children. It was there that she and Michael had spent most of their married life when he wasn't away in Africa, trying his best to stop the slave trade, and, when he could find the time, dealing in salt and rubber.

She looked up at the photograph in the silver frame which took pride of place on the mantelpiece. How handsome her late husband had been. It didn't seem fair that a man like him, who'd done so much good for others, should have caught a disease so foul that it had killed him in a matter of hours.

There were footsteps on the stairs, and Michelle appeared. She was wearing a conservative tweed suit and long button boots. On her head was a flowerpot hat which would have looked much better on an older woman. Her severe steel-framed spectacles – which Becky suspected she hardly needed at all – were clamped firmly on her nose, making it look far less attractive than it really was.

'Sausages and fried bread?' Becky asked her daughter. 'Or there's a bit of bacon left, if you fancy it.'

Michelle shook her head. 'I've no time for breakfast today. Barlow's the butchers have asked me to go over their books this morning, and I'm due at the Northwich Gas Company by twelve o'clock at the latest.'

'You can't go out with nothin' in your stomach, Michelle!' Becky protested.

'I'll get something later,' Michelle promised, then she kissed her mother and brother on the cheek, and was out of the door.

'Flighty thing, isn't she?' Billy said, grinning. 'It's about time she realised life isn't just one big party.'

'You show a bit more respect for your older sister,' Becky said sharply, though she knew really that Billy had nothing but respect for Michelle.

The grin on Billy's face melted away. 'Don't you ever worry about her?' he asked.

Becky turned back the frying pan, cracked an egg against the rim, and carefully slid it into the bubbling lard. 'How do you mean, worry about her?' she said cautiously.

'Sometimes I wish she'd start takin' the world just a little bit less seriously,' Billy said earnestly.

'Your sister's set on makin' a name for herself in the town, an' you can't do that without hard work,' Becky said protectively. 'There'll be plenty of time for havin' fun when she's properly established.' But despite having jumped to her daughter's defence, Becky understood why Billy should feel like he did, because she sometimes felt that way herself.

Michelle had gone away to university a fun-loving kid, but since she'd recovered from her breakdown she'd been acting almost like an old maid. At nineteen, I was already married with a child on the way, Becky thought. And yet there was Michelle, twenty-two years old and apparently showing not the slightest interest in lads. Maybe all those loud men who claimed that women shouldn't be well educated because it would destroy their femininity were not just spouting a load of hot air after all. No, that's a stupid way to think! Becky told herself angrily. But even so, she wished Michelle would be a little more . . . well . . . normal.

When Billy had finished his breakfast and gone off to work, Becky walked over to the mantelpiece and, almost reverently, picked up her husband's photograph.

She remembered when it had been taken, in the early summer, three years earlier. It was just before Michael had been due to sail. They had walked hand in hand through a field of foxgloves. They had seen a yellow wagtail sitting on a tree stump – fresh from the Africa to which Michael was soon to return – and at dusk they had spotted a couple of fox cubs, gambolling near their earth.

The next morning, Becky had travelled with Michael to Liverpool. She had stood on the dock, waving, as his ship sailed slowly out of sight. It was the last time that she would ever see him alive.

She looked now at his smiling face, which seemed to reach

her even from beyond the grave. 'I *do* worry about our Michelle,' she told the photograph, 'an' I don't know what to do about her. But you would have, wouldn't you? You *always* knew what to do.'

Richard Worrell and his son Gerald had not risen early – they had never been to bed. Now, as the sun cast its pale morning rays over the grounds of Peak House, they sat in their breakfast room, topping up the large quantity of alcohol which was already swilling around inside them.

'What a night we had, my son!' Richard said, taking a swig from the large brandy glass he held in his hand.

'What a night, indeed!' agreed Gerald, pouring some more brandy, first for his father and then for himself.

He was lucky to have such a fine son, Richard thought, looking at Gerald through bleary eyes – a son who took after him in so many ways. But there was still one more way in which he wanted Gerald to follow in his footsteps, and perhaps now would be the time to make sure that he did.

'Do you know that when I was your age, I could have had any girl that I wanted,' Richard said, enunciating carefully so as not to slur his words.

Gerald looked vaguely offended, as Richard had intended him to. 'And so could I, if I wished to,' he said. 'But why should I go to the trouble of sweet-talking an amateur into my bed, when for just a couple of pounds I can buy the services of an expert?'

Richard narrowed his eyes. 'What about the thrill of the chase, my boy?' he asked. 'Where's your spirit of adventure?' He paused. 'But perhaps you're right. I mean, it *is* easier to pay for it, and perhaps you wouldn't . . .'

Gerald shot his father an angry glance. 'Perhaps I wouldn't what?' he demanded.

Richard feigned slight embarrassment. 'Well, you're a good-looking boy, there's no doubt about that, but it takes more than good looks to get a woman on her back, you know. You need a certain charm, a certain flair – a little of what the French call *je ne sais quoi*, which means . . .'

'I know what it means, thank you, Father,' Gerald said, a

cold note slipping into his voice. 'Are you saying that while you have it, I do not?'

Richard shrugged. 'Who's to know, unless it's put to the test? But you're probably right. Why bother with amateurs when there are so many willing professionals around?'

Gerald put the brandy bottle carefully on the table. 'I am willing to wager you that I can have any girl in Northwich – *any* girl – if I once put my mind to it.'

At last! Richard thought. For twenty-two years I have been waiting patiently for this moment, and now it has finally arrived. 'When you proposed a wager just now, what *kind* of wager did you have in mind, my boy?' he said aloud.

Gerald smirked drunkenly. 'Anything you care to choose, my dear father.'

Richard pretended to consider the matter. 'For a wager to be worthwhile, both sides must be willing to bet more than they can afford to lose,' he said finally.

'Agreed.'

'Very well, then. If you succeed, I will give you five thousand pounds, which is a considerable amount of money, even for a man in my position.'

Gerald's drunken eyes lit up with greed. 'And if I fail?' he asked.

Richard smiled. 'If you fail, you agree to work for me for two years without pay.'

'But that's preposterous!' Gerald protested.

Richard laughed. 'How thin your confidence seems when your back's up against the wall.'

Gerald reddened. 'Very well, then. Two years without pay,' he snapped.

'There is one more condition,' Richard said.

'And what might that be?'

'I must choose the girl.'

'Why?'

'Because if I left the choice to you, how do I know that you wouldn't pick a homely washergirl whom you could seduce with ease?'

'A washergirl, Father?' Gerald said. 'Do you really think I'd stoop that low?'

'No,' Richard admitted, 'but it would be only human nature to select someone you were sure you would succeed with. That's why we can only be sure it's a *real* challenge if the choice is mine.'

Gerald took another swig of brandy, the expression on his face indicating very clearly that he suspected a trick. 'The girl must be single,' he said cautiously.

'Of course she must,' his father agreed, far too readily for Gerald's liking.

'And by single, I mean that she must not already be intending to marry or even be in love.'

'That goes without saying. I don't want to set you an impossible task, my boy.'

Gerald nodded, slowly and carefully. 'Very well, then. The choice is yours.'

'Your hand on it?' Richard asked, holding out his own.

'My hand on it,' Gerald agreed, taking his father's hand and shaking it firmly.

'The challenge that I have in mind is a very fair one,' Richard said. 'In fact, since I have already trodden an almost identical path to the one I wish you to follow, I do not see how I could possibly make it fairer.'

For a second a vaguely puzzled expression filled Gerald's face, but it was replaced by a look of sheer astonishment. 'Good God, Father! You're going to ask me to seduce my cousin, Michelle, aren't you?'

'Exactly,' Richard agreed.

Chapter Three

It was the afternoon of the first Saturday in July. Signs of new life were everywhere, from the flowering rushes which bloomed pink in the small ponds around the old mine shafts, to the young blue tits who flew from tree to tree, flapping their wings with an urgency which said they were never quite sure they were going to make it.

Becky and Michelle were sitting at the kitchen table, with the back door open to let some of the mild summer air into the room. Michelle was going through some accounts – Why is she *always* doin' bloody accounts? Becky thought – and her mother was reading the *Northwich Guardian.*

Becky frowned at the long article she'd been trying to make sense of, then laid down her paper on the table. 'Where's Serbia?' she asked her daughter.

Michelle glanced up from her ledger. 'Serbia? It's somewhere in the Balkans.'

'Thanks! That really tells me a lot,' Becky said, making a comical face.

Michelle grinned at her. 'Sorry, Mam. It's one of those tiny little countries that are sandwiched between Greece and the Austro-Hungarian Empire.'

Becky shook her head in admiration. 'An' you can say that straight off the top of your head, without even lookin' it up. I wish I'd had your education.'

Michelle laughed, but not entirely wholeheartedly. 'Education's not everything,' she said. 'Anyway, why this sudden interest in far-off places?'

'I was just readin' about it in the *Guardian*. It seems that some feller called the Archduke Ferdinand of Austria has gone and got himself killed there.'

Michelle laughed again, more lightly this time. 'You make it sound like he did it on purpose.'

'I suppose I do,' Becky admitted. 'Anyway, the paper says the Austrians are really mad about it.'

'I expect they are. Wouldn't we be mad if someone assassinated the Prince of Wales?'

Becky frowned. 'Do you think this could mean trouble? I mean, like war?'

Michelle looked out through the open kitchen door. Swallows were swooping effortlessly around the wash-house and beyond the back yard wall she could just see the shining green leaves of a young silver birch tree.

'It's difficult to imagine anything as horrible as a war could happen on a lovely day like this,' she said.

'I know it is,' Becky agreed, 'but your Uncle George thinks there's a good chance that war *will* come.'

'Uncle George!' Michelle said, with just a hint of scorn in her voice. 'I love him dearly, but honestly, Mam, what does he know about it? It's nearly twenty years since he came out of the army. We've had two new monarchs and seen in a different century since then.'

'Don't underestimate your uncle just because he thinks and talks slowly,' Becky warned her daughter. 'He runs very deep, does our George.'

'I didn't mean to be rude about him,' Michelle said contritely. 'Anyway, what if he *is* right? We've had wars before, and it might not be pleasant, but it's not exactly the end of the world, is it? I mean, it won't really affect us here in Cheshire.'

'I'm worried about our Billy,' Becky confessed. 'I'm worried to death that he might be called up.'

'Now why on earth would they call up our Billy?' Michelle asked. 'Fighting's a job for professional soldiers, not master bakers. Just think about it for a minute. How *could* they call up all the young men? If they were gone, who'd work in the factories and the fields?' Michelle laughed. 'You couldn't very well expect the women to do it, could you?'

Becky joined in with her daughter's laughter. 'No, that doesn't seem likely, does it? I'm just an old worry-guts, I suppose. I used to think your gran mithered too much about her kids, and now here I am, doing exactly the same thing. And you'll do exactly the same, when you . . .' She stopped, realising she had said the wrong thing, but not knowing how to get out of it.

'When I what?' Michelle asked. 'When I have some children of my own?'

'Yes, I was going to say that,' Becky admitted. 'Listen, love, I'm not trying to run your life for you, but . . .'

'But . . .?'

Becky forced a smile to her lips. 'But like I said, mothers worry. It's their job. And if there's nothing to worry about, then they worry about *that*.'

An uneasy silence fell, which was only broken when Becky, with some relief, said, 'Blast!'

'What's the matter?' Michelle asked.

'Oh, it's nothin' really. See them three loaves in that basket in the corner? Well, I promised your Uncle Spudder I'd deliver them to him, and then I completely forgot. I'd better take them round to him now.'

'I'll do it,' Michelle said.

'You've got your work to do.'

'Ten minutes away from the ledger isn't going to make a lot of difference. Besides, I think my brain could do with a rest from all those columns.'

A *long* rest, Becky thought, but aloud she said, 'Well, if you're sure you don't mind . . .'

'Of course I don't mind,' Michelle said, standing up and reaching for the basket.

Michelle knocked on the back door of number 47, waited for a few seconds, and knocked again. There was no answer. Maybe Uncle Spudder's gone for one of his walks in the woods, she thought.

She considered leaving the loaves on the back step, but the family of blackbirds perched on the apex of the wash-house roof and looking down expectantly, was enough to persuade her that was not a very good idea.

'I suppose I'd better see if there's anybody in next door,' she decided.

Her knock on the kitchen door of number 49 was greeted by a rich, deep voice which called out, 'Come right in, whoever you are. The door's not locked.'

Michelle lifted the latch and stepped into the kitchen. There were two men sitting at the table – Captain Davenport and Jim Vernon. The Captain was smoking an old briar pipe, which was rapidly filling the room with sweet-smelling grey smoke. Jim Vernon had the paper spread out in front of him and, like Becky earlier, seemed to be reading the foreign news.

The Captain smiled, revealing a row of teeth which were stained yellow by the countless pounds of tobacco he smoked, and ground down by the numerous pipe stems he'd gripped between them. Still, it was a nice smile, Michelle thought, a welcoming smile.

'Well, if it isn't Miss Worrell,' the Captain said. 'This is a pleasant surprise, isn't it, Jim?'

'Aye, very nice,' mumbled Jim Vernon, looking up at Michelle for only an instant, and then turning his eyes back to his newspaper.

'An' what can we do for you on this lovely afternoon, Miss Worrell?' the Captain asked.

'I just brought these loaves round,' Michelle explained, holding out her basket. 'They're for Uncle Spudder.'

'Well, it was kind of you to go to all that trouble,' the Captain said. He screwed up his eyes a little. 'You're lookin' very pale, lass. Workin' hard, are you?'

'I do have rather a lot on my plate just at the moment,' Michelle admitted.

'Do you know what I think you need, young lady?' the Captain asked her. 'A good blast of fresh air. Why don't you come out on the river with us tomorrer?'

'But tomorrow's Sunday.'

'There's no such thing as a Sunday on the river. Salt has to be shifted whatever the day. So if you've got nothin' else planned, why don't you come along for the ride?'

Michelle was surprised and a little confused by the sudden offer. 'But you won't be coming straight back to Northwich tomorrow, will you?'

'No,' the Captain said. 'We'll have to hang about in Liverpool while they unload the cargo.'

'So how would I get home?'

The Captain scratched his head. 'Now that is a problem,' he said. 'Let me think. You could walk back, I suppose. Or swim back. Or maybe you could even wait for winter to come and skate back.' He chuckled. 'Then again, the simplest thing might just be to go to the railway station an' catch a train.'

Michelle was starting to feel very foolish. Imagine getting so flustered over a simple trip to Liverpool, she thought. Those confident girls at the university would have taken it in their stride. 'I suppose I could come back by train,' she conceded. 'But I'm still not sure I should . . .'

'You'd only be away a few hours,' the Captain said encouragingly. 'Go on, lass – say that you'll come with us. We'd both like you to, wouldn't we, Jim?'

'Yes,' muttered Jim Vernon, his eyes still glued to his newspaper and his face slowly turning a brilliant shade of red.

Though she normally had a lie-in on the Sabbath, Becky got up early that particular Sunday morning and was already cooking breakfast when Michelle came down the stairs.

'You shouldn't have bothered, Mam,' Michelle said.

'I just wanted to make sure you got a bit of food in your stomach for once,' Becky replied. Which was not entirely true. She did want to make sure her daughter had a decent breakfast, but she was also curious about what Michelle would choose to wear for her trip up the river, and she was pleasantly surprised by what she saw.

The jacket was blue, complementing Michelle's eyes, had bound edges and trim, and fastened with a single button. Her ankle-length skirt was black, and the long button boots with Louis heels gave her an extra inch or so in height, making her look very elegant.

'Well, have you seen enough, Mam?' Michelle asked.

The hint of annoyance in her voice made her mother jump. 'Nothing wrong with admiring my own daughter, is there?' Becky asked defensively.

'Are you so keen to have me married that you'll even take Captain Davenport for a son-in-law?'

'No, of course not. I wasn't thinking about you getting married at all. Honestly!' But Becky was treading the tightrope between lies and truth again. She didn't see this particular trip as leading Michelle any closer to the altar, but she did hope that it would be the start of her daughter coming out of herself a bit more – and who knew where that might lead?

On all other days of the week, Not-Stopping Bracegirdle rose at dawn, for fear that she might miss something. On Sundays, when everyone stayed in bed later, there was no such urgency, and it was not until after seven that she made her way slowly downstairs. She would be eighty next birthday, and her joints creaked and complained more with every passing year, but her eyes were still as quick as they'd ever been. And her tongue, when she told people she was 'not stopping' but had they heard about so-and-so, had lost none of its sharpness.

There was a fire in the kitchen to be poked back into life and the kettle to be filled, but before she did either of these things, Not-Stopping hobbled into her front room, drew back the curtain a little, and peered out into the street. Another curtain across the road moved slightly, as if there were someone just behind it.

'Huh!' Not-Stopping grunted, realising that Florence Bracegirdle, her daughter-in-law and deadly rival, had already taken up position at her own look-out post.

Half-a-Mo-Flo! That was what people called the detestable woman, though never to her face, and it was just what a busybody like Florence deserved to be called. Must be terrible to have a nickname an' not even know about it, Not-Stopping thought, glad that everybody called *her* by her given name of Elsie.

She heard footsteps coming down the lane, but was disappointed to find that it was only Captain Davenport and Jim Vernon, who were probably only up at that hour because of the tides.

Ten minutes passed and no one else appeared. The curtain in the house across the road flickered once more, and then was still. So Flo had given up for the moment, Not-Stopping thought. She was almost inclined to do the same herself, but there was just the possibility that while Flo was away something might happen, and she decided to give it another quarter of an hour.

Her time was almost up when she heard the click-clicking of heels coming down the street. Not-Stopping opened the curtains a little wider, and gasped at what she saw. Michelle Worrell! Dressed up to the nines! Now where might she be goin' at this time on a Sunday mornin'? Not-Stopping wondered excitedly.

Anything else she might see that morning would only be an anticlimax. Not-Stopping hobbled to her kitchen, thinking of ways to help her get to the bottom of the mystery.

While she waited for the kettle to boil, she glanced through the *Northwich Guardian* to see if she could pick up any gossip secondhand. There was quite a long article about the German Kaiser rattling his sabre – whatever that meant – but foreigners were of no interest to her, and she turned to the local news.

An automobilist had been fined for driving his motorcar at an excessive speed. And quite right too – twenty-three miles an hour was almost unthinkable! Men's suits were advertised for one pound and five shillings. Disgraceful! Why, when she was a girl, you could have kitted out the whole family for that kind of money. And in the last few months, no less than *three* bicycles had been stolen in the Northwich area.

'Three!' Not-Stopping said aloud. 'An' in just a few months.' What with the Kaiser rattlin' his sabre, bicycles bein' stolen and Michelle Worrell out at that time in the mornin', she didn't know what the world was coming to.

The steam barge – or steam *packet*, as Captain Davenport said it should more properly be called – was moored just beyond Northwich Town Bridge. It was a long wooden vessel, with a tall mast, and its name, the *Damascus*, painted on its side.

The Captain and his mate were standing on the deck. Captain Davenport gave a friendly wave when he saw Michelle approaching. Jim Vernon didn't.

'Don't you look as pretty as a picture this morning, Miss

Worrell,' Davenport called to her as she got closer to the boat. 'It'll be a pleasure takin' a real lady down the river, instead of just tons and tons of salt.'

'Thank you, Captain Davenport,' Michelle said, though looking at Jim Vernon, she was already beginning to wonder if this was such a good idea after all.

The Captain held out his hand to help her aboard. 'So what do you think of the old tub?' he asked jovially.

Michelle glanced around her. At one end of the boat was the mast, at the other a funnel belching out smoke as black as any that had ever come out of Richard Worrell's saltworks chimneys. Close to where they were standing was a small rowing boat.

'It looks bigger when you're on it than it does from the riverbank,' Michelle said.

'The old lady's ninety feet long, with a beam of twenty foot – twenty feet wide,' the Captain said proudly. 'An' now, if you'll excuse me an' Jim for a few minutes, Miss Worrell, we've got to cast off. Wouldn't do for us to miss the tide, would it?'

Michelle watched as the Captain and his mate quickly unfastened the mooring ropes and neatly coiled them up. They made it look so easy, but she was certain that if she tried it herself, she would soon be in a dreadful tangle.

It was enjoyable to watch them work, and she couldn't help thinking that seeing Jim Vernon on his boat was like seeing a completely different person to the one she knew from the boarding house. Back in Marston, he seemed unsure of himself – awkward and clumsy – but here on the *Damascus*, his movements were so controlled and confident that they could almost be called graceful. And it was surprising that though she'd seen him dozens of times at Uncle Spudder's, she'd never noticed how strong and muscular his body was.

The boat was finally free of its moorings and all the ropes were coiled.

'Right, I think we're just about ready to go,' Captain Davenport announced.

Michelle looked around again. There was no one else on the deck. 'Aren't there any other . . .?' she began.

'Crew?' the Captain supplied, chuckling. 'There's the engineer, but he's already down in the engine room, lookin' after his boiler. We usually 'ave a cabin boy with us, but he doesn't get paid overtime, so we don't use him on a Sunday.'

'So there's just the three of you?' Michelle asked, half-expecting the captain to say he'd only been joking and the rest of the crew who were needed to handle this big boat would be along in a few moments.

'Just the three of us,' Davenport confirmed. 'Bein' the captain of a steam packet on the Weaver isn't much like captainin' a big ocean-goin' liner, is it?'

It suddenly occurred to Michelle that she might have unintentionally insulted the Captain. 'Oh, I'm so sorry,' she said. 'I didn't mean to imply . . . I mean I never wanted to suggest . . .'

Davenport chuckled again. 'That's all right, lass,' he said. 'I've never been one to stand on me dignity. Anyway, it's time we got crackin'. There's not much for you to see for the first 'alf mile or so, so while I'm steerin' us through that, maybe Jim 'ere'd like to show you round the boat.'

Jim did not look overjoyed with the idea. 'I've got things to do, Fred,' he said. 'You know I usually wash down the deck at the start of the journey.'

Davenport ran his eyes along the deck boards. 'They look clean enough to me, Jim,' he said, 'an' since we've got a guest on board, you can forget that little job for today.'

'Then why don't I, er, take the wheel,' Jim suggested. 'After all, you are the captain, so you're the one who should be showin' Miss Worrell round.'

Davenport shook his head. 'I've never worked with a better mate than you,' he said, 'but you're still inexperienced, and the channels around here can be treacherous. So, if you don't mind, I'll take the responsibility for steerin' us out.'

'All right,' Jim said. He turned reluctantly to Michelle. 'If you'd like to come this way, Miss Worrell.'

He led her to the after end of the steam packet first, right past the funnel and to a part of the deck which vibrated so much it made her toes tingle.

'The engine room's right below us,' Jim shouted, and lifted

the hatch to show her the great steaming monster which was driving the boat forward.

They walked the length of the boat again, past the mast and up to the steam winch. 'That's what we use to lift cargo in and out of the hold,' he explained.

Michelle gazed down at several thick oblongs of glass which were set into the deck. 'What are they?' she asked.

'They're what we call the decklights,' Jim said. 'They're like windows. See, we're actually standin' above the cabin.'

Maybe it was the movement of the boat or the fresh breeze blowing through her hair which made her reckless, but whatever the reason, Michelle suddenly found herself saying, 'Could we go and see the cabin?'

Jim Vernon looked dubious. 'I'm not so sure that's a good idea, Miss Worrell. You see, the cabin wasn't designed for entertainin' young ladies in.'

'Oh, don't be silly,' Michelle told him, her recklessness rising to new heights. 'I'd like to see it. I really would.'

'Well, I suppose it can't do no harm,' Jim conceded. He lifted the hatch cover and gestured towards the ladder.

'I'd rather follow you,' Michelle told him.

'No, I think it'd be much better if you went down first,' Jim said firmly.

It was only when she was halfway down the steep ladder that Michelle realised why Jim had been so insistent. If he'd gone first, he would have put himself in a position to watch her climb down, and it was impossible for her to descend the ladder without revealing more of her ankle than was quite proper.

She was pleased he had such sensibility. Yet at the same time, it was strangely embarrassing, because, for such a thought to come to him, mustn't he already have had her ankles on his mind?

The cabin was an oblong room. At the far end was a table, a simple board which was hinged at one end to the wall and fastened to the ceiling at the other by a long brass rod. Running along the sides of the cabin at the far end were benches which Michelle assumed were bunks at night – though even in her current state of recklessness, she would never have dreamed of asking Jim about that.

It was the grate which really fascinated her. It was next to the ladder and had an oven in it, just like the one at home. The fire was blazing merrily, and resting over it was a brass kettle just coming to the boil.

'We always keep the kettle goin' when we're on the river,' said Jim, who had now reached the bottom of the ladder. 'Well, was it worth the climb down?'

'I think it's very interesting,' Michelle told him. 'And really very cosy.'

Jim walked towards the other end of the cabin. 'That's where we keep all our crockery an' cutlery,' he said, pointing to an alcove behind the table. 'See that bowl? That belongs to the Captain. An' do you know what he uses it for?'

'I've no idea.'

Jim chuckled, seeming at ease for the first time. 'He drinks his tea out of it,' he told her. 'He says that's the way they used to do it in his seagoin' days, and he's got no reason to change his ways now that he's only workin' the river. I can't see it meself. I'd rather have a pint mug any day of the week.'

Jim's sudden relaxation was having the opposite effect on Michelle. The cabin was beginning to feel quite small to her, and she realised that wherever she stood in it, she would never be too far from the muscular young flatman.

'It's . . . it's a little hot down here,' she said. 'I think I'd like to go back up on deck.'

'All right,' Jim said, and this time *he* was the first one to step on the ladder.

The ideal thing about the best room of the New Inn, from Not-Stopping Bracegirdle's particular point of view, was that it had a serving hatch from the bar, and through that hatch, whenever she was ordering drinks, she had a clear view of just what the men were getting up to. Not that there's much to see tonight, she thought.

Archie Sutton, one of the lumpmen from Worrell's, was there, of course, but then it would have been news if that boozin' bugger *hadn't* been there. And there were a couple of ferriers from the Adelaide mine, who Not-Stopping was sure were up to no good – or if they weren't then, they soon would be. But on the whole, the bar presented a poor diet of gossip – bread and dripping, when what she really wanted was roast beef and three veg. Never mind, she already had at least one juicy titbit to feed to her drinking cronies.

'Can I get you anythin', Mrs Bracegirdle?' asked a voice from the other side of the hatch.

Not-Stopping dragged her eyes away from the ferriers and looked up at Walter Dickens, the new landlord. Not that 'new' was perhaps quite the right word. Dickens had taken over the pub when Paddy O'Leary and his wife Cathy had moved back to Ireland ten years earlier, so he wasn't new *exactly*, but in a place like Marston ten short years was new enough.

'I said, can I get you anythin', Mrs Bracegirdle?' the landlord repeated.

Not-Stopping put on her most winning smile. 'Three bottles of milk stout, if it's not too much trouble, Mr Dickens.'

She watched him as he walked to the other end of the bar to get the bottles. He was a solid man of about fifty, with a roundish red face and pale brown hair now reduced to a few thin strands swept across his otherwise bald head. He claimed to have been in the army before he took over the pub – a sergeant major in the Royal Fusiliers, no less – but Not-Stopping was never inclined to believe any stories which weren't her own.

The landlord returned and handed over the drinks. 'It'd make more sense to move the milk stout to this end of the bar,' he said. 'After all, it's you and your mates who drink most of it.'

Not-Stopping shot him a hostile look, then quickly reverted to her smile. There were some people in the world who were too important to fall out with, she'd long ago decided – and pub landlords definitely came within that category.

'You are naughty, Mr Dickens,' she said, wagging her index finger playfully at him. 'To hear you talk, anybody'd think I was always suppin'.'

'An' nothin' could be further from the truth, could it?' the landlord asked, grinning inwardly.

'Of course it couldn't,' Not-Stopping agreed. 'I only have a bottle now an' again. An' then only on doctor's orders.'

'If everybody had a doctor like yours, I'd be in clover,' the landlord said before sweeping her money into the palm of his hand and going off to serve other customers.

Not-Stopping returned to the table where her daughter-in-law, Florence, and her oldest friend, Dottie Curzon, were waiting for their drinks.

'That landlord just told me he wishes all his customers were under the doctor,' Not-Stopping said. 'I think he must be goin' soft in the head.'

'There's a lot of it about,' said Flo Bracegirdle.

Not-Stopping glared at her daughter-in-law. Flo had long black hair, and her nose was somewhat like a beak. In fact, Not-Stopping thought, she resembled nothing so much as a crow. She wondered why her son had married the bloody woman, never realising that he had done what countless men had done before him, and chosen someone who, in so many ways, was just like his dear old mum.

If you had a story of your own to tell, it was as well to launch into it before Florence got started, and that was what Not-Stopping did now. 'You'll never guess who I saw in the lane at half past seven this mornin',' she said.

Flo did a quick calculation and worked out that whatever it was, she'd just missed it. 'Well, if I'll never guess, there's no point in tryin', is there?' she said.

Pointedly ignoring her daughter-in-law, Not-Stopping turned to Dottie Curzon. 'Michelle Worrell,' she said. 'That's who I saw. Fancy her goin' to Northwich at that time on a Sunday mornin'.' She paused for a second, giving time for this information to sink in before dropping her bombshell. 'Still, I suppose she had to leave that early . . .' she continued '. . . if she wanted to catch the tide.'

'Catch the tide?' Flo repeated. 'What's Michelle Worrell got to do with catchin' tides?'

Not-Stopping grinned. 'Oh, you are with us, then, are you, Florence?' she asked. 'I didn't think you seemed that interested a minute or two ago.'

'Stop playin' games, Elsie, an' tell us what you know,' Dottie Curzon said.

'I'd never have worked it out if I hadn't seen them two flatmen from Spudder Taylor's go past half an hour before . . .'

'I saw them,' Flo interrupted.

'. . . but I checked with Spudder himself, an' it's true.'

'What's true?' Flo asked exasperatedly, although if she'd been telling the story, she'd have padded it out for just as long as Not-Stopping was.

'It's true Fred Davenport an' Jim Vernon have taken Michelle to Liverpool on that barge of theirs.'

'That was kind of 'em,' Dottie Curzon said.

Mother-in-law and daughter-in-law exchanged glances. Much of the time they were at each others' throats, but there were occasions when it was necessary to unite against good-natured innocence.

'Kind of them!' Flo said.

'Kindness has nothing to do with it,' Not-Stopping told her. 'It's lust. That young one – that Jim Vernon – *burns* with lust for Michelle Worrell.'

'You can see it in his eyes,' Flo added.

'I allus thought he was such a nice lad,' Dottie said mildly. 'But I have to admit, he's not right for her. Not with her havin' an education an' her father havin' been a gentleman an' all that.'

'So who would you suggest *is* right for her?' Not-Stopping asked, hoping that Dottie would come up with someone totally *wrong*.

'I think she should be seein' somebody more appropriate, like her cousin Gerald.'

This was better than could have been expected. Not-Stopping snorted with disgust. 'After the way that family's been at each other's throats all these years, do you think it's likely they'll kiss an' make up now?' she demanded.

'You never know,' Dottie said. 'People do sometimes forgive and forget.'

'An' folk could walk on water if they wanted to,' Not-Stopping told her.

'It's just that it doesn't happen very often,' Flo chipped in.

The village was in darkness with Michelle Worrell walked up Ollershaw Lane, and she was glad of it, because sometimes being in the dark helped her to think.

It had been quite a day in many ways. She'd enjoyed the trip up the river – taken pleasure in the views of the countryside and been fascinated to see the way the boat locks worked – but she wasn't quite sure what to make of Jim Vernon.

At times, like when he was handling the boat or explaining how it worked to her, he seemed calm and confident, totally in control. But there were other moments, lulls in the work, when he was as awkward as a schoolboy waiting outside the headmaster's door for his punishment.

And her own reactions were, if anything, even more puzzling. She wanted him to be interested in her, and yet she didn't. She liked it when he was close to her, and yet she had to fight back the urge to run away from him. She wondered if this was what people meant when they said you had a crush on somebody. I shouldn't be feeling like this, she told herself angrily. Not at my age.

But that was the problem, wasn't it? During those frozen years at university, all she had learned was mathematics, so that now, although her real age was twenty-two, she didn't feel that old at all – didn't feel any older than a gawky, giggling girl.

She had reached her own back door. With a heavy sigh, she took the latchkey out of her bag and inserted it in the lock.

Chapter Four

Spudder first noticed the girl during the dinnertime rush. She was standing on the other side of the road, next to the Red Lion, but it was the chip shop she had her eyes set on.

She was still there when the last customer had been served and Spudder was about the shut up shop and take his afternoon break. Then, just as he was going to close the front door, she began to walk slowly and hesitantly towards him.

She'd not been much more than a vague shape when she'd been standing across the road, but as she got closer, Spudder got a better look at her. She was a thin girl with a pale, drawn face, and lank, reddish hair. She was dressed in a worn brown frock which was much too big for her, and boots which could have benefited from a long visit to the cobbler's shop. She could have been seventeen or eighteen, or maybe even a little bit older – it was difficult to say.

She walked along the path to the door and looked up at him. 'Is this your chip shop, mister?' she asked in a voice so thin it was a wonder it didn't break.

'Yes, it is,' Spudder said.

'Only I was wonderin' if you've got any chips left over now you've finished servin' all your customers.'

Spudder glanced back into the shop. 'There's a few,' he said, 'but they'll be cold by now.'

'That don't matter,' the girl said.

Spudder remembered his own visit to the shop, when he'd only had enough money in his pocket for chips, but Mam had insisted on him having a fish as well. 'How long is it since you've had a decent meal inside you?' he asked.

The girl shrugged. 'I don't remember.'

'Then you'd better come inside,' Spudder told her. 'Aggie

made me a meat pie this mornin', and I think it should be just about baked by now.'

When Aggie Spratt made a meat pie, she made it as if she was expecting to feed an army, and the one that Spudder pulled out of the oven was no exception.

'Looks lovely,' the girl said.

Spudder placed a knife and fork in front of the girl, and piled a large chunk of the pie on to her plate.

'Ain't you goin' to have none of the pie yourself, mister?' the girl asked.

'I'm not really hungry,' Spudder said. He *was* – Mam once said he had the heartiest appetite she'd ever seen – but he had a feeling that even though it was a huge pie, the girl was starved enough to polish it all off.

And he was right. She didn't eat like some hungry people do, bolting their food down. Instead, she was restrained, almost ladylike, but within half an hour there was not a piece of meat or a trace of pastry left in the baking dish. The girl sat back in her chair, a look of satisfaction spread all over her face.

'Why don't you tell me a little bit about yourself,' Spudder suggested.

The satisfied look disappeared instantly, and the girl glanced at the door as if she was about to make a dash for it.

Spudder put a restraining hand gently on her arm. 'Don't worry,' he said softly. 'If you're in trouble, it won't be me that tells the bobbies on you.'

The girl swallowed gratefully. 'Me name's Ivy,' she told him. 'Ivy Clegg.'

'An' mine's Spudder Johnson. What happened to you, Ivy?'

'How do you mean? Happened to me?' the girl asked.

Spudder shrugged. Using words, explaining himself, was not his strong point, but he supposed he'd better try. 'You're half-starved an' I bet you haven't got two ha'pennies to rub together,' he began. 'But you don't look like the kind of beggar we usually get round here. You look more . . . I don't know . . . more respectable, somehow.'

Ivy smiled gratefully. 'Thank you,' she said. The smile turned into a grin. 'Poor but honest – that's me.'

'You were goin' to tell me somethin' about yourself, weren't you?' Spudder prompted.

Ivy nodded. 'We was brought up in the Crewe Work'ouse, me an' me mam an' me brothers an' sisters, and when I was thirteen I was put into service in a big house just outside Sandbach. It was all right for the first few years. I mean the work was hard – the youngest servants always got the worst jobs – but I didn't mind that. Then the master's nephew come to live with us. An' you can imagine what happened after that, can't you?'

'No,' Spudder said. 'I can't.'

'He started lookin' at me, followin' me everywhere. Oh, I know it's hard to believe, seein' me as I am now, but I wasn't bad lookin' in them days.'

'You're not bad lookin' now,' Spudder interrupted. 'Give you a proper wash and put a bit of weight on you, an' you'd be quite presentable.'

Ivy looked at him strangely. 'Are you takin' the mickey out of me?' she demanded.

'No,' Spudder said. 'Why would I want to do that? Go on, tell me the rest of your story.'

'He started makin' certain suggestions to me. Well, you know what I mean, don't you?'

'No,' Spudder said.

'You don't? Honestly?'

'Honestly.'

The strange look was back in the girl's eyes. 'You're not married, are you?' she asked.

'No.'

'Nor got a lady friend?'

Spudder laughed. 'Me!' he said.

'But you must know how animals behave.'

'Oh yes,' Spudder agreed. 'Before I took over the chip shop, I used to work on a farm.'

'So you know how animals make babies.'

Spudder was thunderstruck. 'You mean this man wanted to give you babies?' he asked.

Ivy sighed. 'Not exactly,' she said. She paused and looked deep into his eyes. 'I don't want to be rude or anythin',' she continued, 'but are you a bit slow?'

Spudder nodded. 'That's what they told me at school,' he admitted. 'An' there are times now when I don't quite understand what's goin' on around me. But one of me gaffers told me I was the fastest 'tater picker he'd ever seen. An' I can make smashin' chips when I set me mind to it.'

Ivy smiled. 'You're a nice man, Spudder.'

Spudder beamed back at her. 'Thanks very much. Now what happened about this man who tried to . . . who wanted to . . .'

Ivy's smile assumed a slightly mischievous edge. 'Give me babies?' she asked. 'Well, he finally got so desperate for me that he followed me down to the cellar, and when I wouldn't do what he wanted, he attacked me.'

'The rotten bugger!' Spudder said.

'Oh, I gave as good as I got,' Ivy told him. 'By the time we'd finished, his face was covered with scratches and I was still as pure as I'd ever been.'

'You what?' Spudder asked.

'He hadn't given me any babies.'

'Oh, I see.'

'Anyway, the master was furious. I mean, it was my fault, wasn't it? It just had to be. He said he was goin' to have me sent back to the work'ouse, an' in the meantime I could stay locked in one of the cellars an' contemplate me sins. But then one of the servants let me out, an' I ran away.'

'An' what have you been doin' since?'

Ivy shrugged again. 'Whatever I could. Sometimes, in the summer, the farmers want extra help in their fields, then when winter comes I usually make me way to Manchester an' get a job in a sweatshop. It's a hard life, but I've not gone the way of many and become a fallen woman.'

'What's a fallen woman?' Spudder asked.

Ivy shook her head. 'You really don't know, do you?'

'I wouldn't have asked if I did.'

'Perhaps there's some things in this world it's better not to know,' Ivy said. 'Anyway, that's my story. What's yours?'

'Well, Mam started the chip shop with the money Mr Taylor got when he was blown up. Down the mine, I mean – that's where he was blown up. Mr Taylor was Mam's husband, an' her name was Taylor an' all, an' she wasn't me real mam or she'd have been called Johnson. Or maybe I'd have been called Taylor. I can't really work that out.'

Ivy laughed. 'You're not tellin' this very well,' she said.

'I know,' Spudder admitted. 'I never do. I'm not good at tellin' stories.'

'Why not start at the beginnin' and take it slow? Where were you born?'

'In Liverpool,' Spudder said. 'Me dad was a lawyer.'

A look of disbelief crossed Ivy's face. 'You don't talk like a lawyer's son,' she said.

'I used to. But when I started workin' on the farms, they laughed at me, an' so I learned to talk like what they did.'

'But how did you ever come to be a farm labourer in the first place?'

'Oh, that was because of me dad.'

'He *wanted* you to work on a farm?'

Spudder shook his head. 'No, it wasn't like that at all. You see, me mam – me real mam, not Mrs Taylor – me mam died when I was still a baby . . .'

'I'm sorry.'

'. . . an' so me dad brought me up on his own. He was dead strict. He never gave me no presents, an' if I did anythin' wrong, I got the strap.'

'How terrible.'

'That wasn't the worst of it. When I was nine or ten, the school I was goin' to told me dad I was backward. So he took me out of it. Said I was goin' to have me lessons at home. Only there weren't no lessons. He locked me up in a little room at the top of the house. I never saw nobody. I had a bucket when I wanted to go to the lavvy, an' he used to bring me food himself. He told the servants I was dangerous – I heard him through the door.'

'What a wicked man.'

'Sometimes he'd get drunk an' give me a beltin' just for bein' backward. Then one day, when I'd grown big enough an' couldn't take it no longer, I hit him back. I knocked him down the stairs. He was just lyin' there, not movin', when I ran out of the house. I thought I'd killed him.'

Ivy gasped. 'But you hadn't, had you?'

'No, but it was years before I found that out, 'cos I never went back to Liverpool.'

'So how did you come to own the chip shop?'

'Well, like I said, Mam – I called her Mam 'cos she sort of adopted me – was runnin' it – an' the boardin' house. An' when I got the money, I bought both of 'em.'

'What money?'

'From me dad's will, when he really did die.'

'I see,' Ivy said.

'Of course, Mam still ran both businesses, an' I was her lodger. But when she died, I thought I might as well have a go at runnin' 'em meself,' Spudder said, his eyes misting over slightly at the memory.

'An' do you enjoy it?' Ivy said.

'Oh yes. Everybody's been very helpful,' Spudder hesitated for a second. 'Where are you sleepin' tonight?'

'I don't know. Why?'

'When I came to Marston, I didn't have nowhere to sleep neither. An' Mam said that if I peeled a dolly tub of 'taters I could have a room for the night.'

'That was nice of her.'

'So I was just wonderin' – are you any good at peelin' 'taters?'

Ivy suddenly bowed her head and her shoulders started to shake uncontrollably.

'What's the matter?' Spudder asked alarmed.

Ivy looked up again, and there were tears in her eyes. 'It's nothin' really,' she sobbed.

'It must be somethin', if it's making you upset enough to cry,' Spudder said.

'It's just that you've been so kind to me, an' after all the hard times that I've been through, it's a bit much to . . .'

Spudder jumped out of his chair and wrapped his arms around her thin shoulders. 'Don't cry,' he cooed softly. 'I'll see that no harm comes to you.'

'An' what's goin' on here?' said a loud voice from the other end of the kitchen.

Spudder sprang away from Ivy, and saw the huge frame of Aggie Spratt blocking the doorway.

'This . . . this is Ivy Clegg,' he stuttered. 'She's a bit upset.'

'I can see that,' Aggie told him. 'What I want to know is what's *made* her upset.'

The girl lifted her head and looked at Aggie through tear-streaked eyes. 'I don't want to cause no trouble,' she said. 'Now I've had me food, I'll be off.'

Aggie advanced into the centre of the room. 'Oh no, you won't,' she said. 'What you'll do is go into the back yard, and you'll *stay* there until I tell you different.'

Ivy was about to protest, then, looking at the formidable cleaner again, she bit back the comment and, head bowed, made her way to the back door.

'Now then, Spudder, what's goin' on?' Aggie said, once the girl was in the yard.

Spudder was so confused that he found it difficult to put his thoughts in order, but he tried anyway. 'She's a work'ouse girl,' he said. 'Or anyway, she used to be. An' now she's got nowhere to live.'

'I see. An' what exactly were you plannin' to do about that, young man?'

Spudder clenched his hands. 'Well . . . er . . . I thought I might offer her a job.'

'An' what kind of job did you have in mind for this work'ouse girl who hasn't got nowhere to live?'

'I don't really know,' Spudder said unconvincingly.

'Oh yes, you do,' Aggie told him. 'You can't fool me, Spudder. Never have been able to. So you'd better come out with your idea right now, and save us both a bit of time.'

'I thought she could do jobs around the house,' Spudder admitted. 'Cleanin' up and things like that.'

Aggie's eyes hardened. 'That's *my* job you're talking about.'

'I know it is,' Spudder continued, 'but I thought what with you gettin' on a bit . . .'

Aggie put her huge hands on her vast hips. 'I could still fling you over me shoulder and carry you for twenty miles without breakin' into a sweat,' she said.

'I know that, but . . .'

'But you still want to take my job off me an' give it to that slip of a girl.'

The idea horrified Spudder. ''Course I don't. You'd keep your job, only she'd be here to help you.'

Aggie narrowed her eyes, as if she was uncertain what to say next. 'And where do you imagine she'd live?'

'I thought she could have my room,' Spudder said. 'See, she'd move in there, an' I'd sleep in the kitchen.'

Aggie shook her head in amazement. 'An' you really think you could do that, do you? Have that girl sleepin' here, in a house with five men?'

'There's only really two of us in here,' Spudder pointed out. 'The other three are in number 49.'

'That's even worse. At least when there's five, there's safety in numbers.'

'I don't understand,' Spudder told her.

'No, that's the trouble. You often don't.' Aggie looked out of the window at the girl, who was standing by the wash-house. 'You stay here,' she said. 'I'm goin' to talk to this Ivy Clegg.'

It was a terrifying sight – Aggie bearing down on her – but Ivy did not flinch.

'Now,' Aggie said, 'you'd better tell me *exactly* what you told Spudder.'

Ivy recounted her tale again, only this time there was no need for her to explain why the young gentleman in the big house had been so interested in her.

'Men can be real sods,' Aggie said when she'd finished. 'Spudder wants you to come an' work for him. How would you like that?'

Ivy Clegg could hardly believe what she'd heard. 'I'd like that very much,' she said.

'Hold out your hands,' Aggie ordered her. Ivy did as she was told, and the other woman examined them carefully. 'Well, from the look of them, it doesn't seem as if you're afraid of doin' a bit of hard work,' Aggie admitted. 'But there's still one thing that bothers me.'

'An' what's that?'

'Spudder's a bit special to people round here,' Aggie explained. 'I mean, by rights he should never be runnin' that chip shop. He's no idea how to handle the money. You could cheat him every time he gives you change. But folk wouldn't do that – not to Spudder. Are you understandin' what I'm sayin'?'

'Yes.'

'Then there's me. If I wanted to, I could rob him blind, but I'd no more think of doin' that than I would of dancin' naked through Northwich.'

'An' you're worried that if I start workin' for him, I might take advantage of him.'

'In a nutshell.'

Ivy looked Aggie straight in the eye. 'I've had people takin' advantage of *me* too often to do it to others,' she said. 'Especially to somebody who's been as kind to me as Spudder has.'

'And you're sure you mean that?'

'I mean it.'

'I see,' Aggie said.

Spudder had been watching the whole thing through the window, but when Aggie returned to the kitchen, he still had no idea what had been said.

'Well, I've had a long talk with Ivy,' Aggie told him. 'Long enough to have found out what I wanted to know, anyway.'

'An' what do you think?' asked Spudder, who was dying of suspense.

'I think she's a decent enough girl, who's been through a few rough times,' Aggie said. 'An' I think she'll be a good worker around the house if she's properly supervised.'

'Oh, I'll make sure of that,' Spudder began with relief.

'You will *not*,' Aggie interrupted him. 'She'll be my assistant, won't she?'

'Well, yes.'

'Then I'm the one who'll see to it that she does her job properly. Now, about wages. I think seventeen an' six a week would be reasonable. You can afford that.'

'Can I?' asked Spudder, who had no idea what he could afford and what he couldn't.

'Yes you can, and she'll need all that, what with havin' to

buy herself some decent clothes an' pay for her board an' lodgin'.'

'But I won't be chargin' her for board an' lodgin',' Spudder protested.

'I know you won't,' Aggie told him. 'Because young Ivy won't be livin' here.'

'Won't she?'

'She will not. I'm not havin' her reputation besmirched by the likes of that Mrs Bracegirdle. An' I'm not about to put temptation in the way of young Jim Vernon. She'll be movin' in with me an' Ned.'

'I see,' Spudder said, though things were moving so fast that he didn't really see at all.

'An' if you can see your way clear to lendin' her a couple of pounds in advance of 'er wages, me an' 'er'll leave a bit early today an' go down to the secondhand shop. That dress she's wearin' now isn't even fit to make dusters out of.'

'I'll get the money now,' Spudder said. 'It's in the cash box under me bed.'

Aggie gave him a despairing look. 'I thought I told you to put your savings in the Post Office.'

'I get very confused in the Post Office,' Spudder said. 'At least with me tin box, I know where I am.'

'All right, keep it in your tin box,' Aggie said, defeated. 'But for goodness' sake, hide it.'

'But it is hidden,' Spudder said. 'I told you, it's under the bed.'

'So now *I* know where it is.'

'But you wouldn't steal from me, Aggie.'

'You're right, I wouldn't. But I wish I could be as sure about the rest of the world. Have you told anybody else about this tin box of yours?'

Spudder looked guilty. 'I might have mentioned it to one or two people,' he admitted.

'Then hide it somewhere else.'

'All right, I'll put it in the ward—'

'An' don't tell me about it, Spudder. Don't tell anybody. Do you understand?'

'Yes,' Spudder said.

'There's one more thing about this Ivy girl,' Aggie said. 'If you suddenly start gettin' any urges when you're with her, come an' talk to me about them.'
'What kind of urges?' Spudder asked.
'You'll know 'em if you get 'em,' Aggie told him.

Chapter Five

It was the Wednesday morning after the Sunday boat trip to Liverpool. The clock had only just struck eight, but this was the glorious summer of 1914, and when Michelle Worrell stepped out of her back door, she noticed that it was already starting to get hot.

She walked briskly down Ollershaw Lane, her briefcase swinging in her hand. Williams the draper's on the High Street was to be her first stop of the day, and after that she had an appointment at the coal depot in Lime Kiln Lane. She looked at her watch. If she didn't hurry, she'd be late for that first call, then it would take her all day to catch up on herself.

She reached the edge of Wincham village and turned left on to the cinder track which served as the main road between Marston and Northwich. Ahead of her she saw a cart, from which two men were shovelling fresh cinders on to the ground. They seemed to be repairing this road every other day, but then there was good reason for that – subsidence, the curse of Northwich.

Sometimes the subsidence would be gradual – almost graceful – and buildings would slowly sink, inch by inch, until it was impossible to open the door or see anything but earth out of the ground-floor windows. At other times it would be dramatic and unexpected – like the occasion when the Northwich to Warrington mail coach was swallowed up by a large crater which hadn't been there a second before. You just never knew when – or how – it would happen.

Michelle checked her watch again and started to walk even faster. She was between two little lakes now, known as 'flashes' locally. The one on her right, the smaller of the two, was called Neumann's Flash. The one on the left, which was connected to the River Weaver, was known as Ashton's Flash, after the Ashton saltworks which clung perilously to its edge.

Neither of the flashes was natural, though it would not be quite true to say that they were entirely manmade, either. Rather, they had been a sort of unintentional team effort. Man had carved out the earth, and Nature had collapsed the ground above, then filled the resultant pit with water.

Somewhere at the bottom of Ashton's Flash lay the remains of her dad's saltworks, which had gone under during the worst case of subsidence Northwich had ever experienced. People who'd seen it still talked about that day with awe. Mines had been flooded, brooks had collapsed. The water pressure had been so great that for several hours, the River Weaver had actually flowed backwards.

A smile came to Michelle's face. And while all that was going on, Mam was in the office, she thought, directing the salvage operation and – when she found that she'd got a bit of time to spare – giving birth to me.

Her dad had not been there to see either the birth of his daughter or the destruction of the business he had worked so hard to build up. While her mam had looked up in horror at the tall chimney toppling over, her dad had been searching the oil rivers of West Africa for Uncle Jack, who had been captured by cannibals. It had been an almost impossible task – scouring thousands of miles of river, hoping to find one individual – and only someone as optimistic as her dad would ever have even considered it. Yes, he'd been a fine man, Michael Worrell, and she still missed him.

'But I don't miss him as much as Mam does,' she said softly to herself. Becky Worrell had always tried to shield her children from her own worries and sorrows, but there were times, when she didn't know Michelle was watching her, that her eyes would express a sadness which almost broke her daughter's heart.

I do so wish that she'd fall in love with someone, Michelle thought wistfully. And she hoped that when she, herself, fell in love – if she ever did – she and the man she married would be as happy as her mam and dad had been.

A rider appeared in the distance, coming from Northwich.

She saw at once that he was tall and well built, but it was not until he got closer that she realised it was her cousin, Gerald.

She felt her heart start to beat faster, just as it always did when she saw him. And then a panic engulfed her. They had been as close as this before, but they had never been so completely alone. What could she do?

Several plans flashed through her troubled mind in rapid, blurred succession: when he was almost level with her, she would pretend that a button on one of her boots had come undone, and bend to fix it as he rode past her. She would act as if she was so absorbed with some private thought that she was hardly even aware of where she was – let alone that he was there, too. She would say hello to him, but do it in such a way as to suggest that she had no idea who he was.

No, all of those were stupid! She would smile at him and say, 'Good morning, cousin Gerald,' even though they had never, in their entire lives, exchanged a single word.

Gerald was perhaps ten yards away from her when his horse suddenly reared up. Gerald flew through the air, hit the ground heavily, and was still.

Almost before Michelle realised what she was doing, she had dropped her briefcase and was running, panting and frantic, towards her supine cousin. 'Are you all right?' she shouted at the top of her voice. 'Please say that you're all right!'

By the time she reached him, he was starting to move his arms and legs a little, though it was obvious to her that any such movement was causing him a great deal of pain.

'Damn and blast that horse!' he groaned. Then he saw her standing over him, and a look of horror came to his face. 'S-sorry,' he stuttered. 'I didn't see you, or I'd n-never have cursed like that.'

'That doesn't matter,' Michelle told him.

'It d-does. A g-gentleman should always remember . . .'

'Forget all about that. How badly are you hurt?'

Gerald shifted position again, and winced with the effort. 'Oh, I'll be fine,' he said bravely. 'Take more than a fall from a stupid horse to keep me on the ground for long. But if you c-could just help me to get up?'

'Of course,' Michelle said, holding out her hand.

Gerald took the hand and began – slowly and gingerly – to rise to his feet. 'My ankle appears to be a little weak,' he said when he was standing again. 'Would you m-mind if I leant on your shoulder for a second or two?'

Mind? Of course she would mind! She had never been that close to a man before – at least a man who was not family. Then she reminded herself that he *was* family, even if he was from a branch of it which hated her side with a passion.

'No, I wouldn't mind at all,' Michelle lied.

Gerald placed both his hands on her right shoulder. The hands seemed to burn, to be almost imprinting themselves on her skin. His smell, a heady mixture of leather and masculinity, invaded her nostrils. She did not know how long she could bear to be so close to him, yet she was afraid of pulling away in case he was not able to stand without her support.

After what felt like hours, he finally removed his hands and painfully hobbled a few feet away from her. 'Nothing broken, anyway,' he said cheerfully. 'But I must admit I am a little shaken up.' His gaze fell on the Townshend Arms which lay further along the road to Northwich. 'I say, you w-wouldn't like to have a drink with me, would you? I don't normally drink myself, but I could really use one now.'

Michelle felt herself beginning to turn red. 'I can't,' she said in confusion. 'I have an appointment in Northwich, at the draper's. I'm going to be late as it is.' Why had she said that about the draper's? she wondered. What did *he* care who the appointment was with?

Gerald looked downcast. 'If you must go, then I suppose you must. But I would be very grateful if you could spare me just a few minutes. You see, I'm not used to p-public houses, and I certainly would feel more comfortable going into one if I had someone else with me.'

His eyes were just like a puppy's, she thought, big and sad and appealing. 'I could make time for *one* drink, as long as it's quick,' she said.

Gerald smiled gratefully. 'Only the one,' he promised her. 'To take the shakes away.'

Michelle went back to where she'd dropped her briefcase. Behind her, she heard Gerald whistling for his horse. After its one act of treachery, the animal seemed to have no more defiance in her, and cantered docilely over to her master.

Gerald led his horse, and Michelle walked beside them. The closer they got to the Townshend Arms, the easier Gerald appeared to find walking.

'Can't understand how it happened,' he said. 'I'm a good horseman – it's one of my few pleasures.' He smiled. 'Perhaps it was seeing you which threw me off balance.'

The Townshend Arms, which for some long-forgotten reason everyone in Northwich called the Witch and Devil, was a two-storey brick building located on the edge of town. When Gerald and Michelle entered it, there were already a few early-morning drinkers standing in the saloon bar.

'Shall we go in there?' Michelle asked.

'I think not,' Gerald replied. 'I believe that in places like this, ladies are not encouraged in the saloon.' He looked around. 'There must be what they call a "best room" somewhere. Let's see if it's through that door.'

The door Gerald had indicated did, indeed, lead to the best room, though except for slightly less grimy wallpaper, there seemed to be very little about it that was better than the saloon. But at least they had the place to themselves.

Gerald led Michelle over to a cracked oak table, and pulled out a chair for her with such ease that it was plain his ankle was no longer bothering him at all.

A young, but fairly plain, barmaid appeared. 'Nice to see you again, sir,' she said with a winning smile.

In return for the smile, Gerald gave her a cold stare. 'I think you must be mistaking me for someone else, girl,' he said.

'No, sir, I'm sure you were . . .'

'I assure you, I have never been into this establishment before,' Gerald said icily.

The barmaid bobbed down into a half curtsy. 'Beg your pardon, sir. Very sorry for the mistake, I'm sure.'

Gerald turned to Michelle. 'I really don't have much experience in these m-matters,' he said to her. 'What do you think I should ask the girl to bring?'

'Brandy is supposed to be good after you've had a shock,' Michelle said.

'But isn't that a spirit? They are supposed to be frightfully strong. Wouldn't it go straight to my head?'

'It might if you're not used to it,' Michelle agreed. 'You could always try a port instead.'

Gerald considered it. 'Yes, a port would be safer, I think,' he said. 'And what would you like?'

'I'll have the same, only with lemonade.'

Gerald dismissed the barmaid with an airy wave of his hand, then looked deep into Michelle's eyes. 'I shall be bruised and stiff tomorrow,' he said, 'but it was worth it.'

'Worth it?' Michelle echoed.

'Of course. How many times do you think I've noticed you when I've been riding through Marston?'

'I wasn't sure you'd *ever* noticed me.'

'I always wanted to speak to you, but n-never plucked up the courage. Couldn't you sense that?'

'No. I never even suspected.'

'Now, because of a happy accident, we're sitting side by side and finally talking to each other.'

'I've often wanted to speak to you, too,' Michelle confessed in a sudden rush.

'And why shouldn't we have s-spoken?' Gerald asked. 'I know that my father has behaved very badly to your family – believe me, he behaves badly to everyone – but is that any reason why *we* should be enemies?'

'No, it isn't,' Michelle said.

'I wanted to come to Uncle Michael's funeral,' Gerald told her, 'but my father wouldn't let me. He is a hard, unyielding man, you know. But let's not talk about him. There are surely more pleasant subjects that we c-can discuss.'

'Do you always stutter?' Michelle asked. The moment the words were out of her mouth, she found herself wishing she could take them back, but it was too late. 'I'm so sorry,' she said. 'I didn't mean to ask you such a personal question.'

But Gerald only smiled. 'It's all right,' he said. 'I don't mind talking about it. My st-stutter comes and goes. When I am n-nervous, as I am n-now, it gets worse. I nearly always stutter in the presence of my father.'

The barmaid appeared with the drinks, and Gerald handed her a silver coin.

'I'll just go and get your change, sir,' she said.

'Keep it,' Gerald told her.

'But you gave me half a crown, sir.'

'Keep the change,' Gerald insisted.

The barmaid thanked him, curtsied again, and left the room.

'That was nice of you,' Michelle said.

'W-what was?'

'Giving her such a big tip.'

'I th-think I was a little rude to her earlier, and I was trying to make up for it.' Gerald took a cautious sip of his port. 'We have put ourselves into a difficult situation, you and I,' he said.

'In what way?'

'Up until now, when we have seen each other on the street, we have looked the other way. Do you think we will be able to go back to doing that?'

'No,' Michelle admitted. 'That would be silly.'

'So how *are* we to act?'

'I'm not sure.'

'Perhaps it would be easier if we got to know each other a little better,' Gerald suggested. 'I have a motorcar – a rather fine one, actually.'

'Do you?' Michelle asked, wondering to herself where all this was leading.

'Yes I do. And sometimes, on Sundays, I like to drive out in the countryside.'

'That must be pleasant.'

Gerald ran his index finger nervously around the rim of his port glass. 'You know, you're n-not making this any easier for me,' he said.

'Aren't I? I'm not trying to be difficult. Honestly. It's just that I'm not sure what you're trying to—'

'Say you'll come,' Gerald interrupted.

'I beg your pardon?'

'Promise that you'll come with me the next time I drive out in the country.'

Michelle frowned. 'I don't think I can promise anything like that on the spur of the moment,' she said. 'I'll have to ask my mam about it first, you see.'

Gerald threw back his head and laughed loudly. 'How old are you?' he asked.

'Twenty-two.'

'The same age as myself. And even I, with a tyrannical father like I have, would not contemplate asking his permission to go out for a simple drive.'

Of course he wouldn't ask for permission, Michelle thought. And when he put it like that, it did seem daft for *her* to want to. But even so, she wasn't quite happy about it.

'Besides,' Gerald continued, a troubled look coming to his face, 'if you *did* ask her, she would be bound to say no.'

'You can't be certain of that.'

'Oh, but I can. She will tar me with the same brush as my father – which is understandable, considering the abominable way he treated her.'

'I don't like doing things behind my mam's back,' Michelle said dubiously.

'Nor would I ask you to – at least not for long. But consider this as a possibility: once we have seen each other a few times, and you tell your mother all about it, she will come to realise that I am of a different mettle from my father. Then, perhaps, she will permit me to visit your home, and I will finally have the opportunity of talking to my aunt and cousin Billy, of whose company I have been deprived all these years.'

Once we have seen each other a few times, Michelle repeated silently in her mind. A drive in the country had seemed a big step to her only a few moments earlier, but what Gerald was now proposing was nothing less than a giant one.

'Do say yes,' Gerald pleaded. 'You can't possibly know how much it would mean to me to have a real family for the first time in my life.'

What to do? What to say? Nothing Michelle had experienced before had equipped her for this moment. But Gerald was waiting, and she had to say *something*.

'We *will* go for a drive together on Sunday,' she told him, 'and I *won't* tell Mam about it. But I'm not promising anything after that, Gerald.'

Gerald smiled and nodded his head. 'I have great admiration for a young lady who will not make promises until she is sure she can keep them,' he said.

The *Damascus,* loaded with salt, steamed slowly downstream towards Liverpool. Fred Davenport looked slowly from bank to bank. On both sides of the river, the wheat was already transforming itself from the green of spring to the gold of harvest time. And over the wheat fields were all kinds of birds, hovering uncertainly and then suddenly swooping down past the ragged scarecrows to do a little harvesting of their own.

Fred turned to his mate, who was standing beside him at the wheel. 'I've seen over fifty summers, an' I can't remember one as good as this,' he said reflectively.

'Hmm,' Jim Vernon replied.

''Course, I shouldn't be at all surprised if it snows tomorrer,' Fred said.

'Hmm,' Jim agreed.

'Either that or a typhoon. Then again, it may just rain fire and brimstone.'

It was the last few words which seemed to finally get through to Jim. 'What was that you just said?' he asked.

Fred grinned. 'So you're back with the world again, are you, young Jim?'

Jim looked sheepish. 'Sorry,' he said. 'I was just thinkin' about the war.'

'Which particular war are you on about? The Crimean War? The Boer War?'

'No, not either of them. I was thinkin' about the one that everyone seems to be expectin' soon.'

'An' *what* were you thinkin' about it?'

'That it'll be a bit of an inconvenience.'

Fred roared with laughter. 'Oh, it'll be that, all right – if it *does* come. For a start, it'll put an end to a lot of buddin' romances, won't it?'

Jim reddened slightly. 'Buddin' romances?' he said.

'Tryin' to pretend to me that you don't know what I'm talking about, are you?' Fred asked. 'Do you think I haven't noticed the way you look at her?'

Jim put his hands into his pockets and shrugged his shoulders. 'It's nothin' but a dream,' he said gloomily. 'Here's me, the mate of a rottin' steam packet. And there's her, with her mother's bakery an' her university education.'

'I'll thank you not to call my boat a rottin' steam packet,' Fred said, though not unkindly. 'The old girl may have seen a fair bit of service in her time, but let me tell you, there's a few good years left in her yet.'

'Aye, you're right,' Jim agreed. 'She's not a bad old boat. But you see what I mean, don't you?'

'Listen,' Fred said, 'you're a steady lad, and you're good at your job. A few more years' service with the company, an' you'll have a boat of your own. I'm not sayin' all that makes you the best catch in the district, but even if her mother does own a bakery, Miss Worrell could do a lot worse for herself.'

'Thanks,' Jim said.

'What for? I was only telling you the simple truth.'

'Maybe you are. But you must see that . . .' Jim suddenly trailed off.

'Somethin' wrong?' the Captain asked.

Jim pointed up the river. About a hundred yards further along the bank was a tall man in a smart brown check suit. At first he was walking fairly rapidly, but then he stopped and seemed to be taking an interest in one of the barges.

'That's Mr Bingham, isn't it?' Jim said.

'Looks like him to me,' Fred agreed.

'An' what do you think he's doin' up here, so far away from Marston?'

'Just out for a walk, I expect.'

'Well, it's a blinkin' long walk if that's all he's doin'. An' look! He's taken a notebook out of his pocket, and he's writin' somethin' down.'

'Maybe barges is his hobby,' Fred Davenport said, unconvincingly.

It was eleven o'clock when Gerald Worrell finally arrived at the saltworks, and once he'd tied up his horse, he went straight to his father's office.

Richard was sitting behind his desk, bent over a thick sheaf of invoices which lay in front of him. When his son entered the room, he looked up and scowled. 'Where the devil have you been until this time of day, Gerald?' he demanded.

'I . . . er . . . had a little business I needed to attend to,' Gerald said lazily.

Richard's scowl deepened. 'In case you've forgotten, your main business – the one which actually pays your salary – is this saltworks of ours.'

Gerald smiled. 'And in case *you've* forgotten, Father, we also have a wager.'

'And just what is that supposed to mean, boy?'

'That the reason I am late is because I've been devoting a little of my time towards winning it.'

'Have you indeed!' Richard said, raising one eyebrow. He pointed to a chair in front of his desk. 'In that case, I think you'd better sit down and tell me all about it.'

Gerald sat, extracted his cigarette case from his pocket, removed one cigarette, and lit it.

'Well?' Richard said impatiently.

'You'll never guess what happened to me this morning, Father. I fell off my horse.'

'Fell off your horse! But you're a superb rider,' Richard said, hardly able to believe what he was hearing.

'And I did it right in front of my dear cousin, Michelle.' Gerald chuckled. 'Well, of course, I didn't *really* fall. But I made it look as if I had.'

A smile began to spread across Richard's face. 'I see,' he said. 'And what did Michelle do?'

'Oh, she was most solicitous about the whole thing. First, she helped me to my feet – not that I really needed any help. Next, she let me rest against her. And then we went to the Townshend Arms for a drink – where the barmaid nearly gave me away.'

'Gave you away?'

'Yes. I'd already decided that I'd no chance of winning a dowdy little spinster like Michelle if I showed her my true self, you understand. So instead I was pretending to be the kind of man I thought *would* appeal to her.'

'And what kind of man is that?'

'I thought – and it seems now correctly – that she would be

attracted to the shy, sensitive, nervous type, and so that is the part I was playing.'

Richard beamed. 'I almost wish I'd been there. It must have been something to see.'

'It was. And in that role, I also had to pretend that I wasn't used to strong drink.'

Richard roared with laughter. 'And the little idiot fell for it, did she?'

'Hook, line and sinker. Then the barmaid greeted me like I was a regular customer.'

'Which you are,' Richard pointed out.

'Exactly. And if I hadn't had Michelle with me, I might have turned my warm reception to my advantage – because she's not a bad-looking girl. And anyway, you don't look at the mantelpiece when you're poking the fire. With Michelle there, of course, I had to act as if she'd mistaken me for someone else.'

'And do you think that you really managed to fool your cousin?' Richard asked.

Gerald smiled complacently. 'I'm absolutely certain of it. Otherwise, she would never have agreed to come out for a spin in the Napier on Sunday.'

Richard shook his head in frank admiration, then a look of caution cane to his face. 'You're not going to try and bed her on Sunday, are you?'

'Of course not,' Gerald said, almost scornfully. 'Women like my little cousin are not driven by passion, as we are. For them to open their legs, they have to imagine that they are in love. And even *I* would be hard pressed to persuade the little fool that she loves me in a single afternoon.'

'So how long do you think it *will* take?'

Gerald shrugged his broad shoulders. 'It's hard to say until I've spent a little more time with her,' he admitted. 'But I should be surprised if I hadn't had her by the end of the summer. And then you, my dear father, will be worse off to the tune of five thousand pounds.'

But it will be worth it, Richard thought. Finally, after all the years of humiliation at the hands of Becky and his brother, he would be avenged.

He pictured the scene in his mind – pictured telling Becky that his son had seduced her daughter, just as *he* had seduced *her* all those years ago. How sweet that would be!

Chapter Six

Early summer slid almost languidly into midsummer. The farm hedgerows were invaded by numerous strands of white-trumpeted bellbind. Meadow brown butterflies flitted from flower to flower, and green woodpeckers fed greedily on flying ants. And still the glorious weather held, with scarcely a cloud in the sky and a benevolent sun always shining down.

'It's almost as if nature was doing her best to make up for the mess that us human beings seem to be makin' of the world,' Becky Worrell said to her daughter.

And the world *did* seem to be in a mess. The newspapers still talked gloomily of the crisis in the Balkans. The Austrians, they said, blamed the Serbian government for the Archduke's assassination, and would almost certainly make the tiny Serbian nation pay a huge price for it – a price which most of the other European powers might not find acceptable.

St Swithin's Day, 15 July, arrived. If it rained on that day, the old superstition had it, then it would continue to rain for the next forty days and forty nights. But as the villagers looked up at the sky, they saw nothing but a vast expanse of brilliant blueness. This, they told themselves, was going to be a summer that they would never forget – a summer that they would tell their grandchildren about.

The footsteps coming down the alley were irregular: one normal, the next something of a clumping sound. Becky, who had been chopping up meat for a hotpot, put down her knife and wiped her hands on the tea towel. 'Well, who would have thought it?' she asked herself.

She opened the back door even before her brother George had time to knock, and for a few seconds they just stood there, grinning happily at each other. Then Becky flung her arms as far around George's massive frame as they would reach, and hugged him tightly.

'You stayin' long?' she asked – just as her mam would have done – as she led him into the kitchen.

'A few days.'

'Business or pleasure?'

'A bit of both. I wanted to see you, an' I need to talk to the bosses of a couple of wood yards in Northwich.'

George placed his cloth bag on the floor, then walked over to the table, laid his crutch against it, and swung himself into one of the kitchen chairs. It was nearly twenty years since he'd lost the lower part of his left leg at the Battle of Omdurman, and though you couldn't fail to notice the fact – his wooden replacement being as big and ugly as a Victorian table leg – he now moved almost as well as if he had both limbs intact.

Becky looked fondly at her middle brother – solid carved features, brown eyes which were steady but cautious, dark hair greying at the temples. At one time he'd been a good footballer and had almost turned professional, she remembered, but the pull of the army had been too strong for him to resist, and he'd seen service in Burma, winning two medals before being wounded in the Sudan campaign. Now he lived in London – a place most of the villagers in Marston had only heard of – and managed a wood yard on the Hibernia Wharf.

'I expect you'll want a cup of tea after your long journey,' Becky said.

George grinned. 'Never been known to turn down a cup of Rosie,' he told his sister. 'That's what they call it in Southwark. Cockney rhyming slang, you see. Rosie Lea – tea.'

Becky put the kettle on. 'They seem like funny folk down in London,' she said.

'They're lovely people once you get used to them,' George told her. 'After bein' down there for so long, I couldn't see meself livin' anywhere else now.'

Becky made the tea and then sat down opposite her brother. 'So how are things with you?' she asked.

George thought for a few seconds. He always did that, even when he was answering the simplest of questions. 'Things are fine with us,' he said finally. 'The kids are growin' up faster than you'd imagine possible, Colleen's still got her job down at the pub, an' she's as fit as a fiddle.'

'An' the wood yard?'

'Business has never been better. How are things with the Worrell family?'

'Billy's makin' a grand job of the bakin',' Becky said. 'He's as good as Monsieur Henri ever was. An' our Michelle finally seems to be comin' out of herself.'

'What d'you mean by that?'

Becky shrugged. 'Well, to tell you the truth, she's been a bit of a mouse since she . . .'

'Got over her illness?' George supplied.

'That's right,' Becky said gratefully. 'Anyway, over the last few weeks, she's really started to blossom. She used to keep her hair in a tight bun, but now she's let it loose. She's got herself some new dresses as well. An' she's stopped wearin' them glasses of hers all the time.'

George's eyes twinkled. 'Sounds to me like she's got herself a young feller.'

'Maybe,' Becky agreed.

'But you're not sure?'

'No, because if she has, she hasn't told me anythin' about it. An' as you know yourself, we've never been a family for keepin' secrets from one another.'

George laughed heartily. 'You mean, we're not a family who can keep secrets from *you*.'

'George!' Becky said, with mock disapproval.

'Becky Busybody was what our Philip used to call you.'

'He always was a fanciful boy.'

'Maybe, but he wasn't far from the mark. You were forever tryin' to find out what our problems were – and then doin' everythin' you could to put 'em right for us.'

'Oh, do shut up, George!' said Becky, who was starting to feel embarrassed.

'Still, I suppose I should thank you for stickin' your nose in,' George continued. 'If you hadn't persuaded Colleen to come over an' talk to me at that bonfire your Michael organised that New Year's Eve, we might never have got married.'

But Becky's thoughts had moved on – or rather, back. 'What bothers me about Michelle is that if she *is* seein' a young feller, why doesn't she tell me about it?' she said. 'I mean, is she ashamed of him, or somethin'?'

George laughed again. 'First you say you're not sure she's got a chap, then you're wonderin' if she's ashamed of him. You want to make up your mind *what* you think.'

Becky joined in his laughter. 'Yes, I am a bit mixed up,' she admitted.

George reached across and took his sister's hand. 'But are you happy in yourself?' he asked.

Becky looked down at the table. 'I'm gettin' by.'

A look of concern crossed George's face. 'Gettin' by? No more than that?'

Becky shrugged. 'I've had my share of happiness, you know. More than my share. Now it's my children's future that I'm lookin' forward to.'

'Good heavens, Becky, you're talkin' like an old woman!' George exclaimed.

'Our Jack said that to me, the last time that he was over from Africa.'

'An' our Jack was right an' all. You've plenty of years ahead of you to—'

'What do you think are the chances of war?' Becky asked, hastily changing the subject.

'High,' George said gravely. 'Very high indeed. An' it'll be a war the likes of which us British have never seen before.'

'What do you mean by that?'

A faraway look came into George's eyes. 'I keep thinkin' back to the Battle of Omdurman,' he said. 'Do you have any idea how many men there were in the Anglo–Egyptian army? Fifteen thousand, all told. An' the Khalifa threw *fifty* thousand of his best troops at us in that battle alone.'

'But you won, didn't you?'

'Oh yes, we won all right. The outcome was never in doubt. We had heavy artillery an' Maxim guns. They were armed with spears an' prayer books. I can still see 'em chargin' our encampment, line after line of 'em. Then we opened fire and none of the poor devils even got within three hundred yards of us. It was just like runnin' a scythe through long grass.'

'I never realised it was anything like as bad as that,' Becky said with a shudder.

'The ground in front of our camp was strewn with their dead. We counted 'em later. Eleven thousand we'd killed – an' it took less than an hour.'

'Terrible,' Becky said.

'It was,' George agreed. 'More like an execution than a battle. While all the shootin' was goin' on, I was standin' next to my officer – Lieutenant Churchill, he was called. Winston Churchill.'

'Isn't he somethin' in the government now?'

'First Lord of the Admiralty,' George told her. 'So you see, we've *both* got on in the world.' He grinned, and then was serious again. 'Anyway, Lieutenant Churchill turns to me, an' he says, "Thank God nothin' like this will ever happen to British soldiers, Sergeant." But if there *is* a war in Europe, Becky, it'll be *just* like that.'

'Are you sure?'

'It's forced to be, because now all the European powers have got heavy weapons – and there's no point in havin' 'em if you don't use 'em. Yes, that's the kind of war it will be – big guns against the poor bloody infantry.' George sighed. 'I'm only glad my Ted is too young to join up.'

'My Billy's not too young,' Becky said sombrely. 'He's just the kind of young man that they'll be lookin' for.'

As Michelle walked past the Post Office at the bottom of Ollershaw Lane, she found herself thinking about her mother. In the previous couple of weeks, she'd caught Mam looking at her strangely, as if she wanted to ask a question, but wasn't sure how to go about it. And Michelle was certain that she knew what that question was. Becky was dying to know if she'd finally got herself a young man.

What would she say if her mam did finally ask? she wondered. She didn't want to lie, but she wasn't keen on telling the truth, either. She was getting to know Gerald better with every meeting, but she still didn't feel confident that she could persuade her mam that instead of being like his father, Gerald was a gentle, sensitive soul. A man she could one day see herself marrying.

Even as these thoughts flashed through her mind, she was on her way to meet him. Another trip to the country was planned – their sixth. He would be waiting for her, as he always was, just outside the Townshend Arms, where – by the happy accident with his horse – they'd first met.

She could picture him, sitting behind the wheel of his Napier touring automobile, with the roof down. He was so absurdly proud of that car, almost like a little boy with a new box of toy soldiers, but that didn't bother her. If anything, his pride in the automobile only made him more endearing.

She had reached the edge of the village when she noticed Jim Vernon. He was dressed in a blue suit which looked like it was his best one, and was leaning casually against some railings. Yet for all his assumed nonchalance, Michelle got the distinct feeling that there was nothing accidental about his being at that particular spot at that particular time. It was almost, she thought, as if he'd been waiting for her to pass by.

It wasn't until she was nearly level with him that he seemed to see her for the first time, and when he did, a smile came to his face. 'Why, Miss Worrell!' he said. 'What a surprise!'

'A pleasant one, I hope.'

Jim looked instantly confused. 'A what? Pleasant? Oh yes, of course it's pleasant. What other kind of surprise did you think I could have meant?'

It was remarkable how much things had changed in only a few short weeks, Michelle thought. When she'd gone to Liverpool with Jim and Captain Davenport, she'd been a shy and awkward girl. All elbows and knees somehow.

She remembered how frightening it had seemed to be alone in the steam packet's cabin with him, almost touching one another. But now that she was an experienced woman of the world, she felt completely at ease about the fact that they were the only people around, and he was the one who was finding the situation embarrassing.

'How is life on the river?' she asked, to fill the unnatural silence that had fallen between them.

'Oh, it's . . . it's fine,' Jim said haltingly. 'We sailed to Liverpool twice last week.'

'And has Captain Davenport let you steer the *Damascus* out of Northwich yet?' Michelle asked, recalling what Davenport had said about the dangerous channels.

The question appeared to put Jim more at ease, and he laughed. 'Let me steer the *Damascus*? No, not yet, he hasn't. He's a cautious old dev— I mean, he's a cautious old man, is Fred Davenport. But before this year's out, I think that he'll trust me enough to let me get behind the wheel.'

'I'm sure he will,' Michelle said, surreptitiously looking at her watch. Half past one. Time was ticking away, and she didn't want to keep Gerald waiting.

Jim took a deep breath. 'I . . . I was wonderin' if you might like to . . .' he said before drying up.

'If I might like to do what?'

'If you might like to come on the river with us again,' Jim blurted out.

Michelle was not sure how to react. She had enjoyed her first trip, but she had been a different person then – one who was much less aware of just how exciting life could be. Jim was still waiting for her answer. 'How kind of you to ask me,' she said, trying not to sound too gracious.

A look of hope appeared in Jim's eyes. 'Well, then . . . will you?' he asked.

He looked so earnest that she couldn't turn him down. 'Yes, I'd love to sail on the *Damascus* again,' she lied.

'When?' Jim said, the light of hope burning even stronger now.

When, indeed? 'You suggest a time,' Michelle said.

'Next Sunday?'

'No, I'm afraid I've already made arrangements for next Sunday,' Michelle said.

It was not quite a lie. Gerald had not yet suggested anything for the following Sunday, but she was certain that he would.

'The Sunday after, then?' Jim said.

'I don't think . . .'

'I'm not sure the *Damascus* will be sailing . . .'

'Well, in that case . . .'

'. . . but that doesn't matter. We could go on the other boats if it isn't, an' because I won't be workin', I'll have more time to explain things to you.'

Michelle sighed softly. 'I really am awfully busy for the next few Sundays,' she said. Then, seeing how crestfallen he now looked, she added, 'But I'll tell you what I'll do. I'll make a firm promise to come with you on the very day Captain Davenport finally lets you take the wheel.'

Jim did not seem in the least cheered up. 'That could be ages,' he said.

Michelle forced a laugh. 'Didn't you just tell me you thought he'd let you do it before the year was out?'

'That *is* ages,' Jim said gloomily. 'Besides, in the wintertime, the river isn't always a suitable place for ladies.'

'The spring, then,' Michelle suggested. 'I'll definitely come with you in the spring.'

She wondered what time it was. Gerald would not be cross with her if she was late – he was *never* cross with her – but she did not want to trespass too much on his good nature. She glanced at her watch again.

'Are you goin' somewhere special now, Miss Worrell?' Jim asked, noticing the gesture.

'Well, I do have an appointment,' Michelle admitted.

'An' would you permit me to escort you to wherever you're goin'?' Jim asked formally.

Michelle imagined arriving at the Townshend Arms with Jim, and introducing him to Gerald. She didn't think it would please either of them. 'I couldn't possibly put you to the trouble of escorting me.'

'It'd be no trouble at all.'

Oh really, he was being impossible. 'I would prefer to be alone,' Michelle said. 'I . . . I have a few things on my mind which I'd like to think over.'

Jim looked from her face to her blue jacket with bound edges and a single button, and from that to her matching overskirt and the ankle-length hobble skirt beneath it – and guessed the truth.

'I won't be botherin' you again, Miss Worrell,' he said, turning on his heel and walking quickly away from her.

As she crossed the cinder track which led to the Townshend Arms, Michelle found that she could not get her conversation with Jim out of her mind. He was a nice young man, and though he wasn't particularly handsome, there'd been a time when he would have been handsome enough for her. But really, he was no match for Gerald, who was charming, graceful and terribly good looking, whatever standards you applied.

She hoped that she had not hurt Jim's feelings too much, and felt a little guilty for not explaining how things were. But if she couldn't tell her own mam, how could she tell a comparative stranger? Then she caught sight of Gerald's shiny Napier, and all thoughts of Jim vanished from her head.

It was Sunday evening. Not-Stopping Bracegirdle, Half-a-Mo-Flo and Dottie Curzon sat at their usual table in the best room of the New Inn with their medicinal milk stouts – the fourth for each of them that evening – easily to hand.

'I went for a walk this afternoon,' Flo said, in that low, conspiratorial tone which announced she had a juicy bit of gossip she was just bursting to come out with.

'Did you now,' Not-Stopping said, feigning disinterest. 'That must have been nice for you.'

'As far as the Witch and Devil,' Flo said.

Not-Stopping felt a twinge of jealousy. For Flo to have abandoned her watching post over Ollershaw Lane, she must have been on the trail of a really good story. And it irked the queen of Marston tale-telling to realise that it was not a story she could have come up with herself – her creaky old joints would never have taken her as far as Northwich.

'Yes, as far as the Witch and Devil,' Flo repeated. 'An' I wasn't on me own, either.'

'You mean you had somebody else with you?' Dottie Curzon asked with the carefully calculated innocence she had cultivated over the years.

'Well, not exactly *with* me,' Flo admitted, 'but there was somebody just *ahead* of me.'

Dottie Curzon glanced at Not-Stopping, but it was plain from the look on the other woman's face that she would rather die than ask the obvious question herself.

So I suppose it's up to me again, Dottie thought. 'An' who might this somebody who was just ahead of you have been, Florence?' she said aloud.

Flo smiled. She was not going to make it that easy for them. 'Why don't you have a guess?' she suggested.

Not-Stopping took a sip of her milk stout. 'The Kaiser?' she said nastily.

'No, I think he's busy rattlin' his sabre somewhere else for the moment,' Flo said. 'But maybe he'll come an' rattle it in Northwich when he has the time.'

This was a good game when you held the key to it, Not-Stopping thought, but when somebody else was in control, it was intolerable. 'Did you hear that George Taylor is back in the village, come to visit his sister?' she asked.

'An' to do some business with a couple of the wood yards in Northwich,' Flo said smugly.

Things were getting worse by the second. All Not-Stopping could hope for now was Flo had seen something and drawn a laughable conclusion from it. 'An' how would you know that he's here to do business?' she asked.

'Because I saw 'im go into 'em meself. An' he had official-lookin' pieces of paper in his hands.'

'That doesn't mean nothin',' Not-Stopping said, but she had no doubt that Flo was right. How she wished that her arthritis would let her get to Northwich a bit more often.

'Anyway, it's a member of that family I was goin' to tell you about,' said Flo, who was determined not to be distracted from her piece of news by talk of someone as uninteresting as George.

'What family?' Dottie asked. 'The Taylors? But there aren't any Taylors livin' in the lane any more.'

'But there's Worrells, aren't there?' Flo said. 'An' that's the same thing.'

Not-Stopping sighed, heavily and theatrically. 'Well, I suppose you'd better tell us all about it, then,' she said. ''Cos you'll never be happy until you do.'

It was about as close as her mother-in-law ever came to asking for anything, and Flo smiled in triumph. 'I saw Michelle Worrell walkin' down the lane, dressed up in all her finery,' she told her two eager listeners. 'An' I said to meself,

"Florence," I said, "she's not just out for an ordinary Sunday walk."'

'So you follered her?' Not-Stopping asked, making it sound like a trick that *she* would never pull.

'I most certainly did not,' Flo snapped, as if she really were offended.

'Then how do you know . . .?'

'But since I was already plannin' on goin' for a walk anyway, there didn't seem no harm in goin' the same way as young Michelle was. An' you'll never guess what.'

'She went to the Witch and Devil,' Not-Stopping said. 'You've already told us that.'

'Yes, but I didn't say who was *waitin'* for her at the Witch and Devil, did I?'

Not-Stopping sighed again. She hated to admit it, even to herself, but Flo was almost as good at spinning out a story as she was. 'Well, out with it,' she said. 'Who was waitin' for Michelle at the Witch and Devil?'

'There was this great big motorcar there. Must have cost a fortune, but some people always did have more money than sense. And sittin' in the front waitin' for her, was . . .' She paused and reached for her drink.

'Who?' Not-Stopping demanded, throwing most of her pride out of the window in her eagerness to learn the truth.

'Why, Gerald Worrell, of course,' Flo told her.

The other two women gasped. Then, slowly, a smile came to Dottie's face. 'I told you people sometimes forgive and forget, didn't I?' she said to Not-Stopping and Flo.

'You what?' Not-Stopping asked.

'We were talkin' about the Worrells, and I said there might be a chance they'd kiss an' make up. An' you said, Elsie – if my memory serves me well – you said, "An' people could walk on water if they wanted." An' you, Flo, said, "It's just that it doesn't happen very often."'

Not-Stopping and Flo exchanged a furtive glance, in which it was quickly decided that the older woman should be the one to handle this sticky situation.

'Don't pay any attention to Dottie,' Not-Stopping told her daughter-in-law. 'You get like that when you're growin' older. You start losing yer marbles an' gettin' things mixed up.'

'I know what I heard,' Dottie said firmly.

And since all three of them knew perfectly well that she was right, they made one of their silent, mutual agreements to let that particular matter drop.

'Just wait till Becky Taylor finds out about it,' Not-Stopping continued.

'Maybe she already knows,' Dottie Curzon suggested.

The other two women gave her looks which said that such an idea was not even worth considering.

'Becky thought that Richard was goin' to marry her,' Flo said, telling the tale as if she'd actually been in the village when it happened, instead of learning it from her mother-in-law at a time when she'd been happy to be just the crown princess of local gossip. 'She'll never forgive him for turnin' her down an' marryin' that posh woman from the south.'

'An' whatever else you might say about Becky Taylor, she's got a strong will,' Not-Stopping added. 'Just look at how she started that bakery from nothin'.'

'Yes,' Flo agreed. 'Once she finds out what's goin' on, the cat will really be among the pigeons.'

On the other side of the hatch, Walter Dickens, the landlord, picked up a glass and began absentmindedly to polish it. He might not have been in the village long by Not-Stopping Bracegirdle's standards, but he had been there long enough to know that what he'd just overheard the three gossips say was perfectly true. Becky Worrell *wasn't* the kind of woman to let anybody mess her around, and when she did find out what her daughter was doing, the cat really *would* be among the pigeons.

Chapter Seven

When Becky arrived home from the bakery, on the afternoon of 24 July, she found her brother George sitting at the kitchen table and studying a long article in the latest edition of the *Northwich Guardian*.

'Are you readin' somethin' about the Balkans?' she asked, as she hung up her hat on the hook behind the door.

'That's right,' George agreed. He took a tin of cigarettes from his pocket, lit one and inhaled thoughtfully. 'I think I'm goin' to have to leave for London as soon as I possibly can.'

'Because of the news?'

'That's right.'

'Then it must be bad.'

'It's about as bad as it could be. The Austrians have sent the Serbs an ultimatum.'

Becky sat down at the table. 'An ultimatum?' she repeated. 'What's that when it's at home?'

'It's like a demand.'

'An' just what are they demandin'?'

'Lots of things,' George told her. 'The details don't really matter very much, but the general principle does. If the Serbs sign the agreement, the Austrians will have the right to poke their noses into Serbian affairs any time they feel like it.' He searched around for a way of making himself clearer. 'It'd be like you agreein' to let Richard Worrell come into your house any time he wanted to and look through all your things. Would you be willin' to do that?'

'Of course not.'

'Neither will the Serbs. So as sure as Not-Stoppin's lurkin' behind her front room curtain right now, there'll be a war between Austria and Serbia.'

'You don't think we might be able to keep out of it?' Becky asked, though there was not much hope in her voice.

George shook his head. 'There's been so many treaties signed in the last few years that we're bound to be dragged in, whether we want to be or not. That's why I have to go back to London right away, you see. To look after me wood yard. Wood's always very important in wartime.'

An' so is bread, Becky thought. She wondered whether she could persuade Billy that he'd be of more use to his country baking loaves than he would be joining the army. But she knew she had very little chance of success – Billy might only be Michael's adopted son, but Michael's spirit still ran through every inch of his being.

'Why do men always have to be so stupid, George?' she asked exasperatedly. 'If they've got problems, like this one in the Balkans, why can't they just sit down together an' discuss 'em, like women would?'

'It's not that simple,' George told her. 'Just wait till you women get the vote yourselves – then you'll soon find out.'

Becky sighed. 'I expect you're right,' she admitted. 'I just wish . . .'

'We all "just wish",' George said. 'But this time, I don't think wishin' is goin' to get us very far.'

The threat of war was also the main topic in the kitchen of number 49, where the four boarders and Spudder were having their supper.

'Maybe I could join the navy,' Jim Vernon suggested. A flicker of sadness crossed his face. 'I think it would do me good to get away from here for a bit.'

Captain Davenport plunged his knife deep into the juicy steak pie which Aggie had baked earlier in the day. 'Mark my words, young Jim, this won't be a naval war at all,' he said. 'It'll be our infantry and cavalry that will flatten the Germans.'

'You think so?'

'I'm convinced of it. So your best plan would be to stay where you are.'

'That just doesn't seem right, somehow.'

'You're doin' a valuable job, Jim. People'll still need salt, even when there's fightin' goin' on.'

The Great Marvello produced a fork out of thin air, and speared a piece of steak with it. 'If hostilities do commence, I might well be called upon to entertain the troops,' he said. 'After all, as I may have mentioned before, I did once . . .'

'Perform before royalty?' Captain Davenport suggested, with a smile on his face.

'Exactly,' the magician agreed proudly.

Spudder looked up from his food. 'I saw France once,' he told the boarders.

Even Mr Bingham – who rarely showed any expression on his face – was amazed by the news. Spudder? Going abroad? It didn't seem possible.

'When were you in France, Spudder?' Jim Vernon asked.

Spudder looked puzzled. 'Never.'

'But you just said you'd been there.'

'No, I didn't. I said I'd seen it.'

'Isn't that the same thing?'

'I think I understand,' Marvello said. 'What Spudder means is that he has seen France from some vantage point on the English coastline. Isn't that right, Spudder?'

'No,' Spudder replied. 'I saw it from the cliffs. In Kent. I was down there pickin' hops at the time.'

'And what impression did it make on you?'

'Pardon?'

'What did you think of it?'

'It seemed ever such a long way away,' Spudder said. 'Is Germany as far as that?'

'Much, much further,' Fred Davenport said.

'Heck!' Spudder exclaimed. 'So if it's *that* far, why don't we just forget it?'

Marvello smiled. 'Ah Spudder, my friend, if only we could do that. But you see, the great nations of the world are like a big family. What happens to one of them will, sooner or later, have an effect on all of the others.'

The back door opened and Ivy Clegg came in to clear away the main course and make room for Aggie's famous treacle pudding.

'You're lookin' very nice tonight, Ivy,' Captain Davenport said gallantly.

It was true. She was not at all the same girl who had come to the chip shop door to beg for leftovers. In the weeks she had worked for Spudder – or rather worked for Aggie, working for Spudder – a great change had come over her. She had put on weight, so that now instead of being skinny, she was merely trim. Her skin had lost most of its unhealthy pallor, and her red hair had started to develop body. Dressed in the secondhand blue frock that Aggie had helped her to choose, she no longer looked like a waif from the workhouse, but could have been mistaken for the daughter of any honest, working-class family in Marston.

'Would you like to come with me when I entertain the troops, Ivy?' Marvello said jokingly, as Ivy loaded some of the plates on to her tray. 'I shall need an assistant to help me with my illusions – especially with my spectacular finish, when that assistant is sawn in half.' He glanced across at his landlord. 'And somehow, I don't think I could rely on Spudder to take part in that particular exhibition again.'

'You're right there,' Spudder agreed. He had once helped Marvello with the trick in a music hall in Warrington, but the moment Marvello had started to cut into the box, he had panicked and tipped the casket off its trestles. The audience, thinking it was part of the act, had applauded furiously, but not all the applause in the world would have made Spudder go through that experience again.

'So what do you say, Ivy?' Marvello asked. 'Will you tread the boards with me?'

Ivy, her hands now full of crockery, shook her head. 'I'm quite happy here,' she said. 'And if it's all the same to you, Mr Marvello, here's where I'll stay.'

'I might join up,' Spudder said.

Ivy's mouth fell open and she almost dropped the tray. 'Oh Spudder, you couldn't!' she gasped. 'You just couldn't.'

'Why not?' Spudder asked.

Ivy seemed lost for an answer. 'Well, you're . . . you're too old,' she said finally.

'I'm only forty,' Spudder said. 'Or maybe I'm forty-one. I

can't remember which of the two it is. But I'm still a big strong feller, aren't I?'

'You are in excellent physical shape for a man of your age, my dear Spudder,' the Great Marvello agreed, 'but nevertheless, Ivy is quite right on that point. You simply do not have the makings of a good soldier.'

'What's a good soldier got to be like? Has he got to have a lot of brains, or somethin'?'

'Brains have very little to do with it. In fact, it might be said that they are a positive disadvantage.'

'Then why couldn't I . . .?'

'Because a good soldier, my dear boy, must not only be prepared to be killed himself, he must also be willing to kill others.'

'I suppose he must,' Spudder said dubiously.

'Can you really imagine yourself, Spudder, standing over a fallen enemy and thrusting your bayonet right into his throat?' Marvello asked.

Spudder looked very shocked and his hand went, involuntarily, up to his own throat. 'Is that what I'd have to do to be a good soldier?' he asked.

'Indeed. It is one of the main requirements of the job,' Marvello told him.

'Then I think I'll just stick to makin' me fish and chips,' Spudder said.

Marvello laughed and Ivy sighed with relief. There were cries of 'Quite right!' from Captain Davenport, and 'Good for you!' from Jim Vernon. Only one person had nothing to say – but then he never did express any opinion.

'What do you think about all this talk about war, Mr Bingham?' Jim asked.

'Me?' Mr Bingham replied, almost absentmindedly. 'Oh, I try never to get involved in politics.'

The sun was setting just beyond the copse of silver birch trees where Gerald had parked his automobile. The passenger and driver were sitting side by side on the plush leather front seats – she with her head on his shoulder – and watching the display.

'You're very quiet this evening, Gerald, my dear,' Michelle said softly.

'I was thinking about everything going on in Serbia at the moment,' Gerald said heavily.

It was natural that he should have the subject on his mind – everyone was talking about the Balkans – yet the words sent a shudder running down Michelle's spine, as if someone had just walked over her grave. Or his.

'What . . . what were you thinking?' she asked, noticing the slight tremble in her voice.

'I was thinking that if there is a war . . .'

'Yes?'

'If there is a war, and we're involved in it, I shall feel compelled to enlist in the army.'

The vague fear which had been growing in Michelle over the previous few seconds erupted in a cascade of what might almost have been blind terror. Gerald in the army? *Her* Gerald risking his life battling the Germans?

'Why must you enlist?' she asked, trying to contain her desperation, because she knew that she needed a clear head if she was to talk him out of it. 'Do you want to fight?'

'Of course not. No sane man would.'

'Well, then, why?'

'Because it will be expected of me. I come from a privileged background, and I went to a good school.'

'But even so . . .'

'I am one of the natural officer class, Michelle. And I will be failing in my duty to my country if I don't take up the position I am qualified to fill.'

'But . . . but . . .' Michelle protested.

Gerald ran his hand through her silky hair. 'Don't worry, little cousin,' he said soothingly. 'Even if the worst does come to the worst, it will all be over by Christmas.'

He turned his head towards her, and kissed her softly on the lips. She responded, moulding her mouth to his. And then she felt his hand straying towards her bosom.

'No, Gerald!' she said sharply.

'Why not?'

'Because it isn't right!'

'You used to say that about kissing.'

That was true enough. The first time he had tried to kiss her – on their third drive – she had been so panicked she'd been shaking. Yet now it seemed the most natural thing in the world. Now, *not* to kiss would have felt strange.

'So why must you always r-reject me?' Gerald asked. 'Is it because you still don't t-trust me? Do you think I'm a philanderer, like my f-father?'

It had been a long time since Gerald had stuttered in her presence, and Michelle felt almost drowned in guilt.

'Of course I trust you,' she said. 'And, of course, I don't think you're anything like your father.'

'Well, then?'

'It's not what nice girls let men do. And it makes me feel uncomfortable,' Michelle said awkwardly.

Gerald chuckled. 'How do you know what nice girls do or don't do?' he asked. 'Do you think they'd tell you, any more than you'd be likely to tell them?'

'Perhaps not,' Michelle admitted.

'And as for it making you feel uncomfortable, how you can possibly say that when you don't really know? You always stop me almost before I've started.'

If it was any other man, Michelle thought, I could ask my mam's advice. But her mother couldn't even know she was seeing Gerald, let alone what he was asking her to do. So the decision had to be hers and no one else's.

'Do you love me?' she asked.

'You know I do,' Gerald said earnestly. 'Deeply and truly. And for all time.'

The sun had set and dusk was falling. Michelle looked at the darkening tops of the trees, as if the answer to her dilemma might lie there.

'If I let you touch my . . . my bosom, would you stop when I asked you to?'

'Of course.'

'And you wouldn't try to go any further?'

'I would never force you to do anything against your wishes, my darling.'

Michelle turned her gaze up towards the moon, which hung large and heavy in pale evening light.

'Very well,' she said.

Her eyes still starwards, she felt his eager fingers unbutton her jacket and her silk blouse. Then his hand was in there, next to her body. Probing and exploring. Stroking and caressing. And suddenly she felt ashamed – not because she was hating it as she'd expected to, but because she was starting to enjoy it.

The hands continued their work, and she knew that her nipples were hard, as hard as they were when she dressed on a cold winter morning. She wanted to tell him to stop, yet she wanted the pleasure to go on. And she knew that if his hand should stray elsewhere, if it should climb up in the inside of her skirt, she would have no power to resist him.

'What's that thing over there, Wilf?' said a voice somewhere in the near distance.

'Under the trees, you mean?' a second man replied.

'That's right.'

'I'm not sure, but it could be an automobile. Think we should take a closer look?'

'That's what we're paid for.'

In the car, Gerald's breathing suddenly quickened, as if he was angry.

'Damn!' he said, and this time he did not apologise for swearing in Michelle's presence.

What had started out as just two vague shapes in the distance became, as they got closer, two uniformed police constables pushing their bicycles.

'I was right. It is a car,' one of them said.

Michelle pulled away, and Gerald did not try to stop her. As she adjusted her clothing, he climbed down from the Napier and began to walk towards the two policemen.

They were now close enough for Michelle just to make out their features. One of them was young and fresh faced, the other older, with a bushy moustache.

'Is anything wrong, Officer?' Gerald asked the older one.

'No, sir, nothing wrong. We're just out lookin' for poachers,' the policeman said. He glanced quickly across at Gerald's car, and as his eyes fell on her, Michelle blushed.

An awkward silence followed, as if the policemen were waiting for Gerald to say something more. Finally, he did. 'Looking for poachers, eh?' he asked.

'That's right, sir,' the older policeman agreed, though it was plain that wasn't what he'd been wanting Gerald to say. 'An' might I ask what you're doin' out here?'

Gerald laughed lightly, but it sounded false. 'It was such a lovely evening that I felt like a drive,' he said.

'You an' your passenger felt like a drive,' the policeman corrected him.

'Yes, I suppose that's what I meant to say.'

'An' are you aware, sir, that this is private land?' the policeman asked gravely.

'Of course I am,' Gerald replied, and the hint of false good humour had completely disappeared from his voice.

'Then it would seem that you're . . .'

'Trespassing?'

'Exactly.'

'On what's my own land, or as good as?'

'I beg your pardon?'

'The land is owned by my father.'

The older policeman sucked in his breath. 'I see,' he said. 'So you would be . . .?'

'Gerald Worrell, son of Richard Worrell, the owner of the saltworks in Marston.'

The older policeman risked another quick glance at the car. 'Well, in that case, sir, we'll wish you good night,' he said. 'And I hope that if you get the chance, you'll mention to your father that you saw us doin' our duty.'

'Yes, yes, I'll mention it,' Gerald said impatiently.

He stood and watched until the two policemen had disappeared in the darkness, then returned to the Napier.

'Now where were we?' he asked, looking down at Michelle, who was hugging herself in one corner of her seat.

'I want to go home,' the girl said.

'There's no need for that,' Gerald assured her. 'Those two policemen know better than to disturb us again tonight.'

'I want to go home!' Michelle said, in a tone which was almost a scream.

'Very well,' Gerald said resignedly. 'If you wish to go home, then that is where I will take you.'

Chapter Eight

Billy Worrell looked around the old barn which had been his mother's bakery for as long as he could remember. The bakers were pulling bread out of the ovens, and the carmen were stacking the loaves in wicker baskets and taking the baskets out to their waiting wagons. The delicious aroma of the recent baking was everywhere.

Billy remembered the first day he had stood on this spot as master baker. How nervous he'd been, waiting for the first batch of baked loaves to appear. Even though he'd baked thousands of loaves himself under Monsieur Henri's watchful eye – even though he'd supervised the whole process while Monsieur Henri had supervised *him* – he hadn't been able to shake the feeling that something would go wrong: the bread would refuse to rise; it would rise, but it would taste like rat droppings; the bread would be fine, but the cakes which followed it – Worrell's *Famous* Cakes – would be nothing more than a pale imitation of the ones the Frenchman had produced.

He was still too young to be a master baker, he had told himself. His mam should never have given him the responsibility. But she had, and it would be the ruin of her. A reputation which had taken years to build up would be destroyed in a single morning.

Then the first loaf had been pulled from the oven, and with trembling hands, Billy had cut off a slice and tasted it. It was perfect – as good as any Monsieur Henri had ever made. Billy had felt wonderful. Better than wonderful. Being a master baker was the most exciting, fulfilling job in the world, and he would never want to be anything else.

As he watched one of the wagons start out for Northwich, Billy tried to recapture the feeling he'd experienced with that first bake. But it was no good – it simply would not come. Why should he feel elated when he *knew* that the bread would be fine? And what if it wasn't? He had only to bake another batch, hadn't he? The problem was he became bored with things too easily.

He supposed that in that way he was similar to his Uncle Philip, Mam's youngest brother. Philip had tried a bit of everything – not all of it legal – and had always given it up when the novelty wore off, even if he was making a good living at it. But even Philip had finally found a job which didn't bore him – making films – and had stuck to it.

'What kind of job could I stick to?' Billy wondered. 'Whatever it is, I'm sure it's not bakin'.'

Pushing thoughts of work aside, Billy turned his mind to the difficult question of his sister. He had been in bed when she got home the previous evening – bakers like him didn't have much choice about going to bed early – but he was sure it had been nearly midnight when he heard her key turn in the door.

His head argued that she was twenty-two, and it was her business. His heart argued back that it was his business too, and the rest of him agreed to follow the heart.

He loved his sister, but there was more to it than that. One of his few memories of the days which followed his rescue from the coal barge was of being absolutely terrified. It was Michelle who had calmed him, Michelle who cuddled him when he was afraid, and who asked for nothing in return. So now he wanted to protect *her*, as if that would somehow pay off the debt he owed.

'Shall I put this first batch of fancies into the oven now, Mr Worrell?' one of the apprentices called to him from the other side of the bakery.

'Aye, you might as well,' Billy replied.

The thing was, he was almost sure that Michelle was seeing a lad. But if she was, why all the secrecy about it? What could be so wrong with him that she couldn't bring him home and introduce him to the family? Billy wanted to meet him, to make sure that he was good enough for Michelle – though privately he suspected that no man would ever come up to the full measure of what he expected from the husband of his beloved sister.

One of the young carmen rushed into the bakery, waving a rolled-up newspaper over his head as if it were a battle-axe. 'Heard the news, Mr Worrell?' he gasped. 'Austria declared war on Serbia yesterday.'

'Are you sure?'

'It's right here, in black an' white. There *is* goin' to be a war, isn't there? Just like everybody said there would be.'

'Maybe,' Billy said cautiously, but he was already beginning to feel the kind of excitement which had been denied him when he'd glanced around the bakery earlier.

'I think you'd better be lookin' for a new driver,' the carman told him. 'If we've got a fight on our hands, I'll be joinin' up.'

'If we've got a fight on our hands, it'll be my mam who has to find a new carman,' Billy said. '*I'll* be goin' with you.'

When Richard Worrell got down to breakfast, his son was already at the table, attacking a plateful of sausages, bacon, liver and devilled kidneys.

'Do I take it that you were out with your cousin Michelle last night, my boy?' the father asked his son, a pleased, yet unpleasant, smile playing on his lips.

Gerald looked up from his food. 'Whatever makes you ask that, my dear father?' he said, with an innocence in his voice which was not quite convincing.

'Because when a man eats as heartily as you're doing now, it usually means he's got something to celebrate.'

Gerald grinned. 'You're quite right, Father. Yes, I was out with Michelle last night. And, yes, I do have something to celebrate this morning.' The grin on Gerald's face widened even more. 'She let me play with her paps.'

'Did she, by God!'

'Well, it was more than just *letting* me, if I'm going to be strictly accurate. I think I would have to say that she actually enjoyed the experience herself.'

Richard shook his head in admiration. 'I never thought you'd manage it, my boy. I'm proud of you.'

'I might have got even further with her if we hadn't been interrupted by two idiotic policemen out looking for poachers,' Gerald told him.

Richard raised a doubting eyebrow. 'Is that so?' he said, somewhat sceptically.

'Yes, it is,' his son replied with confidence. 'It took a great deal of work before she'd let me even kiss her, but last night I'm sure she would have spread her legs for me.' He paused. 'I think it was the thought of losing me which tipped the balance.'

Richard piled food on to his own plate. The knowledge of his son's success had given *him* a hearty appetite, too. 'Why? What did you tell her? That you wouldn't see her again if she didn't give you what you wanted? That was a dangerous gamble, my son, even for one as cocksure as you appear to be.'

Gerald laughed. 'It was nothing so crude as threatening to ditch her, Father. I simply told her that if war came – as appears likely – then I would be joining the army.'

Richard threw back his head and laughed even louder than his son had done. 'Join the army!' he said. 'And the little fool believed you, did she?'

'Yes,' Gerald replied. 'And I have to tell you that she was quite right to do so.'

Richard's cheerful expression froze, to be slowly replaced by one of amazement. 'Are you telling me it wasn't just a lie to get what you wanted from her?' he asked.

'Exactly.'

'Have you gone completely out of your mind?' Richard demanded. 'Why on earth should any man want to fight when there's no need to?'

'You don't think there'll be any need to fight?'

Richard shrugged. 'I suppose there is the possibility of war,' he admitted, 'but if the army needs cannon fodder, it should be provided by the kind of working-class scum we have working for us, not young gentlemen like you.'

Gerald nodded, as if he saw the truth in what his father was saying, but still couldn't quite accept it. 'It took me by surprise, too,' he confessed.

'What did?'

'My sudden feeling of patriotism.'

'Patriotism! That's just a word, as meaningless as the brotherhood and equality that those blasted socialist agitators are always going on about.'

'Perhaps you're right,' Gerald conceded. 'However, if my country needs me, I will have no choice but to answer its call.'

Richard realised that his hands were trembling. 'You *do* have a choice,' he argued with an urgent edge to his voice. 'Even if the government introduces conscription – and it may well in the end – a man of my position and influence can always find some way of keeping you out of the army.'

'But as I've already explained to you, Father, I don't want to be kept out.'

Richard looked down at his food. Only a few seconds earlier, it had all seemed so appetizing. Now it had no more appeal to him than sawdust would have done. He placed his trembling hands in front of him, almost as if he were begging. 'You are my only child, Gerald,' he said. 'If anything happened to you, it would kill me.'

'Father . . .'

'Please listen to me,' Richard said. 'Perhaps I loved Becky Taylor once – I no longer know for certain – but apart from her, you are the only person in the world I have ever really cared about.'

'And I care about you, Father,' Gerald said, both sincerely and sadly. 'I would do almost anything you asked of me, but however much I would like to, I cannot follow your wishes in this matter.'

Billy Worrell followed the news of threatened war with a keen and ever mounting interest. Austria had declared war on Serbia on Tuesday, and the next day, in response, Russia began mobilising her army, an act which the mighty German Empire announced it would not permit to continue. Germany waited for two more days, then, when it became clear that Russia would never back down, it declared a state of war to exist between the two nations.

'An' all that's happened in less than a week,' Billy told his sister over supper on Saturday. 'The speed of it's enough to take your breath away, isn't it?'

'Yes, I suppose it is,' Michelle said disinterestedly, as if she had more important things on her mind than a war which threatened the security of the whole of Europe.

On Sunday night, the Germans invaded Belgium.

'See, they knew if they were goin' to fight Russia, they'd have to fight France as well,' Billy said.

'Why?' his mother asked.

'Because Russia an' France have got a treaty.' Billy moved the crockery around on the table. 'Now that cup's France, that plate's Germany, an' this saucer is Belgium. The Germans want to get to Paris as soon as possible, an' to do that they have to go through Belgium.'

'An' what's all that got to do with us?' Becky asked.

'We signed a peace treaty guaranteein' Belgium's neutrality.'

'A treaty's nothin' more than a bit of paper.'

'That's not true, Mam,' Billy protested. 'If we let the Hun get away with this, we'll never be able to hold our heads up again.'

'So you think we should go to war just to save our pride, do you?' Becky asked angrily.

Billy looked shamefaced. 'No, Mam. Of course not. It's much more complicated than that.'

'Then why don't you say so, instead of making out that we're goin' to send thousands of our young men to their deaths because somebody's hurt our feelin's?'

The following Monday, Germany declared war on France. We've got to do somethin' ourselves soon, Billy thought. We've just *got* to.

The sun was already high in the sky as Michelle walked along the cinder track to Northwich on Tuesday morning. It was going to be yet another beautiful summer day, but she found herself unable to appreciate it.

That night in the woods with Gerald had shaken her considerably. The depth of the passion she had discovered within herself had frightened her – and so had the realisation that, if the constables hadn't appeared when they did, she would have let Gerald do whatever he wanted with her. She had seen him just once since, and they had only kissed. But even that had worried her, because one thing led to another – as she'd already found out.

'I can't let him have his way with me!' she said aloud,

startling a bicyclist who was just passing her. And yet she wanted to. Oh God, how she wanted to.

If only the shadow of war had not been hanging over them. If only they had time for their relationship to develop, time to let her mam get used to the fact that she had fallen in love with the son of their bitterest enemy.

It was late afternoon, and the bakery had closed down for the day. Billy Worrell had been home for a full half hour, but instead of sitting down and relaxing, he was pacing the kitchen floor, checking the clock every two minutes, and softly sighing to himself.

Finally, Becky decided that she could take it no more. 'For goodness' sake, sit down, Billy,' she said. 'You'll wear out the lino if you go on like that.'

'Sorry, Mam,' Billy replied. 'I'm just a bit edgy, what with all this talk about the war.'

'An' prowlin' up an' down like a caged lion will help, will it?' Becky asked. 'Why don't you go up to the pub and have a couple of jars?'

Because the New Inn, like everywhere else, would be full of idle speculation, Billy thought. It was all so frustrating. Everybody knew what was the right thing to do, so why didn't the government just go ahead and do it?

'I think I'll take a walk,' he said moodily. 'I might go an' see what's happenin' in Northwich.'

Becky shook her head in wonder. 'Men!' she said. 'We give you toy soldiers when you're little lads, an' you never grow out of them.'

At half past six Northwich High Street was normally a quiet place, but when Billy reached it that evening, it was seething with people moving around with great energy but no apparent destination.

Billy stopped in front of Hall's newsagent's. A large crowd had gathered, and everyone was pushing and shoving to read a printed notice which had been pasted on the wall.

'Is it war?' Billy asked a black-faced man with chimney-sweep's brushes over his shoulder.

'Where've you been all day?' the sweep asked. 'Of course it's war.' He pointed a sooty finger in the direction of the crowd. 'That's the mobilisation notice they're all fightin' to get a look at. It says that the Reservists and Territorials are ordered to report to their headquarters in Navigation Road as soon as possible.'

Why hadn't he joined the Territorials? Billy thought, angry at his own shortsightedness. Why hadn't he made sure that he would be one of the first men to get a crack at the Hun? But he'd left it too late, and even if he enlisted now, it might be months before they sent him abroad.

'Thinkin' of joinin' up?' the sweep asked.

'I certainly am.'

The sweep shook his head sadly. 'I wish I was your age again, then I could do me bit for me country an' all,' he said.

For the rest of the day people continued to mill about the streets with a kind of excited listlessness. They all wanted to do something, but there was nothing *to* do. They besieged the paper shops, demanding the latest edition of the newspaper, even if they had only bought one half an hour before. They talked of the war as if they had been fighting it for years, whereas the truth was that not a single British soldier had yet fired a shot.

Darkness fell, and still the crowd would not go away. Slowly, people began to drift down to the Bull Ring at the bottom of town, a natural gathering place where in the old days, a bull would be tied to a stake and baited by fighting dogs. Billy looked around him at the hundreds, maybe even thousands of people, all bursting to do whatever they could for the war effort.

'Bloody hell!' he said softly to himself.

At the edge of the Bull Ring a stout, white-haired old gentleman in an old-fashioned frock coat was trying to climb on to a cart.

'Give him a hand,' somebody called out goodnaturedly.

'Yeah, don't let the old feller struggle on alone,' someone else shouted.

Any number of willing hands appeared, and the old man was soon standing on the cart, facing his audience and brushing his hand over his frock coat.

'Some of you good people may perhaps know me,' he said in the booming voice of a practised local politician. 'I am

Alderman Albert Grimshaw.' The crowd cheered loudly, though no one in it could have said quite why, and the Alderman held up his right hand to silence them. 'It warms me to the very bottom of my heart to see you all gathered here tonight,' he said, to more shouts of encouragement.

'Now, as you know, we are at war with the Germans,' the Alderman continued, amidst further cheering, 'and I think all of us here have been presented with a perfect opportunity to show the Hun just what we British are made of. Will you join me in singing a few rousing choruses of "Rule Britannia"?'

'Yes!' the crowd screamed, and sing they all did, so loudly they thought their lungs would burst.

'Rule Britannia, Britannia rules the waves!
Britons never, never, never shall be slaves.'

And when, after several renditions, 'Rule Britannia' finally began to pall, they switched to 'O God, our help in ages past', because there was no doubt that God was on their side this time, just as he had always been.

For Billy Worrell and the hundreds of other people of all ages packed together in the Bull Ring, there had never been a night to equal it.

It was well after midnight, and the crowd was still in full song, when Billy spotted Tom Atherton, who had been at Marston School with him, and now worked as a waller at the saltworks. Tom was leaning against a lamp-post, a cigarette dangling from his lip. He looked exhausted, but very happy. 'How are you doin', Billy?' he asked.

'Never better in me life,' Billy replied warmly. 'Are you goin' to join up, Tom?'

'Well, of course I am,' Tom said. 'An' you?'

'Soon as I can.' That was how dozens of conversations had started that evening.

Tom took a drag on his cigarette. 'Seems like everybody's joinin' up,' he reflected. 'Even that stuck-up cousin of yours.'

'Gerald!' Billy said with surprise. 'Gerald's actually goin' into the army?'

'That's what him an' his dad were talkin' about when they come round to inspect my pan this mornin'. His dad wasn't too keen on the idea, but it sounded to me like Gerald couldn't get into uniform quick enough.'

'Gerald, a soldier! Now there's a real turn-up for the books,' Billy said.

''Course, I shouldn't imagine the idea will please your Michelle much,' Tom said.

'What in heaven's name has our Michelle got to do with it?'

An expression of surprise came to Tom's face, and he looked down at the ground. Tom's grandad, Ha-ha Harry Atherton had stuttered, and when Tom spoke again, it seemed as if Tom himself was developing the habit, too. 'You m-mean, you d-don't know?' he asked.

'Know what?'

'A-about young Master Gerald and your Michelle.'

Billy felt all the patriotic warmth and general well-being which had been building up inside him drain completely away. He grabbed Tom by the scruff of the neck and shook him. 'Don't you go spreadin' untrue stories about my sister!' he screamed in Tom's ear. 'Because if you do, I promise you that I, personally, will flatten you.'

'They're not untrue,' Tom gasped. 'I've seen 'em meself. More than once.'

Billy released his grip on Tom's collar. 'What do you mean?' he demanded.

'Out in his car. Goin' for rides an' that.'

Billy didn't like those last two words – not a bit. '"An' that"?' he asked.

'J-just goin' out for rides together, like I s-said,' Tom stuttered.

'You're holdin' out on me,' Billy said threateningly. 'An' with the mood I'm in, that's not a very good idea.'

Tom looked down at the ground again. 'You sure you want to hear any more?' he asked, and Billy nodded. 'Well, I usually see 'em just drivin' past, but once I saw him lettin' her out of his car. Near the Witch an' Devil, it was.'

'And . . .?'

'He kissed her, Billy.'

'Is that it?'

'That's it,' Tom said unconvincingly.

Billy clenched his fists into tight, hard balls. 'Are you certain?' he said. 'Because if I happen to find out you've been holdin' anythin' back from me, Tom . . .'

Tom held up his hands in front of him. 'All right, all right,' he said. 'There is one more thing, but you mustn't tell anybody it come from me, or you'll get me uncle in trouble.'

Billy thought about it. 'I won't tell anybody it came from you,' he said finally.

'Well, my Uncle Sid, the one that's a policeman, was out lookin' for poachers one night, over on some land the boss owns . . .' Tom gulped. 'He come across Mr Gerald's car parked next to some trees. There was a lady sittin' in it.'

'An' are you tryin' to tell me that this "lady" was our Michelle, by any chance?' Billy growled.

'It was too dark for him to be sure,' Tom said, 'but me uncle *thinks* it was her.'

It couldn't be true, Billy thought. Yet why should Tom lie to him? He had nothing to gain from it, except a bloody nose. The crowd was still singing as enthusiastically as ever, but for Billy the whole occasion had gone sour. He turned his back on Tom and began to walk away.

'You won't forget what you promised, will you?' Tom called after him. 'You know, about not gettin' me Uncle Sid into any trouble.'

Billy had so much coursing through his mind that he didn't even hear him. So Gerald's been triflin' with our Michelle, has he? he thought. Just like his dad trifled with Mam. Well, it's not goin' to go any further – I'll make sure of that.

As he reached the edge of Northwich, the singing from the Bull Ring was so loud that he could still hear it, but now the words meant nothing to him. He turned down the road leading to the Witch and Devil, where Michelle had let herself be kissed by Gerald, according to Tom Atherton.

'But did it all go well beyond that?' Billy asked the night sky miserably. When they'd been disturbed by the two policemen out looking for poachers, had she already let him . . .? If Gerald had robbed Michelle of her good name, Billy decided he would kill the swine – even if it meant ending up on the end of a rope himself.

He laughed bitterly. Just an hour earlier, in the Bull Ring, he had thought there was only one war going on. Now he realised that there were two.

Chapter Nine

Overnight, Northwich turned into a garrison town. From all directions, Imperial Yeomen and Territorial soldiers flocked to Yeomanry Headquarters on Navigation Road. The men belonged to a variety of regiments, so that while each one on his own looked a soldier down to his boots, together the different uniforms made them seem a rag-bag army thrown together in haste. Which was exactly what they were.

The streets of the town were choked with heavy lorries heading for the South. Only the day before, these same wagons had been carrying coal from the Lancashire minefields and cutlery from the factories in Sheffield, but now, with the letters OHMS hastily chalked on their sides, they rumbled importantly through Northwich on government business.

Every man below the age of forty was talking about joining up – four policemen and nine postmen had handed in their resignations that very morning. The chemical firm of Brunner Mond, one of the town's biggest employers, announced that their workers would not suffer loss of pension rights or holiday pay if they went into the army. Their families would not be made to suffer, either, as the company would give their wives ten shillings a week, with an extra shilling for each child.

The shops along the High Street were packed with panicking women, buying anything and everything which could possibly be eaten – and many things which could not. By the end of the day, there was not a tin of meat or pound of butter to be found in any store in the town, and the sellers of candles and donkey stones were rattling the change in their pockets.

Even the countryside did not escape war fever. Army officers and remount purchasers scoured the outlying farms and villages, buying up any reasonably fit horse they could find. 'Our soldiers will need horses to carry them into battle,' they said gravely. 'It's your duty to sell.' And the farmers, driven partly by patriotic spirit and partly by their nose for a good deal, did sell.

Northwich had been hit by a madness the like of which it had never known before, and in those heady days hardly anyone suspected that, over in France, there was an even greater madness yet to come.

Becky sat at the breakfast table with the latest copy of the *Northwich Guardian* in front of her.

'There's an urgent appeal in here from an officer in the Winsford Territorials,' she said. 'He says there's not enough field glasses to go round. He promises anyone willin' to lend them for the duration of the hostilities that his men will take the greatest care of them.'

'I expect they will,' Billy said.

Becky thought of what George had told her about the Battle of Omdurman, of the thousands of Sudanese soldiers charging down the hill and being mown down hundreds of yards away from the British lines. The same thing was bound to happen to the British soldiers over in France. Did this officer from the Territorials really think that the main concern of men coming under that kind of firepower would be to look after the field glasses they'd been lent for 'the duration of the hostilities'?

'My God! Is it only me an' your Uncle George who realise what a terrible war this is goin' to be?' she asked.

'Wars are always terrible,' her son said, 'but somehow they just have to be fought.'

Becky looked up at the clock. 'Isn't it time you were settin' off for work?' she said.

Billy shook his head. 'I'm goin' in a bit later than usual today. I've got some business to attend to first.'

'What kind of business?'

'Just business,' Billy told his mother, and would say no more.

To Gerald Worrell, riding was one of life's great pleasures. He loved the feel of the animal beneath him, and revelled in the knowledge that he could make it do whatever he wished it to. Except in extremely bad weather he always preferred to ride rather than drive to work, and on that fine August morning, which would see the first full day of war, it was his horse he once again selected over his automobile.

That morning he enjoyed the ride even more than usual. The wheat in the fields was almost ripe enough to harvest, and field mice scuttled in and out of the sturdy shoots. There were plenty of birds around, too – sparrows, lapwings, and what were either a couple of pigeons or a pair of turtle doves.

'A pair of turtle doves,' Gerald said aloud, thinking of himself and Michelle. It might be weeks before he was sent to France. There was still plenty of time to win his wager, to ride Michelle as skilfully as he had ridden all his other mounts.

Gerald's pocket watch was just chiming half-past eight as he rode his horse through the saltwork gates and noticed the solitary figure waiting outside the office.

'Billy Worrell!' he exclaimed – his cousin by adoption and his half-brother by blood! What in the devil's name was he doing here?

The hitching rail was some distance from where Billy was standing. Gerald dismounted in a leisurely manner and tied up his horse. Then, as he turned to head for the office, Billy stepped forward and blocked his path.

'I want you to tell me if it's true that you've been seein' my sister,' he said.

'And what business is that of yours?' Gerald asked.

'Like I said, she's my sister, an' I've a right to know,' Billy said, although his clenched fists seemed to suggest that he already thought he had his answer.

'Your sister, you call her, do you?' Gerald sneered. 'She isn't your sister at all. In case you need reminding of the fact, you are the result of a bestial coupling between my – between *our* – mother and one of my father's servants. A common groom, he was, if my memory serves me well!'

At any other time, Billy would have lashed out at Gerald immediately, but on this occasion it was Michelle's honour, not his own, that he had come to defend. 'Answer my question, you bugger,' he persisted. 'Answer it right now.'

Gerald smiled. 'Your sister – if that's what you insist on calling her – is over twenty-one, which means that she may see whoever she wishes, without anyone's permission. Even without the permission of her younger "brother".'

'Leave her alone,' Billy said, 'or you'll have me to deal with.'

'By "dealing" with you, I assume you mean brawling with you.'

'Yes, if you're man enough for it.'

'Oh, I'm man enough for it, all right,' Gerald said. 'You need have no worries on that score.' He examined Billy from head to foot. They were about the same weight and height, he estimated. Working in the bakery had given Billy powerful arms and a broad chest, but then Gerald was no milksop himself.

'Well?' Billy demanded. 'What's your answer?'

'My answer is that I have no intention of leaving Michelle alone – I'd be a fool to – and if you wish to deal with me, then deal with me now. That is, if you'll grant me the courtesy of giving me time to take off my jacket.'

'Take all the time you want,' Billy said. 'I can wait.'

Gerald turned his back contemptuously on Billy and stripped off his coat. That done, he hung it neatly over the hitching rail, and turned to face his opponent. 'Well, come on, then,' he said. 'Teach me a lesson.'

Billy raised his arm and jabbed out with his right fist. Gerald easily side-stepped and countered with a left hook to Billy's jaw. Billy rocked backwards for a second, then made a second lunge. Gerald dodged it and delivered a punishing blow to Billy's midriff.

'I studied the noble art of boxing when I was at school,' Gerald said, almost conversationally. 'I discovered I was rather good at it, as a matter of fact.'

Billy shook his head in an attempt to clear it, then tried another attack. This time, he managed to land a punch on Gerald's cheek, but Gerald retaliated with three of his own.

'Give it up now,' Gerald advised him.

'Leave her alone,' Billy said, spitting out blood.

'You're an idiot,' Gerald told him. 'Can't you see by now that you've no chance of beating me?'

Billy tried one more time, took two more blows, then collapsed on to the ground, groaning.

'I'll say one thing for you,' Gerald said, looking down on him.

'You've more courage than I would have given you credit for. Do you think you can walk?'

'Don't know,' Billy muttered.

'Probably not,' Gerald said. 'I'll get a couple of the men to help you home.'

'Thanks.'

'Oh, don't thank me. I just want a piece of scum like you off our property as soon as possible.'

Becky heard the footsteps first – two pairs of feet walking firmly down the alley and a third making a swishing sound, almost as if one of the men was being dragged. And then she saw the three of them through the window, and realised that was exactly what had been happening.

She flung the kitchen door open. 'Billy,' she sobbed. 'What have you been . . .?'

'Got into a fight,' Billy groaned.

'If you could just step out of the way, missis, we'd be able to get him inside,' one of the saltworkers said.

'Yes, of course,' Becky said. She raked her fingers through her hair. 'What a mess you look, Billy.'

The two saltworkers manoeuvred the injured man through the kitchen door. They helped him over to the table and lowered him into a chair. They were as gentle as they could be, but even so, Billy gasped with pain.

'Thanks, lads,' Billy said, looking up at the saltworkers through puffy eyes. 'I'll be all right now.'

'All right!' Becky stormed. 'You don't look to me as if you'll ever be all right again.'

Billy grinned. It hurt. 'A week or so, an' I'll be back to normal. I promise you I will.'

'Well, if there's nothin' more that we can do . . .' one of the saltworkers said awkwardly.

'No, I'll take care of him from here,' Becky told him, making it seem more like a threat than a promise, and the two men left, closing the kitchen door quietly behind them.

Becky took a handkerchief from her bag, and dried her red eyes. 'Well, what's all this about?' she asked, suddenly sounding all brisk and businesslike.

Billy would have shrugged, but he didn't dare risk what it

might do to his aching body. 'I got into a fight,' he said, 'an' I lost.'

'I can see you got into a fight,' Becky said. 'An' as for losin', I should hope you did – because if the other bloke looks any worse than you, he'll be on his way to meet his Maker by now. But what I want to know, Billy, is who did you get into this fight *with*?'

'I'd rather not say.'

Becky put her hands on her hips. 'An' I'd rather you did,' she said. 'For goodness' sake, Billy, this isn't the school playground, an' I'm not your teacher. You're a grown man, an' I want to know what's at the back of all this. Well?'

He almost wished that she was his teacher, Billy thought, because as terrified as he'd been of Miss Stebbings when he was a little lad, he'd always found her a lot easier to deal with than his mam in one of her moods.

'If you must know, it was Gerald I was fightin' with,' Billy mumbled into the tablecloth.

'Gerald? It's not your cousin Gerald you're talking about, is it?' Billy nodded, and Becky shook her head in exasperation. 'You should know better than that,' she said. 'His side of the family has never been known for fightin' fair.'

'He did this time,' Billy said. 'No dirty tricks. No underhand punches. He won because he was better than me, an' that's the truth.'

'Oh, well, I feel much better knowin' that you got turned into a bloody pulp *fairly*,' Becky said. 'Now are you goin' to tell me what this fight was all about?'

Billy thought about it. He'd tried dealing with this problem his own way, and the results had been disastrous, so maybe it was time he let Mam try.

'Gerald's been seein' our Michelle,' he said. 'I did me best to warn him off.'

Becky frowned. 'What do you mean, seein' her?'

'I mean like goin' out for rides in his car. An' not just in the daytime – after dark an' all.'

Becky slammed her hand down on the table so hard that all the crockery rattled. 'The little fool,' she said. 'The bloody little fool.'

*

Michelle lifted the latch and opened the kitchen door. Her mother and her brother were sitting at either end of the kitchen table. Michelle sensed that they had been there for some time, and though they both looked up when she entered the room, neither of them greeted her. And then she noticed her brother's face.

'What happened to you, Billy?' she gasped.

'Never mind what happened to him,' Becky said harshly. 'Sit down, Michelle.'

'Mam . . .'

'I said, sit down.'

Michelle lowered herself into a chair along the side of the table. She looked first at Billy and then at her mother, and felt two pairs of hostile eyes glaring back at her. 'Perhaps you'd better tell me what this is all about, Mam,' she said, though she knew really that there was only one thing that it *could* be about.

'How long has it been goin' on?' Becky demanded.

'How long has what been going on?'

'How long have you been seein' Gerald Worrell? An' why didn't you tell me about it? What made you go sneakin' around behind my back?'

Michelle sighed. 'I've been seeing him for a few weeks,' she said. 'And I didn't tell you about it precisely because I knew that it would cause this sort of scene.'

'You're a fool, Michelle,' Becky said angrily.

'And you're so narrow minded that you're quite prepared to tar the whole family with the same brush. Was Dad anything like his brother Richard?'

'Of course not. You know he wasn't. Your dad was the kindest, most gentle—'

'Then why should you assume that Gerald can't be any different to him, either? Oh, I know your opinion of Richard Worrell – I've had it drilled into me since I was a baby – but Gerald isn't like him at all. He's sensitive and thoughtful and . . .'

The anger which had filled Becky's face since Billy had told her about Gerald and Michelle now drained away, and was replaced by something which may have been sadness or pity, or perhaps was a little of both.

'You're in love with him, aren't you?' she said.

Michelle stuck her chin out defiantly. 'Yes, I am,' she said. 'And he's in love with me.'

Becky shook her head. 'You always hope your children will learn by your mistakes,' she said. 'But they never do.'

'You know it all, don't you, Mam?' Michelle said bitterly. 'There's nothing anybody can tell you about anything, because you already know it all.'

'Of course I don't know it all, but I know that family. You say I've drilled it into you since you were a kid, so I shouldn't have to repeat this: Richard Worrell convinced me that he was in love with me, just as Gerald's convinced you.'

'He *does* love me!'

'Oh, they're very cunning, are those Worrells, I'll give them that.'

'You're a Worrell, Mam.'

'Only by marriage,' Becky said fiercely. 'When I was seeing Richard, he carved our names on the oak tree . . .'

'I know all about that, Mam, and it has nothing to do with what Gerald and me—'

'. . . carved our names on the oak tree. I couldn't believe that he'd have done it if he didn't really love me. What kind of mind could come up with a scheme like that?' She paused for breath. 'How did you ever meet him, anyway?'

'I was walking to Northwich one morning, on the way to work. He was coming from the other direction. He fell off his horse right in front of me.'

Becky nodded with disgust. 'Now that's a typical Worrell trick,' she said. 'I know about ridin' – Richard taught me – an' I've seen the way young Gerald handles a horse. The only way he'd fall off is if he wanted to.'

'You're wrong about him, Mam. You're terribly, terribly wrong. Gerald would never—'

'If he's anythin' like his father – and havin' been brought up by Richard, he'd *have* to be – then he's only after one thing from you, an' the moment that he's had it . . .' She stopped again, as if something had just occurred to her. 'Gerald hasn't done that to you, has he?' she continued.

Michelle thought back to the evening in the woods, under the trees in the car that Gerald was so proud of. How he'd kissed her, how she'd let him run his hands over her breasts and . . .

'Answer me, girl!' Becky demanded.

'I'm not a girl any longer,' Michelle said angrily.

'That's no answer, and you know it.'

'No, he hasn't!' Michelle screamed. 'All right? He hasn't robbed me of my precious honour like you let Richard rob you of yours!'

She'd meant to hurt her mother, but all Becky felt was relief. 'Well, thank heavens for that, at least,' she said.

Michelle's anger disappeared as quickly as Becky's had earlier, and she was almost in tears. 'He makes me happy, Mam,' she said. 'He makes me happier than I've ever been before.'

Becky reached across and stroked her daughter's hand. 'I know he does, my little love,' she said softly. 'But that happiness isn't real, and when he drops you – an' he will – it'll be like you've fallen off the end of the world.'

'Are you going to try and stop me from seeing him, Mam?' Michelle asked.

Becky sighed. 'How can I? You're past your majority, an' if you insist on carryin' on like this, then all I can do is wait around to pick up the pieces when it's over. But it breaks my heart to see it happenin' to you.'

'So you won't stop me seeing him,' Michelle said, speaking slowly and carefully, to make sure she'd got it right, 'but if I choose to bring him home – and he does so desperately want to come home with me and meet you both – will he be welcome?'

Becky and Billy exchanged a quick, meaningful glance across the table, and even before her mother spoke, Michelle knew what the answer would be.

'No,' Becky said. 'No, I'm afraid that Gerald Worrell will never be welcome here.'

The tears which Michelle had been holding back now streamed freely down her cheeks. 'So what you're asking me to do is choose between the man I love and the only family I've got,' she sobbed.

'It's not like that, love . . .'

'It's *exactly* like that, Mam. And it's not fair on me. It's just not fair.' Michelle stood up, pushed her chair away and rushed to the kitchen door.

'Michelle!' Becky called to her, starting to rise herself as Michelle lifted the latch and flung the door open.

Billy put a hand on his mother's arm and forced her gently back into her chair. 'Let her go, Mam,' he said. 'This is somethin' she has to work out for herself.'

Becky listened to her daughter's footsteps retreating rapidly down the alley. 'Yes,' she said. 'I hate to admit it, but I think you're right there, Billy.'

At the top of the alley, Michelle stopped to catch her breath, then looked frantically up and down the lane. Where could she go now that her own family had turned on her?

She wished that her gran was still alive. Mary Taylor would have understood. She wouldn't have condemned Gerald out of hand, as Mam and Billy had. But she was dead, and Michelle had no one.

Then her eye fell on the brick chimney of Worrell's saltworks, and without even thinking about it, Michelle crossed the lane and headed for the main gate.

The ladies' gossip circle had convened their afternoon meeting at the top of Not-Stopping Bracegirdle's alley, and had a clear view of Michelle's dash towards the saltworks.

'Looked like she was in tears to me,' Dottie Curzon said. 'What do you think it's all about?'

Not-Stopping and Flo both grimaced as if to say that only an idiot would need to ask that question.

'Her mother's found out about her and Gerald at last,' Not-Stopping said. 'They've had a row, and now she's goin' to see Gerald. Well, she'll not get much consolation there.'

'Don't you think so?' Dottie asked.

'No, I do not. Men don't want women bringin' their troubles to 'em. They only really have one use for woman, and it's not cookin' I'm talking about.'

'Maybe young Gerald's different,' Dottie suggested.

'All men have disgustin' habits, even the nice ones,' Not-Stopping told her. 'There was a time when my Ernie wouldn't leave me alone, but he soon got over that.'

'I'm not surprised,' said Flo under her breath, not realising they looked so much alike that people sometimes took them for mother and daughter.

'I think I'll go an' make me tea,' Dottie Curzon said, when Michelle had disappeared through the gates of the saltworks and there was nothing else of interest happening in the lane.

'Me an' all,' Flo agreed. 'Will I see you both in the pub at the usual time?'

'If me joints'll let me,' Not-Stopping said, although they all three knew that only death would stop her from being there – and even then the hearse might call at the New Inn so she could have one more milk stout on the way to the churchyard.

Flo and Dottie made their way back to their own houses, but Not-Stopping stayed where she was in the hope her extra few minutes' vigil would provide her with a really sensational story to astound her cronies with later. But the lane was as quiet as a theatre after the last act has finished – as empty as a church which has seen the final service of the day.

It had provided her with a lot of entertainment over the years, that lane, Not-Stopping thought to herself. And a great deal of it had been connected with the Taylors and Worrells. She remembered George Taylor marching boldly off to war and coming back, crutch in hand, on the back of a carman's wagon. She recalled Becky Taylor's wedding, which the whole village turned out for. And then there was the time that Becky's brother Philip had returned from London in triumph, bringing with him his new bride, a flashy-looking woman called Marie, who said she was a *chanteuse*. Whatever that meant.

It was funny, Not-Stopping thought, but she knew so much about all the Taylors that they were almost like family, and despite her malicious dig at the girl, Michelle was one of her favourites. She hoped that things would work out for the lass and her cousin – but she didn't really think they would!

Gerald's horse was tied to the hitching rail, contentedly chewing at a pile of hay, which had to mean that Gerald was still in the single-storey brick office at the other end of the yard.

'Thank God!' Michelle said aloud. She knew she was in a terrible state, but Gerald would calm her down, know what to do next. Without him her world had no meaning, she thought, but if he was by her side she was ready to take on anything that fate chose to fling at her.

She passed the furnaces, where bare-chested stokers shovelled in the coke which would heat up the brine pans above. A few weeks earlier, before her transformation from dowdy bookkeeper to elegant woman, none of the stokers would have noticed her, but now they all turned their heads and watched appreciatively as she made her way towards the office.

The office door was closed. Michelle knocked once, then, without waiting for an answer, turned the handle. Gerald was sitting at his desk, studying a telegram. He looked up, an expression of irritation on his face, then he saw who it was and how distressed she looked.

'Michelle, I . . . Have you been talking to your brother? Did he tell you about the fight?'

Michelle shook her head confusedly. 'No. Yes. I mean I have been talking to him, but not about the fight.'

'Then you didn't know . . .?'

'It had to be you he'd been fighting with, didn't it? After what we talked about, it couldn't have been anything else. Did you start it, or was it him?'

Gerald stood up. 'He started it, my darling. He wanted me to stop seeing you.'

Michelle took a handkerchief from her sleeve and dabbed her eyes. 'My mother wants me to stop seeing you, as well,' she sobbed. 'But I won't. I *won't*.'

'I can understand why they feel like that. It's only natural they should suspect my intentions—' Gerald began.

'Let's get married as soon as we possibly can,' Michelle said in a rush.

Get married! Gerald's face registered astonishment for the briefest instant, and then the look was gone. 'Your family would, er, never stand for that,' he said. 'If we were to marry, I'm quite sure that they'd have nothing more to do with you.'

Michelle twisted the handkerchief in her fingers. 'I don't care what they do,' she said. 'I love you.'

As good a natural actor as Gerald was, he was finding it harder and harder to keep his amazement from reappearing, and so he did the only thing he could, which was to walk around the desk and hug Michelle's head to his chest.

'You really mean that, do you?' he asked. 'You really would cut yourself off from you family for *me*?'

'Yes,' Michelle replied. 'Wouldn't you do the same for me, my darling?'

'Er . . . yes. Of course.'

Michelle broke away from his embrace and looked up at him. 'You don't sound very sure,' she said, with a tremble in her voice.

'I am,' Gerald said, recovering. 'If I sounded uncertain, it's only because I still find it incredible that you love me enough to sacrifice everything else so we can be together.'

'Then we *will* get married?'

Gerald shook his head. 'We can't.' He reached over to the desk, picked up the telegram, and held it out for her to see. 'This just came. I've been called up. I have to leave immediately.'

'But how can you be going so soon?' Michelle gasped. 'The Yeomen haven't even left Northwich yet.'

'There is a pressing need for officers in the British Expeditionary Force,' Gerald told her, 'and I was in the Officer Training Corps at school.' He grinned. 'Besides, I used my father's influence to pull a few strings at the War Office.'

'You can't wait to get yourself killed, can you?' Michelle said furiously.

Gerald put his arms around her again. 'Don't be a little silly,' he told her. 'Of course I don't want to be killed, but I have to do my duty as best I can. And when this is all over, we *will* get married. I promise you.'

'Do you mean it?' Michelle asked.

'Yes, I mean it. I mean it deeply and truly. When have I ever lied to you?'

Chapter Ten

Richard Worrell stood on the platform at Northwich Railway Station, watching the track for the appearance of the train which would rob him of his son.

'It isn't due for another two or three minutes, Father,' said a voice at his side.

Richard turned to look at Gerald. The boy was dressed in a bold check double-breasted suit, and had a felt homburg on his head. At first glance he could have been taken for any young gentleman who was just off to London for a spot of pleasure, but his stance said that though he was not yet in uniform, he already considered himself a soldier.

Father and son had argued late into the previous night, Richard employing all the powers of persuasion he had acquired over the years, Gerald not budging an inch. Now, although he felt drained by his desperation and his failure, Richard resolved to have one last try at talking his son out of this madness.

'If you'd have told me a week ago that this would be happening, I wouldn't have believed you,' he said.

'I'm still finding it all a little hard to believe myself,' Gerald admitted.

Richard put his hand on his son's shoulder. 'It's not too late for me to use my influence, you know,' he said. 'Even now, I could telegraph my contacts in the War Office and—'

'It *is* too late,' Gerald interrupted him. 'From the moment Archduke Ferdinand was killed in Sarajevo, it was too late. Perhaps it was always too late.'

'What do you mean by that?'

'In some ways, this feels like it was intended to be. It's almost as if I were born for no other purpose than to go to France and fight the Hun.'

'You're talking nonsense!' Richard snapped. 'You're putting your life at risk for some vague, romantic notion of destiny which you can't even justify.'

'Perhaps what you say is true,' Gerald agreed. 'I only know that I find myself in the grip of forces far beyond my control.'

From the distance came the sound of a steam whistle, and looking back down the track, Richard could see that the train was finally approaching.

'Try to accept what I'm doing, Father,' Gerald said. 'Even if you can't understand it.'

The huge locomotive steamed into the station, belching thick black smoke into an otherwise clear blue sky. For a moment, it seemed as if it would keep on going, urged on by Richard's prayers, then the brakes screamed, sparks flew, and the great monster came to a juddering halt.

Two clergymen in long black coats and gaiters stepped out of the first-class compartment in front of Richard and Gerald. Further down the train, a group of workmen, carrying toolboxes in their hands, were disembarking from the third-class section. A family of five – mother, father and three small children – stood by the guard's van, watching their luggage being loaded.

Gerald started to take a step forward, but his father's hand restrained him. 'You'll write to me, won't you?' Richard said.

Gerald laughed. 'Of course, Father.'

'Often?'

'As often as I possibly can. And now, if you don't want me to be court martialed before I've even started to serve, I'd better be getting on the train.'

The two men embraced. Richard wanted to hold on to his son for ever, but Gerald gently disentangled himself.

'I really do have to go, Father,' he said.

He climbed into the first-class compartment the clergymen had just vacated, closed the door behind him, placed his bag in the overhead luggage rack and sat down. Then, when he noticed that Richard was still standing on the platform, he stood up again and pulled down the window.

'You don't have to stay there until we leave, Father,' he said.

'But I'd like to stay,' Richard replied, feeling a sudden catch in his throat. He looked up at Gerald – at the smiling, confident face of his son – and thought his heart would burst. The humiliation he had undergone to retain custody of the boy had all been worth it. He would have suffered it all again gladly, if that would have prevented Gerald from going to France. He wanted to tell his son that the only thing he was really proud of in his entire life was fathering such a fine young man. But he knew that if he tried to put any of that into words, he would break down. It would be best to part on a light note, he thought, best to make a joke. He forced a smile to his lips.

'You might have been a rich man, but for this war, Gerald,' he said.

'Might I?' Gerald asked, looking puzzled.

'Indeed you might. Another few weeks and you might have won our wager. But now we will never know whether you could have done it, will we?'

Gerald smiled. 'Now it's you who's talking nonsense, Father,' he said.

It was Richard's turn to be surprised. 'Surely, it's no longer possible—' he began.

'Do you really think that after I've worked so hard at sweet-talking cousin Michelle into my bed, I'll give up now that I am so close to my objective?' Gerald interrupted.

'But you're off to war.'

'And she will wait patiently for my return, like the sentimental little fool that she is. I'll be back home on leave almost before you know it, and one of the first things that I intend to do is to spend an evening rogering my little cousin.' He grinned. 'And immediately after that, Father, I shall come to you and collect the five thousand pounds which you were foolish enough to bet.'

The station master blew his whistle, and waved his flag. The train began to shunt slowly out of the station.

'Goodbye, my son!' Richard called.

'Goodbye, Father!' Gerald answered cheerily.

Richard stood on the platform until the train was completely out of sight, then turned and walked towards the exit with a single tear making its way slowly down his cheek.

*

Northwich had not been so full or so excited since 'Lord' George Sanger's world famous circus had visited the town over thirty years earlier. The streets were packed with people from all over the area. Street pedlars sold toffee apples, pieces of coconut and brightly coloured balloons. It was like waiting for that long-gone circus, but better: it was the circus and May Day and Christmas all rolled into one. Saturday marked Day Four of the war against the Hun and the first soldiers were about to leave the town.

Spudder Johnson and Ivy Clegg stood with the crowd at the corner of Timber Lane, waiting for the soldiers to march past.

'Isn't this all so thrillin', Spudder?' Ivy asked.

'Yes,' Spudder agreed, politely, but he was not sure that he meant it. Mr Marvello had asked him if he could drive a bayonet into an enemy soldier's throat. He had said that he couldn't, and he didn't really see why anybody else should have to, either. Of course, there were a lot of things he didn't understand about this war. People said it was necessary, and as usual he believed them, but France was so far away that it hardly seemed worth bothering about.

'It was so nice of you to bring me here, Spudder,' Ivy said.

'I didn't bring you,' Spudder told her. 'We just came together, that's all.'

Ivy laughed. 'How gallant you are today.'

'What does that mean?' Spudder asked, frowning, as he always did when he thought he'd missed the point.

'It means you really know how to make a girl feel special.'

'Do I?' Spudder asked, sounding pleased.

Ivy shook her head. 'No, you don't,' she said with a sigh.

'Then why did you say it?'

'I was just tryin' to let you know, the best way I could, that I'd appreciate it if—'

'You *are* special,' Spudder interrupted.

'Am I?' Ivy asked.

'Well, of course you are. I wouldn't have given you a job if I hadn't thought that.'

'So you can be a charmer when you make the effort,' Ivy said.

She slipped her arm through his. Spudder's eyes widened, and for a second she thought he would pull away. Then he looked down at the linked arms, apparently decided there was no harm in it, and relaxed a little.

'There's a lot of courtin' couples turned out to watch the parade,' Ivy said. 'Do you think people lookin' at us might take us for a courtin' couple?'

'No,' Spudder said firmly.

'Why not?'

Spudder was beginning to feel hot under the collar. 'Well . . . they just wouldn't.'

'You can be really hard work sometimes, Spudder,' Ivy said, almost under her breath.

'What was that, Ivy?'

'I said, it's nice to have a break from work sometimes, Spudder.'

'I'm not so sure about that,' Spudder replied. 'I should have been whitewashin' the coal house this mornin'.'

Aggie and Ned Spratt had stationed themselves at the Bull Ring, which would be one of the first places the soldiers would march through. The crowd was quite dense, and there was some good-natured pushing and shoving. Nobody tried to push the Spratts. It wasn't that Aggie and Ned looked the types to get annoyed, it was simply that trying to move them was well beyond most people's capability.

'I don't know what we're doin' here,' Ned said grumpily. 'If they're much longer comin', I'll miss me dinner. An' you know how I get if I miss one of me three squares.'

'One of your five squares, more like,' Aggie responded. 'And that's not countin' what you scoff down between meals.'

'A man's got to eat,' Ned said.

Aggie looked fondly at her husband. He was her second. The first had been a drunk she'd thrown out of the house – through the open kitchen window – when he'd passed out one night. She had no problems of that sort with Ned. Beer was no competition for her cooking, and if it were left up to him, he'd never leave the kitchen table.

'How much longer are we goin' to have to wait?' Ned asked.

'As long as it takes,' Aggie told him. 'Them lads are off to fight for their country, an' the least we can do is be here to cheer them on their way.'

'I suppose you're right,' Ned agreed. 'I just wish I'd thought to bring a meat butty with me.'

From the far end of the Bull Ring, someone shouted, 'They're comin'! They're comin'!' Soon, everyone else joined in the cry.

The Yeomanry appeared first, riding proudly on horses which only a few days earlier had been pulling greengrocers' wagons or fishmonger's vans. Behind them were the Infantry, some in uniform, some not, but all swinging their arms with something like military precision.

The crowd cheered, clapped and whistled, and the soldiers – though they looked neither to left nor right – smiled and basked in the adulation.

It took the parade fifteen minutes to reach Station Road, and all the way it was accompanied by loud cheering. By the time they reached the station yard itself, the smiles on the soldiers' faces were so wide that their mouths looked as if they might be permanently stuck in that position.

'They think that it's all goin' to be so easy,' Becky said softly, as she watched them from her vantage point outside the Lion and Railway Hotel. But she knew they were wrong. George had told her what damage the Maxim gun could do, and what use was a man on horseback against a terrifying machine like that? No, it wouldn't be easy at all – it would be bloody murder.

Billy was suddenly standing by her side, his quick breathing giving away just how excited he was.

'What happened to you?' Becky asked. 'One minute you were here, standin' right next to me, and the next I looked round an' you were gone.'

Her son suddenly became very interested in his boots. 'I've been down to Navigation Road,' he muttered.

'Navigation Road? Do you mean you've been to the recruitment office?'

'Yes, Mam.' Billy looked up again. 'I'd have gone sooner, only after that beatin' Gerald gave me, me face was in such a mess that I thought it might put 'em off.'

'So you're goin' to be a soldier, whatever I say?'

Billy shrugged his shoulders. 'We've got to fight for what's ours, haven't we, Mam?'

Ours! Becky thought. As if the Germans were actually on British soil. As if, even at the moment, a German battleship was sailing up the Weaver.

'When will you be leavin'?' she asked.

'Some time next week, they said.'

'An' what am I supposed to do for a master baker while you're away playin' at bein' soldiers?'

Billy grinned. 'Maybe you can get Monsieur Henri back,' he suggested. 'I shouldn't imagine he's havin' much fun in France at the moment.'

It was pointless being angry for long with anyone as irrepressible as Billy, and Becky did not even try. Instead, she reached up and put her arm fondly around her son's shoulder.

'If you were a bit younger, I'd clip your ear for bein' cheeky,' she said.

'If I'd been a bit younger, I'd have known enough to have got out of range about thirty seconds ago,' Billy told her.

Becky looked into her son's eyes. 'You will be careful, won't you?' she asked.

Billy grinned again. 'You know me, Mam.'

Yes, she did know him. And that was precisely why she was so worried.

The march-past had all but finished, and the crowd was slowly starting to drift away. The first batch of a hundred and forty men – the pride of Northwich and district – had left their home town to journey to the battlefields of France. For many of them, it would be the first time they had travelled further south than Crewe. For nearly all, it would be their first experience of another country.

Becky looked at their strong, confident shoulders, disappearing into the distance, and wondered how many of these fine young men would ever come back again.

PART TWO

A Corner of Some Foreign Field

Chapter Eleven

August drifted lazily into September, and the birds and animals began their preparations for the coming winter. Squirrels and jays gathered acorns and other hard fruits, burying them for later use. Field mice collected their cold-weather rations of hips and stored them in discarded birds' nests. Overhead, the swallows were beginning to flock as a prelude to their long journey to Africa. But though so many creatures of nature were sticking to their normal timetable, nature herself refused to follow suit. Towards the end of the month the leaves on the trees were starting to turn brown, but otherwise there was no indication that the golden summer was ever going to come to an end.

In only a few short weeks, the face of Northwich had changed completely. With so many men already gone away to war, and more due to leave in the near future, the women of the town were stepping into their shoes and taking over their jobs.

There were women chimney-sweeps, and women bill-stickers, too. Anyone unlucky enough to pass away towards that end of that glorious summer would still be laid out by a male undertaker, but was likely to be driven to the final resting place by a female hearse driver, and buried in a hole dug by a woman.

Women were doing anything and everything, from delivering the mail to making bricks, and though such things would have seemed scandalous only a few months earlier, now they seemed quite normal, because, after all, there *was* a war going on.

As the year progressed, so Becky Worrell's worries seemed to mount. She could sell all the bread she could make, but with all her carmen and most of her bakers in the army, it took a tremendous effort to maintain her pre-war production level.

Countless hours were spent instructing her new female drivers and bakers, and more were wasted correcting the mistakes caused by their inexperience. She seemed to spend most of her life at the bakery, and when she did finally get home, it was only to collapse, exhausted, into her lonely bed.

But she could have taken all that if, in addition, she hadn't been fretting about her two children. It was well over a month since Billy had sailed to France. The newspapers contained reports of heavy fighting, and there had not been a single letter from him to say that he was all right. She dreaded each knock on the door, fearing that when she opened it, she would find herself looking at the telegraph boy holding a telegram telling her that her son had been killed in action.

And then there was Michelle. Mother and daughter had been so close for so many years, but since their argument the day that Gerald thrashed Billy, it was almost as if they were nothing more than casual acquaintances.

It wasn't that Michelle was actively hostile, Becky thought. She was always polite, and sometimes, within certain unspoken limits, even friendly. But she seemed to have withdrawn into a world of her own, never sharing her thoughts, never asking her mam's advice about anything. And because Becky didn't know what to do about it, she had done nothing at all.

It was one of those rare mornings when Michelle had time for breakfast. Or perhaps, Becky thought, it was one of those rare mornings when her daughter had something she wanted to say.

Michelle kept quiet until she had finished her food, then she said, 'They're turning the Victoria saltworks over to war production.'

'Oh, are they?' Becky replied, trying to sound interested, because at least they were talking. 'An' what will they be makin'?'

'They're going to be manufacturing nitrates.'

'I'm none the wiser now you've told me. What are nitrates, when they're at home?'

'They're chemicals. They're used in the explosive part of artillery shells.'

'Well, the sooner they get started, the better,' Becky said.

'From what I've been readin' in the papers, our boys are goin' to need all the shells we can send them.'

'They will,' Michelle agreed, picturing Gerald standing by a big gun and waiting for ammunition to arrive. 'And the Victoria works needs all the willing hands it can get to produce the shells. That's why I'm going to be working there full-time.'

'What about all your other clients?'

'They'll just have to do without me. Everybody has to make sacrifices in wartime.'

'I suppose you're right,' Becky agreed. 'An' shell manufacturers need good book-keepers just like anybody else.'

'I won't be working as a book-keeper,' Michelle said. 'I'm going on the production line.'

'But surely, with all your education—'

'It's still the most useful thing I could do.'

Becky frowned. 'I'm not sure I like the idea of you workin' among nasty chemicals. It seems it could be dangerous work, an' all. If you're makin' explosives, there's always the chance of some of 'em accidentally goin' off.'

'You're probably right, Mam,' Michelle agreed, almost indifferently.

'So if you don't mind, love, I'd much rather you didn't have anythin' to do with—'

'You seem to think I was asking your opinion on the matter,' Michelle cut in.

'And weren't you?'

'No, I wasn't. I'm old enough to decide where I want to work – just as I'm old enough to see any man I choose to. So I wasn't asking your opinion at all, I was merely informing you of what I will be doing from now on.'

'I see,' Becky said.

They both relapsed into an uneasy silence.

This was all Gerald Worrell's fault, Becky thought bitterly. If he hadn't set his sights at Michelle, the little fool would never have fallen for him, and there would have been no row to split the family apart. After all those years, when she'd finally come to believe that she and hers were safe, the Worrells had touched them again, and once more created havoc. She had always despised Gerald as Richard's son, but now she had an even more personal reason to hate him.

The morning post arrived just after Michelle had left the house. There were the usual bills and trade circulars, but right at the bottom of the pile was a personal letter in a handwriting that was as familiar to Becky as her own. With trembling hands, she slit open the envelope and pulled out the single sheet of paper.

Dear Mam,
I'm not allowed to tell you *exactly* where I am, but I'm finally in France. It's a funny war, this. I expected it to be all big battles, like the ones we learned about in school, and from what other Tommies have told me, the first few weeks were like that. But now it's all something called trench warfare. We sit in our trenches, and the Germans sit in theirs, and nobody seems to be going anywhere much. We're so close to the German trenches that sometimes we can even hear them talking.

I am very well in myself, and have most of the things I need, but if you could send me a couple of tins of condensed milk and a few packets of Woodbines, it would be much appreciated.

Quite a few of the lads I went to school with are here, and sometimes we have a good laugh about us all ending up so far away from home.

I miss you, Mam, and I miss Michelle as well (I hope she has forgiven me!).

All my love,
Billy.

P.S. I said I had some of my old mates with me, but there is one person here I would rather *not* know. I can't mention names, but he is somebody who has caused our family trouble before and gave me a bloody nose a few weeks back.

As Becky put the letter down on the table, she saw that her hands were shaking even more than when she'd picked it up.

Gerald! In the same regiment as her son! That was bad luck, and no mistake. But maybe they wouldn't have much to do with each other, she consoled herself. After all, Gerald was an officer, and Billy was only a private soldier.

Yes but that was the problem, wasn't it? she thought. Officers had a lot of power over privates, and could make their lives a misery if they wanted to.

Well, there was no point in worrying about it – that would do no good at all. Yet how could she not worry, when in addition to the new enemy, Billy would have to deal with one which went back over twenty years?

She picked up his letter again, and placed it carefully in the box where she kept the ones her husband had sent her from Africa. Like Billy, Michael had always been in danger, and he too had promised that he would be careful. And now he lay in a lonely grave in Marston churchyard.

It was late afternoon when Jim Vernon and Fred Davenport docked the *Damascus* just below Northwich Town Bridge, and by the time they walked up the High Street, all the shops were closed.

'Have you decided yet whether or not you're joinin' up?' Captain Davenport asked.

'No, I haven't,' Jim admitted. 'What do you think you'd do in my place?'

'That's puttin' me on the spot a bit, isn't it? I mean, I'm *not* in your place.'

'No, but what if you were? If you were my age again, do you think you'd stay on the river? Or would you enlist?'

The Captain gave it some considerable thought. 'I'd stay here,' he said finally. 'People need salt, war or no war. An' since you ask me, you'll do a lot more good seein' that they get their salt than you ever could takin' pot-shots at the Germans.'

Jim looked around him. There were flags everywhere. All the shops displayed at least one Union Jack – some had three or four. Flags had been tied to horses' bridles, too, and some people had gone as far as to make Union Jack overcoats for their dogs. Northwich had never been so patriotic, not even during the Boer War.

'Thing is, it's easy for you to say that,' Jim pointed out.

'You mean because I'm gettin' on, an' I don't have any choice any more?'

'No, I mean because you've already had your adventures. You've sailed all the way to China, while I've never been further than Liverpool in me life.' A sudden thought struck Jim. 'You never talk about it, though, do you?'

'Talk about what?'

'China. I mean, I know you've been there, but that's *all* I know. If it'd been me who'd sailed halfway across the world, you'd never get me off the subject.'

The Captain shook his head. 'You young lads are all the same,' he said. 'You're so full of enthusiasm that it's exhaustin' just listenin' to you. You're always expectin' everythin' you do to be full of excitement. But it usually isn't, you know. Let me tell you, Jim – an' remember, I've been there so I know – China's not really much more excitin' than Warrington or Winsford.'

'But how can that be?' Jim asked. 'I mean, Warrington's just ordinary, but you go to China an' there's all them junks, an' rickshaws an' fellers in pigtails . . .'

He trailed off. The Captain was no longer listening to him, but instead had all his attention fixed on the small crowd which had gathered a little further up the street from them, just in front of Heinzmann's pork butchers.

'Now what the bloody hell is goin' on there?' Davenport wondered aloud.

The crowd was about twenty strong, and was looking up at two heads – a man's and a woman's – which were carved above the doorway.

'An' I'm tellin' you that it *is* him!' said one of the onlookers, a burly man with a red face and a broken nose.

'What's goin' on?' Jim asked.

'See that man's head up there?' the man replied, pointing. 'Look at him. Don't he remind you of nobody?'

Jim examined the carving. The head was almost comical, with its rounded cheeks, bulging eyes and puckered lips. Jim remembered looking at it when he was a kid, but it had been years since he'd paid it even passing attention.

'Can't say it does remind me of anybody,' Jim admitted.

'It's the spittin' image of that bloody Kaiser Bill, that's what it is,' the man said belligerently.

'Doesn't look anythin' like him.'

'An' the woman's the spittin' image of the Kaiser's missus. An' just look what they're doin'! They're lookin' down on us, an' laughin'!'

'Oh, don't talk soft!' Jim said, trying to make light of the whole thing. 'Like I told you, it doesn't look anythin' like him. An' them heads have been up there for years – long before the Kaiser was even crowned.'

But the man with the broken nose was not interested in logic. 'It's our patriotic duty as Englishmen to take down that German's sign an' smash up them heads.' Several other people in the crowd murmured their agreement, but Jim was not one of them.

'Mr Heinzmann's lived in Northwich for a long time,' he said. 'I'll bet you've bought your meat from him yourself.'

'Well? What if I have?'

'He's always been a decent honest tradesman, an' you can't turn on him now, just because there's a war goin' on.'

'Oh, I can't, can't I?' Broken Nose asked. 'And who's goin' to stop me?'

Jim bunched his fists, but only loosely. 'Me, if you force me to,' he said.

'What are you?' Broken Nose demanded. 'Some kind of German sympathiser?'

'I'm as against the Germans as you are,' Jim told him. 'But I know what's fair.'

For a second, it looked like Broken Nose was going to take a swing at Jim, then he saw just how determined and tough the young sailor looked, and decided it would be wiser to back down.

'I've no truck with any Germans,' he muttered. 'Nor with them as supports 'em.' Then he turned away and walked off down Witton Street.

Jim looked at the rest of the people who were still standing there. 'If I was you lot, I'd clear off before the bobbies get here,' he advised them. Slowly the crowd began to drift away, but Jim did not move from the spot until the very last of them had gone.

'You took a chance, there,' Captain Davenport told him. 'If that bloke had hit you, some of the others might have joined in – and it wouldn't have been *your* side they were on.'

'Aye, well, we all have to take chances sometimes,' Jim said, wishing he'd been as resolute with Michelle Worrell as he'd been with the man who'd wanted to take the sign down.

They walked up Witton Street, towards the cinder track which led to Marston. There were more flags and posters exhorting men of the right military age to join up.

The two of them had been silent for some time, but now Captain Davenport said, 'It was bound to happen sooner or later—'

'What was? A mob gatherin' outside Heinzmann's?'

'Yes. That – or somethin' like it. I mean, anti-German feelin's been sweepin' through this town like an epidemic of influenza, hasn't it, now?'

It was true, Jim thought. Everybody had been caught up in it. The boy scouts had volunteered to guard the railway bridges against German saboteurs. Men who were too old for the army had announced they would watch the reservoirs in case the Hun tried to poison them. Everybody seemed to be assuming that the Germans either were – or soon would be – active in the area.

'Do you think there really could be any German spies in Northwich?' Jim asked as they passed the Townshend Arms.

Davenport laughed so loudly that a man just entering the pub turned round to see what all the fuss was about. 'Of course there aren't any German spies,' the Captain said. 'Why would they want to bother with a little town like this?'

'Well, you said yourself that salt's important,' Jim pointed out.

'So it is. But I'd imagine the Huns have got a lot more to worry about than whether we've got flavourin' for our Sunday roast.'

'An' I did read in the paper that there's plans to start makin' explosives in the Victoria and Plumley saltworks.'

Davenport shook his head. 'You're not thinkin' this through properly,' he said. 'Say the Germans really *did* want to spy on Northwich, they couldn't very well send somebody here now, could they?'

'Why not?'

'Because now there's a war goin' on, we're goin' to be suspicious of any new arrivals, aren't we?'

'I suppose so,' Jim agreed reluctantly.

'Well, there you are, then.'

Both men relapsed into silence, and the only sound was the crunching of cinders under their feet. It was not until they reached Wincham that Jim spoke again. 'What if they'd had spies here for years?' he asked. 'We know that the Germans have been preparing for war for years, don't we? So why couldn't they have spent years settin' up their spy ring as well?'

Davenport laughed again. 'I can just see it,' he said. 'They send some Fritz to Cheshire an' tell him to pretend he's as English as what we are.' He screwed up his face as if he were wearing a monocle. 'Gut mornink, mine name is Harry Schmitt und I am a Cheshire man, born und bred.'

Jim did not join in the laughter. 'There must be some Germans who speak better English than that,' he said. 'There must be at least a few who could pass themselves off as British if they wanted to.'

'Even if they talked right, there'd always be somethin' about 'em that would give 'em away,' the Captain said.

'Like what?'

'I don't know. I'm no expert in catchin' spies. But it stands to reason that if they're Germans, they'll *act* like Germans, even if it's only in little ways.'

Maybe he was right about that, at least, Jim thought. 'What do they drink in Germany?'

'Drink? Alcohol, you mean?'

'I was thinkin' more of at breakfast. Do they drink a lot of tea, like we do?'

'No,' the Captain said. 'I rather fancy they prefer to have coffee.'

'Mr Bingham never drinks tea,' Jim said ominously.

Chapter Twelve

Spudder looked at the clock on the kitchen mantelpiece of number 49, and slowly worked out the time. The little hand was on six and the big hand was on twelve, so that made it exactly six o'clock. It would be half an hour before the lodgers started to stir, an hour before breakfast was served. He glanced around the room, and felt his hands start to twitch. He recognised the symptom for what it was – a desire to be doing something.

'Don't even think of it, Spudder,' said a voice he recognised as belonging to Aggie. 'Cleanin's what I'm paid to do. I don't appreciate anybody else stickin' their oar in, thank you very much.' He looked around the kitchen again, and saw that he was still alone. So the voice had only been in his head.

Spudder's hands were still twitching. Maybe I'll make some chips, he thought. But that would be nothing but a waste of good food, because any chips he made then would be of no use by dinnertime.

He prowled restlessly around the kitchen, looking for some diversion which would not get him in trouble with Aggie. The newspaper had already arrived, but reading sometimes gave him a headache, and anyway, he was not in the mood. He straightened the mirror over the fireplace, stepped back to examine it, then returned it to its original position.

'Maybe I'll light the fire,' he said. After all, Aggie couldn't object to that, could she? The fire was already laid – all he had to do was strike a match.

He was reaching for the matchbox when it suddenly occurred to him that it wouldn't do the grate any harm to have a black-leading before the fire was lit. He reached for the tin of black-lead, picked up a rag, and set to work. It would have been stretching the truth to say that the grate actually *needed* doing –

in fact, it was hard to tell which parts he'd leaded and which parts he hadn't – but all the rubbing and polishing was soon working its magic on him, and he became oblivious to anything else.

There was the sound of footsteps in the back yard. The kitchen door clicked open. Spudder finally became aware that he was no longer alone. And by then, of course, it was too late!

He spun round, the black-leading rag held guiltily in his right hand. 'I'm s-sorry, Aggie,' he stuttered. 'I know you do as good a job as me, but . . .'

He breathed a sigh of relief. The huge frame of his cleaner was not there in the doorway, blocking out nearly all the light. Instead, there was only slim little Ivy Clegg.

'Aggie's not feelin' very well,' Ivy told him. 'So she's takin' the day off.'

'Good. No, I don't mean good,' Spudder said, getting confused. 'I mean bad, really. 'Cos it's not nice bein' ill, you know. It's unhealthy, bein' ill. So I'm sorry Aggie's not feelin' very well, but I'm glad that she . . . glad that I . . .'

Ivy smiled mischievously. 'You're glad she didn't catch you doin' her job.'

'That's it,' Spudder agreed.

'Well, now you've started, aren't you goin' to finish it off?' Ivy asked.

Spudder looked at the rag in his hand, and then back to the grate. 'You mean, you'll let me?' he said.

Ivy laughed. 'It's your house, Spudder,' she said. 'Besides, I'm a good worker, but I've never been one to find work when there wasn't any. An' if you get pleasure from black-leadin', I don't see why you shouldn't do it.'

'I do enjoy it,' Spudder admitted. 'An' whitewashin', an' donkey-stonin'.'

Ivy took off her hat and hung it up on the hook behind the door. 'When you think about it, you don't really need a maid at all, do you?' she asked.

Spudder looked horrified. 'Oh, I do,' he said. 'I couldn't manage without Aggie.'

'No,' Ivy said quietly. 'In some ways, I don't think you could. You really are a bit of an innocent, aren't you, Spudder?'

'Like I told you before, I *was* guilty once,' Spudder said.

'That time when I pushed me dad down the stairs. But the police let me off.'

Ivy smiled again. 'When you've finished with that grate, I'll make you a good strong cup of tea.'

'That would be nice,' Spudder agreed.

Given the freedom of his own house for the day, Spudder couldn't stop with just the black-leading, and by the time he finally sat down to drink his tea he had swept the floor, cleaned the windows and polished the sideboard.

Aggie never sat at the table with Spudder, and neither did Ivy when Aggie was there. But this time she did.

'It's nice bein' alone, isn't it?' she asked.

'I suppose so,' Spudder said doubtfully.

Ivy looked hurt. 'Don't you like me, Spudder?'

Spudder's face and neck flushed a deep red. 'Well, of course I like you, Ivy. Only . . .'

'Only what?'

'I'm not used to women. Not really. I mean there was Mam, except she wasn't really me mam . . . An' Mrs Becky. An' Aggie. But . . .' He shrugged helplessly. 'I feel more comfortable around men.'

'That's only because you're more used to 'em. Do you know how to row?'

'A boat, you mean?'

Ivy laughed again. 'Now what else could I possibly be talkin' about?'

'I've never done it,' Spudder admitted, 'but I can do most things that I put me mind to – as long as there's not too much thinkin' involved in 'em.'

'Right, well that's settled, then. Next Sunday afternoon, you can hire a boat an' take me out on the river.'

'Take you out on the river!' Spudder felt a sudden pounding in his head and became very hot around the collar. 'I . . . I can't,' he spluttered.

'Why not?'

'Because I'm afraid of water.'

Ivy tilted her head to one side and looked at him questioningly. 'Can't you swim?'

'Yes, but . . .'

'How far? Do you think you could swim from one side of the Weaver to the other?'

'Oh, that's nothin'.'

Ivy nodded, as if that was the answer she'd been expecting. 'So you're not really afraid of water, are you?'

Spudder looked down at the table. 'No. That was a fib. What I'm afraid of is you.'

'Next Sunday,' Ivy told him. 'On the river. You'll be there, won't you?'

'Yes,' Spudder said miserably. He should have known when Ivy had let him do all that cleaning, that there was bound to be a catch to it.

The boarders, with the exception of Jim Vernon, all appeared in the kitchen at their customary time, and Ivy, now that she had extracted the promise from Spudder, set about happily cooking their breakfasts for them.

'I expect you'll be leaving us again soon, won't you, Mr Bingham?' the Great Marvello asked the boarding house's least talkative resident while Ivy was dishing out the food.

Bingham looked down at his plate and then up at the magician. 'Now why should you assume that, Mr Marvello?' he wondered.

Marvello shrugged. 'Well, normally you don't seem to stay very long, but this time you've been here for weeks.'

Bingham gave him a thin, humourless smile. 'I have indeed,' he agreed.

'So naturally, I assumed . . .'

'That I'd be moving on again in the near future?'

'Exactly.'

'I would be gone by now, but for the war.'

'You mean, the war's given you a reason to stay on in Marston longer?'

'Quite the contrary. I mean that the war has merely removed any reason for going elsewhere.'

Spudder frowned. 'I'm not sure I understand that.'

'I don't think he was meant to, was he, Mr Bingham?' Marvello said. He turned to Spudder. 'You see, what Mr Bingham is telling us – in the nicest possible way, of course – is to mind our own business.'

'We never meant to pry. Honestly we didn't,' Spudder assured Bingham.

'I'm sure you didn't,' Bingham said generously. 'And now could we perhaps talk about something else?'

Feeling they had no other choice, the others nodded.

Breakfast was over, and Jim had still not appeared. Captain Davenport rose from his chair. 'Better go an' see what's keepin' my mate this mornin',' he told the other lodgers.

He made his way up the narrow stairs which led to Jim Vernon's bedroom and knocked on the door.

'Who is it?' called a weak voice from the bedroom.

'It's me. Fred.'

'Come in, Captain. The door's not locked.'

Davenport pushed the door open. Jim was lying on top of his blankets, clutching his stomach.

'What the devil's the matter with you, lad?' the Captain asked, walking towards the bed.

'Got these terrible pains in me belly,' Jim gasped.

'D'you want me to call a doctor?'

'No, I . . . I don't think there's any need to go to that extreme. But I'm afraid I'm not goin' to be of much use to meself or anybody else today.'

The Captain nodded. 'You're right there.'

'If you think you can't manage without me, I'll do me best to try and get—'

'There's no need for that. It shouldn't be too difficult to borrow a mate from one of the other packets that isn't sailin' today.' Davenport walked to the door, then turned round again. 'Anythin' I can get you before I go?'

Jim shook his head weakly. 'Nothin'. All I need's a bit of peace an' quiet.'

'Well, you should get enough of that, especially as Aggie won't be in today,' the Captain said. He stepped on to the landing. 'I hope you feel better soon.'

'Me too,' Jim said, through clenched teeth.

As soon as the Captain had closed the door behind him, the look of agony disappeared from Jim's face, and he sat up. 'Sorry about that, Fred,' he whispered. He had never wanted to lie to the Captain, but he'd decided that he couldn't tell the truth, either. Until he had more to go on than just a vague suspicion, he didn't want to start slinging mud at anybody – especially a gentleman like Mr Bingham.

It was a quarter past ten when Mr Bingham left the boarding house and headed off down Ollershaw Lane. He walked at a brisk pace, as he usually did, never once glancing back over his shoulder.

From the doorway of number 49, Jim watched his quarry make his way down the street. Following him without being noticed wasn't going to be easy, but it had to be done.

Bingham passed Cross Street, and reached the mineral railway line which ran from the mines beyond Marston to the station at Northwich. Another minute and he'd be level with the Post Office, then round the bend in the road, and out of sight. Jim set off in pursuit.

There were a few hundred yards between them when the chase began, and caution made Jim maintain that distance. It had its risks – keeping that far behind, he might easily lose the other man, but there were risks the other way, too, because if Bingham spotted him, it was a pound to a penny that anything he subsequently did would be totally innocent.

Jim reached the Post Office just in time to see Bingham turn left into Wincham. Now what the devil was there in Wincham to interest a man like him? Jim wondered. Or in Marston, if it came to that.

Bingham continued to stride ahead, passing the rows of terraced houses which lined Chapel Street, and the large United Methodist Chapel after which the street got its name. And then, just beyond the chapel, he stopped dead. Bingham reached into his pocket, took something out, and examined it. Jim kept on walking, though he had slowed down almost to a snail's pace, worried he would catch Bingham up.

Bingham turned, and walked through the door of the nearest terraced house, the front room of which was a shop. Jim bent down and began fiddling with his bootlace, as if it needed to be retied. He counted slowly to himself: one . . . two . . . three . . . four . . .

He had reached thirty when Mr Bingham emerged from the shop and continued his progress up Chapel Street. Jim let him get some distance ahead, then straightened up and began to follow him again. When he drew level with the shop, Jim entered it, just as Mr Bingham had done before him.

The woman behind the counter was about sixty. She wore her grey hair in a tight bun and had a squint in her left eye. 'What can I do for you?' she asked.

'That feller who just came in. What did he want?'

Suspicion appeared in both the squinting eye and the normal one. 'Why do you want to know?'

'He's . . . he's a mate of mine,' Jim said. 'We've got a bet on.'

'He doesn't look like the kind of feller who'd be a mate of yours,' the woman said dubiously. 'What kind of bet was it?'

'Did he buy cigarettes?'

'He might have done.'

Jim forced a grin to his face. 'I knew he couldn't do without his fags, whatever he said. What were they? Woodbines?'

The woman sniffed, as if to suggest that a gentleman like him would never stoop to smoking such a common cigarette. 'They were Richmond Gem,' she said. 'Imported from America.'

'Thanks,' Jim said. 'He won't half have to take some ribbin' back at our lodgin's tonight.'

He stepped out on to the street again. The problem of following someone who seemed suspicious, he thought, was that everything they did *looked* suspicious. He'd half-expected to meet a German master spy in the shop, and all he'd found was a slightly bad-tempered old dear who'd sold Bingham a packet of cigarettes.

He looked up Chapel Street again. Bingham had reached the crown of Wincham Bridge. Was he going to the Wincham Hotel? Was this entire expedition aimed at nothing more than a drink? But if a drink was what he was after, there were three pubs in Marston, all of them within stepping distance of the boarding house.

Bingham did not go into the hotel. Instead, he turned left and took the path down the canal. Jim increased his pace. Having come so far, he didn't want to lose Bingham now.

By the time Jim reached the top of the bridge, Bingham had travelled some way along the towpath. But he wasn't moving any more. He was standing perfectly still, and appeared to be looking across the canal at the Victoria works.

From that distance, he was little more than a matchstick man, but that situation could soon be altered. Jim pulled his field glasses out of his pocket, and focused them on the man he had a gut feeling was up to no good. He was not the only one with field glasses, he saw. Bingham had a pair of his own, and was training them on the works.

'So I was right!' Jim gasped, triumphantly.

Bingham put his field glasses away, and took a writing pad and a pencil from his pocket. It was difficult to tell what he was doing from such a distance, but it looked like he was sketching something.

Jim turned round and headed back towards Marston. He had seen enough. More than enough.

'You did what?' Captain Davenport exploded, staring across the bedroom at Jim in frank disbelief.

Jim shrugged his shoulders and looked anxiously at his bedroom door, afraid that, even with it closed, the sound of the Captain's voice would carry to the other boarders downstairs.

'I followed Mr Bingham this mornin',' he said, almost in a whisper. 'All the way up Chapel Street, along the canal and down to the Victoria works.'

'Well, there's a complete waste of time if I ever heard of one,' Davenport said.

'It wasn't a waste of time at all,' Jim told him. 'I saw Bingham take out a notebook – just like he did when we saw him down by the river – an' write somethin' in it.'

'I see,' Davenport said heavily.

'An' what does that mean, exactly?'

'It means that I suppose you think you've found yourself a spy, don't you?'

'Don't *you*?'

Davenport snorted with disgust. 'Of course I bloody don't.'

'Then what was he doin'?'

'*I* don't know, but there's bound to be a reasonable

explanation.' The Captain thought for a moment. 'Maybe he's some kind of artist.'

'Artists draw pictures of birds an' little kids, not wharfs an' factories.'

'That's all you know. There's all different kinds of artists. Maybe he's one of them – what-d'-you-call-'em – architects. Yes, maybe that's what he is.'

'There's other things,' Jim said stubbornly. 'He doesn't seem to have a real job, but he's always got plenty of money. He never says much about himself. An' he doesn't drink tea!'

'You can't hang a man for not likin' tea,' the Captain said. 'Look, doesn't he talk English as good as you an' me?'

'Better. But if he *was* a spy, he'd have to speak good English, wouldn't he? I mean, like you said last night, if he talked with a foreign accent, he'd been no good for the job.'

The Captain shook his head. 'Shall I tell you what's the matter with you?' he asked. 'You think you're missin' out on all the adventure of bein' in the war, so you're tryin' to invent excitement where none exists.'

'It's not like that,' Jim protested.

'An' I'll tell you somethin' else for nothin'. I don't know much about Mr Bingham, but I do know he's a gent.'

'Are you sayin' gents can't be spies?'

'No, that's not what I'm sayin', though I'm sure he isn't. What I mean is that gents have influence.'

'I'm not followin' you,' Jim said.

'Then listen closely, an' you will. If you go makin' trouble for him, he'll start makin' trouble for you. An' he could do you more harm than you could ever do him.'

'If he is a spy, then I'd be failin' in my duty if I didn't report him.'

'When you've had a bit more experience of life, you'll see the way the world really works,' the Captain said. 'The poor stick together, don't they?'

'By an' large.'

'Well, so do the rich – that's how they manage to *stay* rich. Mr Bingham's only got to drop a few quiet words to one of the bosses at the Salt Union, an' you'll find yourself without a job. Then what will you do?'

'I could always join the army.'

'If they'll have you – which I doubt.'

'They keep sayin' in their recruitment drives that they want all the young men they can get.'

'Young men with clean records. But you won't have that, will you? You'll have been dismissed from your job, and there'll be a black mark against your name.'

'So you're sayin' that I should just forget the whole thing?' Jim asked.

The Captain sighed. 'Yes. That's exactly what I'm tellin' you.'

Supper at the boarding house was over. The Great Marvello and Mr Bingham had gone up to their rooms, Ivy had left for Aggie's house, and Spudder was still working in the chip shop. The only two people left in the kitchen of number 49 were Jim Vernon and Captain Davenport.

'D'you fancy a pint?' the Captain asked.

Jim shook his head. 'Not tonight.'

'So you're turnin' in early for once, are you?'

Jim shook his head. 'I'm not tired. I think I'll go for a short walk.'

'You want to watch the night air at this time of year,' the Captain advised him. 'It can be treacherous, an' once you've got it on your chest, nothin' will get it off.' He paused. 'You're not still thinkin' about tryin' to dig up anythin' more on Mr Bingham, are you?'

'No, I'm not,' Jim said. 'You were quite right. It's best to let matters rest.'

Davenport clapped him on the shoulder. 'Now you're talkin' like a sensible young man,' he said. 'An' about time, too, in my opinion.' He stood up. 'Well, since I can't talk you into havin' a drink, I think I'll have an early night meself.'

Jim waited until Davenport had reached the top of the stairs, then opened the back door and stepped into the yard. It was a warm, pleasant evening. The Captain had been wrong about the night air, he thought – just as he'd been wrong about Bingham!

He made his way down the lane, which was unnaturally dark

due to the black-out restrictions, and stopped in front of Becky Worrell's house. He remembered the Captain's warnings about what harm gentlemen could do to ordinary working men, and hesitated for a second before walking down the alley to Becky's back door. Through a chink in the black-out curtains, Jim could just see a light burning in the kitchen. He took a deep breath, and knocked loudly on the door.

From inside a voice called out, 'Who is it?'

'Jim Vernon.'

'Come on in, Mr Vernon.'

Jim lifted the latch and swung the door open. Becky Worrell was sitting at the kitchen table, holding the *Northwich Guardian* near to the oil lamp.

'This is a surprise,' she said. 'An' what can I do for you, Mr Vernon?'

Jim coughed awkwardly. 'I was hopin' . . . I was hopin' you'd answer some questions for me.'

Becky smiled, a little sadly, he thought. 'This isn't about our Michelle, by any chance, is it?' she asked.

Jim felt himself start to blush. 'No, it's not, er . . . not about Miss Worrell. It's about Mr Bingham.'

The smile changed to a puzzled look. 'Well, sit yourself down,' Becky said. 'Would you like a cuppa?'

'No thanks,' Jim said, sitting down opposite her and starting to wonder if this had been such a good idea after all.

'Are you sure?'

'Well, if you're havin' one yourself.'

'I never did know a man who'd turn down a cup of tea when it was offered,' Becky said, putting the kettle on.

'Not an Englishman, anyway,' Jim said, under his breath.

The kettle boiled, and Becky made the tea. 'So what did you want to know?' she asked, as she poured Jim a cup.

'Mr Bingham – when did he first move into the boardin' house?'

'Oh, it was years an' years ago,' Becky said. 'Me mam was still alive then.'

'An' when he arrived, did he say anythin' about where he'd come from?'

Becky smiled again. 'No, he didn't. He's always been a bit tight lipped, has Mr Bingham. But why do you ask?'

'I was just curious,' Jim lied.

Becky's eyes narrowed, and a stern expression came to her face. 'Are you tellin' me that you took the trouble of comin' down here at this time of night out of idle curiosity?'

'Yes.'

Becky's frown deepened. 'I think you'd better come clean with me, Jim Vernon,' she said firmly.

Jim told Becky what he'd seen Bingham doing down by the river, and how he'd followed him to the Victoria works that very morning.

'Captain Davenport thinks I'm just after a bit of excitement in me life,' he said when he'd finished. 'An' he told me that if I did go any further with it, I might land up in hot water.'

'Well, he was probably right about that part, at least,' Becky admitted.

'An' what about the other part?'

'You mean Mr Bingham bein' a spy? To be honest, I don't know. But I *do* know it wants lookin' into some more.'

'The problem is, I've got me own work to do,' Jim said gloomily. 'I can't pull that sickness stunt again – the Captain'd never wear it twice, especially now I've told him I wasn't really sick at all. Which means there'll be days at a time when Bingham could be up to anythin', an' I'd never know about it.'

'Yes, that is a problem,' Becky said. 'What you really need is help. Now if I was to use one or two of my people from the bakery . . .'

Jim put his hands up in horror. 'Oh no, Mrs Worrell! I could never get you involved in it.'

'Why do you think Mr Bingham's makin' all these sketches?' Becky asked.

'I don't know,' Jim said. 'Maybe it's so that somebody can plant bombs.'

'Or perhaps because the Victoria works will be a target for zeppelins?'

'Could be that 'an all.'

'Which would put anybody workin' there in danger?'

'Well, yes, of course it would.'

'As soon as they start making nitrate, my daughter Michelle's goin' to take a job there,' Becky told him. 'So, you see, I am involved already.'

Chapter Thirteen

It was on Friday morning that Billy's second letter arrived. As Becky bent down to pick it up, she felt her pulse starting to race. 'Don't be an idiot,' she told herself. 'As long as he's still writin' to you, everythin's all right. It's when the letters stop that you need to worry.' She walked back to the kitchen, sat down at the table, and slit open the envelope.

Dear Mam,
Thanks for the condensed milk and the cigarettes that you sent me. They have made me the most popular feller in my trench.

And I'll tell you somebody else who's popular – Cousin Gerald! I can just imagine the look on your face when you read that, Mam. Yes, I know it's hard to believe, but it's true. And the most incredible thing of all is that he really deserves all the admiration he is getting.

Believe it or not, Gerald has turned out to be a very good officer. And a brave one, as well. When we go into battle ('going over the top' is what we call it) it is always the officers who lead us. They are a pretty fearless bunch on the whole, but even among them, Gerald is exceptional. His men (and I am one of them!) would follow him to hell and back if we had to. He seems to have quite forgotten our fight at the saltworks, and sometimes, when there's nobody else around, we have a quiet smoke together and talk about life back in Marston.

I think he really does love our Michelle, Mam. You should see the look in his eyes when he's talking about her. And I'm sure that an officer and a gentleman like he is would never do anything to take advantage of her.

I can hear our sergeant bawling for us to muster, so I will close now. I'm taking good care of myself and looking forward to seeing you when this horrible war is over.

Your loving son,

Billy

Becky read the letter three times, then took down her box and put it inside. 'So now you think that you had Gerald all wrong, do you, Billy?' she asked her son, talking to him as if he were actually in the room with her instead of hundreds of miles away, trying to kill people he'd never even met.

Yet she should not have been surprised. It was only natural that he should be taken in – the Worrells had a charm and a cunning that went well beyond his experience.

She closed her eyes and thought back to that summer Sunday so long ago. In her mind's eye, she could see it as if it were only yesterday . . .

There were butterflies in Becky's stomach as she approached the oak tree where she always met Richard. She saw the heart the moment she reached the tree. It hadn't been there the previous Sunday. It had been carved into the bark at her eye level. There was an arrow through it, and it contained two sets of initials – RW and BT.

'Richard Worrell and Becky Taylor,' she said softly to herself.

The sound of a whinnying horse made her turn her head, and she saw Richard in the distance, riding Caesar and leading Midnight behind him. The closer he came, the faster she felt her heart beat. He was Sir Galahad, Robin Hood, William Tell – all the heroes she had read about in her childhood storybooks rolled into one.

They didn't go riding as they usually did. Instead, Richard produced a Fortnum & Mason hamper and announced that they would have a picnic. They laid the tablecloth on the grass and unpacked the feast. There were cheeses which smelled unlike any Becky had ever known before, glazed hams and turkey legs, and a kind of meat paste Richard said was called pâté. And to wash it all down, there was champagne, a drink Becky had only heard about from music-hall songs.

It was wonderful food, finer than any Becky had ever tasted before. Yet it was not so much the food itself which gave her the warm, contented feeling in the pit of her stomach as the fact that they had eaten it together. *She felt like a newlywed who was not just sharing a meal with her husband, but who also knew that everything in life – the troubles as well as happiness – would be shared between them from now on.*

When the picnic was finally over, Becky lay back in the grass and closed her eyes. Tiny insects buzzed busily close to her ear and the sun cast its gentle warmth on her face. She heard Richard stand up, but she did not move, not even when he walked towards her – not even when he knelt down beside her.

'What would you do if I kissed you now, little Becky?' he asked softly. 'Would you run and hide? Or would you give yourself to me as I'd like to give myself to you?' He was not talking about just kissing, and they both knew it.

'Did you mean what you said last Sunday?' Becky asked. 'About wanting me to be with you always.'

'Of course I meant it.'

Becky opened her eyes and looked deep into his. 'If you were to kiss me now,' she said slowly and carefully, 'I wouldn't run and hide. If you kissed me, I'd give myself to you as you'd like to give yourself to me.'

He kissed her passionately and lingeringly, and she did not resist him. She made no effort to fight him off when his hand found her breast, nor when it burrowed under her skirt. And as he was mounting her, she made no move save for the slightest quiver of anticipation. Even when he entered her, only the softest of moans indicated how much it had hurt . . .

Becky opened her eyes again, and was back in her own little kitchen, back in the house she had shared with Michael – the house Billy wanted her to sell, but which she knew she never would.

'Damn you and your son, Richard Worrell!' she said aloud. 'Damn you both to hell!' The curse of the Worrells had hung over her like a black shadow for so many years. And it was *still* hanging over her.

It crossed her mind for the briefest of instants that Gerald might be a different man from his father, but she knew it wasn't possible. If his mother, Hortense, had lived, Gerald *might* have been different. But she hadn't. There had been no force for good in Gerald's life. He had been brought up by a monster, and so could be nothing less than a monster himself.

There was an urgent knocking on the door, and when Becky opened it, she found Jim Vernon standing there.

'He's gone!' the young flatman said.

For a second, Becky's mind was so wrapped up with thoughts of the Worrell family that she didn't know what he was talking about. Then she said, 'You mean Mr Bingham? When did this happen?'

'A few minutes ago, just after breakfast. A taxi cab pulled up outside the boardin' house. We didn't know who it was for at first, then Mr Bingham came downstairs with his bag in his hand an' said *he'd* ordered it.'

'Did he tell you why he was leavin'?'

'Told us he'd been suddenly called away on urgent business. He told Aggie that she should keep his sheets aired, but he didn't say when he was comin' back.'

'An' I don't suppose he left a forwardin' address?'

'Of course he didn't. He never does.'

Becky sighed with what may have been relief. 'Well, that's it, then,' she said. 'Until he *does* come back, there's nothin' more we can do.' Which meant – thank heavens – that there was at least *one* problem which could be put on the back burner for a while.

Spudder had spent the whole week hoping – *praying* – for rain on Sunday, but when Sunday came, though it was now early October, the weather was as mild and soft as if it were still midsummer. And so, forced to recognise that even nature was against him, Spudder saw no alternative but to keep his promise and take Ivy Clegg out on the river.

They had arranged to meet by the Town Bridge, but when Spudder arrived there was no sign of Ivy. He didn't like having nothing to do, especially when he was nervous, and for the first five minutes he stood there fretting and fidgeting.

'I should have brought a brush an' pot of paint with me,' he told himself, looking at the chipping paint on the bridge. 'I could have touched that up lovely while I was waitin'.' Maybe he could have even talked Ivy into letting him make a proper job of it, instead of wasting his time in a boat, he thought. But he hadn't brought any paint with him, so that was that.

Another few minutes passed, and Spudder's nervousness turned to hope, born of the possibility that maybe she wasn't coming at all! But no sooner had that hope begun to grow than it shrivelled and died. Ivy appeared, walking towards him as if she had all the time in the world.

'You're late,' Spudder said grumpily, when she finally drew level with him.

'Lady's privilege,' Ivy said gaily.

Spudder wondered what that meant, but decided it might be safer not to ask.

Ivy had obviously dressed up for the occasion. She was wearing a black skirt which had a hem dangerously above the ankle, a white imitation-silk blouse, and her wide-brimmed hat was decorated with artificial flowers. Spudder didn't think he'd seen any part of this particular outfit before.

'Do you like me new get-up?' Ivy asked, reading his mind. 'Me an' Aggie bought it down at the market, yesterday afternoon.'

Spudder looked down at his boots, and mumbled something.

'Speak up!' Ivy said.

Spudder lifted his head again. 'I said, I think it's very nice,' he told her. And though he didn't want to, he couldn't help noticing that her bosom – no bigger than a sparrow's when he'd first met her – had started to fill out as a result of Aggie's cooking.

Ivy grinned. 'So where's me flowers, then?'

'Flowers?' Spudder repeated.

'Of course. When a young gentleman takes a young lady out on the river, he always brings her flowers.'

'I didn't know that,' Spudder said, gazing up at the sky and pleading for a change in the weather. 'I'm sorry.'

'It doesn't matter,' Ivy replied. 'I was only jokin', anyway. I didn't *really* expect you to bring me anythin'. Shall we go an' hire that boat, now?'

'Might as well,' Spudder said gloomily.

The man who rented out the boats had a jolly red face and a white beard. A nautical cap was perched on his head, and he wore a blue and white striped jersey which clung to his ample belly. When he saw Spudder and Ivy approaching, a twinkle appeared in his eye and a smile began to play on his lips. 'Want to hire a boat, sir?' he asked.

'Suppose so,' Spudder replied.

'The river's a bit crowded round here,' the man said, 'but it shouldn't take a strong feller like you long to row beyond Winnington Bridge, an' then you'll have the water pretty much to yourselves.' He winked at Spudder. 'Can't beat a rowin' boat for a bit of privacy, can you?'

'Can't you?' Spudder asked, pulling some coppers out of his pocket and handing them over.

The man gave Ivy a quizzical look, which asked if she really knew what she was doing.

'Don't worry about Spudder,' she told him. 'He's sometimes a bit slow to catch on, but he usually gets there in the end.'

It took Spudder a couple of minutes to master the technique of rowing, but then he was well away. Pulling on the oars with his powerful arms, he was soon overtaking every other rowing boat on the river. Some of the other young men out with their girls took this as a challenge and tried to catch up with him, but Spudder continued to pull furiously on the oars, as if by doing so he could escape from Ivy. Instead, he was merely taking them both further away from the watchful eyes of the rest of the boaters.

Ivy leant against the prow of the boat and opened up the parasol she'd bought the day before. 'Here we are, out on the river, like real toffs,' she said. 'Isn't it grand, Spudder?'

Spudder didn't reply, because he was thinking – and that never came easy. He wished he knew what he was supposed to do next. He wished he'd been to see Mrs Becky and asked her advice. But now it was too late. Now there were just the two of them, in a boat, leaving Northwich Town Bridge far behind.

The sun continued to shine down benevolently on them, and they could see the leaves of the trees, turning a golden brown now, reflected in the water. And still Spudder rowed as if he was going all the way to America, and had to be there by nightfall.

As they passed under Winnington Bridge and, just as the boatman had promised, they had the river to themselves.

'Stop for a bit, Spudder,' Ivy said. 'I want to take a look at the scenery.'

Spudder did stop, though he felt even more uncomfortable now that he had nothing to do.

'Did you mean what you said about never havin' had a girl of your own?' Ivy asked.

'Uh . . . yes,' Spudder mumbled, his hands twitching at the oars, desperate to be rowing again.

'Why not? I mean, you might be a bit slow sometimes,' Ivy continued relentlessly, 'but you're not a bad-lookin' feller, an' you're *very* kind hearted.'

'I'm too busy with me chip shop to think about things like girls,' Spudder said, looking down at the oars again. 'An' speakin' of the chip shop, I think we'd better be gettin' back, 'cos there'll be customers waitin'.'

'You know you don't open till six o'clock on a Sunday,' Ivy reminded him.

'Oh yes, I'd forgotten that,' Spudder lied.

'We're a right pair, the two of us,' Ivy said. 'What with you never havin' had a girl, an' me never havin' had a lad . . .'

'Maybe we're both a lot better off that way,' Spudder suggested hopefully.

'I don't think we are,' Ivy said. She shifted her weight slightly, as if she were about to move. 'What would you do if I kissed you, Spudder?'

'Kissed me!' Spudder repeated, suddenly going pale. 'I . . . I don't know.'

'Want to try it, so we can find out?'

Spudder looked up and down the river for another rowing boat, or a steam packet – anything which would rescue him from this terrible situation.

'Well?' Ivy asked.

'I . . . I don't think we should start kissin'. It might be dangerous in a boat.'

Ivy laughed. 'It isn't dangerous at all. Not as long as you don't make no sudden moves. An' *you* won't make no sudden moves, will you, Spudder?'

Spudder's mouth flapped open as if he were a fish which

had just been landed and was gasping for air. 'Ivy,' he said. 'It isn't . . . we couldn't . . . this boat's only rented . . .'

'And what difference does that make?' asked Ivy, who was on all fours and slowly crawling along the boat towards him.

'You'll get your skirt dirty.'

'I can always wash it later.'

As Ivy moved forward, Spudder moved back, until he could feel the wooden prow pressing hard against his spine. And suddenly Ivy was on him, her hands gripping his shoulders, her lips searching for his mouth.

It was a nightmare, Spudder thought – like the time Mr Marvello had tried to saw him in half. And now, he did exactly the same as he'd done then – twisted and turned in a desperate effort to avoid the awful fate which awaited him. History was about to repeat itself in more than one way. On the music-hall stage, Spudder had succeeded in rolling the magician's cabinet off its trestles and on to the floor. Now, all his squirming and struggling caused the boat to tilt first this way, then that, and finally to capsize.

As he sank, Spudder felt the cold, cold river engulfing him. He opened his mouth to call out for Ivy, then quickly closed it again, as it started to fill with water. He had to find her, he told himself. Using his strong arms to propel himself upwards again, he broke the surface of the water. He could see the boat. It was upside-down, and was floating slowly away, like some huge wooden turtle. But where was Ivy?

'Spudder!' a frightened voice called out. 'Spudder, please help me! I can't swim!'

He twisted round and saw her, waving her arms desperately and kicking up hundreds of bubbles. It only took him a couple of seconds to reach her. 'Don't be frightened,' he said, as he put his hands under her armpits.

'I'm not,' Ivy replied. 'Everythin'll be all right now that you're here.'

Spudder towed the girl towards the riverbank and pulled her ashore. Once on dry land, he stood up, but Ivy just lay there, gasping for breath.

'Can you walk?' he asked.

Ivy looked up at him. 'I . . . don't think so,' she said. 'Not for a few minutes, anyway.'

He couldn't really leave her lying in the mud like that. Spudder bent down, scooped her into his arms and set off up the gently sloping bank towards the grassy knoll at the top.

It was only when he had nearly completed his journey that he realised he had a *girl* in his arms, her body pressed against his. What was even more disturbing was that the water had made Ivy's clothes cling to her so tightly that they were almost a second skin, and that wasn't proper. It took all his self-control not to drop her then and there.

But he didn't drop her. By some miracle, he made it to the top of the bank, where, with a huge sigh of relief, he lowered her on to a patch of grass. Ivy lay there, looking at him. There was a strange expression in her eyes, but he didn't think it was anger. Still, he had better make his apologies.

'I'm sorry that I turned the rowin' boat over, Ivy,' he said. 'Honestly, I am.'

Ivy laughed. 'It was as much my fault as it was yours. Anyway, I don't really mind.'

'Don't you?'

''Course not. It was the most thrillin' thing that's ever happened to me. An' you were *ever* so brave, Spudder.'

'I . . . it wasn't nothin',' Spudder said. 'I think I'd better go an' fetch the boat.'

Spudder took off his sodden boots and walked squelchingly back down the bank.

Ivy watched him as he entered the water again, and followed his progress as he swam towards the capsized boat with powerful, confident strokes. There had been a river running through the grounds of the big house she'd worked at, she remembered. She and the other maids had gone there on their days off. What fun they'd had – what innocent pleasure.

She couldn't do many things well, she thought, but at least while she'd been working at the big house she'd taken the opportunity to learn to swim like a fish.

Chapter Fourteen

The leaves of the beech trees were turning a coppery brown, and the woodland floor was carpeted with acorns from the mighty oaks. Bats had stopped flying at night, the goldfinches were leaving for the south, and starlings had started to arrive from the north. Though the air was still pleasantly warm once the sun had risen, there were sometimes early morning frosts, a grim reminder to every living creature that there could be no glorious summers without the chilling winters which followed them.

Richard Worrell, his mind far from thoughts of nature and her cycles, nervously paced the railway platform in Northwich Station. His hand hovered over the pocket watch which he had consulted five times in as many minutes. 'Why is it that the important trains are nearly always late?' he asked himself unhappily.

Not that this train was actually late yet, but he was certain it was going to be. Though he knew it was pointless, he opened his watch and checked the time again. One minute! The train had one minute left to arrive, and if it did not do so, it would definitely be late.

He heard the steam whistle blow and saw a cloud of smoke in the distance. His heart leapt! The train would be on time, and in no more than a few frantic heartbeats, he would be seeing his beloved son Gerald again!

The locomotive screeched to a halt, and Richard anxiously scanned the first-class carriages – anxiously because, although the telegram had clearly stated that this was the train his son would be arriving on, it was just possible that the boy had somehow missed it, or been recalled to France, or . . . Or any of the million other things which would mean that the moment

Richard had been looking forward to for so long would be denied him.

One of the carriage doors at the far end of the first-class section swung open, and there was Gerald, stepping down on to the platform. He was wearing his battledress: peaked cap, well-tailored khaki jacket and trousers, and puttees which ran from the top of his boots almost to his knees. How drawn and tired he looks, Richard thought anxiously. And yet how much more of a man he appears than when he went away, he added with pride.

Gerald saw his father and waved. The two men approached each other, weaving in and out of the other passengers – not exactly running, but not far from it. The gulf between them seemed vast, and the time taken to cross it endless. Then they met and flung their arms around each other. Richard could not remember a moment when he had been happier.

'It's good to have you back,' the father said as they walked towards the ticket barrier. 'But how in God's name did you manage to get leave so soon?'

'It isn't leave,' Gerald replied. 'Not *real* leave, anyway. I've come home to recruit more men for the Front.'

They passed through the barrier and out on to the forecourt. Gerald saw that his Napier was parked there, and gave his father a quizzical look.

'I thought you'd like to be behind the wheel of your own vehicle again,' Richard said, feeling suddenly awkward.

Gerald looked touched. 'That was kind of you, Father,' he said. 'And you were quite right. After a couple of months of madness, it will be wonderful to get back to doing something normal.'

They climbed into their seats, and Gerald sighed with contentment as he smelled the expensive leather and looked down at the gleaming brass dashboard.

'A couple of months of madness, you said. Is France really as bad as that?' Richard asked.

Gerald slipped his Napier smoothly into gear and pulled away from the station. 'It's worse than you could ever imagine,' he said. 'There was some real fighting when I first went out there, but now we're reduced to trench warfare.'

'And that isn't good? I should have thought that you'd have been safer in a trench.'

Gerald laughed hollowly. 'Imagine it, Father. A line of trenches stretching almost all the way from Switzerland to the sea – and by Christmas they *will* go all the way. We sit in our trenches, behind acres of barbed wire, and the Germans sit in theirs. Both sides have machine-guns, so it would be madness to ever think of attacking each other. But we do!'

'Why?'

'Because we're supposed to be at war, and we can't just sit there, can we? So, for the sake of gaining a few yards, we send thousands of brave men out to their deaths.'

'This is a big country. We have men enough to spare,' Richard said indifferently.

'I break my heart every time one British soldier dies unnecessarily,' Gerald said.

It didn't sound like Gerald talking. Richard gave his son a hard, assessing look. Was the boy making a very wry joke? If he was, it certainly didn't show on his face. And then Richard understood – or thought he did.

'I see what you mean now,' he told Gerald. 'When you say it broke your heart, it's *officers* you're talking about, men of your own class – not ordinary soldiers. Well, I suppose that's understandable. You probably went to school with some of them.'

'I was talking about the enlisted men. Brave chaps who only a few months ago were toiling away in factories and sweatshops, and are now willing to lay down their lives for their country.'

'But they're the sort of people you used to call working-class scum!' Richard said in amazement.

Gerald laughed again. 'Yes, I did, didn't I? And after the war, I will probably call them that again. But for the moment they are comrades-in-arms, *my* men, and their welfare is as important to me as my own. *More* important.'

'The war's changed you,' Richard said, as they drove through the gates of Peak House, where Gerald had been born and brought up.

Gerald grinned. 'In some ways, Father,' he admitted, 'but not in others.'

'In what ways are you unchanged?'

'Cousin Billy is serving under me. The boy's a good soldier, but he's also an idiot. So easy to charm, so easy to fool.'

'You talk to him, then?'

'Of course. Billy's part of my plan, and he's been doing valuable groundwork for me.'

'What plan? What groundwork?'

'He's been writing touching little letters to his family, telling them what a wonderful man I really am – and how much I love his sister Michelle.'

'You mean . . .?'

'That our wager is still on? Of course! Get the money together, Father. By the time I return to France, I expect to be five thousand pounds richer.'

Michelle sat at her dressing table, looking into the mirror and running a brush through her golden hair. Her mother, meanwhile, hovered anxiously in the doorway.

'So are you goin' to tell me how your first day at the Victoria works went?' Becky asked.

'I found the work hard,' Michelle confessed. 'A lot harder than adding up columns of figures. But then it's of a great deal more use to the war effort, too.'

'Yes, it is. An' as for it bein' hard, I expect you'll get used to it in time.'

'Oh, I'm sure I will.'

They were fencing with each other, neither of them saying what was on her mind – and they both knew it.

'So you're goin' out with Gerald Worrell tonight, are you?' Becky said.

Michelle put down her brush for a second, and looked up at her mother. 'You know I am.'

'An' where is he takin' you?' Becky asked, trying her best not to sound like an inquisitor, but knowing that she was making a very bad job of it.

'He's taking me out to supper. Dinner, he calls it,' Michelle replied, tilting her head to the left and examining her nose from a different angle. 'He's booked a private dining room at a quiet little inn out in the country.'

'Private dinin' room,' Becky repeated. 'I don't like the sound of that at all.'

Michelle transferred the brush to her other hand. 'You have to trust me, Mam,' she said.

'Oh, I trust *you* all right, love. It's that Gerald I've got me doubts about.'

Michelle looked appealingly into her mother's eyes. 'He loves me, Mam. He really, truly does. And when the war's over, we're going to get married.'

'If he survives. I read in the papers that there's been a lot of young officers killed in action already.'

'If I can't marry him, then I'll never marry anyone,' Michelle said firmly.

'I thought the same about his dad,' Becky reminded her. 'An' then I fell in love with your father, an' I realised that what I'd felt for Richard was nothin' in comparison.'

Michelle slammed her brush down hard on the dressing table. 'You always know best, don't you?' she shouted. 'Well, you don't know best this time. I'm not reliving your life, Mam. I'm finally having one of my own!'

Becky bowed her head. 'You're right,' she said, 'so I won't try to stop you. All I do ask is that you're careful. Your dad gave me my second chance – you might not be so lucky.'

There was the sound of a horn being hooted outside in the street. The noise seemed to calm Michelle down. 'That'll be Gerald now,' she said. She hesitated before speaking again. 'You . . . you wouldn't like him to come inside and meet you, would you, Mam? It'd make me very happy.'

Becky shook her head.

Michelle's anger erupted again. 'All right, have it your own way! But when we're married, and Gerald won't have anything to do with you because of the way you're treating him now, don't go blaming me.' She grabbed her hat and jammed it down on her head, destroying most of the careful work she'd done on her hair. Then she stood up and pushed past her mother.

'Michelle . . .' Becky called, as her daughter stamped down the stairs. 'I don't want . . . if I *could* bring meself to ask him in . . .'

At the foot of the stairs, Michelle stopped and turned around.

'Don't wait up for me,' she told her mother, 'because I may not come home at all. Ever!'

Motorcars driving through the village were still enough of a novelty to attract attention, and this one had certainly attracted Not-Stopping Bracegirdle's.

Imagine Gerald Worrell driving up to Becky Taylor's front door, as bold as brass, she thought as she peered from behind her parlour curtain. And imagine Michelle being brave enough to allow him to. There was obviously a lot more to the girl than there seemed to be at first sight.

She heard the sound of footsteps, then saw the girl walking towards Gerald's automobile. She could not see Michelle's face under the hat, but from the way she was moving it was easy to tell that she was very agitated.

When Michelle reached the automobile, Gerald got out and opened the passenger door for her, which, to give him his due, was a gentlemanly thing to do. So they were going straight out, without Gerald seeing Becky. Well, Not-Stopping had never thought it would be otherwise.

The gossip queen glanced up at her clock. Half past seven. Where could they be going at that time of night? Not for a drive – it was already too late in the year for that.

Not-Stopping found herself wondering exactly what posh people did when they were courting. 'You've led a very sheltered life, you have, Elsie Bracegirdle,' she told herself. But sheltered or not, she would get to the bottom of this particular mystery if it was the last thing she did.

The inn, which was on a country road just outside Macclesfield, was called the Jolly Miller. It had a moss-covered slate roof – and mullioned windows with leaded glass. The gas mantles in the private dining room had not been turned on, and the only illumination came from half a dozen flickering, very romantic candles.

Michelle looked across the table at Gerald. Had it only been two months since she'd last seen him? It seemed like years. He was thinner than she remembered him, and the strain marks around his eyes were new, but she still thought he was the handsomest, most wonderful man she had ever seen.

'Are you very brave?' she asked.

Gerald considered it. 'Yes,' he said finally. 'But only because any man can be brave when he has to be.'

'And you do have to be?'

'Indeed. That's what being an officer means.'

'Is Billy brave?'

'Billy is *too* brave,' Gerald said. 'Almost foolhardy. Yet for all that, I'm proud to call him one of my men.'

A waiter entered, and they were self-consciously quiet while he cleared away the plates. When he had left, Gerald said, 'You know I love you, don't you?'

'Yes,' Michelle said. 'I believe you really do.'

'That's why it's so hard to go back. I don't want to leave you. I don't want to die a . . .'

Michelle reached across the table and took his hand in hers. 'Don't talk about dying,' she pleaded.

'Out there, it is difficult to think of anything else,' Gerald said. 'But if I live to see the end of the war, we'll be married. And then I'll be glad that we waited.'

'Waited?'

'But what if I don't live?' Gerald asked, a look of anguish coming to his face. 'What if I *am* killed in action? Then I will have died without ever knowing . . .'

'Go on,' Michelle said, gently stroking his hand.

'It's so difficult to say,' Gerald explained. 'I don't want to shock you.'

'You won't shock me, my darling. Nothing you could ever say would shock me.'

Gerald took a deep breath. 'I have seen so many young men go out to their deaths in no-man's land without ever having known what it was like to be in a woman's arms,' he said in a rush. 'I don't want to die a . . . a virgin, Michelle.'

She should have been expecting it, but she wasn't. Her heart started to beat faster, and the hand which had been stroking Gerald's began to tremble. 'You . . . you want me to let you make love to me,' she said.

Gerald covered his face with his hands. 'Oh, what a cad I am,' he said, his voice filled with remorse. 'Why couldn't I have spared you this? Why couldn't I just have done what other men – better men than me – have done?'

'I don't understand.'

'There are ladies – professional women – who I could have gone to. Women who think no more of doing that for a man than they would of washing and mending his shirts. Yes, that's what I could have done, but I knew, deep inside myself, that it wouldn't be the same if it wasn't you.'

Michelle's mind was in turmoil. She knew if she did what he asked, she would be a marked woman for ever. And that if Gerald was killed, or ceased to love her, she was doomed.

Your dad gave me my second chance – you might not be so lucky, her mother had said to her, only hours earlier. But I don't want a second chance, she told herself. I love Gerald, and if I can't have him, I don't want anybody.

She reached up and gently eased Gerald's hands away from his face. He looked as if he were about to cry.

'Forgive me, my sweet,' he croaked. 'Forgive me for my one moment of weakness.'

Michelle shook her head. 'You were quite right to say what you did to me just now,' she told him, doing her best to control the tremble in her voice. 'We must have no secrets from each other, you and I.'

A look of hope came into Gerald's eyes. 'And you don't think me evil for even having such thoughts?'

'Of course not. Because I've had them, too.'

'Then . . .?'

'Then we'll do what you want . . . what we *both* want, if I'm to be honest. But where can we go, my darling?'

Gerald's whole body relaxed. 'I'm told that the landlords of inns such as this are usually quite willing to rent out their upstairs rooms,' he said.

'They are?'

'Certainly. Dinner guests often feel the need to rest for a while, before resuming their journey. If I were to ask him now, he wouldn't even raise an eyebrow.'

'Then do it, Gerald,' Michelle said. 'Do it now, before my courage fails me.'

Gerald had assured her that the landlord would not be shocked, but as she walked up the stone stairs to the first floor, it felt to

Michelle as if every eye in the inn was watching her disapprovingly, and her skin glowed with shame.

Yet what had they to be ashamed of? she demanded angrily of herself. If war hadn't broken out, she and Gerald would already be married. They *were* married, at least by their own lights, and that was all that mattered.

At the top of the stairs Gerald opened the door, then stood aside to let her enter. There were candles in this room, too, and a fire blazing away in the hearth. Since they had only asked for the room a few minutes earlier, Michelle wondered how the inn's staff had managed to get such a strong fire burning already. It was probably a trick of the trade, she decided.

She looked across at the big four-poster bed – the bed she would soon be sharing with Gerald. It was not too late to back out, she thought, then Gerald closed the door behind them, and she knew that it was.

She looked uncertainly at the man she loved. 'What do we . . .?' she asked.

'Just leave everything to me, my darling,' he said, walking towards her.

'Would it be all right if I closed my eyes?'

'Of course, if you feel happier like that.'

Michelle closed her eyes, and then Gerald's lips were on hers. They kissed, long and lingering. After what seemed like hours, Gerald broke away from her, and Michelle could feel him unfastening the buttons and straps which held her dress. She shuddered as his hands ran over her breasts. She flinched, then forced herself not to, as his fingers probed between her legs. It crossed her mind that Gerald seemed very knowledgeable for a man who had had no experience with women, and then she brushed the thought away as unworthy.

There was a rustling of silk as Gerald removed her underclothes. Now, completely naked, she finally opened her eyes again. Gerald had stepped back, and was looking at her. 'Do I please you?' she asked timidly.

'You're beautiful,' Gerald gasped. 'You're the most beautiful woman I've . . . I mean, you're more beautiful than I'd ever imagined you would be.'

She felt naked under his burning gaze, she thought. Then she laughed inwardly, because she *was* naked. And the laugh made her feel slightly uncomfortable, because this was neither the time nor the place for joking.

She shut both eyes tightly again, and felt Gerald lift her effortlessly off her feet and carry her over to the bed. She was surprised that the sheet on which he laid her was so smooth, then realised that it must be satin. Still in her world of self-imposed darkness, she heard Gerald's footsteps as he walked away, and then the sound of swishing material as he started to undress.

She opened her eyes for a second. Gerald was in the corner. He had removed his jacket and shirt, and was standing in only his sporty striped trousers. His skin shone in the firelight, and his firm, hard muscles made her shiver in anticipation of what was to come. He reached for the buttons at the top of his trousers, and she closed her eyes again.

He padded across the room then lay down beside her. His thigh was pressed against hers, and his hands were everywhere. She remembered how she had felt that night in his car. It had been wonderful – but it had been nothing like this. And suddenly, though she had not willed them to, her hands were exploring too, running down his broad back, grasping his solid shoulders.

He shifted positions, and his head was between her legs, his tongue exploring where she had never considered any tongue would ever explore. It was marvellous. It was frightening.

She thought she would explode, and didn't mind if she did. She wondered if she would end up burning in hell-fire for this, then realised she was already burning and had never been happier in her life.

He placed his sturdy trunk between her legs, and entered her. It hurt at first, but not as much as she'd been expecting it to. And almost immediately the hurt disappeared, to be replaced by a feeling even more intense than all that had gone before.

She wanted to scream, but wasn't sure if it was the right thing to do, so held her peace. She lifted her legs and locked her ankles behind Gerald's buttocks. She didn't know if that was the right thing to do, either, but it *felt* right. Then he was out of her, and kneeling by her side.

'Is it finished?' she asked, trying to keep the disappointment out of her voice.

'No, my darling, it's only just started,' Gerald said softly, and then he picked her up with his big, gentle hands, and laid her on her stomach.

Richard Worrell had determined to wait up for his son, but he had consumed well over half a bottle of brandy, and at half past ten he fell asleep in his armchair. It was the noise of a motorcar entering the grounds that finally woke him up.

Gerald! he thought, sitting upright and feeling the anticipation course through his veins.

Richard glanced at the grandfather clock which ticked away remorselessly in the corner. A quarter past two in the morning! If Gerald had been out with Michelle until that time of night, then he must have succeeded in having his way with the little fool.

The lights of the Napier lit up the study wall as Gerald drove past. Richard stood up, walked across to the far wall and took down the oil painting of a hunting scene which hid his safe.

As he dialled the combination, he thought about Becky. They had not spoken to each other for over twenty years, but he would make sure that they spoke again soon. Perhaps he would wait for her outside the bakery. And what would he say to her when she emerged? There were so many possibilities!

'I've been talking to my son, Becky. It seems that Michelle takes after her mother in more ways than one.

'My boy would like to pay your daughter for her services the other night. Would five shillings be enough?'

'I don't expect Michelle will have told you this herself, Becky, but Gerald and she . . .'

Oh, there were so many good lines he might employ. He could just see the look on Becky's face when she realised what he was saying, when she finally understood that the likes of Richard and Gerald were *always* meant to triumph over the lesser folk of the world.

He opened the safe and took out the money he had withdrawn from the bank that very day. Five thousand pounds! Was such sweet revenge ever bought so cheaply?

The door opened, and Gerald entered the room. The boy looked as tired as he had when he'd got off the train from France.

'You did have her, didn't you?' Richard asked, suddenly alarmed that he'd read the signs wrongly.

Gerald nodded his head. 'Oh yes, Father, I did indeed have her. Several times.'

Richard beamed with happiness. 'Several times,' he repeated, savouring the words.

'Are you proud of me?' Gerald asked.

'Prouder than I can ever begin to tell you.' Richard held out the money. 'And here's your winnings, my boy. Wake up the servants. We must have champagne.'

'Must we?'

'But of course. An occasion like this demands champagne, doesn't it?'

Gerald shook his head. 'No, Father,' he said. 'It doesn't. It doesn't at all.' Then he turned on his heel and headed for the stairs.

Chapter Fifteen

Michelle lay snugly in her own bed, only half awake. Outside her window, the dawn chorus had begun, and though she knew she was being fanciful, it seemed as if the birds were singing just for her.

'Gerald!' she murmured softly. She could still smell his body on her own, and when she closed her eyes she could almost feel his firm thigh pressing against her.

How right she'd been to go to bed with him the night before. How stupid it would have been to wait until after the war. At the inn, Gerald had talked about the possibility of his being killed. But she knew that couldn't happen to her Gerald. In the glow of the early morning, which was just now peeking through the bedroom window, Michelle saw the golden future which lay ahead of her.

Gerald would survive the war, and return home a hero with a suitcase full of medals. Becky would at last have to admit that she'd been wrong about him. And then? And then they would get married, and live happily ever after.

It sounds just like one of the fairytales that Mam used to tell me, Michelle thought. But she knew that it wasn't. Gerald was real, their love was real – the whole thing was all incredibly, amazingly true.

From downstairs came the noise of Becky moving around in the kitchen. Michelle frowned. Knowing her mam, she was sure there would be an interrogation about what had happened last night. She didn't really want to face that – didn't want to have her blissfully happy mood temporarily shattered by another row with Becky – but she supposed she'd better get it over with. She threw off her blankets, swung her legs out of bed, and felt her feet touch the cold linoleum floor.

★

Becky had wanted to talk to her daughter the moment she'd woken up, but she'd forced herself to wait. Yet now, as she heard Michelle's footsteps on the stairs, she almost wished the next few minutes could be postponed indefinitely.

Michelle entered the kitchen, already wearing the baggy uniform the munitions factory had issued her with. Becky looked straight into her daughter's face, and knew immediately that something was wrong. Well, not wrong, exactly, she told herself, but not quite as it should have been.

'I waited up for you last night,' Becky said, as Michelle took her usual seat at the table.

'There was no need for you to do that.'

'Then at about half past one I went upstairs. I didn't mean to fall asleep, but I did.'

'As I said, there was no need.'

'What time did you finally come home, Michelle?'

'It must have been around two o'clock.'

'Did the car break down or somethin'?'

Michelle sighed. 'No, Mam, it didn't.'

Becky sat down opposite her daughter. 'So why were you so late?'

'We went out to dinner . . .'

'It must have been a very big meal if it took you that long to eat it.'

On her way downstairs, Michelle had decided that in order to keep the peace, she would lie about what had happened. But now she realised she couldn't lie. More than that, she didn't want to. 'The inn had bedrooms upstairs,' she said, 'and after the meal we went up to one of them.'

'An' did you . . .?'

'Well, of course we did.'

Becky dug her fingernails into the palms of her hands. 'You little idiot!' she hissed. 'I thought I told you to be careful.'

'I was careful,' Michelle replied angrily. 'I was careful to make sure that he really loved me before we ever went upstairs.'

'*I* thought that Richard—'

'And don't start telling me about you and Richard, because I'm sick to death of hearing about it.'

'All right,' said Becky, whose own anger was growing apace

with her daughter's. 'Let's talk about you an' Gerald. Do you think he'll have any interest in you, now you've let him have what he wanted? An' I don't mean buyin' you another meal an' takin' you off upstairs again. I mean *real* interest.'

'We're going to be married.'

'You're livin' in a fool's paradise.'

Michelle stood up and walked over to the door. 'You're wrong,' she said. 'And before you come to our wedding – if you're invited – I'll make you eat your words.'

'I only wish I *was* wrong,' Becky said, as Michelle pulled open the door and stepped into the back yard. 'I only wish I was.'

Gerald Worrell looked down at the hundreds of eager faces below him. He was standing on the back of a wagon decorated with Union Jacks for the first of the recruitment rallies he'd been sent home to conduct.

'The war is not the adventure we were led to expect it would be,' he said. 'It is harsh, and it is brutal.'

A low, uneasy murmur ran around his audience. Harsh? Brutal? This was not how the recruiters usually talked about the fighting.

'I have seen men die before they even got close to the enemy,' Gerald continued. 'Mowed down by machine-gun fire. Slaughtered like cattle.'

The feeling of unease was spreading. 'What are you – some kind of traitor?' one of the crowd called out.

'No,' Gerald replied. 'I am as patriotic now as I was when I first joined up, but since I am asking you to enlist, I think I owe you the truth.' Gerald paused. 'Before this war is over, many, many of our soldiers will die in the most horrible ways imaginable. It will be a tragedy, but it will not be a waste. The winning side will be the one which is prepared to sacrifice more of its sons.' He paused again. 'And that is why I am here today. Not to offer you excitement. Not to lure you to France with false hopes of adventure. I am here to ask you – to beg you – to put yourselves forward as willing sacrifices. The future of your children, and of your children's children, depends on men like you. Do not let your country down.'

The cheering started at the back, then travelled through the crowd like a wave, until everyone had joined in, even the man who had called Gerald a traitor earlier.

The young soldier looked at his watch. He had four more meetings to address that day, and though he didn't want to, he knew he must also find the time to write a letter to Michelle.

As she made her way up Ollershaw Lane, Michelle was thinking about just how wonderful life could be. She had spent the entire day counting down the hours until she would see Gerald. Now it was five-thirty, and in only two more hours she would be reunited with the man she loved with all her heart.

Michelle turned down the alley which led to her back yard. Another couple of minutes had ticked by, bringing her time with Gerald even closer. She opened the back door and stepped into the kitchen. Her mother was home already, ironing on the kitchen table. She did not look up from her work, even when her daughter sat down opposite her.

'Can't we stop this stupid fighting, Mam?' Michelle asked. 'Maybe I'm right, and maybe you are. Only time will tell. But in the meantime, we've still got to live together, haven't we?'

'There's a letter for you on the mantelpiece,' Becky said, as if she hadn't heard a word Michelle had spoken. 'It came this afternoon. Delivered by hand.'

Michelle picked up the letter. It was addressed in copperplate to Miss Michelle Worrell. It was probably from Gerald, Michelle thought, but she didn't know for sure, because she had never seen his handwriting before. There were so many things she didn't know about him, she realised. She turned the letter over, and examined the flap.

'It's all right. I haven't opened it,' Becky said, her eyes still on her ironing.

'I wasn't suggesting that . . .'

'I'm through pokin' me nose in your business,' Becky said relentlessly. 'An' now I expect you'll want to take your letter up to your own room, where you can read it in private.'

'No, I'll read it here,' Michelle said. She slit the flap and took out the single sheet of expensive paper.

My dear Michelle,

I am afraid that there is a great deal more work involved in this recruitment drive than I had ever imagined, and so I will not be able to meet you as we agreed. However, I will be in Northwich for several more days, and I hope to be able to see you before I go back to France.

Yours sincerely,

Gerald.

The words swam before Michelle's eyes, and she clutched the mantelpiece for support. None of it sounded like Gerald – *her* Gerald – at all. It was as if it had been written by a stranger with whom she'd made a casual arrangement, which he was now forced to break with little regret.

'It's from Gerald,' she told her mother.

'Is it?' Becky asked woodenly.

'Yes. We were going to go out this evening, but he's so busy with his recruitment drive that he's not going to be able to make it after all.'

'You surprise me.'

'It's not like you think,' Michelle protested.

Her mother finally looked up from her ironing, and Michelle could see that there were tears in her eyes. 'Listen, love,' Becky said, 'when you finally realise the truth an' need a shoulder to cry on, you know where I am. But until then, I don't think we should talk about Gerald Worrell any more.'

Michelle looked down at her right hand, and saw that she had crumpled into a tight, angry ball the only letter Gerald had ever sent her.

It was already dark as Michelle walked down Ollershaw Lane, the coppers she needed for her phone call clutched tightly in her hand. The letter had to be a mistake, she told herself as she passed the Nelson Pumping Station. Or if it wasn't a mistake, there must at least be some explanation for it.

The phone box was empty. Michelle stepped inside, picked up the receiver and told the operator which number she wanted. She heard a ringing tone at the other end, and then a man's voice said, 'Peak House. This is Chesworth speaking. How may I help you?'

'I . . . I'd like to speak to Mr Gerald Worrell, if he's there,' Michelle said.

'Certainly, madam. And whom shall I say is calling?'

'Just tell him it's Michelle.'

There was a slight pause, then the butler said, 'Would that be Miss Michelle *Worrell*?'

'Yes.'

'I'm afraid Mr Gerald is not at home.'

'But a minute ago, you said I could speak to him.'

'A minute ago, madam, I was under the impression that he *was* at home. But I appear to have been mistaken.'

'Could you tell me when he'll be back, then?' Michelle asked desperately.

'I'm afraid I can't, madam. Mr Gerald, as you probably know, is very busy with important war work. He does not expect to be spending much time at the house.'

'I see,' Michelle said miserably. 'I'm sorry I bothered you.'

'It was no trouble, madam,' the butler said, and hung up.

Michelle replaced the receiver on its cradle. She stepped slowly out of the box as if her legs were made of lead, then looked up the lane in the direction of her home.

'You can't be right about him, Mam,' she said desperately. 'I just know you can't.'

Chapter Sixteen

It was the third day of the recruitment drive, and young men were heading towards the Northwich Drill Hall from all directions. They were a mixed bunch: some of them were saltminers, others agricultural labourers, and a few worked in the brewery or served behind the bars of the town's hotels. But they all had one thing in common – they wanted to be told about the war by someone who had actually seen it for himself.

Michelle, standing on the corner near the main entrance, caught herself listening to the animated conversation of a couple of young carmen.

'Once you an' me get over there, we'll soon teach the Huns a thing or two,' one of them said.

'You're right there, Len,' the second replied. 'I wonder what it's like to kill one of 'em with your own hands?'

'We'll soon find out, won't we? But it won't all be fightin', you know. From what I hear, them French mamzelles are somethin'.'

'How d'you mean?'

'Well, they're a lot more . . . er . . . generous than what our English girls are.'

'Oh, I see what you're gettin' at.'

Michelle, who also saw what he was getting at, shuddered. She had been generous herself. But only for Gerald – it had only ever been meant for Gerald.

The doors of the hall opened, and the young men streamed in. Soon Michelle was left standing alone. Was it possible she'd missed Gerald? she wondered. No, she couldn't have. He wouldn't have come to the hall more than an hour before the meeting, and she'd been waiting for him for two.

She heard the sound of approaching footsteps. It was Gerald

at last! He was striding confidently towards the main door, looking neither to left nor right. She hesitated for the briefest of instants, then stepped out of the shadows, blocking his path.

Gerald came to an abrupt halt. Their eyes met, then he quickly looked away. 'Michelle, what are you doing here?' he asked.

'We have to talk.'

'Perhaps we do. But this isn't the right time. I have an important meeting to address.'

'Then when *will* be the right time?' Michelle asked desperately. 'It's been three days since . . . since we last saw each other . . .'

'I have been extremely busy.'

'. . . and you'll be going back to France soon.'

Gerald pulled out his watch and checked the time. 'The meeting should last about an hour,' he said. 'I have another appointment after that, but I think I can spare you a few minutes before it.'

Spare her a few minutes! she thought. As if she was nothing to him. 'Can I come into the hall and listen to you speak?' she asked.

Gerald shook his head irritably. 'I'm afraid not. The meeting is for men only. But as I said, I should only be in there for an hour. Or maybe a little more.' And with that, he stepped smartly to one side of her and marched towards the door.

'Not a kiss, not a hug,' Michelle said to herself as she watched him disappear into the hall. 'He didn't even ask me how I'd been.'

She could have gone away during that hour, but where would she have gone *to*? She wanted to be with him, and this was about the closest she could get. Besides, she was afraid that the meeting might end early, and she would miss him.

So, instead of seeking the comfort of a cosy best room in one of the nearby pubs, she stood in the cool night air, listening to the cheers coming from the Drill Hall.

It was an hour and fifteen minutes after Gerald had entered the building that the men who had gone to see him started to stream out. They were even more excited now than they had been when they'd arrived.

'He's a real firebrand, that Lieutenant Worrell, isn't he just?'

'Yeah, mind you, he didn't make the war out to be no picnic, like some of the other officers I've heard talk about it.'

'That's what I like about him. Straight as a die an' as honest as they come.'

'He's made me want to join up.'

'Me, too.'

Soon, the men had all dispersed to their homes or the pubs, and still Gerald had not come out. Michelle waited for another five minutes, then pushed the door open and stepped inside.

There was only one person in the hall, an old man who was sweeping up. He had his back to her, but turned when he heard Michelle's footsteps and said, 'Can I help you, miss?'

'I'm looking for Lieutenant Worrell, the officer who just addressed the meeting.'

'Oh, him! Didn't catch his name, but I listened to his speech all the way through. I tell you, just lookin' at him was enough to make me feel proud to be British.'

'Where is he now?' Michelle asked, trying her best not to show her impatience.

'Haven't got a clue, love.'

'But he must be somewhere in the building, mustn't he?'

The old man smiled. 'Why, bless you, no. He's long gone from here. Nipped out of the back door real smartish he did, as soon as he'd finished givin' his speech.'

The Marston ladies' gossip circle was assembled, as usual, in the best room of the New Inn.

'Michelle Worrell's lookin' down in the mouth just at the moment,' Dottie Curzon said.

'I've noticed that meself,' Half-a-Mo-Flo chipped in. 'Do you think it's got anythin' to do with her cousin Gerald?'

She doesn't know! Not-Stopping thought triumphantly. I may not have me legs any more, but when it comes to piecin' things together, I'm still the champion.

'You're very quiet tonight, Elsie,' Dottie Curzon said.

'Am I?' Not-Stopping asked. 'Maybe it's because I was thinkin' about young girls that have lost their reputations.'

'You what?' Dottie said.

Not-Stopping drained the last few drops of her milk stout. 'I think it's your round, Dottie,' she said.

'It is, but you were sayin' about—'

'Talkin's thirsty work,' Not-Stopping said firmly.

With great reluctance, Dottie stood up and walked over to the serving hatch.

'So what's all this about, Mam?' Flo asked, her tongue almost hanging out in anticipation.

'Let's wait till Dottie gets back, shall we?' said Not-Stopping, who was really starting to enjoy herself.

Dottie returned with the drinks, and while the others waited eagerly, Not-Stopping made a great show of slowly pouring out her stout and taking the first sip.

'Well, are you goin' to tell us, or what?' Flo said. 'Not that I'm really interested, you understand.'

Not-Stopping smiled. Not interested? Flo wouldn't sleep if she didn't hear the story. 'The other night, Monday it must have been, I happened to be looking out of me parlour window,' Not-Stopping began.

'And . . .?'

'An' I saw that big, fancy car of Gerald Worrell's pullin' up outside Becky Taylor's place.'

'Did he go inside?'

'Well, of course he didn't. Becky don't want no truck with that side of the family.'

'Well, then?'

'But Michelle came out, dressed up to the nines. Then she got in the car, and they drove off.'

'I don't call that much of a story at all,' Half-a-Mo-Flo said dismissively.

'Neither would I, if that was all there was to it,' Not-Stopping agreed.

'So there's more?'

'It got to be ten o'clock, which, as you know, is long past my bedtime . . .'

'An' she came back?'

'. . . an' she still hadn't come back.'

'So you don't know when—'

'Well, I wasn't really feelin' sleepy that night, so I thought to meself, I'll stay up a bit longer. Anyway, I didn't mean to, but I must have dozed off, 'cos the next I knew, I was woken up by the sound of Gerald's car pullin' up.'

'Very interestin',' Flo said, making it plain from her tone that she thought it was anything but.

'I really think that people should have more consideration than to drive them big, noisy machines through the village at that time of night,' Not-Stopping said. Then she sat back, took a sip of milk stout, and waited.

There was a strained silence for perhaps a minute, before Flo finally cracked. 'What time of night?' she asked.

'Didn't I say?' Not-Stopping asked innocently. 'It was two o'clock in the mornin'! An' you know what that means, don't you?'

'What?' Dottie Curzon asked.

'Well, all the pubs had been closed for two hours by then, an' it was too cold for drivin', so they must have . . .' Not-Stopping lowered her voice to a dramatic whisper '. . . they must have been to some hotel together.'

Though she really didn't want to, Dottie Curzon found herself nodding her head in agreement.

'An' yer know what men are,' Not-Stopping continued. 'Once you've given them what they're after, they don't want nothin' more to do with you. That's why Michelle's lookin' so down in the dumps – because he hasn't been near her since that night.'

'You might be right there, Mam,' Flo admitted, trying to hide both her admiration for her mother-in-law's powers of deduction and her envy of them.

'So the same thing's happened to Michelle as happened to her mother,' Not-Stopping said. She paused. 'History's a bit like pickled onions,' she went on, delivering the line she had thought up while she was doing her mangling earlier in the day. 'It's always repeatin' on you.'

Flo sniggered, but Dottie Curzon didn't. 'I don't think it's somethin' you should make jokes about,' Dottie said. 'Michelle's a nice lass who's always been very pleasant to you. Now she's had her life ruined, and there'll be no Michael Worrell to rescue her. So I just don't think that's somethin' that you should make jokes about.'

'Aye, you're right,' Not-Stopping agreed.

'What did you just say?' Flo asked in amazement.

'I told her she was right.' Not-Stopping took another sip of her drink to hide her confusion. She was experiencing an emotion which was so alien to her that it was almost a complete stranger. She was feeling ashamed of herself.

Michelle arrived at Northwich Station ten minutes before the London train, which would take Gerald on the first leg of his journey back to France, was due to arrive.

'You're acting like a fool,' she told herself as she bought a platform ticket and stepped through the barrier. 'A complete bloody fool.' She took the letter out of her clutch purse, and read it for perhaps the tenth time.

My dear Michelle,

I must apologise for my behaviour over the last few days. Leaving you waiting outside the Drill Hall was inexcusable, but though I am brave enough on the battlefield, I did not have the courage to face you then.

There is a great deal I have to explain to you, but time is short and my duty must come first.

I will be leaving Northwich on the six o'clock train. If you could arrive a few minutes before that, we could talk.

Please be there. It is very important.

Yours,

Gerald.

He ignores me for four days, and then when he whistles, I come running like a dog, Michelle thought angrily. But what else could she do? A dog will still love the master who savagely beats it, and she still loved Gerald – however badly he had treated her.

The big clock hanging at the end of the platform loudly clicked the passing of another minute. A chill breeze blew in from along the track. Michelle hugged herself and started walking towards the ladies' waiting room, then realised that she might miss Gerald if she went in there.

She stopped, and turned around to face the barrier just as Gerald and his father arrived.

Even from a distance, it was clear that both men were agitated. Richard was pointing at the platform, as if that was where he wanted to go, and Gerald was shaking his head firmly, as if what *he* wanted was to say their goodbyes at the barrier. The argument went on for perhaps half a minute before Richard finally nodded his head and accepted defeat.

Father and son put their arms around each other. Another minute ticked noisily away on the big station clock. Gerald gently broke free of his father's embrace. Richard said something, then turned and walked away. Gerald watched his father's back for a few seconds, then took his travel warrant out of his pocket, and handed it over for inspection. The big clock clicked off another minute.

Gerald passed through the barrier and walked towards Michelle. She wanted to run to him, fling herself into his arms, and tell him that she loved him. But after what had happened in the previous four days, she didn't dare to. And so she just stood there, as motionless as a statue, and watched him getting closer and closer.

Gerald stopped a few feet away from her. 'It was good of you to come,' he said awkwardly.

'You asked me to come, and so I did,' Michelle told him. 'I would have done the same yesterday, or the day before that. Wherever you were, I'd gladly have come and waited for you until you were finally free to see me.'

Gerald lowered his head. 'I know.'

'Were you really so busy that you had to leave me standing outside the Drill Hall, Gerald?'

Gerald lifted his head again, and looked into her eyes. 'No,' he admitted. 'I was not so busy – but I was so ashamed.'

'Ashamed? Why are you ashamed? Because of what we did together at the inn? But if we love each other, Gerald . . .' She hesitated and a look of doubt came to her face.

'There's so much I want to say, Michelle, but I've told you so many lies that I don't know where to begin.'

Michelle felt her stomach churn. If this went on for much longer, she was sure that she would be sick. 'Perhaps it would be best to start at the beginning,' she said, as firmly as she could.

'That night at the inn, before I asked you to go upstairs with me, I told you I was a virgin.'

'I remember.'

'Nothing could be further from the truth. I had my first woman – a prostitute – on my sixteenth birthday . . .'

'I see.'

'. . . and there must have been dozens since then.'

Michelle's lip trembled. 'I should have guessed from the way you took me that you knew what you were doing,' she said. 'What other lies have you told me?'

'When I fell off my horse in front of you, I said I'd lost control. I hadn't. I did it deliberately.'

'So Mam was right about that.'

'And when I said I was not used to strong drink, I was lying again. I can drink a bottle or two of port with ease, and wash that down with a half-bottle of brandy.'

There was the sound of a shrill whistle, then the London train steamed into the station.

'You seem to have deceived me in any number of ways,' Michelle shouted over the noise.

'And not only you. I lied to your brother Billy, when I told him that I loved you.'

Michelle felt her world collapsing around her. Her mam had been right about that, too. The Worrells were no good. Gerald was just like his father, and had destroyed her just as Richard had almost destroyed Becky. Why had he done it? *Why?*

'Do you wish to know why I told so many lies?' Gerald asked, as if he could read her mind.

'Yes, I think you'd better tell me,' Michelle said, though she was dreading the answer.

'I had a wager with my father.'

'What kind of wager?'

'He bet me five thousand pounds that I couldn't get you into my bed.'

It was worse – far worse – than she had ever imagined it could be. If Gerald had been driven by a burning lust, it might have been bearable. But to be the object of a cold, calculating bet – to be treated like a whippet or a racing pigeon – that was too much.

'I hope you burn in hell, Gerald Worrell!' she said, turning towards the exit.

She felt Gerald's powerful hands grab her shoulders and swing her round. 'Don't go!' he said in a voice which was half pleading, half command. 'Let me finish what I have to say.'

Why not? she asked herself. What could he tell her that would be worse than the things she'd already heard. 'All right,' she said with dignity. 'Let me hear the rest.'

'I didn't take the money. I won the wager, but I told Father I didn't want his money.'

'And am I supposed to be grateful for that?'

'I didn't take it because, in a way, I'd lost. You see, the other night the lying stopped, and when I said I loved you up in that bedroom, I meant it.'

'You loved making love to me,' Michelle said bitterly. 'What a fool I was!'

'Yes, it was wonderful doing it with you,' Gerald admitted. 'I've never had a woman who wasn't getting a payment of some sort before – never had a woman who did it because of what I meant to her.'

'You enjoyed it all the better because it was free, you mean,' Michelle said bitterly.

'No, that's not what I meant at all. I suddenly realised, as we were lying there in each other's arms, how much I was going to miss you, how my only real reason for wanting to survive this dreadful war was so I could be with you.'

Michelle was trembling from head to toe. 'How do I know you're not lying again?' she demanded.

'Why should I lie now?' Gerald asked, looking frantically around at the station master, who was already walking along the platform with his whistle and flag. 'If all I wanted was your body, I've already had that. But I want more, Michelle. Much more.'

Michelle noticed that he was trembling, too, almost as much as she was. 'What *do* you want from me, Gerald?' she asked.

'If you can find it in your heart to forgive me for the way I've behaved, I will marry you as soon as I can. And I promise, I'll never make you unhappy again. Can you forgive me, Michelle?'

It had all happened so quickly. First he did love her, then he didn't, and now he was telling her again that he did. The wager, the lies, the tricks he had played – it was too much to take in.

'*Can* you forgive me?' Gerald repeated.

'I . . . I don't know,' Michelle said, and behind her she heard the station master blow his whistle. 'I . . . oh God, yes, I forgive you. I can't make myself do anything else.'

Gerald hugged her to him so tightly that she thought he would crush her. Then, just as quickly, he broke free and began to chase the train, which was already chugging out of the station.

He leapt for the last carriage, and for one dreadful second, Michelle thought he would fall on to the track. Then he was on the running board and turning round to wave to her.

She thought his last words, as the train steamed away, were 'I love you', but the locomotive was making so much noise that she couldn't be sure.

Chapter Seventeen

The middle of October brought with it some of the fiercest storms the villagers had ever seen. Night after night, people awoken from an uneasy sleep would climb out of their warm beds and go to their windows to look at the spectacle.

For a spectacle it was. Bolts of brilliant white lightning slashed their way savagely across the dark sky. Thunderclaps boomed as menacingly as the big guns just across the water, and heavy raindrops bombarded windowpanes and slate roofs with the ferocity of enemies trying to break through.

Then, quite suddenly, the skies were clear again, and the inhabitants of Marston experienced a gentle autumn which was a fitting successor to the golden summer which had just gone.

'Shall the two of us go for a walk this afternoon, Spudder?' Ivy suggested, one morning before the boarders had come down to their breakfasts.

'I can't go takin' walks,' Spudder replied, without even a second's hesitation.

'Why not?'

'I've got me chip shop to consider.'

'I don't mean a big walk,' Ivy said. 'Not anythin' that'll keep you away from your precious chips for long. Just a little one, down the woods after dinner.'

'I don't think . . .'

'It's lovely there at this time of year, you know. Everythin's all golden brown. An' we could gather some chestnuts an' roast 'em over the fire.'

Spudder thought about it. 'A walk?' he said. '*Just* a walk? No tryin' to kiss me?'

Ivy smiled. 'I haven't tried to kiss you since we were in that boat, have I?' she asked.

'Well, no.'

'An' I promise I won't again. The next time we do any kissin', it'll be you that starts it.'

There was the sound of footsteps on the stairs, and then Captain Davenport and Jim Vernon entered the room.

Spudder had been standing quite close to Ivy, but now he jumped guiltily across the kitchen. 'We . . . we were just talkin',' he said. 'About walks. The woods are lovely at this time of year.'

Captain Davenport grinned. 'Oh aye.'

Jim Vernon smiled, too, but there was a sad edge to it. 'If you've got somebody to take for walks in the woods, you take 'em while you've got the chance,' he advised.

The Great Marvello was the last down. As was his custom, he immediately picked up his newspaper and began scanning it for news of the war. 'The Germans have attacked Wipers again,' he announced. 'This war's turning into a bad business.'

'It is that,' Captain Davenport agreed. 'It's about time somebody struck a decisive blow.'

'What d'you mean, "somebody"?' Spudder asked.

The Captain looked startled by the question. 'Well, I mean either us or the French,' he said. 'Because it's no good relyin' on the Russians, you know.'

'Isn't it?'

'It is not. They've got the men – millions more than the rest of us put together – but they're that short of weapons that they're sendin' 'em into battle with no rifles.'

'So if they haven't got rifles, what are they supposed to fight with?' Spudder asked.

'They're supposed to wait until one of their comrades who *does* have a rifle gets killed, then they can take his,' the Great Marvello explained. He shook his head again. 'As I said, a bad business. A very bad business.'

The back door latch clicked, and the door swung open. They all turned to see who was calling on them so early in the morning. In the doorway stood a tall man with a clipped moustache.

'Oh, hello Mr Bingham,' Spudder said. 'It's good to have you back with us.'

*

Michelle stood naked in front of her mirror, something she would never have done before Gerald had convinced her that her body was beautiful. Her stomach was as flat as it had ever been, she decided, but it was early days yet.

She put on her underwear, then stepped into the baggy trousers the munitions factory had issued her with. Another day's hard work was ahead of her, but she did not resent it because, as she'd told her mother, it was useful work. She liked to think that some of the shells she helped to make would find their way to Gerald's company, and that he, in some mystical way, would sense that they had come from her.

'You're being fanciful,' she told herself. Just like her dad had been. Just like her mam was, sometimes. Maybe it had something to do with the condition she was in.

She finished dressing and made her way downstairs. She was just entering the kitchen when the sudden wave of nausea hit her. She wanted to clutch her stomach, then she looked at her mother – who was sitting at the kitchen table, watching her – and knew she didn't dare.

'Anythin' the matter, love?' Becky asked.

Michelle shook her head, and made her way quickly to the kitchen door.

'Where are you goin'?' Becky said, with an edge of concern to her voice.

'The lavvy,' Michelle managed to gasp, as she opened the door and stepped outside.

'The lavvy!' she heard Becky repeat behind her. 'You seem to be spendin' half your time in the lavvy these days. You might as well move your bed in there.'

Michelle laughed weakly, as she was expected to. 'Must have been something I ate,' she said over her shoulder.

As she made her way down the yard, her vision began to blur slightly, and it was all she could do to keep down the bile. She flung open the lavatory door, bent down over the pan, and was immediately and violently sick.

It was still eight months before the baby would be born, she thought as she heaved for a second time. And it would be a couple of months before it even started to show, so she could keep quiet about it for a little while longer. But she couldn't keep it from Mam for ever. Sooner or later, she would have to know.

It was shortly after Michelle had left for work that Jim Vernon appeared at the back door.

'Mr Bingham?' Becky asked, the moment Jim had entered the kitchen.

The young flatman nodded. 'He arrived back at the boardin' house about half an hour ago.'

'Sit yourself down and I'll brew us a cup of tea,' Becky said, all brisk and businesslike, although she felt far from it. Instead, she felt as she had when she'd helped Dr Doyle track down the murderer of Septimus Quinn; as she had when she'd confronted a criminal called Caper Leech, and told him to leave her brother Philip alone; as she had when rival bakers tried to drive her out of business . . .

Ever since Michael's death, she'd existed in a shadow world, living only for her children. Now there was a bubble of excitement building up inside her, and she knew the time had finally arrived for her to step out of the shadows and start taking on the real world again.

The kettle boiled, and she made the tea. 'Right,' she said, taking the pot over to the table. 'What we need now, Jim, is some kind of plan.'

The next day, Mr Bingham strolled down to Northwich Railway Station, where, Becky noted, he showed great interest in the track. The following day, when one of Becky's bakers was following him, he visited the Pool mine, which was being converted into a warehouse for ten thousand boxes of picric acid. On the third day, with Jim as his tail, he returned to the Victoria works, and made some more sketches.

If he wasn't a spy, then what the hell *was* he? his watchers asked themselves.

It was late afternoon. Jim and Becky sat in Becky's kitchen, a pot of tea and a seemingly insurmountable problem between them.

'We *know* he's a spy,' Jim argued.

'We're *almost* sure he is,' Becky countered. 'But whether we have enough evidence to convince the bobbies of it is another matter.'

'Look at where he's been. Look at what he's done.'

'He likes to go for walks, an' sometimes he makes sketches. You can't arrest a man for that.'

'I suppose you're right,' Jim agreed reluctantly.

'Besides, he may not be workin' on his own. Maybe he's part of a gang, an' if the police do arrest him . . .'

'Then the rest of 'em will get away?'

'Exactly.'

'So what are we goin' to do?'

'I don't know,' Becky admitted. And then, out of nowhere, an idea came into her head. 'He's goin' to have to make his move soon,' she said excitedly.

'How do you mean?'

'It doesn't do the Germans any good just to know what the Victoria works and Pool mine look like. What they want is to have the places destroyed.'

'You're sayin' that you think he'll try his hand at . . . what's the word . . . sabotage?' Jim asked, starting to get as enthusiastic as Becky.

'It would make sense.'

'An' if we caught him in the act, we'd have all the proof that we needed.' A look of gloom came to Jim's face. 'But how will we know when he's goin' to do it?' he asked. 'I mean, we can't follow him all the time, can we?'

'We won't have to. Look, if he's goin' to plant a bomb or start a fire, he's not goin' to do it in the daytime, when he can be seen, is he?'

'Probably not.'

'So he's no choice but to work at night.'

'I still don't see how we're goin' to know when he's ready to make his move.'

Becky smiled. 'You live in the same house as he does, Jim. It looks like you won't be gettin' much rest for a while, doesn't it?'

Chapter Eighteen

Mr Bingham had tied her to the kitchen chair, and was piling up dynamite round her ankles. 'Zis is how we Chermans deal with those who oppose us,' he said, laughing like a maniac.

She had all the proof she needed now, Becky thought. But it wouldn't do her any good, would it? Because as soon as the dynamite reached her knees, Mr Bingham would light the blue touchpaper and retire.

How did she know that, she wondered – the bit about the dynamite having to reach her knees? Bingham hadn't mentioned it, yet she was convinced that was the case.

She needed a plan, she told herself, but it was hard to think one up, because someone was tapping on her head.

Tap, tap, tap.

Perhaps if she could loosen the strings of onions that Bingham had tied her up with, she might be able to . . .

Tap, tap, tap.

Why had he used strings of onions in the first place? And how long had dynamite had blue touchpaper?

Becky opened her eyes. She was at the kitchen table, just as she had been in the dream. And someone was knocking gently but insistently on the back door.

She looked up at the clock. It was twenty past two in the morning. It all came back to her. This was the third night she'd stayed up waiting for Mr Bingham to make his move. It was no wonder that she'd fallen asleep.

The tapping continued. Becky stood up and walked quickly over to the door. 'Jim?' she whispered.

'Yes, it's me.'

Becky drew back the bolt and opened the door.

Jim was standing in the back yard, a look of flushed

excitement on his face. 'Bingham!' he said, as if he could be calling about anything else at that time of night. 'I heard a noise in the back yard about ten minutes ago, and when I looked out of my window, I could see Bingham standin' there. An' he wasn't alone!'

'Who was with him?'

'I don't know. There's nearly a full moon tonight, but the other feller was standin' in the shadow of the wash-house.'

'But you're sure he was there?'

'He was there, all right. Because after they'd left, I followed them. An' there were definitely two of em' walking down the lane. They were both carryin' packages as well!'

'Explosives?'

'I don't know, but they could have been.'

'An' where are they now?'

'When I came to get you, they were nearly at the pumpin' station.'

'Then we'd better get movin' ourselves,' Becky said.

It would have been an exaggeration to say that it was as bright as day, but the full moon lit up Ollershaw Lane clearly enough for them to see that there was no one else around. That was hardly surprising – unless Bingham and his companion were walking at a snail's pace, it was only to be expected that they would have reached the Post Office and turned the corner by then. Jim and Becky made their way quickly down the lane. They walked as quietly as they could, but the sound of their footsteps seemed to echo like cannon shots.

'Maybe it'd be better if you went back home, Mrs Worrell,' Jim whispered.

'Not a chance,' said Becky, who felt more alive than she had for years.

'It's too dangerous for you. There might be more than just the two of 'em.'

'Even if there's only two, we can't tackle them, can we?'

'Well . . . no.'

'So if all we're goin' to do is take a look, I can't be in any danger, can I? Stop fussin', Jim. I'm comin' with you, an' that's the end of it.'

They had reached the Post Office and had a clear view of the road as far as the corner of Chapel Street. There was no sign of the men they were following.

'We've lost 'em,' Jim said.

'Maybe they went down the mineral line,' Becky suggested.

'If they did that, we'll never find 'em now,' Jim said despondently. 'We might as well go to the police.'

'They'll laugh at us. Besides, we've only got Bingham's name to give them. If we can catch up with them, we might be able to identify the whole gang.'

'But we've no idea where they've gone.'

'I know that. But we could make an educated guess. They're headin' in the general direction of the Victoria works – an' Mr Bingham has seemed more interested in that than he has in anythin' else.'

'Bit of a long shot, isn't it?' Jim said.

'It might be,' Becky agreed. 'But it's the only one we've got.'

The moon had clouded over, and Becky and Jim made their way along the canal bank to the Victoria works in almost complete darkness.

'We're wastin' our time,' Jim whispered.

'If that's what you think, then why are you talkin' so quietly?' Becky whispered back.

Jim grinned shamefacedly into the blackness. 'You're right, Mrs Worrell,' he admitted. 'There's not much chance they will be there, but we have to check anyway.'

The shape of the works loomed up ahead of them. Another minute or so, and they would be at the main gate.

'Can you see them, Jim?' Becky asked.

'I can't see a bloomin' thing.' Jim replied.

The dark cloud over the moon shifted, exposing a small sliver of yellow. It moved a little further, and the sliver became a quarter.

Ahead of them, they could see a bush. 'Let's get down behind that,' Becky said.

'What for?'

'Because if it gets any lighter – an' they *are* there, they'll be bound to see us.'

Jim grinned again. 'Good job you insisted on comin' along. I'd have made a right mess on me own.'

They had only just crouched down behind the bush when the rest of the cloud was blown away. The works was once again bathed in the moon's eerie blue light, and they saw two men standing by the factory gates.

'The tall one's Bingham,' Becky said, 'but who's the other?'

'I don't know,' Jim confessed, because although the second man's body reminded him vaguely of someone he knew, both men had handkerchiefs wrapped around their faces, just like bandits in the cowboy books.

A minute, then two, ticked away, with Becky and Jim hiding behind the bush, and Bingham and his partner standing by the gate.

'What are they waitin' for?' Becky whispered.

'I think they must be expectin' somebody else.'

'Well, I've seen enough,' Becky said, 'You stay here an' watch them, an' I'll go an' fetch the police.'

Behind them, a twig cracked as if it had been trodden on, then a harsh voice said, 'I have a gun in my hand, and if either of you try any tricks, I will not hesitate to shoot.'

Becky's heart started to gallop. She turned her head and saw that there were two masked men standing there, and one of them really did have a gun. 'We'll behave,' she said. 'Won't we, Jim?'

'I wouldn't dream of arguin' with a gun,' Jim answered, and though he was trying to put on a brave face, she didn't miss the slight crack in his voice.

'You will both stand up very slowly,' said the man behind them, 'then you will raise your arms in the air and walk to the gate.'

He's goin' to kill us, Becky thought as she stood up. He might not do it yet, but he will in the end. He doesn't have any choice now that we know about Mr Bingham.

A few days earlier, the idea of death would not really have bothered her. She'd have told herself that she'd had her share of happiness, that now she'd lost her husband and her children didn't really need her any more, she'd be quite content to go. But that was before this business of Mr Bingham had brought her back to life again.

'Remember, no sudden moves,' the man with the gun said.

They walked towards the works entrance, Jim and Becky leading the way, the gunman and his partner behind them. When they reached the gate, the gunman gestured that they should stand to one side, and turned his attention to Bingham.

'Caught these two hiding in the bushes,' he said.

'You've got a pistol,' Bingham replied, sounding very angry. 'You were told that there would be no weapons on this expedition.'

'Why is he worried about that?' Becky wondered. 'Why isn't he more concerned about the fact that we know what he's up to?'

'You were told to bring no weapons,' Bingham repeated. 'You deliberately disobeyed an order.'

The gunman shrugged. 'If I hadn't brought the gun, these two could have been a real problem,' he said. 'As it is . . .'

Bingham switched to a language which sounded like gibberish, but which Becky assumed was German. The gunman did the same. It was more of an argument than a discussion, and though Becky could still not understand a word of it, she was sure that she and Jim were the subject of it.

Suddenly, the sound of a whistle cut through the night air, and out of nowhere several figures appeared, each wearing a pointed helmet.

'*Politzei!*' said the gunman. He pointed his pistol in the direction of the nearest policeman and was just about to pull the trigger when Jim flung himself at him, knocking him to the ground.

The two men rolled over and over, first Jim on top and then the German. The young flatman grabbed the German's wrist and twisted hard. The German grunted and released his grip on the pistol.

'Get the gun, Mrs Worrell!' Jim shouted. 'Pick up the gun!' As he rolled again, he saw Becky bend down and pick up the weapon.

The German was on top again, his hands on Jim's face, trying to claw out his eyes. Then, with no warning, he was gone. Jim looked up, and saw that he was now being held between two burly constables.

Jim quickly took in the rest of the scene. The gunman's partner was also being restrained, and Bingham, who seemed to be putting up no resistance, was talking to another constable. But the fourth man – Bingham's companion whom they had followed all the way from Marston – was running towards the canal. Jim hauled himself to his feet, and set off in pursuit.

At the edge of the canal the man hesitated, then dived in. He was already halfway across when Jim plunged in after him. The water was so cold that it felt as if it were stripping the flesh from Jim's bones. 'Just a few more strokes an' I'll be on the other side,' he encouraged himself. He touched the opposite bank, and pulled himself out.

The man he was chasing was already running down the towpath towards Northwich. Jim started running, too. His clothes were heavy with water and clung uncomfortably to him, and his boots squelched as he moved, but he had no time to do anything about that. If he didn't catch up with the other man soon, he would simply slip away into the night.

His quarry was slower than he was, and Jim started gaining ground almost immediately. Once more, it crossed Jim's mind that there was something familiar about the man he was chasing.

There were ten yards between them, then five, then three. When Jim was almost close enough to reach forward and touch him, the other man stopped and turned round. Jim tensed himself for a struggle, but it was plain from the way the other man stood that he would offer no resistance.

'I'm too bloody old for playin' these sorts of games, Jim,' Captain Davenport said.

The room the policemen had taken Becky and Jim to was at the back of the police station. With one small window set high in the wall, and containing only a plain table and two chairs, it might as well have been a cell.

Becky and Jim sat at the table. One of the policemen had brought a blanket for Jim and mugs of steaming tea for both of them. Beyond asking how Jim was feeling, he hadn't spoken. Nobody, it seemed, wanted to tell them anything.

'It's almost like *we're* the spies,' Jim complained.

'I expect they have their reasons for doin' things this way,' Becky said.

The door swung open, and a man they had never expected to see again walked into the room.

'What are you doin' here, Mr Bingham?' Jim demanded. 'You should be behind bars by now.'

'I'll explain later,' Bingham said crisply. 'But first, I shall require you to sign these.' He laid a printed document in front of each of them.

'Official Secrets Act,' Becky said. She scanned the document: '. . . felony punished by imprisonment to approach or enter any prohibited place . . . to obtain or to communicate to any other person any information which might be or which is intended to be useful to an enemy . . .'

'What if I don't want to sign it?' she asked Bingham.

'After what you've witnessed tonight, I'm afraid you don't have any choice,' Bingham said. 'And why should you object to signing something which is in the interest of your country?'

'All right, I will sign,' Becky agreed. 'But after I have, I shall want some questions answerin'.'

'I suppose that's reasonable,' Bingham conceded.

Becky signed her document, and Jim his, and Bingham put them in his pocket.

'Now, Mr Bingham, just what *is* your game?' Becky asked.

'As you rightly deduced, I am a German spy, but—'

'You what!' Jim interrupted.

'But I am also working for the British government.'

'An' which side are you really on?' Becky asked.

'Yours, of course. Otherwise, I'd be locked up by now.'

'What does it amount to, all this spyin'?'

'Until recently my job has been to pass on information about what might be described as strategic targets, most of which has been hopelessly inaccurate.'

'But why did you choose to live in the boardin' house?' Becky asked.

'There are two ways a spy can shield his true purpose,' Bingham told her. 'One is to blend into the community. The other is to clearly stand out, to be so conspicuous that you are above suspicion. The man who called himself Captain Davenport took the first route, but I have duties in other parts of the country which made that impossible. So I chose the second route. By living in the boarding house, I was drawing attention to myself, but only as a harmless eccentric. You two people, as far as I know, are the only ones who have ever thought I might be a spy.'

'Tell us about tonight,' Becky said.

'I have known there were other German spies operating in the area for quite some time,' Bingham said. 'Given the strategic importance of the chemical factories and the shipping lanes, it would have been surprising if there hadn't been. But I didn't know who these other spies were.'

'You mean, you didn't know about Fred Davenport?' Jim asked.

Bingham laughed. 'Though we lived in the same house, I had no idea,' he admitted. 'But I have reason to believe that he knew about me.'

'He must have done,' Jim said. 'That would explain why he tried to talk me out of doin' anythin' when I told him I thought you were a spy.'

'At any rate,' Bingham continued, 'when war was declared, German Intelligence evidently decided that it would be necessary for us to reveal ourselves to each other.'

'Because you could do more damage workin' as a team?' Becky asked.

'Exactly. Captain Davenport contacted me late yesterday afternoon, and told me what our first target would be. And I, of course, immediately informed the local police.'

'What about the other two men?'

'I met them for the first time at the factory gates.' Bingham laughed again. 'It was a rather short meeting, wasn't it?'

'Why would any man betray his own country?' Jim wondered.

'Are you referring to Captain Davenport?'

'Yes.'

'He wasn't betraying his country. He may have one English parent – just as my own mother is German – but from his accent, I would say he comes originally from Hamburg.'

'So all that about sailin' on the tall ships to China was a lie, was it?' Jim asked.

'Almost certainly, a lie which he will have used to cover the time while he was probably a serving officer in the German navy.'

'What will happen to him now?' Becky asked.

'We shall turn him,' Bingham said.

'What does that mean?'

'It means that he'll be working for us. He and the other members of his network will continue to send reports back to Berlin, but like the reports I send myself, they will be grossly inaccurate.'

'So we're not likely to read about his arrest in tomorrow's *Guardian*, are we?' Becky asked.

'You may never read of his arrest,' Bingham said. 'We like to keep our activities as secret as possible, and publicity of that nature is the last thing we want.' Bingham checked his watch. 'It will be light in an hour or so. I suggest you do your best to reach your homes while we are still in darkness.'

'You mean we're free to go?' Jim asked.

'Yes,' Bingham replied. 'But please remember that you are now bound by the Official Secrets Act.'

'As if we're likely to forget,' Becky said.

She stood up and discovered how exhausted she was. But it was only her body which tired. Her mind still raced with excitement over what had happened during the night. She had not felt so alive for years!

Chapter Nineteen

It was the twelfth of December. The woods, which Ivy had tempted Spudder to walk in only a few weeks earlier, were no longer golden brown. Now the trees were stark and bare, and it was impossible to walk between them without crunching the thousands of frosted leaves which lay at their roots.

Blue tits and long-tailed tits hung from the topmost branches of the skeletal trees, in a desperate search for the tiny insects which would give them the strength to carry on. Owls slept by day and hunted voles by night, and the robins fluttered around the back yards of Marston in the hope that their splendid red breasts might coax the householders into giving them a little charity.

It was a bleak midwinter, yet it was not entirely without signs of hope. In some sheltered spots, the wrinkled leaves of the next season's primroses were already breaking through the ground, and the lamb's-tail catkins on the hazel bushes were already formed and yellowing, in anticipation of shedding pollen early in the new year.

In the midst of life we are in death, it said in the prayer book. And nature, which knew about such things, replied that in the midst of death, we are also in life.

Becky placed the Christmas tree in the corner of the front parlour, then stepped back to take a proper look at it. It was a good tree, she decided, one of the nicest that they'd ever had.

She searched around in the battered, ancient box which contained the tin ornaments, and finally produced the big gold star. Start at the top of the tree and work your way down, she told herself. That was how she and her family had always done it, and she saw no reason to change her habits at this stage.

It was daft, in a way, to go through all this palaver, she thought. After all, there were only the two of them left at home now, and Michelle a grown woman. Yet somehow, she couldn't quite bring herself to give it up.

As she hung a lantern from one of the upper branches, she remembered the Christmases of her childhood, spent in number 47 with her man, dad, three brothers and two sisters. Now Mam and Dad were dead, and though her sisters had never moved far away from home, the lads were scattered all over the place. Jack was still working the oil rivers, despite what had happened to Michael; George was in London, looking after his wood yard down by the river; and Philip – well, Philip, as mad as ever, was talking of moving to America, because, he said, that was where the *real* pictures were going to be made.

Becky's mind drifted slowly on to the Christmas when Billy had finally learned to talk, after all the worry that he never would. Then there was the one when Spudder had first moved into number 49 as Mam's lodger. And the one when Michael didn't come home because . . .

The tree decoration was completed. Becky stepped back and inspected her handiwork. She'd done a good job, and it looked pretty much like every other tree she'd decorated, but somehow it didn't *feel* the same. 'Next year, I won't bother,' she said to herself. Next year, instead of gazing over her shoulder at the past, she would look to the future.

She heard the back door open. It would be Michelle, returning from the Victoria works. She was worried about the girl, and she had good reason to be. There were moments when Michelle looked happy – almost radiantly so – and then a black mood would settle over her, and she seemed to be carrying the whole weight of the world on her shoulders. It was all the fault of Gerald Worrell, of course.

'I told you that you were wrong about him, Mam,' Michelle had said when she'd returned from seeing him off at Northwich Station, a month earlier.

'And just *how* am I wrong about him?'

'You said once I'd given him what he was after, he'd want no more to do with me. Well, he does! He loves me, and he wants to marry me as soon as he can.'

But Becky had still not been convinced. His sort always talked like that. Probably all he was after was another roll in the hay the next time he was home on leave. 'But can I convince Michelle of that?' she asked the newly decorated tree. 'Can I hell as like!'

She went back to the kitchen. Michelle was sitting at the table, still dressed in her baggy munitions factory uniform.

'Aren't you goin' to get changed out of your work clothes, love?' Becky asked.

'In a minute,' Michelle replied. 'When I've just had a little bit of a rest.'

She was always so tired these days, Becky thought. Maybe it was the work at the factory that was taking it out of her. Yet she was a strong enough girl – she should have been able to take the extra strain in her stride.

Michelle rested her head in her hands, almost as if it would not stay upright without their support. 'You wouldn't fancy making me a cup of tea, would you, Mam?' she asked.

'Is somethin' wrong? Are you feelin' ill, love?'

Michelle shook her head, weakly. 'Like I said to you, I'm just a bit tired.'

Becky sat down and looked her daughter in the face. 'You look more than tired to me,' she said. 'You look positively drained.'

'I'll be all right,' Michelle insisted, irritably. And then both her eyes went completely blank and she fainted dead away.

When Michelle came round again, she was lying in her bed and her mother was sitting in the chair beside her. It was hard to read the expression on her mam's face. There was worry there, certainly, and perhaps a little confusion, but also, bubbling away just below the surface, there was a raging anger.

'I had the doctor round to examine you,' Becky said, and Michelle could tell that it was taking her mother all her effort to keep her voice steady.

'Did you hear what I said to you?' Becky repeated – 'I had the doctor round.'

'I heard, Mam.'

Becky stood up, and began pacing the room. 'I should have

guessed meself, without the doctor's help, but I suppose there's none so blind as those as won't see.'

'Mam . . .'

Becky had reached the window, and had her back to Michelle, but now she swung round to confront her daughter. 'It's a bit of a bugger when you have to learn from other people what you should have been told by your own family,' she said angrily.

'I was going to tell you, Mam. Honestly, I was.'

'When?'

'Soon.'

Becky began pacing again, and now she had her arms crossed hugging herself. 'An' don't go pinnin' your hopes on Gerald Worrell,' she said, 'because he won't marry you. As soon as he finds that out you're expectin', he'll run a mile.'

'He knows already,' Michelle said calmly.

'You mean to say that you told him before you told me, your own mother?'

'You might be my mother, but he's the father of my child. He had the right to know first.'

'I see,' Becky said. 'An' how did wonderful Gerald, who loves you so much, take the news?'

'He wrote to me.'

'Did he! Well, that was nice of him.'

'The letter's in my top drawer. You can read it yourself, if you want to.'

'Oh, I do want to. Indeed I do,' Becky said, opening the drawer and taking the letter out.

My Dearest Michelle, she read aloud,

I don't know what to say to your letter. Of course, I want us to have children when we are married, but it came as a great shock to me to hear that you are already pregnant.

'You see,' Becky said. 'He's tryin' to get out of his responsibilities already.'

'Read the rest, Mam,' Michelle pleaded.

However, if that is the situation, we must make the best of

it. I calculate the baby will be born in June. I cannot possibly expect to be given any leave immediately . . .

'It's just like I told you,' Becky said.

'You won't give him a chance, will you?' Michelle demanded, angrily. 'Whatever he does, whatever he says, you won't give him a chance.'

'Give one of the Worrells a chance and they'll . . .'

'Finish the letter, Mam! Finish the bloody letter!'

There was a commanding edge to her daughter's voice which Becky had never heard before. She looked down at the tight, neat handwriting once more.

. . . cannot possibly expect to be given any leave immediately – nor would I ask for it while the position here is so critical – but I promise you I will return to England not later than February, and then we can be married right away.

Your loving
Gerald.

P.S. I have just reread this letter, and it sounds as if I am not pleased about the baby. But I am. Really I am.
P.P.S. You will not have to go through the humiliation of marrying a humble lieutenant. I have just received a field promotion to captain.

'Well?' Michelle asked.

Becky walked over to the window, and looked out. A rook was hopping along the back wall, and a finch perched, shivering, on the wash-house roof. In the distance, she could see the holly bushes, though not clearly enough to distinguish their bright red berries.

'Maybe I was wrong,' Becky said grudgingly. She turned slowly and faced her daughter. 'No, damn it, there's no question about maybe. I *was* wrong – totally an' completely wrong. I was lettin' my feelin's about the father cloud my judgement of the son.' She walked over to Michelle's bed and put her hand on her daughter's head. 'I'm sorry, love. I must have given you a very hard time.'

Michelle smiled. 'That's all right, Mam. We all make mistakes now and again.'

'You're bein' nicer to me that I deserve,' Becky told her daughter.

Michelle hesitated before she spoke again. 'But if you really are sorry . . . there's something you could do to make up for it.'

Becky's smile matched her daughter's. 'Just tell me what it is, an' I'll do it.'

'You can go and see Uncle Richard. Go and see him, and make your peace with him.'

Becky had started to stroke her daughter's hair, but now her hand froze. 'I can't,' she said.

'You *have* to,' Michelle told her. 'In a few weeks' time, he's going to be my father-in-law.'

Becky sighed. 'The last time I was in the same room as Richard Worrell was when you were a little girl. I went to see him about adoptin' Billy. I didn't want to see him, but I knew that speakin' to him directly was the only way I'd get what I wanted. I had to force myself to do it, Michelle, an' even though it was so important, I almost backed out at the last minute.'

'That was a long time ago, Mam.'

'Not to me, it isn't,' Becky said fiercely. 'Even when I just catch sight of him in the street, it makes my flesh crawl. You'd have to be me to understand how I feel, Michelle. I just can't be near him – not even for you.'

Richard Worrell strode furiously up and down his study. He was not alone. Sitting in one of a pair of matching leather armchairs was a small man with a bald, heavily veined head, and teeth which had been rotting for years, but refused to fall out.

'He says that he actually wants to marry the little slut!' Richard thundered.

Horace Crimp took a dirty toothpick from his waistcoat pocket and probed one of the gaps between his teeth.

'Did you hear what I said?' Richard demanded of his attorney. 'He wants to marry her.'

'I not only heard you, Mr Worrell, but I have also read the letter in which he conveyed the information,' Crimp replied mildly.

'And what are you going to do about it?'

Crimp sighed. 'Over the years, Mr Worrell, I have been of considerable service to you.'

'You've been well paid for it, haven't you?'

'It was I who arranged the deal which robbed . . . er . . . perhaps I should say which "relieved" your late brother of his share of the saltworks.'

'I know that, you fool!'

'And it was I who contrived to have your wife committed to a lunatic asylum.'

'And you who helped me fight Hortense and that bitch Becky Taylor when they tried to take permanent custody of my son from me. I know all that. The question I'm asking you, Crimp, is what are you going to do now?'

Crimp continued to explore his rotting stumps with the toothpick. 'That is exactly the point I am trying to make,' he said. 'I have pulled you out of some very difficult situations in the past, but this is different. Your son is over twenty-one, and therefore legally an adult. If he wishes to marry his cousin – or the hag who washes your soiled underclothes, for that matter – then there is nothing that I, or anyone else, can do to stop him.'

'Nothing!' Richard repeated, finding it almost impossible to believe that Horace Crimp, who had always come up with a solution to his problems before, was failing him this time. He looked out of the window, and remembered the days when he had watched little Gerald bravely jumping his pony over the hurdles that his doting father had had erected for him.

'I'm prepared to pay whatever it will cost, if only we can stop this disastrous—'

'It is not a question of money,' Crimp interrupted him. 'For once, Mr Worrell, you will simply have to face the fact that you have been defeated.'

What a fool he'd been, Richard thought. If only his thirst for revenge hadn't been so strong, he would never have made that foolish wager. And if he had not done that, then Gerald would never have fallen in love with his cousin.

'Might I offer one piece of advice?' Crimp asked. 'And for once, it will not be *legal* advice.'

'Have your say,' Richard said gruffly.

'You cannot prevent the marriage, and if you attempt to do so, you run the risk of alienating your son's affections.'

'Rubbish!'

'I would go one step further. Even if you do not fight the marriage, but still maintain this rift between the two branches of your family, you will be forcing your son to make a choice between yourself and his new wife's closest relatives. And I think that he may well choose the other side.'

'He would never do that!' Richard exploded. Yet he was no longer as sure of himself as he had once been. The old Gerald, whom he had taken whoring with him, was not the same person as the Gerald who had come home on leave. The old Gerald would never have talked about the common soldiers in the way this new one did. Nor would he have been foolish enough to be trapped into marriage by his scheming cousin. So it was just possible that Crimp was right.

Could Gerald become so infatuated by his new wife that he never came near Peak House? he wondered. If that happened, then what did he, himself, have to look forward to, except a lonely old age and a solitary death? He just couldn't take that.

He bowed his head in defeat. 'What do you advise me to do?' he asked Crimp.

'It could do no harm for you to go and see Mrs Rebecca Worrell,' the attorney said.

'What!'

'After all, you have the perfect excuse for doing so. Time is short, and there are a considerable number of arrangements to be made with regard to the wedding.'

Richard pictured himself sitting across the table from Becky, discussing carriages and receptions, helping to plan his own son's destruction. He had been prepared to compromise – to make sacrifices, even – but that was just too much.

'Talk to *her*?' Richard shouted. 'Talk to that bitch who has tried to thwart me at every turn? Never!'

The Christmases of Spudder's childhood – spent imprisoned in an upstairs room by a father who'd been ashamed of him – had been no more and no less miserable than the rest of the year.

Then he'd come to Marston, become Mam's boarder, and learned what a wonderful event the holiday could be.

Yet this year, despite having the usual trappings of a tree and decorations, he couldn't seem to raise his normal enthusiasm for the festivities.

Maybe it's because I've got somethin' else on me mind, this year, he thought. Yes, that might be it – his mind never had been able to cope with two things at the same time.

It was Christmas Eve when he decided he had to do something about his dilemma. He and Aggie Spratt were alone in his kitchen. He was sitting at the table, and Aggie was doing some last-minute dusting before she went home to prepare the gargantuan feast that her husband, Ned, expected not just for Christmas, but on every day of the year.

'Aggie?' Spudder said tentatively.

'Yes?'

'You remember when Ivy first arrived?'

'It's only a few months, so I'm not likely to have forgotten, am I, now?'

'No, I suppose not.'

'Why don't you tell me what's on your mind, Spudder?'

'When Ivy arrived, you told me I should . . . er . . . should talk to you if I started gettin' feelin's about her.'

'That's right. I did.'

'Well, I think I am.'

Aggie never sat down at work, but now she put her duster on the Welsh dresser and levered her massive frame into the chair opposite Spudder's. 'What kind of feelin' are you startin' to get, Spudder?' she asked softly, her huge forearms covering half the table.

'I don't really know,' Spudder admitted. 'It's just that sometimes, when I look at Ivy, I get this sort of flutterin' in me stomach.'

Aggie nodded her head. 'Butterflies,' she said. 'A sure sign of love. That's how my Ned goes whenever he sees one of my meat pies. Anythin' else?'

Spudder started to redden. 'There is somethin' else, but I don't really want to talk about it.'

Aggie grinned. 'I've watched six kids of me own grow up –

four of 'em lads – so if you think you're goin' to shock me, you couldn't be wronger.'

'Maybe your lads were different to me,' Spudder said. 'Did they . . .?'

'Did they find that a part of them which is usually soft can go hard sometimes?'

'Yes, that's it,' Spudder admitted guiltily.

'Well, of course they did. Every young man does. It's only natural.'

Spudder took out his handkerchief, and mopped his brow. 'That's a relief,' he said.

'The question is, now you've got these feelin's, what are you goin' to do about them?'

'I could ask Ivy to marry me,' Spudder said quickly. 'Do you think she would?'

'She might,' Aggie told him, 'but it's never a good idea to rush into things.'

'How do you mean?'

'You need time to get to know one another proper – decide if you're right for each other.'

'But I do know her,' Spudder protested. 'I see her every day, don't I?'

'You see her when she's at work, when you're her employer. That's not what I'm talkin' about. You have to get to know the person she is *outside* work.'

'An' how do I do that?'

Aggie shifted her forearms, and the table wobbled dangerously. 'Gettin' to know people is what they invented courtship for,' she said.

Spudder looked confused. 'But I don't know anythin' about courtin' anybody,' he said. 'How would I do it?'

'Well, you can stop lettin' her make all the runnin', for a start.' Aggie told him. 'Instead of Ivy always askin' you out, *you* should ask *her* out for a change.'

'But I wouldn't know where to take her.'

'I'm sure you could come up with somethin' if you just put your thinkin' cap on.'

An expression of panic came to Spudder's face. 'But I don't have a thinkin' cap,' he said. Then he relaxed again. 'I'll get one. As soon as the shops open tomorrer, I'll go into Northwich an' buy one. Are they very expensive?'

Aggie sighed. It wasn't always easy getting through to Spudder. 'All I meant was that if you really try, you're bound to come up with an idea.'

'Oh, I see,' Spudder said, sounding far from convinced. 'Is there anythin' else I should be doin'?'

'Yes. You should give her little presents now an' again, to show her that you care for her.'

'I gave her a bag of chips the other day,' Spudder said. 'An' a fish to go with it.'

Aggie sighed again. 'Chips – even if you throw in a fish as well – aren't exactly romantic, are they? You want to give her flowers, an' things like that.'

'But if she wants flowers, she can go down to the woods an' pick as many as she wants.'

'I'm not talkin' about *wild* flowers, you daft 'a'p'orth. I mean bought flowers. From a shop!'

'An' she'll like that, will she?' Spudder asked, although now he thought about it, he did remember that Ivy had mentioned flowers when they had gone out on the river, the day she had tried to . . .

'She'd be a rum sort of woman if she didn't like havin' flowers given to her,' Aggie said.

Spudder frowned. 'This courtin' lark all seems very complicated to me,' he said. 'Couldn't I forget about it, an' just ask her if she'll marry me?'

'No,' Aggie said firmly. 'No, you could not.'

From the air, the trenches looked like a huge wound, gashed savagely across the landscape. To the men on the ground they were more like endless tunnels which cramped and confined them – and eventually served as the gateway to death.

The bad weather had set in with a vengeance. Most mornings there was a sharp frost which clung to the creases of the cheap khaki uniforms and gave the furrows in the ground razor-sharp edges. Sometimes the heavy snow clouds would mass menacingly above the trenches, then bombard the shivering souls below with millions of tiny missiles. Men from the far north of

Britain, who had known cold all their lives, said they had never experienced anything like it. The rats, which outnumbered even the soldiers, moved with the lethargy that extreme cold can bring.

Winter had slowed down the fighting on the Western Front, but not brought it to a complete halt. Shells were still fired by both sides, and snipers sometimes got in a lucky shot. Overhead, tiny aeroplanes battled it out, gaining no strategic advantage from their victories, and only oblivion from their defeats.

And then there were the ordinary soldiers – the poor bloody infantry, as they were known – ordered over the top for the occasional sortie because someone in Divisional Headquarters had decided that the Devil finds work for idle hands – and to avoid that happening, sent innocent men into hell.

It was just after dawn. Gerald and Billy stood side by side in a trench which had been named Witton Street since the Cheshires arrived in it, but was Oxford Street the week before that, and would acquire another new name when a fresh regiment made it their temporary shelter. Gerald took out a packet of Woodbines, and offered one to Billy. They both lit up and inhaled deeply.

'My request for leave's been processed at last,' Gerald said.

'When's it to be?'

'The middle of February.'

'An' you'll be gettin' married as soon as you're back in good old Cheshire?'

'That's right.' Gerald took another drag of his cigarette. 'I'm sorry you won't be there for my wedding. I did try to swing it, you know. I would have liked you to have been my best man.'

Billy grinned. 'Well, you know how things are in the army,' he said, goodnaturedly. 'If you're an officer, you can get your trips back to Blighty any time you want them. Yellow parchment on demand, as you might say. It's only us poor bloody privates who are stuck with the Hôtel des Ramparts.'

The relative silence was suddenly shattered by the booming of artillery from the German lines.

'They're a little late with the Morning Hate today, aren't they?' Gerald asked.

'Maybe the Huns are finally runnin' out of ammunition,' Billy said hopefully, but neither of them believed that the Germans were running short. They had both been in the trenches long enough to know that as long as there were men to kill, there would be the bullets and the shells to do it with.

There were roars from behind them, as the British guns returned the fire of the Germans.

'Sorry you joined up?' Gerald asked, as a shell exploded close enough to the trench to shower them with small fragments of frozen earth.

'No,' Billy said. 'Are you?'

Gerald shook his head. 'It's a bloody awful war, and the brass hats on *both* sides are idiots to fight it the way they are. But we're stuck with it and we're stuck with them, and I don't see how I could ever hold my head up high again if I let someone else do my fighting for me.'

Gerald's sergeant – a regular soldier with a solid fifteen years' experience behind him – approached, saluted, and handed Gerald a sheet of paper. 'Fresh orders, sir,' he said. 'Just come through.'

Gerald unfolded the paper and quickly scanned the message. He frowned, then checked his watch. 'We're going over the top in exactly half an hour, Sergeant,' he said.

'I thought we might be, sir.'

'Very well, then. Put the men on stand to.'

The sergeant looked questioningly at Billy.

'It's quite all right,' Gerald told him. 'I haven't finished talking to Private Worrell yet, but I'll make sure that he doesn't miss the big show.'

The sergeant grinned, saluted again, and was gone.

'Got the wind up, Billy?' Gerald asked.

'A bit,' Billy admitted, then added 'sir,' because now they were going into action, Gerald was no longer his half-brother or even his future brother-in-law, but Captain Worrell, a commander he trusted with his life.

Another shell exploded near the trench. More frozen earth rained down on them like a plague sent from heaven.

'I'm a little windy myself,' Gerald confessed. 'Though God knows why. We'll either get killed, or we won't.'

'Yes, those are the only two outcomes,' Billy agreed, forcing himself to grin again.

Gerald stubbed his cigarette against the side of the trench. 'About ready to move out, Private Worrell?' he asked.

'Yes, sir,' Billy replied.

They walked down Witton Street side by side. They knew, as they did every time they went over the top, that it might be their last chance to do so.

Chapter Twenty

It was a bitterly cold mid-January day on Northwich Railway Station. The wind screamed down the track, carrying with it sheets of old newspapers, empty tin cans and other assorted rubbish. On the platform itself, doors banged and the gaslight brackets rattled in protest. It was not a morning when anyone would have chosen to be outside.

Becky looked at the poster which had recently been pasted up next to the third-class waiting room.

I WILL BE A MAN
AND ENLIST TODAY it read.

George was right, she thought. They should never have let this war happen.

She turned to her daughter, who was standing next to her, dressed from head to foot entirely in black. 'How you bearin' up, love?' she asked.

'Not too well,' Michelle admitted, taking out her handkerchief and dabbing her eyes.

'I know it's hard,' Becky said. 'Just do your best, love. Your brother Billy's entitled to a little respect.'

'I know he is, Mam,' Michelle said tearfully. 'And I will try. Honestly I will.'

How many trains had she met and seen off on this very station? Becky wondered. There was the one her brother Philip had taken to avoid a beating from Cedric Rathbone. The one George and Colleen had caught when they'd made their move to London. The one that had brought Michael's body home. So many trains – a lifetime of saying hellos and goodbyes. No more lookin' back, she promised herself. From now on she would look to the future – whatever it held in store for her.

'It's comin', Mam,' Michelle said, and in the distance they could hear the faint chugging of the train.

Becky looked up and down the platform. There were plenty of women standing there: women in nurses' uniforms; women from the Volunteer Reserves; women factory workers in their baggy pants. There were far fewer young men waiting to catch the train than there would have been six months earlier, but then there were far fewer young men around the town than there used to be.

The train steamed into the station. 'Where do you think he'll be, Mam?' Michelle asked.

'In his condition, I should think they'll have put him in the guards' van.' The two women walked quickly down the platform, towards the point at which the back end of the train would stop.

The locomotive came to a complete halt, and the station was suddenly full of life.

Carriage doors were flung open, and young soldiers stepped out to be greeted by happy, weeping sweethearts. Two members of the Women's Police Patrol, their broad hats pulled down tightly against the wind, moved up and down the platform, looking for any girls or young women who might fall easy prey to the returning warriors.

A team of women football players, who had a match arranged against the Plumley munitions works, shivered as the wind hit them, then wrapped their coats tightly around themselves to protect their bare knees from the cold.

The whole station echoed with the organised chaos that only comes in wartime.

Becky and Michelle threaded their way through the mob, and finally reached the guards' van. One of the guards was sliding the heavy door open, and just behind him they could see Billy lying flat out on a stretcher. Becky reached for one of the iron grips to pull herself up and into the van.

'You can't come in here, missus,' one of the guards protested. 'Only persons on official railway business are allowed access to the guards' van.'

'Oh, get away with your nonsense,' Becky said impatiently, heaving herself up and brushing the guard aside with a sweep of her hand. 'That's my son lyin' there.'

She knelt down by the stretcher. She wanted to hug Billy, but in his condition she wasn't sure if she should.

Billy looked up and smiled at her. 'How have you been keepin', Mam?' he asked.

Becky smiled back. 'Better than you, by the look of you.' The smile retreated and a worried look replaced it. 'How bad are you feelin' really?'

'Not too bad,' Billy said. 'I've got a bullet wound in me leg, an' three of me ribs were smashed . . .'

'Oh, God!'

' . . . but the quacks in the field hospital said that with a bit of the right care and attention it shouldn't be that long before I've mended almost as good as new.'

'You better *had* mend as good as new,' Becky said threateningly, 'or you'll have me to answer to.'

Billy looked down at his bandaged chest. 'You hear that, ribs?' he asked. 'Start knitting together quick, or you'll have me mam to answer to.'

Becky turned her attention to the guard. 'Can I take him home now?' she asked.

'As soon as you've signed this chitty for him,' the man replied, producing an official-looking piece of paper.

Becky signed, and then signalled to her two carmen, who were waiting next to the ticket office.

'You'll get so much motherin' from me, you'll wish you were back in France,' she told Billy.

Standing alone on the platform, still well out of her brother's range of vision, Michelle did her very best to force a welcoming smile to her lips.

The moment she had learned of Gerald's death would stay in Michelle's mind for ever. She'd been at the factory, just one of an army of baggy-overalled women whose sweethearts were overseas. She had no more or less worries than anyone else, until she'd heard the two girls next to her talking.

'You know me Uncle Dave, the one that's a waller at Worrell's saltworks?'

'What about him?'

'Well, he told me that Mr Worrell's had one of them telegrams.'

'What telegrams?'

'The ones your closest relatives get to tell them that you've been killed in action.'

'Which Worrell's saltworks are you talking about?' Michelle had demanded.

'As far as I know, there is only one. Right next to the bridge in Marston.'

'And are you sure it's Mr Worrell who's got the telegram?' Michelle had asked, hoping – praying – that the girl would tell her she'd got confused, and it was really one of Mr Worrell's foremen she was talking about.

'It was Mr Worrell, all right. Accordin' to me Uncle Dave, he was really cut up about it. But then that's only to be expected under the circumstances, isn't it?'

Disbelief had come first, rapidly followed by shock and then despair. Yet in the days that followed, she forced herself to work through it, because even if the man she loved was dead, there were other boys over there who were depending on the shells. And if she let them down, she would, in some mysterious way, be letting her beloved Gerald down, too.

She tried to tell herself that she'd been lucky – that she could have lost Billy, too – but it didn't work like that. Life wasn't some neat balance in which you could weigh the good against the bad and end up with some kind of mental equilibrium.

The days passed, and though she learned to believe in Gerald's death, she did not learn to accept it. As far as she was concerned, her own life had ended at the same time as his. True, she was still walking around, eating and going through her normal daily chores, while he lay dismembered in some foreign field, but inside she felt just as dead as if she'd been in that foxhole with him when the shell landed.

Richard Worrell had been drunk for days, ever since he got the telegram. 'It can't be true!' he told himself, again and again. 'It just isn't possible!' His Gerald, his wonderful golden boy, wasn't dead. It was all a mistake. Some other Captain Gerald Worrell had been shot, and his son would walk through the door any second and say that he hoped his father had not been too worried about him.

Yet deep in his heart, he knew it was no mistake – that there was only one Captain Gerald Worrell, and he would never be coming home again.

Images of Gerald flashed before his eyes. The baby who had been born the day Michael's saltworks had been flooded. The small boy who had not wanted to admit he was afraid of jumping his pony over the hurdles Richard had set up in the grounds, so had bitten his lip and urged his mount forward. The soldier, who had spoken of his responsibility to his men. All of them Gerald – all of them gone for ever.

He cursed the war, and cursed the men who had survived while his son had paid the ultimate price. He wished they were dead, all of them, Germans and British alike.

It was time for another shot of booze. He reached out drunkenly, grabbed the bottle and drank straight from the neck.

'Why *my* son?' he moaned. 'Why not someone else's?'

He heard footsteps, and looked up to see that his butler had entered the room. 'I didn't ring for you,' he snarled. 'What you doing coming disturbing me when I didn't ring for you?'

'With respect, sir, you asked to be informed the moment Mr William Worrell arrived in Northwich, sir.'

Richard did his best to focus his bleary eyes. 'Billy?' he said. 'Billy's back home?'

'I have just been told that he arrived on the ten-thirty train, sir.'

'Run me a bath,' Richard said. 'A cold one. And I want coffee. Lotsa coffee.'

The butler raised a discreet eyebrow. 'Certainly, sir. And will you be at home for luncheon?'

'No,' Richard slurred. 'I will not be at home for luncheon. I'm going visiting.'

Billy was resting upstairs, and Becky and Michelle were just making themselves a soothing pot of tea when they heard the knock on the kitchen door.

'Could you answer it, Mam?' Michelle asked miserably. 'I don't think I could face anybody right now.'

'I know you can't, my poor little love,' Becky clucked sympathetically. 'Why don't you go an' have a lie down an' I'll bring your tea up to you as soon as it's brewed?'

Michelle nodded gratefully. 'Thanks, Mam,' she said, standing up and walking over to the stairs.

Becky opened the kitchen door. She'd had no idea who would be standing there, but never in her wildest dreams would she have imagined it to be *him*.

'Oh, my God!' she gasped. She blinked, still hardly able to believe it. But it was true. Richard – whom she hadn't spoken to for nearly twenty years – was standing on her step. She felt a tightness around her throat and her head began to swim. She clutched the door jamb for support.

'I'm sorry, Becky. It wasn't my intention to startle you,' the apparition said.

'Wasn't your intention to . . . How the . . .' Becky groped for words and finally found the right ones. 'What the hell do you think you're doin' here?' she demanded.

Richard looked her straight in the eyes. 'I want a favour from you,' he said.

Now that she had recovered a little from the shock of seeing him, Becky began to realise what a bad state Richard was in. His eyes were red and his face was drawn. He stank of alcohol, but she was sure he was not drunk at that moment.

'What kind of favour do you want?' she asked fearfully.

'They tell me your son arrived home today. I'd like to see him.'

Becky felt her panic increasing with every second which passed. Why should Richard want to see Billy? To hurt him? To rant and rave at him, because he was alive and Gerald wasn't?

'He's very tired after his journey,' she said. 'He can't see you now. Maybe another day.' But there wouldn't be another day – not if she could help it. She would do all in her power to keep this evil man away from her poor wounded son.

'It's very important,' Richard said. 'Billy was with Gerald when he was killed. I just want to talk to him about it, to learn how my son died.'

'That's all?'

'That's all. I promise. It really matters to me. Please let me see him, Becky!'

She had never heard him plead for anything before. She saw the tears forming in his eyes and sighed. 'You'd better come in,' she said. 'Pour yourself a cup of tea while I see if he's feelin' strong enough to see you.'

Richard angled the bedside chair so that Billy could see him without moving, and sat down. 'It was very kind of you to agree to talk to me,' he said.

'You're me captain's dad. If I don't owe it to you, I owe it to him,' Billy replied.

'Thank you, anyway.'

There was a pause, and then Billy said, 'I suppose you want to know how it happened.'

Richard gritted his teeth. 'Yes, that's exactly what I want to know,' he admitted.

They lined up in front of the trench ladders. They were not the first to go over the top, and already there was the manic clatter of a machine-gun from somewhere out there.

Billy's turn came. He placed his hands on the ladder and began to climb, but though he could feel the wood against the palms of his hands, none of it seemed real.

And then, almost before he knew it, he was out of the trench and advancing towards no-man's land, his bayonet pointing the way and the kit on his back feeling as heavy as if it were made of lead.

Ahead of him, he could already see fallen comrades – some he knew and some he would now never meet.

'We'd nearly reached the Hun's front line when the machine-gun opened up,' he told Richard.

It had been to the left of them, sweeping round in a wide arc, scything men as if they were nothing more than blades of corn. Though his own company was out of its reach, Billy felt his bowels turn to water, and wondered where he would find the courage to go on. Then, suddenly, Captain Worrell was standing next to him.

'We have to knock that blighter out before he can do any more damage,' Gerald said.

'Just like that?' Richard asked. 'Without any thought of the possible danger?'

Billy smiled. 'Oh aye, that was the Captain for you,' he said. His face turned sombre again. 'To tell you the truth, it's a wonder he lasted as long as he did.'

'Go on with the story,' Richard said softly.

They moved up on the Germans' blind side, though they were well aware that the closer they got, the greater the possibility that they would be spotted. They could see men from other companies falling as if they were puppets whose strings had been cut.

'We were nearly at their dug-out when they saw us,' Billy said.

'And what did they do?'

'Swung the gun round on to us, of course.'

'And was that when my son was killed?'

'No, not then.'

Gerald had reached the wire, and however much the Huns swung the gun round, they could never get the right angle, and they knew it, so they didn't even waste their time trying. Instead, the machine-gunner concentrated on knocking out the back of the column.

Almost before he knew what was happening, Billy was down on the ground, rolling around in the frozen mud and wishing he was dead. But he wasn't dead, not even seriously wounded, and he still had his duty to do. He forced himself to stop writhing, and raised his head to see if he could be of any further use.

The Captain, and a few other members of his company, had reached the wire, and Gerald had managed to cut a hole in it. As Billy lay there, gasping with agony, Gerald led his remaining five or six men through the gap.

They were too near to the enemy to use their rifles, so they relied on their bayonets instead. Even in the watery winter sun, the steel glinted as it slashed its way through the air. Gerald had his pistol in his hand. He pulled the trigger twice, and two of the Germans guarding the machine-gun nest went down. But he was in far too close. A Hun, no more than a scared kid, came up from behind Gerald and bayoneted him in the back.

The German lad was still looking at his bloody bayonet – as if he was wondering how it ever got to be so red – when Gerald rolled over and shot him.

By then, Billy was moving again, dragging himself slowly and painfully towards the machine-gun nest, because he knew that however bad a state he was in, Gerald was in a worse one. And Gerald was his captain, his half-brother and, most of all, his friend.

Then the shelling started.

'From the German side?' Richard asked.

'No, from our side. See, what our gunners were tryin' to do was to get beyond the German lines, but a few of the shells were fallin' a bit short, an' one of 'em landed right on top of the German machine-gun nest.'

'So he was killed by British artillery.'

'Yes, I'm afraid he was.'

'And if he'd only waited a few more minutes, there'd have been no need to make the sacrifice at all, because the shell would have destroyed the machine-gun nest anyway. Isn't that right?'

Billy shrugged. 'Maybe, but a soldier like your son wouldn't see it that way, Mr Worrell.'

'How *would* he see it?'

'He'd have seen it as somethin' he had to do anyway. That's the way it is with war. You never know what you could have done, so you just have to get on with doin' what you *can.*'

Richard had been controlling himself well for most of the conversation, but now an expression of pain flashed across his face. 'Did you see his body?' he asked.

Billy looked uneasy. 'I don't think you want to hear about that, Mr Worrell.'

'I have the right to know,' Richard said. 'I have the right to know *everything*.'

'All right,' Billy agreed reluctantly. 'If you really insist, then I'll tell you.'

He crawled along the frozen ground, sometimes hauling himself over fallen comrades, sometimes merely staining his uniform with their blood. It was not far to the dug-out, but it was the longest journey he had ever made.

Finally, after a greater struggle than he'd ever have believed he could endure, he reached the gap which Gerald had cut in the wire – and wished he hadn't.

'You've no idea what kind of damage a direct hit from a shell can do unless you've actually seen it for yourself,' Billy said. 'There were arms and legs all over the place. Heads, as well, though by then they didn't look very much like they'd ever belonged to real people.'

Richard nodded solemnly. 'I see,' he said. 'Is all you've told me true?'

'Every word of it.'

'You haven't changed any of the details, to put Gerald in a more favourable light?'

'I swear I haven't.'

Richard sighed with what may have been relief. 'So my son really did die a hero's death.'

'It was just about as heroic as it could possibly have been,' Billy agreed.

Richard stood up. 'Thank you for your time. It was very kind of you.' He had almost reached the door, when he stopped and turned around. 'Er, Billy . . .'

'Yes, Mr Worrell?'

'I don't know how much you've been told about this, but I treated you very badly when you were young.'

'Are you talkin' about fosterin' me out to the woman on the coal barge?'

'Yes, God help me, that's what I'm talking about. Was it a really terrible place?'

'Well, me mam an' Uncle Spudder tell me that it wasn't no picnic, but I don't really remember it meself.'

'It was a wicked thing for me to have done,' Richard said. 'I see that now. I see so many things now.'

'We all make mistakes.'

'But some are worse than others. I hope that in time, you can learn to forgive me for treating you so badly.'

'Forget it,' Billy said generously. 'All water under the bridge, isn't it? Besides, if you'd looked after me like you should have done, I'd never have got adopted by Mam, would I? An' I wouldn't have missed bein' brought up by her for the whole world.'

Richard smiled sadly. 'I admire you, Billy,' he said. 'You know when you're lucky.' A faraway look came into Richard's eyes. 'I only wish *I'd* been able to recognise good fortune when it was staring me in the face,' he continued. 'Thank you again for telling me about my son.' And then he turned and was gone.

PART THREE

Rising From the Ashes

Chapter Twenty-one

It was late January, and the cold weather had really started to bite. The wealthy of Northwich ordered their servants to light fires in their bedrooms, but for the ordinary folk, this was a luxury well beyond their budgets. And so, for the less well-off, it was simply a case of removing the copper bedwarmers from between their sheets, diving under as many blankets as they could afford, and praying that the temperature wouldn't drop so low that frost would form on the insides of their windows.

Getting up was even worse than going to bed. Lying in the midst of a layer of warm air that had taken all night to create, it was hard for people to persuade themselves that it was a good idea to throw off their blankets, place their feet on the icy linoleum and face another day of teeth-chattering cold.

But it had to be done, they told themselves – and, after all, there were worse things happening in France.

Whatever the weather, Ned Spratt never had any trouble getting out of bed. He would have gone through fire and water for a good meal, and with Aggie around, there was always a good meal waiting for him. So when Ivy Clegg entered the kitchen that particular January morning, she was not in the least surprised to find Ned there. Nor would it have come as a shock to her if she'd been told that he had already polished off three eggs, five sausages and half a dozen slices of bacon.

'Grand day, isn't it?' Spratt said.

'Is it?' Ivy asked, looking out of the window at the sheen of frost which had formed like a skin on the yard, and listening to the wind howling furiously up the back alley.

Ned glanced fondly across at big Aggie, who was frying him half a loaf of bread. 'It's always a grand day when you've been well fed,' he said.

Aggie turned and smiled affectionately at him. 'We're the perfect match,' she said, 'a good cook and a bottomless stomach.' She paused. 'By the way, Ivy, I won't be goin' to work today, so you'll have to manage on your own.'

'Are you not feelin' well?' Ivy asked, although she didn't think that Aggie looked poorly.

'Oh, I'm feelin' fine,' the big woman told her. 'You know me. I'm always as fit as a fiddle.'

'So why are you takin' the day off?'

'I'm not takin' the whole day off,' Aggie said awkwardly. 'Just part of the mornin'. I've got some, er, business to attend to in Northwich.'

This wasn't like Aggie at all, Ivy thought. She hardly ever missed work, because she was afraid that if she did, Spudder would grab at the opportunity to do some of his own cleaning.

'Is it serious, this business of yours?' she asked.

'No, it's just somethin' I have to do,' Aggie said. A twinkle came into her eye. 'You will be sure to give Spudder my best, won't you?'

Ivy turned to Ned Spratt and saw that he had the same sort of expression in *his* eye. Strange, she thought. Very strange.

Despite the cold, Spudder was standing at the back door of the boarding house, as if he'd been waiting for her to arrive. And that wasn't the only thing which was strange. He was wearing his best Sunday suit and had obviously had his hair cut since the last time she'd seen him.

'Hello, Spudder,' Ivy said.

But Spudder was too distracted to be bothered with commonplace things like greetings. 'Come into my kitchen, Ivy,' he said urgently.

Ivy looked through the window at the big clock on the boarding-house kitchen wall. It was already nearly seven o'clock.

'But what about the lodgers' breakfasts?' she asked.

'That can wait,' Spudder said agitatedly. 'I've got somethin' I have to show you now.'

Mystified, Ivy followed Spudder round the front of the houses and into the kitchen of number 47.

'Sit down on the sofa,' Spudder said.

Ivy sat, as instructed, and Spudder crossed the room to the pantry under the stairs. 'What's this all about?' Ivy asked.

'You'll see,' Spudder said, from inside the pantry. He emerged holding a huge bunch of roses. 'I bought these for you,' he said. 'From a real shop.'

'They're lovely, Spudder!'

'I didn't think you could get 'em at this time of year, but the man said they was grown under glass.' He looked at the tumbler which was sitting on the table. 'Must have been a really big one.'

Ivy took the roses in her arms. 'They smell absolutely smashin',' she assured him.

'I've not finished yet,' Spudder told her. He returned to the pantry and came back with a bunch of carnations. 'Maybe these was grown under glass an' all.'

'Two lots of flowers!' Ivy exclaimed. 'Spudder, you really shouldn't have.'

'There's more.' And so there was. Spudder made a further four trips to his pantry, re-emerging with dahlias the first time, then chrysanthemums, daisies, and finally, tulips.

'You must have bought up the whole shop,' Ivy said, as she sat there, surrounded by flowers.

'Well, she said that I should buy you some flo—' Spudder began.

'*Who* said?'

Spudder reddened and looked down at the floor. 'A woman I know,' he mumbled.

'It was Aggie, wasn't it?'

Spudder nodded.

So that was what lay behind Aggie's evasive answers and the twinkle in her eye. She'd known this was going to happen. But she could never have guessed how far Spudder would go, or she'd have told him to scale it down a bit.

'An' . . . an' I thought we could go out together some time,' Spudder said.

'Oh yes?'

'Yes. There's this public meetin' bein' held at the Town Hall on Thursday. Summat about plannin' persimmon. I thought we might go to that.'

'You really are a hopeless case, aren't you?'

Spudder frowned. 'Is that good or bad?' he asked.

'I'm not sure,' Ivy said, very seriously.

Billy sat in the armchair next to the kitchen fire, watching his mother preparing dinner. He had made great progress since he'd been shipped back to England on a stretcher. His ribs were mending nicely, and now, except when exposed to the cold, the wound in his leg hardly throbbed at all.

But he was not happy. He'd never been one for reading, like Michelle was, and having to spend so much time just sitting around was mind-numbingly boring. An' the future doesn't seem exactly bright for me, either, he thought.

He could always go back to the bakery, of course, but that had started to bore him even before he'd joined up. The war itself had changed things for him for ever.

He could still picture the Western Front in his mind's eye. Desolation, where there had once been fields of golden corn. Endless miles of tangled barbed wire and gash-like trenches, which had killed the countryside as surely as the men crouching in those trenches were killing each other. He could hear the screaming noise that the whizzbangs made when they were coming over, and could smell the cordite stinking out his nostrils.

It had all been dreadful in so many ways, and he didn't want to romanticise it, yet there was a part of him which had enjoyed it – a part of him which only came alive when he was climbing up the ladder out of the trench, knowing that seconds later he'd be facing a hail of bullets and having shells exploding all around him. Could he now return to the humdrum work of the bakery, after all he had seen and done? No, it was impossible.

'You look like you're miles away,' Becky said. 'Thinkin' about France?'

'In a way, I suppose I was,' Billy replied, and though his mother looked questioningly at him, he didn't say anything more to enlighten her. But if he was not to be a baker, what else could he do? he wondered. He was not as clever as his sister, nor did he have the training for anything but bakery work.

'Do you think that it's too late for me to go to college, Mam?' he asked.

'Caterin' college, do you mean?' Becky said. 'But there's no need to. You're a smashin' baker already.'

'It wasn't caterin' college I was thinkin' of.'

'What then?'

'I don't know. I was thinkin' of studyin' somethin' serious, like our Michelle did.'

Becky shook her head slightly. 'You're the best son a woman could ever wish for,' she said. 'An' as I told you before, you're a smashin' baker. But let's be honest, lad, you just haven't got our Michelle's brain.'

'That's true enough,' Billy admitted.

'Which doesn't mean that if you want to try, I won't be right behind you,' Becky added.

'No, it was only a thought.' And it wasn't the answer. Studying would bore him just as much as baking had begun to. What he needed was something which would help him recapture the thrill of being in France. And suddenly, he knew what that was!

'Do you know what I'd really like to do when I'm better, Mam?' he asked.

'What?'

He'd been going to tell his mother all about it, he really had, but now he realised how upset his plan would make her. Coping with Michelle's problems was enough of a burden on her for the time being.

'Well?' Becky said. 'What *will* you do when you're better?'

'I'll go straight up to the New Inn, and drink the place dry,' Billy told her.

It was Saturday afternoon, and yet another recruitment drive was being held in the Bull Ring in Northwich. The man in charge of it this time was a major who sported the kind of moustache which was very popular among officers, but which the enlisted men called a Charlie Chaplin. He was standing on a wagon smothered in red, white and blue bunting, and addressing the group of overcoated and mufflered young men who had gathered below him.

'Don't wait to be called up,' he told his audience. 'Join now of your own free will. Join now, and when your children ask you what you did in the Great War, you can tell them that you acted like a man and volunteered to fight for your country.'

Richard Worrell stood at the edge of the crowd, deep in thought. His son had died a hero's death – and Richard was glad of it – but brave or cowardly, he was still dead. And for what? So that the British would gain a few yards of territory that they would probably lose again the next day?

No, he hadn't even laid down his life for something as insignificant as that. Gerald had died attacking a machine-gun nest which would have been destroyed by shelling a minute later anyway. What was it Billy had said?

'That's the way it is with war. You never know what you *could* have done, so you just have to get on with doin' what you *can*.'

Gerald's death had been no less than murder, Richard thought. But his murderers were not the men who had actually wielded the bayonets and fired the guns. The real killers sat in London and Berlin, signing pieces of paper which condemned thousands to death, and then going out for a good luncheon. The real killers were the politicians and generals who played out badly conceived chess games with human lives.

Richard remembered what Gerald had said on his last, and only, home leave: 'I break my heart every time one British soldier dies unnecessarily, Father.' Richard hadn't understood it at the time, but, by God, he was convinced that he did now.

'Why should you stay in your dreary jobs, shackled to the workbench or the plough?' the Major asked the crowd.

'You're right, there!' someone shouted.

'Why stay shackled, I say, when out there is a great adventure waiting for you?' The Major stopped for a second to acknowledge his audience's cheers with a gallant wave of his hand. 'A great adventure, and a great crusade,' he continued. 'Help us defeat the evil Hun. Make us proud of you.'

A number of the young men below were already squaring their shoulders and puffing out their chests, as if they were ready to march straight from the Bull Ring to the recruitment office.

Richard pushed his way through the crowd until he had reached the front and was standing by the wagon.

'Do the duty you owe your king, your God and your country,' the Major urged.

Richard placed his foot on one of the spokes of the nearest wheel, and hoisted himself on to the cart.

The Major, caught up in his own oratorical flow, was not aware at first that he had been joined on his platform. Then, from the corner of his eye, he detected a movement. He turned, his face full of fury, but when he saw that Richard appeared to be a gentleman, his expression changed to one of mild irritation.

'If you don't mind, sir, I'm trying to conduct a meeting here,' he said.

'You've been ranting on for hours and hours. Now it's my turn,' Richard replied.

'I beg your pardon!' the Major said, almost unable to believe his own ears, but Richard was no longer interested in the soldier. Instead, he had turned his attention to the sea of eager young faces gathered around the wagon.

'It's lies, all lies!' he told them. 'War isn't glorious. It isn't a great adventure. It's crawling through lakes of mud. It's being shot before you've even seen the enemy. It's dying in agony, with a bayonet in your belly.'

A murmur of surprise rose from the crowd.

'Now just one minute, sir . . .' the Major said.

'If the soldiers on all sides refused to fight, there couldn't be any war!' Richard shouted. 'If every soldier on the front line ignored the orders of the generals – generals who are living in the lap of luxury, far from the fighting – then our leaders would have no choice but to talk to each other.'

'I think you'd better get off that wagon, sir,' said a voice at his feet.

Richard looked down. Two middle-aged policemen – a sergeant and a constable – were standing just below him.

'Let him finish!' somebody in the crowd called. 'Let's hear what he's got to say for himself.'

'Can't you hear them?' Richard asked the policemen. 'They want me to talk to them.'

'*Some* of them might want you to talk to them, sir,' the sergeant said, 'but that isn't the point, is it? You don't have no right to be up there in the first place.'

'Pull the traitor down or I'll do it meself,' said a man in the crowd.

'We don't want to listen to no friend of Kaiser Bill's!' shouted the man standing next to him.

'You see the trouble you're causing, sir?' the sergeant asked Richard. 'Wouldn't it be better just to climb down now, before you start a fight?'

'I demand my right as an Englishman to free speech,' Richard told him.

The sergeant shook his head, wonderingly. 'Don't make us drag you off, sir,' he said. 'It wouldn't look dignified.'

He was right, Richard thought. He didn't give a damn about his own dignity any more, but the dignity of his cause must be protected at all costs. Reluctantly, he turned and climbed off the wagon.

'What about his rights as an Englishman?' shouted the man who'd said Richard should be allowed to finish.

The two policemen flanked Richard and frogmarched him through the crowd.

'Traitor!' men hissed as he passed. 'German spy! You should lock the bugger up an' throw away the key.'

'Where are you taking me?' Richard asked the sergeant.

'Down to the police station, sir.'

'Do I understand that to mean that I am under arrest?'

'No, sir, you're not under arrest. But I do think you need to be somewhere quiet for a while – somewhere you'll have a bit of time to calm down.'

They reached the edge of the Bull Ring. 'There are always those who will attempt to decry our noble crusade against the enemy,' the Major said. 'But the Hun must be stopped at all costs, and that is why I am here today, to ask you to . . .'

Richard turned his head. 'Don't throw away your lives!' he shouted to all the young men behind him. 'Please, I beg you, don't throw away your young, precious lives!'

The sergeant increased his pressure on Richard's arm. 'Been drinkin', have we, sir?' he asked.

'No,' Richard replied, and he hadn't. He'd not touched a drop since his talk with Billy Worrell. It was very hard to live up to the memory of a hero, but he was doing his best.

The man standing at the back door of the boarding house was twenty-three or twenty-four years old. He had sandy hair and a handsome face, though his green eyes were perhaps a little too sharp, and his mouth was the kind which finds it easy to form slightly unpleasant smiles.

'Can I help you?' Spudder asked him.

'No, you can't,' said the man, who had already noticed the slightly vacant look in Spudder's eyes. 'I want to talk to the organ grinder, not his monkey.'

Spudder scratched his head. 'I beg your pardon,' he said. 'I don't think I'm follerin' you. Mr Marvello's got some pigeons – he uses them in his act – but we don't have any monkeys.'

The man sighed. 'I'm lookin' for the feller that runs the boarding house.'

'That's me.'

'You run it?' the man asked incredulously.

'Yes.'

'On your own?'

Spudder laughed. 'Not on me own, no. I've got Aggie an' Ivy to help me.'

The man nodded, as if to suggest the fact that Spudder had help explained everything. 'The name's Toby Pickup,' he said. 'I've just got meself a job at the munitions factory in Wincham, an' somebody told me you've got a room goin' spare in your boardin' house.'

'I have,' Spudder said. 'You see, it used to be Captain Davenport's, but he—'

'Aye, well, I'm sure that's all very interestin' in its own way,' Pickup said dismissively, 'but if you don't mind, I'd like to see the vacant room.'

Spudder led him upstairs and showed him the room. 'It overlooks the back yard,' he explained.

'Well, I'd never have guessed that,' Pickup said sarcastically, looking out of the window.

Spudder laughed, though he was not entirely sure that the other man was joking or not. 'It's quieter than bein' at the front,' he said. 'You don't get no noise from the chip shop.'

Pickup took another look around the room. 'I suppose it'll have to do,' he said ungraciously.

They went back down to the kitchen again. 'What about terms?' Pickup asked, when they were both sitting at the table.

'Terms?'

'How much will you want payin''?'

'It's fifteen shillin's a week,' Spudder said. 'But that includes breakfast an' supper every day of the week, an' a hot dinner on Sundays.'

Pickup's eyes flashed with cunning. 'That might be a bit difficult for me just now,' he said.

'How d'you mean?'

'Well, I've been out of work for some time, you see, and I've got debts.'

'I'm sorry to hear that,' Spudder said. 'Debts is a terrible thing to have hangin' over you.'

'Now I suppose I could just tell me creditors to go an' drown themselves,' Pickup continued, 'but I'm not that kind of feller. I like to pay what I owe, but I can't do that *and* cough up fifteen shillin's a week for rent.'

Spudder's brow pursed, like it always did when he was thinking through a problem. 'I tell you what we could do,' he said finally. 'You could give me ten bob a week an' owe me the rest. An' when you're back on your feet, you could make it up to me.'

Pickup smiled. 'That would be fine,' he said. 'I think I'm goin' to like it here.' He hesitated, as if deciding how far he could push his luck. 'There is one other thing.'

'What's that?'

'It'll be Saturday before I draw me first pay.'

'I can wait till then for the rent.'

'Yes, but the problem is, what am I goin' to live on in the meantime? There's me dinners to buy for a start, not to mention me smokes. An' a man deserves a couple of pints after he's been workin' all day, now doesn't he?'

Spudder saw what he was getting at. 'Would you like me to lend you some money?' he asked.

'That's very kind of you.'

'How much would you like?'

'A quid, if you can manage it.'

It seemed to Spudder that a pound was an awful lot of money for one week's dinners, cigarettes and drinks, but Pickup would have more idea what they cost than he did, and if the man asked for a pound, that must be what he needed.

'So are you goin' to lend me the money or what?' Pickup asked.

'I don't see why not,' Spudder said cheerfully. He stood up. 'I won't be a tick. I keep me money in a tin box in me bed—' He stopped, suddenly, remembering Aggie's warning about telling people where he kept his money. 'I mean, I think I have the odd pound lyin' around somewhere,' he finished unconvincingly.

'I'm sure you do,' Pickup said.

Spudder went back upstairs, and the new lodger leant back lazily in his chair. He had got his feet under the table and no mistake, he thought.

The back door opened, and Ivy walked in.

'An' who might you be?' Pickup asked.

'Ivy Clegg, I work for Spudder.'

'An' I'm Toby Pickup. I'm goin' to be the new lodger.'

Ivy did a pretty half-curtsy. 'Pleased to meet you, Mr Pickup,' she said.

Pickup ran his eyes hungrily up and down Ivy's slim body. 'An' I'm very pleased to meet *you*, Miss Clegg,' he told her.

Chapter Twenty-two

February started with a cold snap which froze the flashes and ponds around Northwich, much to the discomfort of the families of swans who had decided to spend the winter there. Then, quite unexpectedly, the thaw came, and with it signs that nature was coming to life again.

Snowdrops emerged almost shyly in the shadow of the hedgerows. Then the primroses burst proudly into bloom, while on the banks of the River Weaver the purple-tinted alder catkins began to shed some of their pollen.

In the sky above newly green meadows, lapwings swooped and spiralled, and pairs of bullfinches flitted between flowering shrubs, selecting the juiciest buds before going off to mate. It was even possible, on some mild days, to catch sight of brimstone butterflies, coaxed from their winter hibernation by the promise of kinder days to come.

The summer, it seemed, was just around the corner. Perhaps it would be as hot as the one which had preceded it, but it could never be as glorious: even the brightest sun, shining in the clearest blue sky, could not completely vanquish the shadow of war.

It felt as if the bloody conflict across the water had been going on for ever, had always been as much a part of life as waking up or going to sleep. People were surprised, when they counted back, to realise that only eight months earlier there had been no such thing as the Western Front. Yet though so little time had passed since the start of the war, the changes it had brought to the lives of so many families in the area were immense.

There had been fifty thousand British casualties at the Battle of Ypres alone, and everyone in Northwich and district knew someone who had lost a son, a husband, a brother or – like poor

Michelle Worrell – the man she had only been *planning* to spend her life with.

Michelle was four months pregnant as February drew to a close, and it was beginning to show. But though the tongues clicked as much as they had ever done, there was now a more sympathetic edge to them.

'After all, young Gerald Worrell was a soldier, fightin' for his king an' country, an' I suppose it was only reasonable that he should take his consolation when he could,' Not-Stopping Bracegirdle said to Dottie Curzon and Half-a-Mo-Flo as they sat around their usual table in the best room of the New Inn.

'It's nice to hear you talkin' that way, Elsie,' Dottie Curzon said, taking a sip of her milk stout.

'Assumin', of course, that Gerald Worrell *is* the father of the baby,' Not-Stopping added, finding that, despite her good intentions, she was not quite able to relinquish *all* her old ways.

Dottie slammed her glass down on the table. 'He was the father, all right,' she said sharply.

Instead of arguing, Not-Stopping merely nodded her head. 'Yes,' she said. 'Yes, I believe he was.'

'It's a pity she can't find herself some nice young man who'd be willin' to marry her despite her condition,' Half-a-Mo-Flo said, sounding sincere.

Not-Stopping looked at her daughter-in-law in astonishment. 'You what?' she asked, shaking her head wonderingly. 'I can understand me an' Dottie startin' to turn soft,' she said. 'That comes with old age. But what's your excuse, Florence?'

If Michelle was aware of being pointed out in the street, she showed no sign of it. In fact, she showed no sign of anything very much. She reported to the munitions factory on time every morning, did her work conscientiously, and went home. She ate whatever food her mam had prepared for her almost without comment, helped to clear away, and then retired to her room.

Once her bedroom door shielded her from the outside world, she would finally let her emotions show. Sometimes she would reread Gerald's letters and cry a little. Sometimes she would simply stare at the wall, seeing on it visions of the life they might have had together, but for the terrible, terrible-war.

Just as the brimstone butterflies had been seduced by the warm weather, she had been tempted out of hiding by the warmth of Gerald's love – only to find herself left alone in a cold, cold world.

It was at the end of her shift on the last Friday in February that Michelle came across Jim Vernon standing outside the main entrance of the Victoria works.

'Are you waiting for someone, Mr Vernon?' she asked, not because she really wanted to know the answer, but just for something to say.

Jim took off his cap, a nautical one which she hadn't seen him wearing before. 'I certainly am waiting for someone, Miss Worrell,' he said. 'I'm waitin' for you.'

It came as a shock. For Michelle, Jim Vernon – and virtually everyone else in Marston – had not really existed for months. Only Gerald was real, and he was gone.

'Did you hear what I said, Miss Worrell?' Jim asked.

'I heard you,' Michelle replied, 'but I'm not quite sure that I understand you. Why should you be waiting for me?'

'Because you don't look like the kind of young lady who breaks her promise.'

'But I haven't made any promises, as far as I can remember,' she said, puzzled.

'Oh yes, you have. You said that when Captain Davenport finally agreed to let me steer out of Northwich, you'd come on the river with me again.'

'Oh, that!'

'Well, Captain Davenport isn't around any more, but that doesn't matter because the new captain's more than happy to have me steerin'. An' d'you know who he is?'

'No,' Michelle said, and if she told the truth, she didn't much care, either.

Jim poked himself in the chest with his thumb. 'Me. I'm the new captain. So, I'll see you on Sunday, will I?'

Why couldn't people leave her alone? Michelle wondered.

Aloud, she said, 'It's really very thoughtful of you to ask me, Mr Vernon, but—'

'None of that,' Jim said severely. 'When all's said an' done, a promise is a promise.'

Didn't he understand? Didn't he know what suffering she was going through? 'A great deal has happened since I made that promise to you,' she said.

'All the more reason to come out on the river with me. Take you out of yourself a bit.'

'Thank you very much, but I don't want taking out of myself, Mr Vernon,' Michelle said, starting to get angry.

'You might not *want* it, Miss Worrell,' Jim told her, 'but you certainly *need* it.'

It was all fuel to Michelle's growing rage. 'You're being very presumptuous, Mr Vernon,' she said.

Jim should have looked shamefaced and mumbled an apology. Instead, he merely grinned.

'Bein' presumptuous, am I?' he asked. 'Well, don't you think it's about time *somebody* was, Miss Worrell?'

'What's happened to you?' Michelle asked. 'You used to be so quiet, so unsure of yourself.'

Jim nodded, as if he accepted the truth of the statement. 'Maybe it was bein' made captain that changed me,' he said. 'Or maybe if you suffer a bit, it makes you grow up quicker. Anyway, it doesn't really matter what's made me different.' 'We're here to talk about you, not me. An' I know that's bein' presumptuous again, but there's not much I can do about it.'

Michelle smiled for the first time in months. It was a sad smile – one which showed her the true depth of her misery – but at least it was a smile. 'You're very kind . . .' she said.

'First I was presumptuous, then I was kind, now I'm goin' to be serious,' Jim told her. 'There's some women around here who can afford to wrap themselves up in their grief, but you're not one of 'em, Miss Worrell.'

Michelle felt her anger bubble up again. 'How dare you!' she demanded, almost screaming the words.

'I'm not speakin' for myself,' Jim said calmly.

'Then just who are you . . . ?'

'I'm speakin' on behalf of the little mite that you're carryin' inside you.'

Michelle was as outraged as she could ever remember being. 'I've never been so—' she began.

'An' there's no need to look offended,' Jim interrupted, with such quiet confidence that she fell silent. 'I didn't want to mention your baby, but you forced me into it. Anyway, as I was sayin' before you started gettin' all huffy, every new baby's got the right to expect a happy home. How can yours possibly have one as long as you're mopin' away like this?'

He could not have shocked her more if he'd slapped her across the face. She had been doing all she should have done to care for the child she was carrying, but ever since Gerald's death, she had never really thought of it as her baby.

'I . . . I never looked at it that way,' she confessed, ashamed of her selfishness.

'Course, you didn't,' Jim said chirpily. 'That's what I mean about you needin' to be taken out of yourself, so you can look into the future, instead of dwellin' on the past.' He put his hand on her shoulder, something he would never have dared do in the old days. 'Come out on the river with me. Please . . . Michelle.'

Michelle bit her lower lip. 'All right, Jim,' she said. 'I'll see you on Sunday.'

He was making enemies everywhere, Richard Worrell thought as he walked down Witton Street.

Men he'd known most of his life were crossing the road to avoid him. Members of his club started earnest conversations with each other the moment he entered the room. The editor of the *Northwich Guardian*, who had been a close friend for years, refused to print any of his letters about the war. None of it mattered. Let them think him mad, let them treat him like a leper. If he could save only one young life, it would have all been worth it.

He reached the Bull Ring, and, as he had suspected, there was yet another recruitment rally going on. The man on the wagon this time was a captain, just as Gerald had been. He had a florid face with the marks of too much drinking clearly mapped out on it. Well, why shouldn't he have a drink?

Richard asked himself. If conditions in France were even half as bad as Gerald had said they were, who could blame a man for taking to the bottle? But why, after all he'd seen, did he have to come to Northwich and tell all these young men a pack of filthy lies?

The usual two policemen were standing on the edge of the crowd. Richard could just make out the tops of their pointed helmets. It would take them a while to reach him, and if he acted quickly, he might just be able to disrupt yet another meeting.

He edged his way through the crowd, and had almost reached the wagon when he heard the sergeant's voice call out, 'Don't do it, Mr Worrell!'

As Richard placed his foot on one of the wheels and pulled himself onto the wagon, someone shouted, 'Look who's turned up! It's that lunatic again!'

There were jeers from many of the spectators, but not, Richard noticed with a flicker of hope, from everyone.

'Don't listen to him!' Richard shouted at the crowd. 'He's not telling you the truth. None of them does!'

The captain with the drinker's face broke off from his own speech and turned to face Richard. 'I will not have my meeting interrupted in this way, sir,' he said angrily.

The police, edging their way through the crowd, had almost reached the wagon. He wasn't going to have the chance to make his usual impassioned plea this time, Richard thought. Yet he felt the need to do something, to make some kind of gesture.

'Why don't you throw the mad bugger off the platform?' a voice in the crowd called up to the captain.

'I have no intention of lowering myself to the level of a common street brawler,' the captain replied.

'Oh, you haven't, haven't you?' Richard said. 'Well, I have!' With one hand he grabbed the seat of the captain's pants and pulled upwards. With the other, he pushed as hard as he could against the soldier's shoulder. The captain wobbled on the edge of the wagon for a second, then fell forward into the crowd.

Richard looked down at the captain, who was only just starting to disentangle himself from the crowd and struggle to his feet. One thing was certain: after such a loss of dignity there was no way the man could carry on with his speech.

The policemen climbed on to the wagon. The sergeant's face was flushing bright red with anger. 'Do you have any idea how many meetings you've disrupted, Mr Worrell?' he said.

'It must be four or five,' Richard said cheerfully.

'It's six! An' this time, you've used violence. I'm afraid we can't turn a blind eye any more.'

'I wouldn't expect you to,' Richard told him. 'I have done my duty, now you do yours.'

The sergeant coughed, as if he was suddenly starting to find the situation embarrassing. 'I'm, er, goin' to have to use the handcuffs, sir,' he said. 'I'm afraid that the regulations don't leave me no choice. So if you wouldn't mind turnin' round an' puttin' your hands together behind your back . . .'

'Of course,' Richard agreed, doing as he'd been instructed.

'Who'd have ever thought I'd end up cuffing a gent,' the sergeant said, as Richard felt the cold metal on his wrists and heard the handcuffs click shut.

Spudder walked along the towpath towards Burns Bridge with his hands in his pockets and his head bent low. Somehow, he just couldn't seem to get the hang of this courting thing, he thought.

Like the flowers, for example. Ivy had told him they were lovely, but had forbidden him to buy her any more. And then there were the outings. He'd suggested a number of them: a trip to Hodge's farm, so they could take a look at the pigs; another council meeting – somethin' to do with the rates this time; the town's annual angling competition. Scores of ideas – and she'd turned him down every time.

'You're tryin' too hard, Spudder,' she'd told him. 'You've been listenin' to Aggie too much. Don't do what she wants you to do – just be yourself. That's all that's necessary.'

The problem was, though, that he didn't really know *who* he was any more. When he'd been the old Spudder, life had been so simple. Breakfast with the lodgers, then peeling spuds and frying them, a bit of cleaning on the side, when Aggie would let him, and his day was complete. Then he'd met Ivy and everything had got jumbled up.

He was still pondering on his problems when he heard a conversation coming from round the bend in the canal.

'I mean, whichever way you look at it, you have to admit that he's not all there, don't you?' said a voice which Spudder recognised as belonging to Toby Pickup.

'You might have found a nicer way of putting it,' said the second voice, unmistakably Ivy Clegg's. They were talking about him! Spudder realised. And any second they would turn the corner and see him!

He hadn't meant to eavesdrop, but now he had, he didn't think he could face them. He looked around him in a panic. There was a hawthorn hedge growing alongside the canal, and with his natural athleticism augmented by a surge of desperation, Spudder flung himself over it. He landed badly and felt the wind being knocked out of him. 'Ouch!' he said, and then he fell silent, because the two voices were getting closer.

'Whatever you might say about him, you have to admit that Spudder's got a big heart,' Ivy said.

Toby Pickup laughed, as if he were enjoying some private joke. 'Oh, he's got that all right,' he said. 'But even with a good heart, he's not exactly every young maiden's dream, now is he?'

'No, but I used to think he might be mine,' Ivy said sadly. 'I really did.'

Spudder, lying on his back, felt some small twigs digging into him, and shifted his position slightly, to get more comfortable. The hedge rustled.

'What was that?' Ivy asked.

'It's probably just a water rat,' Toby Pickup replied. He laughed again. 'Unless, of course, there's a two-legged creature lurkin' down there. Maybe Spudder's spyin' on us.'

Ivy joined in his laughter. 'It wouldn't be him,' she said. 'Now if I was out with him, and he told me that you were hidin' behind a hedge, I might believe it. But Spudder's a simple soul. He doesn't go in for clever tricks like that.'

'Does he know you're out with me?' Pickup asked.

'I'm on me own time,' Ivy said. 'I can go for a walk with whoever I choose to.'

'You haven't answered my question.'

'I know I haven't.'

'I suppose you think it's none of my business.'

'That's right. I do.'

'You've got a fine spirit, Ivy Clegg,' Pickup said. 'An' if that wasn't enought to recommend you to a man, you've been blessed with the face of an angel.'

Ivy laughed again. 'I'm not listenin' to you no more, Toby Pickup,' she said. 'You've got such a smooth tongue on you, you could charm the birds out of the trees.'

'Get away with you. I'm nothin' but a plain-spoken man who says what he feels.'

'A charmer,' Ivy repeated, her tone more serious now. 'An' I'm afraid that if I *do* listen to you, you just might be able to talk me into doin' somethin' I don't want to do – somethin' that isn't right.'

'Or it could be you're afraid that I'll talk you into doin' somethin' that *is* right,' Pickup said. 'Right for both of us.'

The footsteps receded and the voices drifted away in the distance. Still in his hiding place, Spudder felt large, bitter teardrops trickling down his cheeks.

Chapter Twenty-three

Michelle stood on the fore-deck of the *Damascus*, looking down the river. An hour earlier, the wind had been blowing so forcefully that if she'd not held on tight to her new ostrich-feathered hat, she would almost certainly have lost it. But now the wind had dropped, and though the early March sunshine did little to warm the air, it was still very pleasant to be out on the water.

She turned to look at Jim, who was standing at the wheel. He waved cheerily, then handed the wheel over to his mate, and made his way towards her.

'Not too rough for you, is it?' he asked, with a hint of concern in his voice.

'It's fine,' Michelle assured him. 'And I'm sure it's doing me a lot of good.'

Jim grinned. 'Told you it would.' He raised his arm and pointed. 'Look over there.'

Michelle followed the line of his finger, and her gaze settled on a stark black tree on the nearer river bank. 'What exactly am I supposed to be looking at?' she asked. 'The tree?'

'No, the nest right at the top of it. The same pair of rooks have been nestin' in it for years.'

'Don't birds build new nests every year?' Michelle asked.

'Some species do, but not your old rooks. They feel more comfortable with familiar things around them.'

Michelle gave the nest a second look. It seemed far too insubstantial to have served year after year.

'Oh, it needs repairin' every now an' again,' Jim said, 'but they'd rather do that than chop an' change.'

'They're a bit like my mam, then,' Michelle said. 'Billy's been trying to get her to move to a bigger house for ages, but she simply refuses to budge from where she is now.'

'I bet she doesn't steal her neighbours' slates, though,' Jim said.

'Whatever do you mean by that?'

'See that rook hoverin' over the nest? It comes from another nest. An' it's waiting for the owners of this one to go away, so it can swoop down an' pinch some of their twigs. Your rooks prefer pinchin' to gatherin' any day of the week.' He laughed. 'Say people *did* behave like that. What if you came home one day an' found there were no slates on your lavvy roof because Mrs Bracegirdle wanted them for hers?'

Michelle joined in the laughter. 'Yes, that would be funny,' she agreed. 'But don't the rooks ever catch each other stealing?'

''Course they do,' Jim said. 'An' when they do, there's a right barney about it, an' a lot of pullin' an' tuggin'. "I believe that's my slate, Mrs Bracegirdle," says one of 'em. "I think you're wrong, Mrs Worrell," says the other one. "I distinctly remember nickin' this from off of Spudder Johnson's lavvy."'

Michelle punched him lightly in the ribs. 'You are a fool sometimes,' she said, 'but if you wanted to impress me, I suppose you could say you've succeeded.'

'Have I?' Jim asked, sounding surprised.

'Yes, you have. I've lived on the edge of the countryside all my life, but I don't seem to know half as much about nature as you do. Where did you learn it all from?'

'Just watchin'. You get a lot of time for watchin' on the old river, you know.'

Michelle looked at him almost as if she was seeing him for the first time. 'There's a lot more to you than meets the eye, Jim Vernon,' she said.

'Do you think so?' Jim asked, reddening slightly. 'I've always seen myself as a simple soul.'

'I've been meaning to ask you about Captain Davenport,' Michelle said, changing the subject.

'What about him?' Jim asked, a look of caution suddenly appearing on his face.

'Well, he just disappeared, didn't he? One day he was in the village, and the next he was gone.'

'Maybe he just got fed up with workin' the river, an' moved on to somewhere new,' Jim suggested.

Michelle's eyes narrowed. 'I think I'm getting to know you, Jim Vernon,' she said. 'I'm starting to be able to distinguish between when you're telling the truth, and when you're lying.'

'I would never lie to you!' Jim protested.

Michelle laughed. 'There goes another one,' she said.

Jim looked down at the deck. 'What I mean is, if I did lie to you, it wouldn't be a bad lie, one that could hurt you.'

The conversation seemed to be getting very intimate, and Michelle had a sneaking suspicion that she was the one who'd started it moving in that direction. 'So you admit that you lied to me about Captain Davenport,' she said, trying to sound more businesslike.

'Yes, I did,' Jim agreed. 'But I had to. I made a promise to someone that I would.'

'So who did you make this promise to?'

'I can't tell you that, either.'

'You really are a bit of a man of mystery on the quiet, aren't you?' Michelle said.

Jim looked quite flustered. 'I don't mean to be mysterious. It's just that as I see it, a promise—'

'Is a promise?'

'Exactly.'

He really looked sweet when he was bothered, Michelle thought, and she realised that the newfound confidence which he showed could sometimes be wafer thin.

'Have you ever been to the tea shop in Northwich?' she asked on impulse.

'No,' Jim confessed. 'I can't say that I have.'

'They do some lovely cream cakes,' Michelle told him. 'From my mam's bakery, of course. So if you're not sailing next Sunday, we'll go and have our tea there. My treat – a way of thanking you for this trip.'

'That would be nice,' said Jim, who was, in fact, supposed to be sailing, but had just decided that he'd rather lose his job than take salt to Liverpool the following Sunday.

It was Monday morning, and the magistrates' court attached to

Northwich Police Station was packed to capacity with local tradesmen, day labourers, housewives and a few general layabouts. 'After all,' people said when the word was getting around, 'it's not every day you get a chance to see a toff in the dock.'

Richard Worrell, the toff in question, gripped the dock's iron rail and looked straight into the eyes of Councillor Holdroyd, the senior magistrate – yet another of the town's elite whom he had counted as a friend for years.

'You are charged with a breach of the peace and with common assault,' the clerk said. 'How do you plead?'

Richard shrugged. 'If it will speed up the proceedings, I am quite willing to plead guilty.'

There was only one witness – the police sergeant – who described precisely what he had seen, and what he had done about it.

'Since you do not appear to have any legal representative in court with you, do you wish to question the sergeant yourself?' the senior magistrate asked Richard.

'There would be no point,' Richard replied. 'The sergeant's evidence is perfectly accurate, as far as it goes.'

The magistrates put their heads together and conferred. 'I don't like it,' one of them whispered. 'I don't like it at all. It's never good for the common people to see their betters being humiliated.'

'I don't like it either,' the second magistrate said. 'But what can we do? He's pleaded guilty – we have no choice but to find against him.'

'Perhaps if he would apologise and put forward some mitigating circumstances,' the first magistrate suggested.

'I will certainly give him the opportunity to do so,' the chairman promised.

The three men came out of their huddle. 'We find the charges proved to our satisfaction,' Holdroyd said gravely. 'I trust that you have some explanation for your behaviour, which was no better than that of a common hooligan.'

'Of course I have an explanation. I was doing my duty as I saw it.'

Holdroyd's brow furrowed with a deep frown. 'Was it your

duty as you saw it, then, to throw a senior army officer off a platform and send him sprawling in the street?'

'I got tired of listening to him tell lies, tired of listening to all of them tell lies,' Richard said. He smiled. 'You should have seen it for yourself. One minute that captain was up on the wagon spouting all kinds of pompous falsehoods about adventure and holy crusades, and the next he was going arse over tit towards the cobblestones.'

Had it been possible, Holdroyd's frown would have become even deeper. As it was, he had to be content to let his mouth drop open in astonishment. 'Levity and bad language will win you very few friends in this court, Mr Worrell,' he said, when he had finally recovered himself.

Richard took a long, slow look around the room. 'I hope I am more selective in my choice of friends than to wish to choose any from this assembly,' he said. 'Unless, that is, there is anyone here with the guts to stand up next to me and say that we must do all we can to stop this evil war as soon as possible.'

There was a horrified gasp from the spectators, followed by a dozen or so whispered conversations.

'Evil war, did he say?'

'The man's a traitor. There's no doubt about it.'

'They ought to string him up from the nearest lamp-post.'

'Silence!' the senior magistrate ordered, and slowly the noise in the courtroom subsided. Holdroyd turned back to Richard. 'Do not think I am unaware of the fact that though this is the first time you have appeared before us, it is by no means the first time that you have attempted to prevent officers in His Majesty's forces from going about their legitimate business . . .'

'The business of lying.'

'. . . of going about their legitimate business, I say. The local police force, out of respect for your position in the community, have dealt leniently with you on the other occasions – perhaps too leniently, as it now appears – but that state of affairs simply cannot be allowed to continue. Before you leave this courtroom today, Mr Worrell, I shall require from you your assurance that you will behave yourself in future.'

'You have my assurance that I will do what is right,' Richard told him.

'That is not what I meant, and you know it. I shall have to insist that you promise, on your word as a gentleman, that you will refrain from committing further breaches of the peace.'

'That is one promise I cannot give you.'

Holdroyd sighed exasperatedly. Richard Worrell was, after all, one of their own, he thought. Why in God's name was the man making things so difficult for all of them? 'Perhaps you are not aware of the alternative to giving your word, Mr Worrell,' he said aloud.

Richard shook his head. 'On the contrary. I am very well aware of the alternative. If I won't give you the assurances you require – and I refuse to – then the only course of action left open to you would seem to be locking me up.'

Damn the man! 'A custodial sentence is indeed a possibility,' Holdroyd admitted.

Richard shrugged. 'I'll not be the first man who has ever gone to prison for his beliefs.'

The magistrates put their heads together again. 'We can't send him to prison,' the first one said. 'The man rides with the hounds, for God's sake!'

'He's not leaving us any choice,' the second argued. 'If we don't send him to gaol, we'll have the local papers screaming that there's one law for the rich and another for the poor.'

'He's put himself beyond the pale,' Holdroyd said. 'Whatever befalls him now is entirely of his own making.'

'But even so, we have to consider how his incarceration would reflect on the rest of Northwich society . . .'

Richard watched the magistrates' deliberations with an ironic smile on his lips. If he'd been one of his workers, they'd have had him locked up long ago, he thought. He wondered how he could ever have seen the world through their eyes – could ever have valued a man solely by his bank balance.

The magistrates separated again. 'I am loath to send a gentleman to gaol,' Holdroyd said, 'even if the gentleman in question appears to have forgotten that he is one. Nevertheless, you leave me very little choice. You will go to prison for a period of two weeks. And I can only hope that while you are serving your sentence, you will have time to come to your senses.'

'I *have* come to my senses,' Richard said. 'It took me a long time, but now I finally realise what's important and what isn't. And there is nothing more important than human life. So lock me up if you want to. It won't change me. It won't change anything.'

Holdroyd shook his head. The man was impossible. He wouldn't save himself, and he wouldn't let anyone else save him. 'Take the prisoner down,' he said to the bailiff.

The 13th of March did not fall on a Friday that year, but it was a black day for the news anyway.

'Another big battle,' the Great Marvello said gloomily, putting down his newspaper and looking across the breakfast table at the other lodgers.

'Where was it this time?' Jim Vernon asked.

'Somewhere called Neuve-Chapelle – a place which, I should imagine, most of the poor bloody infantry on the firing line probably couldn't even pronounce.'

'An' what happened?' Spudder asked.

'What always happens?' Marvello asked in disgust. 'We attacked, the Huns counter-attacked, and when it was over there were over thirteen thousand casualties on each side.'

'Well, that's war for you,' Toby Pickup said indifferently.

'It's sheer bloody stupidity, you mean,' Marvello countered. 'We advanced about a thousand yards—'

'How far's that?' asked Spudder, who had never been very good at distances.

'About as far as it is from Four Lane Ends to the Post Office, Spudder.'

'But that's no distance at all.'

'Exactly. A thousand yards gained along a front that was only a mile and a quarter wide. Do you realise what that means? We lost thirteen men for every yard of territory that we won.'

'Tragic,' Jim Vernon said.

'If you ask me,' Marvello continued, turning to the court reports section of newspaper, 'Richard Worrell – for all they say about him in the village – has the right idea.'

'Any man who joins up when there's such good money to be made in the munitions factories is a fool,' Toby Pickup said. 'Why, look at me, I'm makin' a fortune. Of course,' he added hurriedly, looking at Spudder, 'most of the money I earn goes towards payin' off me debts.'

Ivy came in from the back yard, and Spudder suddenly seemed to find his breakfast plate very interesting.

'Another cup of tea, Spudder?' the girl asked.

Spudder shook his head. 'Don't feel like it,' he said, still not looking up.

'I wouldn't mind one if you're offerin', Ivy, my love,' Toby Pickup said.

Ivy smiled at him. 'Comin' up right away, Toby,' she said. 'An' what about you, Mr Vernon?'

Jim jumped as if she'd startled him. 'What?'

'I asked you if you'd like another cup of tea. Is your mind somewhere else or somethin'?'

'Yes, it is,' Jim admitted. He'd been struggling to reach two separate decisions for days, and now, on this crisp March morning, he'd finally made up his mind on both of them.

Chapter Twenty-four

From his bedroom window, Toby Pickup watched as Aggie, a wicker basket on her arm, walked towards the back gate.

Goin' shoppin', he thought. That means she'll be away for at least half an hour.

And he didn't need half an hour. Five minutes, he calculated, would be more than enough, especially as he had a good idea of exactly where he needed to look for what he wanted.

Aggie lifted the latch, opened the gate and squeezed her huge frame through the gap.

'Goodbye, you fat sow,' Toby said softly. He opened his bedroom door, and stepped on to the landing. With Aggie out at the shops, and Spudder gone for a walk in the woods, he would never get a better chance than this.

Toby made his way to the back gate of number 47. It was open, as he'd expected it to be. He tried the kitchen door and found that it was locked. That would cost him a few extra seconds, he thought, but it was no real problem.

He made his way quickly to the wash-house, and once inside headed straight for the brick boiler. There was a grate at the bottom of it, where, on Mondays, a fire was lit to heat the water. Pickup knelt down, stuck his hand inside the grate, and felt his hand brush against cold metal. 'You never could keep anythin' to yourself, could you, Spudder?' he said, as he withdrew the key.

He opened the back door, crossed the kitchen and mounted the stairs. He imagined the look on Spudder's face the next time he went to his room, and chuckled to himself. Still, it serves him right for bein' so careless, the stupid bloody half-wit, he thought.

He had reached the top of the stairs. He opened Spudder's

door and stepped inside the bedroom. 'I keep me money in a tin box in me bed—' Spudder had started to tell Pickup, before he'd realised it might be wiser to keep quiet. But he'd already said more than enough for the other man to get the picture.

'Now where will he keep it?' Pickup asked himself as he looked around the room.

The chest of drawers was a possibility, as was the wardrobe, but Pickup was betting on the third possibility.

He bent down, peered under the bed, and saw the battered metal box. He pulled it out. There was a lock on it, but he knew a lot about locks, and it was the work of a few seconds to open it with the piece of wire he'd brought with him. He lifted the lid, and his eyes lit up when he saw all the banknotes inside.

'It must be more than a hundred quid,' he gasped.

He stuffed the money into his pocket and replaced the box under the bed. He had only just straightened up again when the door opened, and Ivy walked in.

Pickup gave her one of his most winning smiles. 'Hello, Ivy, my love,' he said. 'You've saved me the trouble of havin' to come an' look for you.'

Some of the girls at the munitions factory took their dinners to work with them, but Michelle always went home for hers. It was all a bit of a rush – no sooner had she got home than it seemed it was time to go back to work again – but it was worth it. After a morning of working in the fetid, chemical atmosphere of the factory, she needed a break. And anyway, exercise was good for the baby.

It was as she was coming out of the main entrance that she noticed Jim Vernon standing there. 'I'm surprised to see you here,' she said, and she was. When he was not working on the river, he had fallen into the habit of escorting her home in the evening, but he had never appeared at dinnertime before. And she didn't ever remember seeing him wear his best suit in the middle of a working day.

'I was at a bit of a loose end,' Jim said unconvincingly. 'An' I thought I might as well go for a stroll as mope around the boarding house all day.'

'But why aren't you at work?'

'I was owed some time for all the Sundays I've been workin', so I decided to take a day off.'

He was such a bad liar, Michelle thought, looking into his eyes. But knowing he was not telling her the truth got her no closer to finding out what was actually on his mind.

They walked along the towpath towards the Wincham Hotel. Michelle told him about a new girl from Liverpool who had just started work in the factory, and Jim grunted occasionally, as if he wasn't really listening.

Finally, when they had reached the path which led up to Chapel Street, Jim said, 'It's time we had a serious talk.'

Michelle laughed. 'I thought we'd had our serious talk the first time you met me from work.'

Jim looked troubled. 'That talk was about you comin' out of yourself a bit more,' he said. 'Well, you have, an' I'm glad about it. Now I want to talk about somethin' else entirely.'

She shouldn't have laughed, Michelle thought guiltily, not when he was being so earnest. 'All right, I'm listening,' she said, trying to match his tone.

They turned left, towards Marston. In the distance, they could see the brick chimneys of Worrell's saltworks, pumping thick, black smoke into the atmosphere.

'How many times have we been out together?' Jim asked her, and from the slight quiver in his voice, she could tell that he was quite nervous.

'I'm not sure we've ever "been out together" at all,' Michelle answered.

Jim winced, as if he were in pain. 'Well, whatever you want to call it, then.'

'Let me see. We've been out on the river twice, we've had a few walks along the canal and we went to the tea rooms in Northwich a couple of times.'

'So you know me pretty well by now, wouldn't you say?' Jim asked.

'*Quite* well,' Michelle said cautiously.

'I'm a steady feller, honest and hard-workin' . . .'

'I know all that, Jim,' Michelle said. 'But when are you going to get to the point?'

Jim bit his lower lip. 'The baby's goin' to need a name,' he blurted out.

Michelle stopped dead in her tracks. 'What did you just say?' she asked.

'When the baby's born, it's goin' to need a name, Michelle. A father's name.'

Was she misreading what he was saying? Michelle wondered. Was she finding a meaning in his words which simply wasn't there? No, she couldn't be. She looked deep into his eyes. 'You're . . . you're asking me to marry you, aren't you?' she gasped.

'I am,' Jim replied, his own gaze matching hers.

She did not know what to feel. Part of her was flattered, of course, and another part of her wondered guiltily if she had unintentionally led him on. But most of all, she was sad – sad that she was going to have to hurt a nice feller like Jim Vernon.

'Can you say somethin' quick?' Jim asked. 'All this waitin' is just about killin' me.'

Michelle took a deep breath. 'I like you a lot, Jim,' she said. 'I really do. But I can't honestly say, hand on heart, that I love you.'

'I know that,' Jim said.

'You do? Then how can you even think . . .?'

'Didn't you tell me once that your mother didn't love your father when they got married? That she didn't fall in love with him for nearly a year after they became man an' wife?'

'Yes, that's true, but—'

'So if it worked for them, how do you know that it can't work for us?'

'But what if it doesn't?'

Jim shrugged his shoulders. 'If it doesn't, it probably won't matter much anyway.'

'How could it not matter?' Michelle asked. 'Once we're married, we're stuck with each other for life. "Till death do us part," as the vicar says.'

'That's the point,' Jim told her. 'Till death do us part. I'm goin' to join the army.'

'Join the army! But you can't. You've read the papers. You know what's happening in France.'

'Yes, I do,' Jim agreed. 'That's why I've got to go.'

'You're not making sense.'

'I was talkin' to your brother, Billy,' Jim said. 'An' he told me what must have been almost the last words Gerald Worrell said before he was killed.'

She hated him for mentioning Gerald. Yet at the same time she admired his bravery for doing so now – for reminding her of her lost love at the moment he was asking her to marry him. 'What did Gerald say?' she asked.

'He said somethin' about it bein' a bloody awful war, with idiots in charge on both sides. But he also said that he figured we were stuck with it, an' he didn't see how he could ever hold his head up again if he let other fellers do his fightin' for him. Well, that's how I feel meself.'

'You're not really offering me the chance to become your wife at all, are you?' Michelle asked. 'You're giving me the chance to become your widow.'

Jim shrugged again. 'Not everybody'll get killed. That stands to reason. Your Billy survived an' I might as well.'

'And if you don't?'

'If I don't, then at least the baby'll be legitimate. So what do you say?'

'I don't know,' Michelle admitted.

'I only want to protect you,' Jim said. 'An' you don't have to worry about the other side of marriage . . .'

'The other side of marriage?'

'You know what I mean. What goes on in the bedroom. I won't expect you to . . .'

Michelle tried to imagine herself in bed with Jim as she had been in bed with Gerald. It seemed strange, but not unpleasant. 'I'm not having that,' she said. '*If* I marry you, then I'll be your wife in every way.'

A glimmer of hope flickered in Jim's eyes. 'Does that mean I've got a chance?' he asked.

Michelle looked at him helplessly. 'Give me a bit of time to think it over,' she pleaded. 'A couple of days. Maybe three. I want to be fair to both of us.'

'I know you do,' Jim said heavily. 'All right. Three days. But if you *could* make it quicker than that, I'd appreciate it.'

Michelle smiled. 'You'll know as soon as I do,' she said.

Aggie heard the hooter at Worrell's saltworks blasting out its call for a return to work. The fish and chip shop would be closing soon, she thought – which would mean that for the next few hours, until it opened again, Spudder would be hanging around the house, fretting that he had nothing to occupy himself with, and wishing she'd at least let him do a bit of cleaning.

She smiled and shook her head. He was a case, that Spudder, and no mistake about it. But she was very fond of him. She had hoped, not so long ago, that he and Ivy might get married. There was still a chance they would, but she was not half as optimistic about it as she had once been.

'Well, I suppose it's time I made a start on the ironin',' Aggie told herself. She cleared the kitchen table and put the two flat irons on the hob over the fire. Give the irons a couple of minutes to heat up, and they'd do the job champion.

She heard the door from the chip shop open, and then the sound of Spudder's footsteps as he went upstairs. It's a pity about him an' Ivy not workin' out, she thought. A real pity.

She'd start with the big jobs first, she decided, picking up a sheet and laying it across the table.

There was the sound of footsteps again – like thunderclaps this time – and Spudder burst into the kitchen. It was immediately obvious that something was wrong. His usually ruddy complexion had turned a deathly pale, and there was a look of pure panic on his face.

'It's gone!' he moaned.

'Calm down, Spudder,' Aggie said, laying aside her iron. 'Just what exactly is it that's gone?'

'Me money.'

'The money you keep in the tin box?'

'Yes.'

'Is the box gone as well?'

'No, that was under the bed, where I always keep it. But it was empty.'

'You're sure you didn't put your money somewhere else?'

'Why would I do that?'

Aggie placed her hands on her huge hips. 'Right,' she said. 'If it's not in the box, an' you didn't put it somewhere else, then it must have been stolen. An' I bet I know the bugger who pinched it.' She walked to the door. 'Come on, Spudder.'

'Where are we goin'?'

'Round to number 49.'

There was no one in the boarding-house kitchen – as might have been expected at that time of day – but it was not the kitchen that Aggie was interested in. She marched straight to the top of the stairs, and knocked loudly on the door to the right.

'Are you in there?' she demanded in a voice loud enough to bring the wall down.

'Mr Pickup'll be at work at this time of day,' Spudder said from behind her.

'That's what you think,' Aggie said, turning the handle and stepping into the room.

Toby Pickup's bedroom, like those of all the other lodgers, had a bed, a chest of drawers, a wardrobe and a table with a water jug and enamel basin on it. It looked tidy enough, but then it should have done, if Ivy had been doing her job properly.

Aggie threw the wardrobe doors open. 'Empty!' she said. 'An' you look under the bed, I bet that you'll find that his suitcase has gone, an' all.'

Spudder bent down and peered under the bed. 'It has gone, Aggie!' he said.

'I never did really trust that feller Pickup,' Aggie told him. 'There was somethin' about his eyes. An' I wasn't keen about the way he played up to Ivy, either.'

'So what do we do now?' Spudder asked, looking as miserable as she'd ever seen him.

'We call the police, of course. But before we do that, we'd better find out when he was last seen. Ivy'll know that.' She looked around the room, as if expecting to see her assistant lurking in one of the corners. 'Now where is the girl?'

Spudder remembered what he had heard when he was hiding behind the hawthorn hedge: *'I'm afraid that if I listen to you, you just might be able to talk me into doin' somethin'*

I don't want to do – somethin' that isn't right,' Ivy had said.

'Or it could be you're afraid that I'll talk you into doin' somethin' that is *right,'* Pickup had replied. *'Right for both of us.'*

'I said, where's Ivy got to?' Aggie repeated.

'I don't know,' Spudder said. 'I haven't seen her around for ages.'

The middle-aged police constable who came to the boarding house was very sympathetic, but it was obvious he thought there was little he could do.

'How much was in the box exactly?' he asked.

'A hundred an' twenty-three pound,' Spudder told him.

'That's a lot of money.'

'Aye,' Spudder agreed. 'An' I had to sell a lot of fish an' chips to make it.'

'You should have put it in the Post Office, you know,' the constable said.

'Oh, for heaven's sake!' Aggie exploded. 'Don't you think the lad feels bad enough about it already, without you remindin' of what he *should* have done?'

'You're right,' the policeman agreed. 'Sorry, missis.' He turned his attention back to Spudder. 'Now I think you'd better tell me about this girl.'

Spudder's misery seemed to be growing by the second. 'Her name's Ivy Clegg,' he mumbled. 'She works for me – or she *did* work for me, anyway.'

'When I think of how ungrateful that girl's been after you took her in an' gave her a job, I could spit,' Aggie said. 'I'd never have believed it of her. She took us both for a right pair of fools, didn't she, Spudder?'

'She did that,' Spudder agreed.

He'd realised the day he'd seen her walking down the canal with Toby Pickup that he'd lost her, but he'd never thought she'd do this to him. And though the theft of the money hurt him, it was Ivy he was really breaking his heart over.

Chapter Twenty-five

As they were walking up the lane, Becky and Billy saw the policeman leaving number 47.

'I wonder what he wanted,' Becky said, sounding slightly worried.

Billy grinned. 'Who knows? Maybe Uncle Spudder's given up makin' chips and started robbin' banks instead.'

Becky relaxed a little, and grinned back. 'Yes, I can just see Spudder pointin' a gun at the bank clerk – probably the wrong way round, if I know him – an' tellin' him to hand over the money.'

'I want all the cash you've got!' Billy said, in an affectionate imitation of his uncle, 'but if you're too busy now, I don't mind waitin'. An' while I'm here, I might as well polish your windows for you – they look like they could do with a good clean.'

Becky laughed, and then the anxious look returned to her face. 'Still, I don't like it,' she admitted. 'Bobbies usually mean trouble.'

'There's hundreds of reasons he could have gone to see Uncle Spudder,' Billy said reassuringly. 'But if it's really botherin' you, why don't we call in on the way back from our walk?'

'Yes, I think we might do that,' Becky said.

They walked up the cartroad and on to the canal towpath. These strolls together had become a regular thing since Billy had been well enough to leave the house. At first, it had been a strain on him, but now, though he still had a slight limp, he had no difficulty in keeping up with his mother. In a couple of weeks, I'll be fightin' fit an' ready to make me move, he thought. But before he could make the move, he had to talk about it to his mam, and he was definitely not looking forward to that at all.

'You've got somethin' on your mind, haven't you, our Billy?' Becky said.

Billy sighed. Nobody in Mam's family had ever managed to keep anything secret from Becky for long. Well, he supposed now was as good a time as any to get it over with.

'I think I'm almost ready to start working again, Mam,' he said.

Becky looked at him anxiously. 'Are you sure?' she asked. 'It's heavy work, bakin' bread.'

'That's the thing, Mam. I've been weighin' it up, an' I don't want to be a baker any more.'

Becky smiled indulgently. 'So you have decided to give college a try after all, have you?'

Billy shook his head. 'No, Mam.'

'Then if you're not goin' back to the bakery, an' you don't want to go to college, I don't really see . . .'

'I want adventure. I want excitement.'

'You never want to go back in the army again?'

'They wouldn't have me,' Billy said. 'There's plenty of eager young men without gammy legs who are more than willin' to take my place. Besides . . . I've never really told you much about the war, have I, Mam?'

'No,' Becky agreed, 'you haven't. You never seemed to want to talk about it, an' I thought I shouldn't push you.'

'Well, maybe it's time to talk about it now. I've killed men, Mam.'

'I thought you must have.'

'I've plunged me bayonet into 'em an' watched 'em die. An' they weren't monsters, you know. They were just ordinary, decent workin' fellers like me.'

'You had to do it, Billy,' Becky said.

'I know I did, but that doesn't make it right. An' that's why, when I do start work again, I want to be sure that I'm doin' somethin' which is good an' useful. You understand what I'm sayin'? I'd like to think that I'd be leavin' the world a better place than I found it.'

Becky closed her eyes and saw the marble gravestone in

Marston churchyard, could read the inscription that she had composed for Michael – the inscription that Billy had just quoted back at her. But why had he chosen just those words? she wondered. And then it hit her with all the force of a bolt of lightning. No! she told herself in horror, it couldn't be true! Yet she knew that it was.

'You want to go to Africa,' she said, praying that he would reply that wasn't what he wanted at all – that he'd decided to become a clergyman or hospital porter.

'That's right,' Billy agreed. 'I wrote to Uncle Jack a few weeks ago, an' he's written back to say he's prepared to take me on as his assistant.'

When Richard had heard that his son had been killed, images of the boy's life had flashed through his mind. And now, though Billy was still with her, Becky experienced the same thing: Billy as she had first seen him – dirty, naked and crawling round the floor of a filthy coal barge; Billy the first time he had spoken, when he thanked his Uncle Spudder for the toy soldiers; Billy on his first day at work – nervous, worried, intimidated by the giant presence of a fat little French baker called Monsieur Henri. All those Billy's leading up to this one. He was a fine boy, a wonderful boy, and now she was about to lose him.

'Africa robbed me of your father. Don't let it rob me of you,' she pleaded.

'Dad was just unlucky,' Billy told her. 'Look at Uncle Jack. He went out to work on the oil rivers long before Dad did, an' he's still as fit as a fiddle.'

'It's your Uncle Jack who's been lucky, not your dad who was unlucky,' Becky said. 'They don't call that coast the White Man's Grave for nothin'.'

'It got that name years ago, when conditions were a lot worse than they are now.' Billy smiled and put his arms around his mother. 'You fuss too much, Mam.'

'That's what mams are for,' Becky said. She looked down into the canal, almost if she was expecting to see a vision of the future in it, but all she saw there was the green water and gentle ripples.

'I can't talk you out of it, can I?' she asked.

'No, Mam,' Billy said. 'I'd cut off me own arm rather than

hurt you, you know that. But this is somethin' I've just got to do.'

Though she fought against it, large tears began to appear in Becky's eyes.

'Don't cry, Mam,' Billy begged her.

'I can't help it,' Becky said. 'Sometimes you're so much like Michael that I just can't stop myself.'

Jim Vernon made his way slowly up Ollershaw Lane. His feet ached from so much walking, yet he felt so restless that he couldn't bring himself to stop. He took out his watch. It was only a few hours since he had proposed to Michelle, but it seemed like an eternity. And she might take two or three days before she made up her mind, she'd told him. He didn't know how he would ever last that long.

He was passing her house when she suddenly appeared in the alley and called to him.

'How did you know I'd be comin' by now?' Jim asked.

'I didn't,' Michelle replied. 'But I wanted to see you. So I was sitting in the front room, watching the street.' She giggled. 'Not-Stopping Worrell, that's me.'

'An' what did you want to see me about?'

Michelle's face became serious again. 'Would you like to go for a drink? she asked.

'I'm not bothered one way or the other,' Jim told her.

'Well, I think I could use one,' Michelle said, taking his arm, and leading him towards the New Inn.

Though it was customary for women to do their drinking in the best room of the pub, Michelle couldn't bear the thought of having her conversation with Jim scrutinised by the village gossips, so she steered him into the public bar instead.

'So what's this all about?' Jim asked, when he had paid for their drinks and taken them over to a table in the corner.

'I just want to be certain that when you proposed, you knew what you were doing,' Michelle said. 'I'm carrying another man's child.'

'No, you're not. If we're married, it'll be my baby.'

'There'll be people who call you a fool.'

'Let them. I don't care.'

'It's easy to say now.'

'I'd be a fool if I *didn't* want to marry you.'

'Suppose we did get married, and then next year, or the year after, you met a decent girl who'd been saving herself for her husband?'

'It won't happen. You're the only one I want. You're the only one I'll ever want.'

'I've got one more question, and then I'll give you my answer,' Michelle said.

'You'd better ask it, then.'

'If I made a condition of agreeing to marry you that you didn't become a soldier, what would you say to that?'

'I'd say you were breakin' my heart,' Jim told her.

'You mean you'd join up anyway?'

'I'd have to. You see, I can choose to propose to you, but I don't feel as if I have any choice at all about the other thing. It's as if I've got to go, whether I want to or not.'

'I don't want to lose a second man to that terrible war,' Michelle said.

'An' I don't want you to have to spend the rest of your life livin' with a feller who's lost all respect for himself, because he knew what the right thing to do was, an' he didn't do it,' Jim countered.

Michelle sighed. 'It feels like we're just going round in circles,' she said.

'So do you want more time to think about it?' Jim asked.

'No,' Michelle replied. 'No, I don't think I do.'

Not-Stopping Bracegirdle glanced through the hatch at the occupants of the bar, then picked up the three milk stouts and made her way arthritically back to the table.

'What's the matter with you, Mam?' Half-a-Mo-Flo asked.

'Why should there be anythin' the matter with me?' Not-Stopping asked, pouring out her drink in the infuriatingly slow way she always did when she had a good story.

'You've a grin on your face like the cat who's got the cream, that's what's the matter.'

'Have I?' Not-Stopping said innocently.

'You know you have.'

'Michelle Worrell an' Jim Vernon were in the bar,' Not-Stopping said. 'They were too far away for me to hear what they were sayin', but I did hear somethin'.'

'What kind of somethin'?'

The grin on Not-Stopping's face broadened. 'I heard weddin' bells,' she said.

It was half-past nine in the evening. Becky had been round at number 47 offering her sympathy, but now she had gone home. Aggie should have left hours ago, but though she knew Ned would be pining for his supper, she couldn't abandon Spudder, not in his state. And so they sat opposite each other in the kitchen, he miserable because he had been betrayed, and she because she had not protected him from it.

'You know them feelin's I had?' he asked.

'Yes, Spudder.'

'I think they were love.'

'Maybe they were,' Aggie said. 'But you'll have to learn to put them behind you now.'

'Why did she ever have to come here, Aggie? I was happy enough before she arrived, an' now I don't think I'll ever be happy again.'

'You'll get over it in time,' Aggie said soothingly, but she was not sure that he would. Spudder was a special case, and even if it *was* possible for him to fall in love a second time, she didn't think he'd ever trust any woman enough to let it happen.

They heard the back gate click open, and then footsteps crossing the yard.

Aggie looked out of the window. 'Well, I never would have believed it!' she said. 'Not in a million years.'

The back door opened, and Ivy Clegg walked into the kitchen.

'Ivy!' Spudder said. Then, though his mouth remained open, he seemed incapable of finding any other words.

It was not a problem Aggie Spratt shared with him. 'You've got a brass nerve showin' your face again, Ivy,' she said. 'What are you doin' here, anyway? Did you leave in such a rush this mornin' that you forgot to take somethin' with you?'

'No,' Ivy said. 'I—'

But Aggie hadn't finished. 'Because whatever it is you left behind, it'll cost you dearly,' she continued. 'Make no mistake, you'll find yourself talkin' to the police before long, my girl.'

Ivy looked bewildered. 'But I've already talked to the police,' she said. 'In Manchester.'

'Manchester!' Aggie repeated. 'What the hell were you doin' in Manchester?'

'Followin' Toby Pickup.'

'I don't understand,' Spudder said, finding his voice at last.

'Neither do I,' Aggie admitted. She pulled out a chair. 'You'd better sit down an' tell us all about it, Ivy,' she said in a voice still far from friendly.

Ivy sat. 'It all started late this mornin',' she said. 'About eleven o'clock, it was. You were out shoppin', Aggie, an' Spudder had gone for one of his walks in the woods.'

'That's right,' Spudder agreed. He had taken to walking in the woods a lot since he'd seen Ivy and Toby together. But it hadn't helped – nothing had really helped.

'Anyway, I went upstairs to do the dustin',' Ivy continued, 'an' found Toby Pickup in Spudder's room.'

'What did he say to you?' Aggie asked.

'He said he'd been lookin' for me.'

'An' did you believe him?'

'No, I didn't. He wouldn't have had to go right into Spudder's room to find out whether I was there or not. If I had been there, he'd have heard me workin'.'

'That's true enough,' Aggie agreed. 'So what did you do next?'

'Well, I knew that he was thinkin' of leavin' Northwich for good an' all . . .'

'Just how would you know that?' Aggie asked sharply.

'He told me himself a few days back. He . . . he said that when he went, he wanted me to go with him.'

'An' you said yes?'

Ivy shook her head. 'I said no. Don't you believe me?'

'I'll reserve judgement till I've heard the rest of it,' Aggie told her. 'You were sayin' . . .?'

'Well, since I knew he was plannin' to go, I thought he might have gone into Spudder's room to pinch somethin', but—'

'That's exactly what he did do!' Spudder interrupted.

'But thinkin' somethin' an' knowin' it for sure are two completely different things,' Ivy continued. 'So what I decided to do was keep an eye on him and see what he did next. Not fifteen minutes later, he came out of the back door of number 49 with his suitcase in his hand an' set off down the lane. That's when I knew for certain that he'd pinched somethin'.'

'How could you suddenly be so sure?'

'Because he's not just goin' to walk off an' leave nearly a week's pay uncollected unless he's got a lot more money from somewhere else, now is he?'

'That's smart thinkin',' Aggie admitted, 'if you're really tellin' the truth. So he set off down the lane. What did you do?'

'Followed him, of course.'

'Why didn't you just call a bobby?'

'I would have done if I could have found one, but there weren't any about, not even on Northwich Station.'

'Is that how you ended up in Manchester?'

'Yes. Toby Pickup got on the Manchester train, so I did, an' all. An' when we reached Victoria Station there was a bobby on duty, an' I told him all about it. Pickup tried to talk his way out of it – he's got a smooth tongue in his head, that one – but even he couldn't explain how all them banknotes had found their way into his suitcase. So they arrested him.'

Aggie still did not look convinced. 'If all you've been sayin' is true, where's Spudder's money?' she asked.

'The Manchester Police have got it.'

'What do they want with it?'

'They said they needed it for evidence at the trial. But Spudder'll get it back in the end.' Ivy reached into her bag, took out a piece of paper and handed it to Aggie. 'They gave me this.'

'What does it say?' Spudder asked.

'It's a receipt for your money,' Aggie said when she'd read it. 'It looks like Ivy was tellin' the truth.' She turned to the girl with a look of remorse on her face. 'Sorry I didn't trust you, love, but—'

'But you only had Spudder's best intentions at heart, an' you know how easy it is to take advantage of him?'

Aggie smiled gratefully. 'Yes, that's it.'

'Did you foller all that, Spudder?' Ivy asked.

'I'll be gettin' me money back in the end?'

'Yes, you will.'

'An' will you still be workin' for me?'

'Well, of course I will. Why should you ever imagine that I'd want to leave?'

'I don't know,' Spudder admitted. 'But it's all a bit confusin', isn't it? Up until a few minutes ago, I thought that you an' Toby Pickup were . . .' He stopped, and began to redden.

'Were what?' Ivy demanded. 'Stealin' your money between us?'

'No. Well, you know,' Spudder said uncomfortably.

'No, I don't know.'

Aggie stood up. 'If you'll excuse me, it's time I was gettin', home to my Ned,' she said, 'Anyway, I don't think I want to listen to this particular conversation.'

They sat in silence while Aggie put on her coat, but the moment they heard her close the yard gate behind her, Ivy turned to Spudder and said, 'Now what's this about?'

'I don't want to talk about it,' Spudder mumbled.

'Spudder!' Ivy said severely.

'I saw you an' Toby walkin' along the canal together. So I thought that you and him must be . . .'

'Courtin'?'

'Yes.'

'But I only ever went for a walk with him once,' Ivy said. 'An' even then, you were the reason behind it.'

'Was I?'

'Yes. You see, I think I knew even then that Toby wasn't a very nice man, but he was a lot cleverer than I am – an' I thought that he might be able to tell me a way to get you to do what I wanted you to do.'

'And what was that?' Spudder asked, completely mystified.

Ivy sighed. 'If I have to tell you meself, it's no good.' She searched around for some way of dropping a hint without giving away the whole thing. 'Let's face it, Spudder,' she said finally, 'you're not cut out for this courtin' lark, are you?'

'You mean I should give up on you?' Spudder asked.

'I didn't say that.'

Spudder frowned. 'But if you don't want me to court you, and you don't want me to give up on you, what in the dickens do you want me to do?'

'Think about it,' Ivy said, as she had done that day in the rowing boat. 'I'm sure it'll come to you in the end.'

And suddenly, it did. Spudder stood up quicky, then sank down on to one knee. 'Will you marry me, Ivy?' he asked.

'I'll give you your answer in a minute,' Ivy said. 'But first, I really think you ought to kiss me.'

Spudder rose again as if his pants were on fire. 'Do I have to?' he asked.

'Yes, you do,' Ivy said firmly. 'In fact, I rather think it's somethin' you're goin' to have to get used to on a regular basis.'

Spudder leant forward. He pressed his lips gingerly against hers, and would immediately have withdrawn them again had not Ivy clamped her arm around the back of his neck. And then, as their lips began to move, Spudder found that he didn't want to pull back. This was much easier than he'd expected, and a lot nicer.

It was Ivy who finally broke away. 'You're like a tiger when you're roused, aren't you?' she said.

'Am I?' Spudder asked, starting to feel very proud of himself.

'An' now I expect you'll want an answer to your question.'

'What question?' said Spudder, whose head was reeling.

'Whether I'll marry you or not.'

'Oh, I'd forgotten that,' Spudder admitted. 'Will you?'

Ivy smiled. 'Of course I will, you daft 'a'p'orth,' she said.

Chapter Twenty-six

The first thing which came into Billy Worrell's head when he woke up was thoughts about the weather. It had been overcast for the whole of the previous week, and he prayed that on this day which was so important to his sister and his friends, the sky had at last learned to behave itself.

He climbed out of bed and walked over to the window. The clouds had all disappeared, and it looked as if the last Saturday in April was going to be a truly glorious day. Well, that's one big weight off me mind, at any rate, he thought. Because although he knew that no one could possibly blame him for the weather, he was responsible for so much else that he'd started to think that if it *did* rain, it would somehow be his fault.

He ran through his mental checklist of the things he should have done. 'The cars have been ordered,' he murmured to himself, 'the church has been booked, an' so has the hall . . .'

'The rings!' a voice screamed from the back of his mind. 'What have you done with the bloody rings?'

'I've put them in the top drawer, of course,' he told his panicking brain. But even though he knew they should be there, his hands still trembled as he slid the drawer open. He looked down, and breathed a sigh of relief. Yes, they were still there – all four of them.

He grinned as he remembered the expression on the vicar's face when they'd told him the arrangement they wanted.

'Who is to be your best man?' Reverend Birchall had asked Jim, as they all sat in one of the rectory's larger sitting rooms, taking a polite afternoon tea.

'Billy, er, William's goin' to do the job,' Jim had replied. 'He's a good mate of mine, as well as bein' Michelle's brother.'

The vicar, a rather self-important man in his early fifties, nodded his head to show that he considered that to be a very sensible arrangement. 'And who is to be your best man?' he asked, turning to Spudder.

'Billy,' Spudder said.

The vicar laughed that dry, reserved laugh that some vicars seem to cultivate. 'Another Billy, I assume,' he said.

'Pardon?'

The vicar laughed again. 'I said, it's another Billy you're talking about, isn't it? It couldn't be this one, could it?' he asked, gesturing towards Michelle's brother.

'But it is,' Spudder said.

The vicar's smile disappeared. 'You want to share a best man?' he asked incredulously.

Spudder became flustered as only he could. 'Well, he's me nephew, you see, Vicar. I mean, he's not really me nephew. He couldn't be, could he, 'cos Mam wasn't really me mam? But I was with Mrs Becky when she found him on that coal barge in Liverpool, an' he's always called me Uncle Spudder, ever since I gave him them toy soldiers, even though I'm not.'

'I'm not sure that I quite understand,' Reverend Birchall said. 'What exactly is all this about mothers not being mothers and people being found on coal barges?'

'Well, you see . . .' Spudder said.

Ivy squeezed his hand tightly. 'Shush, Spudder,' she said. 'Let Jim an' Michelle do the talkin'.'

'Is there anything in the Bible or the Book of Common Prayer which says they can't both share the same best man, Reverend Birchall?' Michelle asked.

'Well, no I suppose not,' the vicar admitted reluctantly. 'It's just that I've never heard of such a thing happening before.'

Michelle smiled sweetly and persuasively. 'In that case, it really would make us all very happy if you could see your way clear to starting a new tradition.'

Starting a new tradition! The vicar rather liked the sound of that. He could imagine future discussions in ecclesiastical circles up and down the country: 'Of course, it's quite common to have only one best man for two couples now, but it was a novel idea, almost revolutionary, when Birchall first came up with it.'

'Could you, Vicar?' Jim asked anxiously.

'All right,' Reverend Birchall agreed. 'But I'm sure I don't know where it will lead. I shouldn't be at all surprised if I had two brides and only one groom at the next wedding I conduct.'

'Oh that happens already,' Spudder said. 'Mr Michael told me all about it once. It's called poly-somethin'-or-other.'

'Shush, Spudder,' Ivy said again, pinching his hand quite hard this time.

Michelle sat in front of her dressing-table mirror, brushing her long, golden hair. Well, Jim's got what he asked for, she thought. I *am* going to marry him. But though he was getting what he asked for, was he also getting what he really wanted, she wondered, what he really deserved?

She imagined her mam asking herself the same questions the day she married her dad. 'And that worked out all right, didn't it?' she said to her reflection. 'Better than all right.'

Yet she couldn't help thinking about all the difficulties which lay ahead. The doctor had told her that, for the next month or so at least, she and Jim could live, as he so tactfully put it, 'like any normal married couple'. And she was determined that they would. She didn't love Jim, but she wanted him to share her bed.

Would that be hard – to make love to a man you were only fond of? Should she try to forget that night with Gerald and let Jim make all the running in bed, or should she do things that were sure to please him?

Becky appeared in the doorway. 'How are you doin', my little love?' she asked.

'Did you have any doubts on your wedding day, Mam?' Michelle asked, returning to her earlier thoughts.

'Doubts!' Becky repeated. 'I had nothin' *but* doubts. Do you know, when your Uncle Jack was drivin' me over the bridge to the church, I kept wantin' to jump out of the carriage an' run away.' She laughed. 'Of course, it was easier in those days. Try jumpin' out of a motorcar, and you'll really be in trouble.'

'I have actually thought about running away myself,' Michelle confessed.

'Well, of course you have,' her mother said. She put her hand on Michelle's shoulder. 'Jim's not Gerald, and he never will be,' she continued softly. 'But then your dad wasn't Richard, either. If my experience is anythin' to go by, you'll learn to love Jim in a quite different way to the one in which you loved Gerald.'

'Thanks, Mam,' Michelle said.

She stood up and walked over to the window. Only a month earlier, the trees which grew just beyond the back yard had been black skeletons. Now they sprouted thousands of buds, which would soon open and shroud them in a cloak of green. Up in the sky, birds swooped and swirled and sang their songs, as they celebrated the coming of spring.

New life – wonderful, miraculous new life – was starting everywhere, she thought. In the flowers. In the trees. In her belly. So maybe it was not too much to hope that her own new life might have a little wonder in it, too.

Up the lane, in number 47, Spudder Johnson was in a real champion of a panic. 'I can't find me collar studs,' he told the Great Marvello. 'I had them a minute ago, an' now I just can't find 'em.'

'Maybe you'll find them in your collar studs box.'

'I don't know where that is, neither.'

'Isn't that it, on the mantelpiece?'

'So it is,' Spudder said. 'Thank heavens for that.'

'Why don't you try to relax?' Marvello suggested.

'How can I when there's so many things that can go wrong?' Spudder fretted. 'Say Ivy forgets that we're gettin' married today.'

'I don't think that's likely.'

'But she could.'

'If she'd forgotten, she'd have turned up for work, as usual, wouldn't she?'

'Oh, that's right,' Spudder said, but his relief did not last long. 'What if I forget the words of the marriage service? I do forget things, you know.'

'All you have to do is repeat what the vicar says,' Marvello assured him.

'You see! I'd forgotten that! I don't think I want to get married after all.'

'You can't let Ivy down now,' Marvello told him.

'Oh, I want to be married to Ivy,' Spudder said. 'More than anythin' in the world. It's just the ceremony I don't fancy.' Spudder looked hopefully at his old friend. 'There isn't any way we could just forget about the church bit, is there?'

'No,' Marvello said. 'I'm afraid there isn't.'

'I think I'd rather have you saw me in half again than go through all this,' Spudder told him.

Jim was just fastening his tie when there was a discreet knock on his bedroom door. 'Come in,' he said.

'Good morning, Jim,' said the tall man with the neat moustache who entered the room.

'What are you doin' back here in Marston, Mr Bingham?' Jim asked.

'Checking up on a few things,' Bingham said. 'And I've come to attend your wedding. If I'm invited, that is.'

'Well, of course you're invited,' Jim said, wondering if he would ever get his tie straight.

'I'm also here to make you a proposal,' Bingham said, with a more official edge creeping into his voice.

'Oh yes?' Jim said cautiously.

'I hear that you're thinking of joining up.'

'I *am* goin' to join up. But not right now. I'll do it after the baby's born. Michelle'll need me around till then.'

'I was very impressed with the way you handled yourself during the Captain Davenport affair,' Bingham told him.

'I didn't do nothin',' Jim said.

'Don't be so modest. You built up a good case against me – even if your conclusions *were* completely wrong. And the way you disarmed one spy and then chased another shows that you react very well in a crisis.'

The tie would still not come straight. 'What's all this leadin' up to, Mr Bingham?'

'I would ask you to consider the possibility of joining Military Intelligence, instead of enlisting in the army.'

'I don't think so,' Jim said, without hesitation.

'It's vitally important work, and not without its moments of excitement.'

'I'm sure you're right.'

'So why won't you even consider it?'

'War changes people,' Jim said. 'It's changed Michelle's brother Billy, for one. He can't bring himself to go back to the bakery after what he's been through.'

'What's your point?'

'Maybe I'll feel the same, if I survive. Maybe the river won't be enough for me when I get home, an' I'll be lookin' for a bit of excitement. Come an' see me again after the war, Mr Bingham, an' you'll probably get a different answer to the one I'm givin' you now.'

'I still don't see why you're turning me down, Jim,' Mr Bingham persisted.

'Because I wouldn't feel comfortable sittin' in an office, while all the time I knew there was other fellers gettin' blown to bits on the Western Front.'

'I admire you for your principles,' Mr Bingham told him, 'but I still think you're making a mistake.'

The tie was straight at last. 'Maybe I am makin' a mistake,' Jim admitted, 'but it's a mistake that I can live with – or die with, if I have to.'

Ivy examined her outfit in the mirror. It was green – the colour of spring. The jacket had a wing collar, a wide buckled belt and fur trim, and there was a wraparound skirt to match. They were the first new clothes she had ever worn in her life.

'Do I look all right?' she asked anxiously.

'You look a real treat,' Aggie assured her. 'That outfit's champion, and you've got the figure to show it off – just like I had when I was your age.' It was hard to believe that the mountainous cleaner had ever had any figure other than her current one, but then Aggie smiled and Ivy could *almost* see her as the slim young girl she once might have been.

'Where's me breakfast, Aggie?' Ned Spratt called up plaintively from the kitchen.

'You'll have to wait a bit longer,' Aggie shouted back. 'For once, there's somethin' more than your stomach to consider.'

Ivy was still looking at her clothes. 'I feel awful guilty,' she said. 'This dress an' skirt must have cost Spudder a fortune.'

'They did,' Aggie said. 'I was with him when he bought 'em, so I should know. But it was nothin' like the fortune you saved him when you had Toby Pickup arrested.'

'Still . . .' Ivy said doubtfully.

'Besides, it's right that your man should spoil you on your weddin' day.' She raised a thick finger in warning. 'Just don't let him go on spoilin' you too much, because you know what Spudder's like.'

'I do. An' you don't need to worry on that score.'

'I know I don't. Otherwise, I wouldn't have let you get near him in the first place.'

Ivy smiled. 'You really care about him, don't you?'

Her words made Aggie look distinctly uncomfortable. 'Well, you know how it is.'

Ivy grinned mischievously. 'No. How is it?'

Aggie looked down at her ham-like hands. 'Me an' Spudder have worked together for a long time, an' I've sort of got into the habit of lookin' after him. But I won't have to do it much longer, thank the Lord, because that'll be your job after the weddin'.'

'An' I'll make a good one of it,' Ivy promised.

'I'm sure you will,' Aggie said. 'I'll be off to make Ned's breakfast for him in a minute, but there's just one more thing I've got to say before I go.'

'And what's that?'

'I never called anybody ma'am,' Aggie said, almost defiantly. 'Not even Mrs Taylor – an' I worked for her for years.'

'I'm not sure I'm followin' you.'

'Spudder's my boss,' Aggie said, 'an' as from this mornin', you'll be Spudder's wife an' takin' charge of the household affairs. Which means that *you'll* be my boss, doesn't it?'

'I'd never really thought about it like that, but I suppose it does,' Ivy admitted.

'But just because you'll be my boss doesn't mean I'm goin' to start callin' you ma'am.'

'I wouldn't want you to,' Ivy assured her. She giggled. 'Me, a ma'am! That would be awful.'

★

Billy's earlier worries proved groundless. The cars arrived on time, the weather held, and by eleven o'clock that morning, most of the interested parties had arrived at St Paul's Church, Marston, to celebrate the weddings of Mr James Vernon to Miss Michelle Worrell, and of Mr Clarence 'Spudder' Johnson to Miss Ivy Clegg.

'I want to go to the lavvy,' Spudder whispered to Jim and Billy, as they stood facing the altar.

'Take it easy, Uncle Spudder,' Billy whispered back. 'You don't really want to go – it's just nerves.'

'It might well be, but I know just how he feels,' Jim said sympathetically.

Spudder looked down, saw that one of his bootlaces had come untied, and wondered if bending over and fastening it again was allowed in church. If he did fasten it, he argued, the vicar might shout at him. But if he didn't fasten it, that might cause trouble, too. The boots were new, and a little loose, and if one came flying off his foot when he was walking back down the aisle with Ivy, then she'd *shout* at him.

'Won't be long now,' Billy said. 'I can hear the bridal cars pulling up outside.'

Spudder glanced down at his boot again, hoping that the lace had magically retied itself. It hadn't. He would walk out of the church very slowly, he decided, and then, with any luck, the boot would stay where it was supposed to.

Becky heard the cars pull up outside. Soon, her only daughter would be married. An' I suppose that when it happens, I'll cry like most mothers do, she thought. Partly, she knew, she would cry with happiness, because Jim Vernon was a nice lad who would make Michelle a fine husband. But there would be sadness behind the tears, too, because when Becky saw Michelle walking down the aisle on her Uncle Jack's arm, she knew she would wish with every inch of her being that it was her beloved Michael who was giving his daughter away.

Spudder shifted his weight from one foot to the other, and then remembering his untied lace, stopped moving at all. Behind them, the organist struck up the wedding march.

'Does that meanin' they're comin' into the church at last?' Spudder asked.

'Yes, that's what it means,' Billy assured him.

'Can I turn round an' have a look?' Spudder asked.

The vicar scowled, and Billy said, 'No, Uncle Spudder. Somehow, I don't think that would be a very good idea.'

Then, suddenly, Ivy was standing beside him, and beyond her was Mr Marvello, who was giving her away.

'You look relieved to see me,' Ivy said impishly. 'Did you think I'd back out at the last minute?'

'No,' Spudder said. 'But I want to go to the lavvy, you see.'

Ivy shook her head in mock despair. 'Well, if it was romance I was lookin' for, I've come to the wrong shop,' she said. 'But then I already knew that.'

'Wilt thou have this Man to thy wedded husband . . .' the vicar intoned.

It was too late to think about backing out now, Michelle told herself. She turned her head slightly, so she could see Jim. Standing there, so straight and proud, he almost looked handsome. No, she corrected herself – he *was* handsome, at least to her.

' . . . and forsaking all others, keep thee only unto him, so long as ye both shall live?'

'I will,' Michelle said firmly.

'Who giveth this Woman to be married to this Man?'

'I do,' said Uncle Jack, the man who would soon be showing her brother the dangers and mysteries of the Oil Rivers.

The vicar took Jim's hand and placed it in Michelle's. Jim gave her an encouraging squeeze.

'Say after me, I James, take thee, Michelle, to my wedded wife . . .'

What would her father have made of Jim? Michelle wondered. But she already knew the answer. Michael Worrell had never been one to be taken in by outward appearances or trappings. He would have looked right into Jim's inner self – and would have approved of what he saw.

'Say after me, I Michelle, take thee, James . . .'

'I Michelle, take thee, James . . .'

It was going to be all right, she thought. *It was going to be all right.*

Spudder had stood perfectly still – trying not to think about either his stomach or his bootlace – while the vicar married Jim and Michelle, and then it was his turn. It wasn't as bad as he'd feared it would be. Reverend Birchall said the words nice and slowly, and Spudder repeated them with only one or two mistakes.

It was only after he had slipped the ring on Ivy's finger – without dropping it once – that the trouble started. 'I now pronounce you man and wife,' Reverend Birchall said. 'You may kiss the bride.'

Spudder looked around to see who the vicar was talking to, and then realised with horror that the remark was being addressed to him. 'Kiss her?' he said.

'Yes,' the vicar replied.

'Here? In front of all these people? I couldn't.'

Then Ivy took control, pulling his head down to the level of hers, and Spudder soon forgot about all the people who were watching him, and sighing sentimentally to themselves.

Michelle and Jim led the procession out of the church. Spudder and Ivy followed them.

Spudder had not forgotten about his bootlace, and walked slowly, almost dragging his foot along the floor.

'What's the matter with you, Spudder?' Ivy asked. 'Why are you dawdlin'?'

He didn't dare tell her about the boot, he decided. Better think of some excuse quickly. 'Oh, er, it was such a lovely service that I don't want it to be over,' he said.

He felt Ivy's hand clutch his arm a little more tightly. 'There you are,' she said. 'You can be romantic when you want to be.'

'Can I?' Spudder asked.

Not-Stopping Bracegirdle's aching joints had been kind enough to allow her to make the walk over the bridge to the church, and she and her cronies were gathered by the gate to watch the wedding party emerge.

'They've not put on much of a show, really, considerin' that

Michelle Worrell's mam's got more money than she knows what to do with,' Half-a-Mo-Flo said, sniffing.

'There's a war goin' on,' Dottie Curzon reminded her.

'And what's that got to do with anythin'?'

'We've all been told to avoid waste, haven't we? Why, you're not even supposed to throw rice at weddin's any more.'

'Anyway, I don't think it's all *that* bad a show,' said Not-Stopping, with a generosity which seemed to occur so often these days that it was starting to worry her.

'Well, all I can say is, you're not much of a judge of weddings, Mam,' Flo said.

I hate it when she calls me Mam, Not-Stopping thought. If people hear her, they might think we're blood relatives or somethin'. Aloud, she said, 'The one advantage of bein' old, Florence, is that you've usually seen a lot more than them what's younger. I watched Michelle's mam get married. Aye, an' her granny as well. So when I say it's not a bad show, I know what I'm talkin' about.'

'Just because you're old—' Flo began.

'An' you'll see I'm right when they come out,' Not-Stopping continued. 'So if you'll just wait half a mo, Flo . . .' She stopped and chuckled to herself.

'What's the joke?' Flo asked suspiciously.

'Maybe I'll explain it when you're old enough to understand,' Not-Stopping said.

Flo relapsed into sulky silence, and Dottie Curzon – who derived a great deal of innocent pleasure from these skirmishes – wondered if, while each of them knew the other's nickname, either had even the slightest suspicion that she had one of her own.

Not-Stopping looked around her. The Adelaide Mine Brass Band had already taken up its position outside the church porch. It had played at Becky's wedding, too, she remembered, when Becky's dad had been lead trumpeter. It wasn't the band now that it was then, and there was reason enough for that. The saltmining industry had been in decline for a quarter of a century, and the Adelaide mine no longer employed half the miners it used to. At the time Becky got married, the bandmaster had had any number of willing volunteers to choose from. Now, he had to take who he could get. And then there was the war – there was *always* the war. Several young bandsmen had already joined up, and others were talking of going.

Still, it would be nice to hear them play again, Not-Stopping thought. And maybe if she tried very hard, she could convince herself that they were playing for her – an old woman who would probably not live to see another performance.

The wedding party emerged from the church and posed for the photographers. Spudder seemed as if he were in a daze, but Ivy, by his side, still looked up at him adoringly. Jim and Michelle held hands, and looked both happy and brave – but mainly brave.

The Adelaide Mine Brass Band played its usual selection of Gilbert and Sullivan, and then it was time for the wedding breakfast in the church hall – meat from Trundley's the butcher's, bread and cakes courtesy of Worrell's bakery.

It was a good reception, considering there was a war going on, but even so, most of the guests couldn't help noticing how many familiar faces were absent – overseas or in their premature graves – and when it came to the dancing, most of the women had to settle for female partners.

At four o'clock in the afternoon, the cars turned up to take the honeymooning couples away. Spudder and Ivy were going to New Brighton, and Jim and Michelle had settled on a few days in Blackpool. For this part of the proceedings at least, they were going their separate ways.

'You're in for a rare treat tonight,' Billy whispered to Spudder, just before his uncle got into the car.

'Am I?' Spudder asked. 'Will we be havin' a special supper or somethin'?'

'I'm talkin' about after that, when you go upstairs to bed,' Billy said.

The light of comprehension came to Spudder's eyes. 'You mean, when we try to make babies?'

'Yes, that's what I mean.'

'Is it more fun than kissin'?'

Billy grinned. 'I couldn't speak from experience,' he said, 'but I'm told it's a lot more fun than kissin'.'

'Bloody hell!' said Spudder, though he hardly ever swore.

Becky and Billy Worrell sat facing each other across the kitchen table. Outside, night was falling.

'I thought it went well,' Becky said.

'Very well,' Billy agreed.

'An' I thought you made a wonderful job of bein' best man. You didn't get the rings mixed up or anythin'.'

'Keepin' Uncle Spudder calm was the most difficult part,' Billy told her.

Becky looked around the kitchen and sighed.

'What's the matter?' Billy asked.

'I was just thinkin' how strange it will be not to have Michelle to cook an' wash for any more,' Becky said.

'Well, she needed a house of her own, what with startin' a family,' Billy pointed out. 'An' it's not as if she'll be miles away. She's only livin' down the road.'

'I know all that. But the house always used to feel so full – so burstin' with life. Now your dad's dead, our Michelle's married, and you'll soon be gone away as well.'

'Not until the end of July, Mam.'

'That'll come quicker than you think.'

'You're feelin' just a little bit sorry for yourself, aren't you, Mam?' Billy said.

'I suppose I am,' Becky agreed. She forced a smile to her lips. 'Isn't it funny,' she said. 'However much you promise yourself that you're never goin' to end up talkin' like your mother did, you always do.'

Spudder and Ivy lay side by side in their New Brighton boarding-house bedroom. Spudder had a broad smile on his face.

Ivy snuggled up to him. 'Mrs Worrell told me a joke the other day,' she said. 'It was about Queen Victoria.'

'I remember her. She was a nice little old lady.'

'Well, this joke isn't about when she was an old woman. It's about her weddin' night, when she was even younger than I am. Do you want to hear it?'

'All right,' Spudder said. He spoke without enthusiasm,

because although he wanted Ivy to do whatever she liked, he didn't usually understand jokes.

'Well, the first time her and Prince Albert are in bed together, he rolls off her, an' she just lies there, very quiet. "What's the matter, love?" he says.

'"Do the workin' classes do this?" she asks him.

'"Well, yes, they do," Albert says.

'The Queen clicks her tongue, like Aggie does when she disapproves of somethin'. "There ought to be a law against it," she says.

'"But why?" Albert asks her.

'"Because it's much too good for them," the Queen says.'

Spudder scratched his head thoughtfully. 'I don't get it,' he admitted.

Ivy bit his chest, but not hard. 'The point is, it's not too good for us, is it? It's just right for us.'

'Yes,' Spudder agreed happily. 'An' Billy was right – it's bags better than just kissin'.'

Jim was awakened from his sleep by the sound of Michelle sobbing softly to herself.

'What's the matter?' he asked.

'It's nothing,' Michelle replied.

Jim switched on the bedside light, then shifted position so that he was looking into her eyes. 'We're married now,' he said. 'An' part of bein' married, as I see it, is not hidin' things from each other, however much them things might hurt.'

'What do you mean?'

'You were thinkin' of Gerald, weren't you? You were wishin' that it was him in this bed with you, instead of me.'

'I wasn't thinking that,' Michelle said.

'There's no need to be ashamed of it. It's only natural. You never pretended to feel about me like you felt about him.'

'I wasn't thinking about Gerald,' Michelle insisted. 'Honestly I wasn't.'

'Then what started you cryin'?'

Michelle hesitated. 'When we made love just now . . .'

'Yes?'

'It was the first time for you, wasn't it?'

Jim looked away from her. 'Yes, it was,' he admitted. 'Was I that terrible?'

'You weren't terrible at all,' Michelle said. 'A little clumsy, perhaps, but you'll improve with time. That's not the point.'

'So what is the point?'

'I could feel that your whole heart was in it. I could tell that you really loved me.'

'I do, Michelle. I think that I have since the first moment I saw you.'

He was still looking away from her, but now Michelle put one hand on each of his cheeks, and turned his head towards her.

'It's a wonderful feeling to know that you're loved,' she said. 'That's why I was crying. Not for Gerald – but for you. Because you haven't experienced it yet. But you will. I promise you, you will.'

EPILOGUE

July 1915

Young rusty-brown blackbirds strutted confidently through the grass of Marston churchyard, and whole families of tits flitted from treetop to treetop, feeding on the juicy grubs. It was the end of July – the time of the young – and inside the church, a christening was in progress.

Becky Worrell, standing close to the font, looked at the tiny baby held in Ivy Johnson's arms, and thought her heart would burst with love. 'She's a beautiful baby,' she said softly to herself. 'The most beautiful baby in the world.'

And then she laughed inwardly and told herself that she was turning into the over-indulgent granny that she'd vowed she would never, ever, be.

Becky forced her eyes from her granddaughter and looked at the other people around the font. Next to Ivy stood the other godparents. One was Spudder, the other was Colleen Taylor, her oldest friend and sister-in-law. The years had treated Colleen well. She had never been a great beauty, but what good features she did have seemed to have improved with age.

And then there were the parents, Michelle and Jim, watching the whole event with obvious pride. Michelle was wearing a light blue dress which was much higher above her ankles than would have been thought quite proper only a couple of years earlier. The war again – somehow it seemed to have changed everything. Jim was already in uniform, and though he was only a private, he managed to wear it with some dash.

Becky turned her head so she could see the others. Her son, Billy, was wearing his best suit, but in a few days' time he would be swapping his normal clothes for tropical gear. He would be eaten alive by insects – Michael had told her all about that – and the sticky heat would cling to him like a second skin. It would be the closest thing imaginable to hell, but he was a man now, and that was his choice. All she, as his mother, could do, was to pray that he wouldn't add one more body to the White Man's Grave.

She looked further along the semi-circle. There was her

brother George, with his two kids, and beyond them her older sisters Jessie and Eunice, with their husbands and children.

Both Jack and George had told her that she lived too much in the past, and she agreed with them. But when she saw them all gathered together like this, it was impossible not to remember things which had happened long ago: the day George came home from the wars with his wooden leg; visiting Philip in Strangeways prison; her dad's accident down the Adelaide mine; her mam opening the chip shop, even though Ted had said it was the daftest idea he could imagine . . . A great many happy memories, and not a little heartbreak.

Families! Becky thought. They can be a right nuisance sometimes, but who'd want to be without them?

Richard Worrell stood at the top of the hump-backed bridge next to his saltworks and gazed down at Marston Church. He had been in that position for some time, ever since he had seen the christening party pass the works. He could imagine them inside the church now. Happy people. People with something to celebrate.

He thought of his son – not a man any longer, but just a collection of body pieces, lying in an unnamed grave in Flanders. 'Gerald should have been there!' he said to himself. It should have been Gerald walking to the church, holding in his arms the baby he had given to the woman who – in spite of himself – he had fallen in love with.

How long would the ceremony take? he wondered. Ten minutes? Fifteen?

He was torturing himself, standing there on the bridge, and he knew it. His most sensible course of action would be to go back to his office and immerse himself in work. A mountain of orders and invoices had built up while he'd been out disrupting the recruitment rallies and serving his prison sentence.

He knew he should make some provision for the next time he was in gaol. A two-week sentence had been hard enough on a middle-aged man used to living in the lap of luxury, and he was sure he would not get off so lightly again – but there would be a next time. Because he could not give up now, could not abandon his personal crusade against the devils in the War Office.

So whichever way he looked at it, he argued, going back to his office was by far the most intelligent, and least painful, thing that he could do. Richard looked back at his works once more, then set off down the bridge towards the church.

The godparents had just finished reading their vows, and now Ivy stepped forward to the font.

'What is the child to be named?' the vicar asked.

'Mary,' Ivy said.

Mary! After Granny Taylor. Michelle looked up at her husband, and was touched by the way she saw him watching the baby. He loves her with all his heart, she thought, even though she isn't his. And she loved Jim, not perhaps with the burning longing she had felt for Gerald, but with a warmth and affection which, in its own way, was just as deep and passionate as the love she felt for her dead cousin.

In a few days, Jim would be heading for France himself – towards the trenches, the miles of cruel barbed wire, and the machine-guns which mowed men down as if they were nothing more than blades of grass. Michelle wondered if his death would devastate her as much as Gerald's had, and knew that it would.

'I baptise thee in the name of the Father, and of the Son, and of the Holy Ghost,' Reverend Birchall intoned, splashing font water on the infant's head.

Michelle moved closer to her husband, and squeezed his arm. 'Come back safely,' she whispered. 'Come back safely, so you can watch your daughter grow up.'

The christening party stood in front of the church chatting happily and petting the baby.

Becky wandered over across to the front wall, to a grave which had new flowers on it. There was a new inscription on it, too.

'ELSIE BRACEGIRDLE 1835–1915'

'Beloved wife of Ernest and mother of Geoffrey. Rest in Peace.'

What changes old Not-Stopping had seen in her lifetime, Becky thought. The steam train had been a novelty when she was born. Now there were cars and aeroplanes – and ways to kill a man which had never been dreamed of back then.

Not-Stopping hadn't been a bad old stick really, especially in her later years, and if there really was a heaven, she'd probably be there now, sitting in the Celestial Arms and chatting to her old friend Ma Fitton about what St Peter did on his night off.

Becky looked up from the grave and was shocked to see Richard Worrell on the other side of the church wall, a couple of yards away from her. Her first impulse was to ignore him. Yet how could you ignore a man who had suffered so much, a man who had lost his only son?

She walked over to Richard, and was surprised to discover that her old revulsion of him was not quite as intense as it used to be.

'We always seem to be readin' about you in the papers, these days,' she said, smiling.

Richard smiled back. It was a touchingly sad smile. 'Yes, I'm making quite a name for myself in these parts, aren't I?' he said. 'I don't think most people can decide whether I'm a madman or just a hooligan. Perhaps some of them think that I'm both.'

'I don't think you're either of them,' Becky told him. 'I'm not sure I agree with the way that you're goin' about things, but I admire you for doin' it anyway.'

The sad smile was still on Richard's face. 'It's a long time since you've admired me.'

'It's a long time since there's been anythin' to admire.'

'You're right,' Richard agreed. 'I've done some pretty rotten things in my time, haven't I?'

'Yes, you have.'

'But that's all behind me now.'

Becky cocked her head slightly to one side, and tried to look at Richard as if she were seeing him for the first time. 'I wish I could believe you,' she said. 'I wish I could really believe that the old Richard wouldn't suddenly come poppin' up again like some kind of evil jack-in-a-box.'

'He won't,' Richard promised her. 'The leopard's finally changed his spots. The old dog's learned some new tricks at last.'

'Maybe he has,' Becky said, but she still did not sound completely convinced.

Richard looked longingly at the rest of the family, who were still standing in front of the church porch. 'Becky? I want a favour.'

'What kind of favour?' Becky asked the man who had once used every trick in the book in order to bed her.

For a few seconds, Richard was silent, as if he were plucking up the courage to speak. Then he said, 'The baby.'

'What about her?'

'She's all that's left of Gerald. I was wondering if . . . if I might visit her, sometimes.'

'It's up to Michelle, not me,' Becky said severely.

'Of course. But I thought that if you could have a word with her . . . tell her that you think it would be all right if I . . . if I . . .'

Against all her instincts, Becky found herself softening, and the smile came back to her face. 'Like I said before, it's Michelle's decision,' she told him. 'But I can't see that my daughter'll have any objections to the baby seein' her grandad.'

'Then when could you . . .?'

'Why not now?' Becky turned towards the porch. 'Michelle!' she called. 'Can you come over here a minute, love? An' bring little Mary with you.'

Michelle walked over to them, looking puzzled. 'Yes, Mam? What do you want?'

'You wouldn't mind if your Uncle Richard held the baby for a minute, would you?'

Michelle hesitated, then she saw the expression of agony forming on Richard's face and said, 'Of course I wouldn't mind.'

She passed Mary over the wall to him, and Richard took the baby into his arms as if he was afraid she might break.

'She's beautiful,' he said softly. 'She's the most beautiful baby in the world.'

Becky grinned at her daughter. 'I told you I wasn't bein' biased,' she said. 'Your Uncle Richard can see it, too.'

Richard rocked the baby gently back and fro. 'Would it be all right if I gave her presents now and again?' he asked. 'On her birthday? At Christmas? Times like that.'

'Yes, that would be nice – just as long as you don't spoil her too much.'

'And perhaps when she's older, I could teach her to ride?'

'I'm not sure about that,' Michelle said doubtfully.

'I'm a good riding teacher, aren't I?' Richard said, appealing to Becky.

'Yes, you are,' Becky admitted. 'You might never have been very good with people, but you've always known your horses.'

Richard turned back to Michelle. 'So could I teach her? I promise I'll be very careful.'

Michelle smiled for the first time. 'I suppose so,' she said. 'If it's what Mary wants.'

The rest of the christening party was heading for the lych gate, but Richard still held on to the baby as if she had become a part of him.

'Hand Mary back to Michelle now, Richard,' Becky said softly.

Slowly, as if it were costing him a great effort, Richard leant forward and passed the baby to her mother.

Michelle shot Becky a questioning look, and Becky, understanding what the question was, nodded.

'We're having a christening tea back at Mam's house, Uncle Richard,' Michelle said. 'Would you like to come?'

'More than anything in the world.'

It was early evening. Richard and Becky walked slowly along the canal towpath towards Burns Bridge. The sun was low in the sky, and in its golden light metallic dragonflies flitted across the water, hunting their tiny prey.

'You're as beautiful as you were when I first met you,' Richard said.

'Get on with you,' Becky replied. 'I'm a granny now. Almost an old woman.'

'And I'm a grandfather. I was a fool to ever let you go, Becky Taylor.'

'You thought you could have your cake and eat it. That was your problem.'

'You would have married me, wouldn't you?'

'You know I would.'

'I should have asked you. Instead of offering to make you my mistress, I should have made you my wife.'

'There's no point in rakin' up the past,' Becky said. 'You were a different person back then. An' I was happy with Michael, you know, blissfully happy. So probably things turned out for the best.'

'Probably?'

'Well, we can never really know, can we?'

'Look at that!' Richard said, stopping and pointing to a multicoloured butterfly which was hovering delicately over a clump of ragged robin.

'You never used to notice that kind of thing in the old days,' Becky said.

'I never used to notice a lot of things in the old days,' Richard replied. 'Do you know what it's called?'

'The butterfly?'

'Yes.'

'It's called a painted lady.'

'And where does it come from?'

'North Africa, I think.'

Richard whistled softly. 'Imagine a frail little thing like a butterfly travelling all that way.'

'It's remarkable what you can do when you put your mind to it,' Becky said.

'It is,' Richard agreed. 'Do you think we could ever become friends again, Becky?'

'Oh, I think so.'

'Do you think we could ever become more than just friends?'

'Careful, Richard!' Becky warned him. 'You're pushin' things far too hard, an' far too fast.'

'You're not saying no though, are you?'

Becky looked him straight in the eye. 'You're right,' she admitted. 'I'm not sayin' no.'